THE ISLAND SWIMMER

Lorraine Kelly CBE has worked in breakfast TV for forty years, joining TVam as Scottish correspondent in 1984 and now presents *Lorraine* on ITV.

She is married to cameraman Steve and they have one daughter Rosie, a journalist and broadcaster.

Lorraine is a Dundee United fan and gets her best ideas when out for a walk with her beloved border terrier Angus.

She first visited Orkney in 1985 and goes back every year.

Lorraine Kelly

THE ISLAND SWIMMER

ORION

First published in Great Britain in 2024 by Orion Fiction,
an imprint of The Orion Publishing Group Ltd.
Carmelite House, 50 Victoria Embankment
London EC4Y 0DZ

An Hachette UK Company

1 3 5 7 9 10 8 6 4 2

A CIP catalogue record for this book is
available from the British Library.

ISBN (Hardback) 978 13987 1445 8
ISBN (eBook) 978 13987 1447 2

Typeset by Born Group
Printed and bound in Great Britain by Clays Ltd, Elcograf S.p.A.

MIX
Paper from
responsible sources
FSC www.fsc.org FSC® C104740

To my mum Anne who gave me the greatest gift of all by introducing me to a lifelong love of books.

Prologue

Orkney, 2004

Freya was the only person Evie trusted to help and who wouldn't bombard her with questions. In a blind panic, she got in her car and drove to Freya's house.

The driving rain lashed down on the windscreen, but the noise was drowned out by the sound of Evie's laboured breathing and beating heart.

When she arrived at Freya's, the lights were off, but she could see a glow from the dying fire. Outside, Evie took a moment to try to think. She couldn't tell Freya the whole story, she just couldn't. She burned with guilt and shame.

She pushed open the door and called for Freya, her voice sounding like a lost lamb.

'Evie?' said Freya, coming into the hallway in her dressing gown. 'Evie, what on earth is the matter?' Evie flung herself into Freya's arms, sobbing and almost incoherent.

'Freya, I need your help. Please. I need to get away.'

I

Orkney, 2024

Maybe the plane will fall out of the sky, and it will all be over. No more pain and no more guilt. Evie was only half kidding. She didn't really wish a horrible death on herself and her fellow passengers on the short flight from Dundee to Kirkwall, she just didn't want the flight to land in Orkney at all.

Yet here she was, travelling north against her better judgement and with ice in her stomach. She looked down through the tiny window at the choppy grey sea and felt a deep sense of dread. She had been terrified of water ever since she was a little girl and all of her life the sea had meant tragedy and trauma.

She shuddered as the thoughts tumbled through her head. *This is a massive mistake, everyone is going to find out exactly why I left in the first place and they won't be able to forgive me, and why should they? I can't even begin to forgive myself.*

The pilot announced they were coming in to land. Racked with nerves, Evie clumsily grabbed her handbag to place it under the seat and her phone tumbled onto the floor.

The one member of the cabin crew in a cheery red tartan uniform picked it up and asked if she was OK. Evie nodded but wished she could tell this kindly woman all her fears and worries.

Looking at her phone she thought of all the unanswered calls and texts from Jeremy. She hadn't told him where she was going, and he'd be pacing the floor of their London flat. She pushed thoughts of him away – it was just too exhausting and draining.

Evie was only thirty-eight, but she looked so much older. Her once-bright green eyes were dull with pain, her skin dry and sallow, and her fair hair was scraped back into a greasy ponytail. She had a wide, generous mouth that was made for smiling, but these days was usually downturned or tight with stress. She was too thin for her frame and sat with her shoulders hunched as though she was waiting on an insult or a slap. Her mother would have told her tartly that she had 'let herself go'.

As the plane began its descent, the sun broke through and the islands of Orkney stretched out below, glinting like fat mermaids covered in emeralds. The grey sea had turned azure and turquoise, lapping onto bone-white beaches merging into impossibly vivid green fields. Evie felt her heart being squeezed.

I'd forgotten just how beautiful it is here, she thought. *There's nowhere like it in all the world. That's why it was so hard to leave and to stay away for so long.* But now she had no choice but to come back. She hoped it wasn't too late. She had to ask her father for forgiveness – and face her sister and her mother.

Old wounds would be opened, but she couldn't run away from her past any more.

2

Orkney, 1960

Cara was from the island of Hrossey and – like all the children scattered throughout the northern islands of the Orkney archipelago – she had to leave her home at the age of fourteen to finish secondary school in Orkney's capital, Kirkwall, living in a hostel and going home on the ferry most weekends.

She was a tiny little teenager, with fair dandelion-clock hair and enormous brown eyes in a sharp little face fizzing with energy and curiosity.

Her mother, Sheila, said she'd come out of the womb shrieking 'Why?' and had never stopped asking questions ever since. Some of them had been harmless – 'Why couldn't she have a pet seal and keep it in the house? Why did she need to go to bed when it wasn't even dark? And why did she even have to go to school in the first place?' – but when she was five years old, she'd piped up in the middle of the queue in Linklater's (the shop on Hrossey, which sold everything) demanding to know: 'Why was Mr Linklater staggering about on the beach yesterday singing to himself? Why were his eyes all funny?'

There was a deafening silence in the shop, and behind the counter Mrs Linklater's mouth turned itself into a cat's bottom.

Cara's mother felt her face burn fiery red. This was even worse than those dreaded hot flashes she'd been trying to ignore for months now.

Everyone knew poor Mr Linklater would go on the occasional bender when he was driven to distraction by his prissy wife and demanding bairns, and he would be made to pay dearly for such behaviour, but they chose to ignore his antics because he was such a harmless soul and they felt sorry for him.

Sheila left her grocery basket on the floor and bundled her daughter into the street.

'Don't ever ask questions like that again,' she said to Cara.

'Why?' Cara fired back as usual.

Sheila sighed. 'They make people uncomfortable.' Sheila felt that although Cara was only a child, she knew exactly what she was doing and it was all about being the centre of attention.

It was quite some time before her mother took Cara back into the shop, bribed with the promise of sweeties if she promised to keep quiet. That tactic worked, but it didn't stop the little girl asking questions all the way home, even though she seldom listened to the answers.

'Why,' Cara demanded to know, 'was her best friend Anne Marie's big brother Magnus wearing his mother's dresses when she went over to play at their house? And why did he always want to be with the two of them instead of playing with the boys?'

Cara took a real dislike to Magnus and always made fun of him at school, mimicking his voice and mannerisms, and encouraging the rest of the bairns to call him a 'jessie'. She didn't seem to care how much it hurt both Magnus and Anne Marie and that most of the others thought she was downright mean for picking on Magnus, who was sweet, funny and kind. She was friends with Anne Marie because the two of them happened to sit beside each another in the classroom, but they gradually drifted apart, mainly due to her unkindness towards Magnus.

As she grew older, Cara had a knack for alienating most of the people who started off on her side, but everyone on Hrossey felt sorry for her and cut her a lot of slack because she had grown up not knowing her dad.

Cara's mum and her father had met late in life. James worked on the fishing boats off the Scottish mainland in Fraserburgh and came to Orkney to attend a monumentally drunken stag do for one of his mates. Sheila was working in a bar in Stromness at the time, and the two of them struck up a conversation.

They clearly did a helluva lot more than talk, and just under nine months later Cara was born. James wanted nothing to do with his daughter. As far as he was concerned, she was the result of a barely remembered one-night stand, but he did at least pay child support. Sheila went back to Hrossey where no one judged her, apart from a couple of old biddies who tut-tutted about her not being able to keep her legs together, but their gripes were soon drowned out, and everyone else quietly rallied round to help.

James was rarely spoken of and even Cara eventually stopped asking questions but, as a child, she would make up stories about him being a rich and famous movie star who would return to take his beloved daughter to Hollywood where she would eat ice cream all day and wear pink, sparkly dresses and spangly high-heeled shoes.

Cara was happiest with her own company. She arranged her books in alphabetical order. Her toys were always put away, and her room so neat and tidy it was as though no child actually lived there. Her mum's sister, Cara's aunty Betty, said it was all highly unnatural. Her own gaggle of wild red-haired daughters made her want to tear her hair out with the state of their bedrooms and their messiness, but she would rather pick up their dirty clothes from the floor every single morning than deal with the complicated, tightly wound Cara.

Cara drove her mother and teachers to distraction with her restless energy and feverish questions, especially when she paid no heed to their patient answers. There were sighs of relief when she left to finish her education in Kirkwall. Unlike many of her homesick fellow pupils, Cara relished the freedom. She desperately wanted to get away from her mother, and from Hrossey, where she wrongly believed people looked down on her because she didn't have a dad.

Teenaged Cara, with her flushed good looks and vital energy, was popular at first among pupils at Kirkwall Grammar School, who were amused by her ability to ask the most cheeky and personal questions – even of the teachers. The girls wanted to be her friend and the boys wanted her to be their girlfriend, but she had already made her choice.

She had her eye on Duncan, a big bear of a boy with hands like shovels and a shock of angry black hair that stood to attention, but he had the kindest brown eyes, and, despite his size, he was gentle, kind and very shy.

When Duncan was just ten years old, his father had died in a car crash, and the sorrow and responsibility of being the only child taking care of the farm and his mother, was etched on his face, making him look sadder and older than his years. He'd adored Cara since they first met in school, and he vowed there and then she was the girl he would marry.

All he had to do was screw up the courage to ask her out. He practised what he was going to say to her over and over again, but, when it came to striking up a conversation with Cara, he blushed brick red and couldn't string a sentence together.

Cara saw how kind Duncan was, helping his widowed mother on their small farm, and how hard he worked, getting up brutally early to do the milk run before school, but what really made her mind up was when the class went to the beach for a picnic on the last day of term and she saw him in his swimming trunks. She was hugely impressed by his muscular body as he plunged into the sea.

Cara stuck to paddling up to her knees in the cold water but shouted to Duncan that she didn't want to get her feet all covered in sand, so he effortlessly gave her a piggyback and she clung to him like a koala bear as he carefully placed her on her fluffy towel on the grass above the beach.

She thanked him for being such a gentleman, whereupon he blushed furiously, mumbled something incoherent and ran back into the water to cool off.

Duncan was just so bashful he couldn't find the courage to tell Cara how he felt. So, she decided she'd have to be the one to make the first move. Her campaign began by asking Duncan for a share of his massive lunches, packed with such loving care by his mother.

As they munched on fat ham-and-cheese sandwiches thick with butter, Cara asked him endless questions about the farm and his plans for the future, gradually winkling him out of his shell.

She knew she'd enjoy complete freedom with Duncan, and he'd always let her have the upper hand, and also realised he would forever take great care of her, and they could build a good life together. Cara was so tiny that Duncan could lift her off her feet without the slightest effort and circle her waist with the span of his big hands.

The two of them sneaked kisses in the school playground and walked around Kirkwall hand in hand, Cara chattering endlessly and Duncan beaming with pride at the wonderful prize he had on his arm. When she visited the farm, Duncan's mother tried to fatten Cara up with glasses of creamy milk and home cooking. She was happy her shy, hardworking son had fallen for someone so full of life who brought noise and energy into their quiet lives.

As for Duncan, he couldn't believe his luck that this glorious, clever, vital young girl had actually chosen to go out with him of her own free will, and never believed he was worthy of her.

3

Kirkwall airport, 2024

Evie walked down the few steps of the plane and had to grip the handrail. She felt emotional and lightheaded to be back breathing fresh, clean Orkney air. Her knees buckled and she almost crashed into the bulky backpack of the man in front of her, but somehow managed to stumble down onto the tarmac.

She staggered the short distance into the terminal building but could feel herself losing touch with reality. Nauseous, her head swimming, and finding it increasingly difficult to breathe, she slumped to the floor. The man with the backpack managed to catch her and break her fall, and everyone rushed to try to help.

'Give her some room,' he said. 'The poor lass, she's as white as milk.'

Evie slowly opened her eyes and looked into the concerned face of the man holding her and saying everything was going to be OK. Her chest was tight, and she was struggling to take a breath.

'My inhaler. It's in my pocket,' she whispered. 'I'm so sorry for all this fuss.'

'Don't be daft. My sister is asthmatic. I'm used to this. You just take your time.'

The airport first-aider was quickly by Evie's side.

'Look,' said the man. 'Don't worry. This lovely medic is going to check you over.'

She vaguely registered that he had the kindest blue eyes and a reassuring gentle Irish accent. She took a big puff of her inhaler and started to feel less panicky. The colour came back into her face, and the world slowly regained focus. The kind-eyed man had unruly black hair, was slim and wiry with an outdoorsy tan and just handsome enough not to be intimidating.

His checked shirt needed an iron and was frayed at the collar, his chinos were faded and worn, and he'd obviously walked miles in his scruffy hiking boots.

'Can I get you a cup of tea?' he said. 'That might help.'

'No. I need to get to the Balfour Hospital as quickly as possible,' Evie whispered.

'Do you feel that bad? I'll take you, don't worry. I've hired a car and the hospital is only about ten minutes away.'

'No, it's not me. I'm fine. It's my dad.'

Evie could feel the tears threatening to choke her as she realised she might already be too late to see her father. She hoped she would be in time to say goodbye. She owed him that much at least.

'Look. Let me take you. I'm Finn by the way.'

'Evie. And thank you so much.'

As always on Orkney the keys were left in the hired car's glove compartment, so, after making sure Evie was comfortable by taking an old jumper out of his rucksack and placing it over her knees, all Finn had to do was drive off.

On the short trip to hospital, he chatted about his work for the RSPB, monitoring sea eagles on the island of Hoy, the 'high island' with its imposing hills and abundant wildlife, but Evie wasn't really listening, lost in a world of anxiety and worry.

She looked out of the window as a light rain started to fall while the sun continued to shine. She had always loved this kind of weather as a child, because usually it meant vivid rainbows reflected in the puddles. Everything always looked newly washed after the rain. She saw plump sheep and cows grazing contentedly on bright green grass. There were more brand-new bungalows than she remembered, but it was all so reassuringly familiar. Maybe everything would be all right.

As they approached Kirkwall, Evie was amazed to see the massive new state-of-the-art hospital dominating the outskirts of the town. It hadn't existed when she'd left, and she wondered what else had changed since she'd been away.

As a child she had loved going into Kirkwall for an ice cream, a look around the shops and meeting up with her pals. She never came with them to the nearby beaches, even on the sunniest days. Even when it was calm, she was terrified of the water.

In the hospital car park, Finn asked if she wanted him to come in and help, but Evie said he had done enough.

'I'm so grateful to you. Honestly, and thank you for not asking me loads of questions. I'm all over the place right now.'

He nodded. 'Look, here's my number. I wouldn't feel right leaving you with no one to call on. I hope your dad's OK. Let me know if you need a lift anywhere.'

He tapped his number into Evie's phone.

Walking into the huge entrance, Evie nervously approached the reception desk. Medical staff bustled past purposefully and she recognised one of them right away, even after all these years. The hair wasn't as ruddy. He'd lost weight and gained posh glasses, but it was Edwyn, one of her best pals from school. He'd always wanted to be a doctor and here he was, all grown up and in a white coat.

He saw her and broke into a huge grin. 'Evie Muir. Is that really you? I can't believe it after all this time.'

Evie was so relieved. She'd always felt safe around her friends, Edwyn and Kate. The three of them had been inseparable as teenagers and she hoped that despite everything, they might somehow be able to go back to how they'd been. But this was Edwyn – he'd always been easy-going. Kate might be another matter altogether.

'Oh, Edwyn. It's so good to see you. I'm here for my dad. Can you tell me how he is?'

His smile swiftly faded.

'Let's sit down somewhere quiet where we can talk in private.'

He took Evie to the peaceful family room and held her hand. 'I'm so very sorry, Evie,' he said gently. 'Your dad never regained consciousness after suffering a massive stroke. He died yesterday. He was such a lovely man, and we did all we could.'

Evie felt faint again, but she was able to whisper.

'He's really dead? Are you sure? Can I see him?'

'I'm sure you can. Of course you can. Give me a minute.'

Evie couldn't believe it. She was too late. She would never hear her dad's voice again. No one would ever call her Teenie or love her as much as he did.

Why did I leave it so long? she thought in despair. *Now I will never get a chance to make it up to him.*

Edwyn put a supportive arm around her, and she leant on him gratefully.

'Here we are, Evie. He's in this room. Are you sure you are ready?'

Evie nodded. Tears blinding her as she gazed down at her father's ice-cold, wizened body. He looked like a yellow waxwork, so old and frail with sparse, matted grey hair and a thin, wispy beard. Where was the big, bold giant who could lift her up as though she was a newly hatched chick?

'That's not my dad,' she said. 'There's been a mistake. That's not him. He was a such a big man. You've got it wrong. There's obviously been a mix-up.'

She could hear herself becoming shrill and slightly hysterical. Edwyn held her firmly but kindly.

'I'm so sorry, Evie, but Duncan was very ill when he was brought in.'

'But what happened? He was always so strong and healthy.'

Edwyn sighed. 'He wasn't looking after himself. We all tried to help but ever since your mother went away, he just seemed to lose the will to live. He was brought in a week ago after suffering a bad fall at home. He'd been on the floor all night and was in a terrible state. He suffered another massive stroke in the ambulance on the way here and despite our best efforts, he never woke up from that.'

She looked down again at the shrunken old man and felt such overwhelming love that it drowned out the deep sorrow and crushing guilt for just a moment. 'Goodbye, Dad,' she said. 'I'm sorry we didn't get to say it properly. I will never forgive myself for that, and for not being here when you needed me.'

She touched his cold cheek tenderly.

'Look, I'm off shift in about ten minutes,' Edwyn told her softly. 'Take your time here to say goodbye and meet me in the hospital café.'

She nodded again, not trusting herself to speak.

Quarter of an hour later, cradling a scalding, over-sweetened tea in the hospital canteen, Evie struggled to take in what had happened. 'Freya just wrote in her letter that I had to get here quickly. I didn't know he was so ill,' she explained.

Edwyn sighed. 'I had an idea she was still in touch with you,' he said. 'But she never told us exactly where you were.

You know what she's like. She would never break her promise to you. To be honest, Freya was the one person who really got through to your dad near the end. She was the only one he would let in the house, and it was her who found him and called the ambulance. She did her best to try to encourage him to stop drinking and eat properly, but there's only so much she could do. All of us tried, Evie. We really did.'

Evie looked stricken. 'And, of course, I wasn't here. I should have been here looking after him.' *All because I was too scared to face up to what I did. This is all my fault. The whole sorry mess. It's down to me.*

Edwyn couldn't help a slight coldness creeping into his voice. 'I'm sure you had your reasons for not coming home, Evie, and for not getting in touch. But it was hard on all of us. We missed you. You just disappeared.'

Evie was near tears.

'I know. I'm so sorry.' She was exhausted, a careworn woman with eyes full of pain. 'Does Liv know about our dad?'

'As far as we know, your sister never visited him here, and never saw him unless she wanted money,' said Edwyn.

Evie gave a quivering sigh and put her head in her hands.

Edwyn looked stricken. 'Evie, love. I never know when to shut up. You've had a horrible shock and I'm making things worse. Look, why don't you come back to my house and see Kate and our bairns? We can help you with all the arrangements that need to be done, and you are welcome to stay as long as you like.'

Evie gave him a watery smile. 'That's far more than I deserve. I booked a room at the Foveran because I wasn't sure if I could stay at my dad's. I won't be here long. I'll see if I can get a flight out as soon as I can.'

Edwyn hesitated. 'You'll need to be here to sort out the paperwork for your dad. That could take a few days at least.'

Evie choked up again and Edwyn gave her a hug.

'We will help you with all of that. I can drive you to the hotel now and call me later or in the morning if you need anything. Here's my number.'

Evie remembered another man who just an hour ago had also given her his number and offered to help. She'd forgotten what it was like to live somewhere where people actually looked out for one another. As Edwyn handed her phone back with his number stored, she saw that Jeremy had left her another text. *Call me back immediately when you receive this or you will regret it.*

She barely registered his latest threat as she settled into her hotel room in a daze. The sympathetic receptionist knew her family and made the check-in as easy as possible.

Despite the traumatic events of the day, she fell into a deep sleep but was abruptly wakened when the phone by her bed started ringing.

She'd been having the most horribly realistic dream and could have sworn her mother had come into her room ranting and raving and accusing her of ruining their family with her selfishness and wickedness.

'Wretched girl,' she'd kept shrieking. 'Wretched, wretched girl.'

Evie reached for the phone feeling disorientated and a wave of grief hit her when she remembered her dad was dead.

'Hello,' she whispered shakily.

'Evie? It's Freya. Edwyn called to tell me where you were. I would have picked you up at the airport and been there for you when you heard about your dad. I'm so sorry, my lamb. How are you holding up?'

'Oh, Freya, I was too late. You were right; I should have come sooner. I am so sorry. I know I should have been in touch with you, but it all happened so fast. I never got the chance to say goodbye or tell him I was sorry and that I loved him.'

She broke down and started to sob.

'Stay where you are; I'm not far away. You shouldn't be left on your own and you are coming home to stay with me. No arguments.'

4

Orkney, 1962

When Cara and Duncan turned sixteen, Duncan's timid mother died as she had lived, quietly and with very little fuss. She just went to bed one night and never woke up. Everyone was convinced it was because her poor heart had simply worn out with the grief of losing her fine, handsome husband.

The funeral was small and dignified. Duncan gave the eulogy, which was simple but so sincere that the women in the congregation sniffled into their handkerchiefs and the men had to clear their throats so as not to be thought overly emotional.

Duncan was deeply uncomfortable with everyone's eyes upon him and only managed to get through the whole ordeal by never taking his eyes off Cara. At the graveside, when she gripped his hand tightly, he knew he couldn't live without her.

Duncan now had to run the farm with the help of two hired hands. It was a big burden on such young shoulders, even with the help of his mother's friends, who rallied round to support him with advice and practical help.

Duncan had to quit school, and, on his last day, Cara asked him to drive them both in his battered old van to Yesnaby

Castle as she had something important to say to him. The 'castle', an impressive natural sea stack, was well worth the twenty-minute hike from the car park. She had brought a simple picnic of homemade bread and Hrossey cheese and set it up on the scrubby green grass of the clifftops.

The two of them sat close together looking out at the spectacular view, the sound of the waves breaking against the sharp rocks. The summer wind was soft and caressing, the kittiwakes were putting on an impressive aerial display, puffins were being effortlessly cute and there was a pod of dolphins frolicking in the sea. It couldn't have been more idyllic.

'You know dolphins mate for life?' said Cara, trying to make her voice all soft and sensual like she'd seen in the movies.

'No, they don't, Cara. They are totally at it all the time with any dolphin who is up for it. They are terrible shaggers.' His eyes narrowed. 'And anyway, why are you talking in such a daft way?'

Cara sighed in exasperation.

'Duncan John Muir, you really do know how to ruin the moment.'

'What do you mean?'

'I had it all planned. I knew you'd never get round to it, so I had to take matters into my own hands. I was going to go down on one knee and everything. I even got you a ring. Well, it was so cheap it'll probably turn your fat finger green, but we need to save up and we don't want to spend cash on stupid trivial things.'

Duncan looked stunned. 'You really want to marry me? Are you sure? This isn't a joke, is it?'

Cara began to giggle. 'No, you gigantic oaf. I WANT to marry Elvis, but you will have to do, I suppose.'

Duncan gave a roar and lifted Cara into the air.

'Put me down, you eejit, or we will both fall over this cliff and there won't even be a wedding,' she said, laughing, but, really, she loved the feeling of being held in his strong arms.

He set her down, gave her a massive hug and told her he was sorry for not asking her first, but he just couldn't believe she would agree to spend the rest of her life with him. Cara leant into him, and he kissed her heartily.

Then he looked into her eyes and said gravely, 'Cara, I am going to make it my life's work to be sure you are happy. I love you so much and I will take care of you always. And I can't wait for us to have bairns. As long as they have your looks and your brains.'

Cara's heart lifted. 'We will have to build a bigger house then.' Cara's dream was a home full of fat, happy babies that would grow up with a mum and a dad.

Of course, before the wedding there had to be a traditional blackening. Duncan was nabbed by his pals, stripped, covered in a foul mixture of treacle, feathers and flour, then driven around Kirkwall on the back of a truck with all of them banging drums and bin lids, making enough noise to waken the dead.

His hands and feet were tied up and he found himself tethered to a lamp post outside Kirkwall Cathedral, luckily with his underpants still intact. Some poor grooms-to-be weren't so fortunate. and their hairy arses and more were exposed to passers-by. A fair bit of drink was taken before Duncan was released, taken to the beach, rolled about in the sand, and then pushed into the cold sea, which instantly sobered him up and got rid of most of the sticky mess that had attached itself to the most intimate parts of his body.

After they'd dried off and were walking back, Duncan's friend Hugh dropped back to speak to him. He was gangly and awkward with mousy hair and freckles.

'Duncan,' he said. 'You know you're my best mate?'

The two of them had been firm friends since science classes when Duncan had struggled to light his Bunsen burner and nearly set himself on fire. Hugh had patiently shown him how to do it safely. He also helped him with his homework, and no one dared make fun of Hugh, the class geek, with his big pal by his side.

'Aye,' said Duncan.

Hugh cleared his throat.

'It's not easy to say this. But are you sure Cara's the one for you? You're just so different from each other.'

Hugh was blushing furiously. Duncan was baffled. He thought everyone adored Cara.

'It's those very differences that make us work,' he said.

'I'm sorry if I spoke out of turn,' Hugh stuttered.

Duncan clapped him on the back. 'I know Cara can be a lot to handle. But don't worry. She's the one for me.'

Cara's blackening was more of a sober affair, mainly because the girls she had gone to school with were afraid of her, and, also, because she didn't have as many friends as Duncan, but both had to have several long soaks in the bath to get totally rid of all the gunk.

The wedding ceremony was held in Hrossey with Cara's mum and her clan of aunts, uncles and cousins squeezed into the small plain white kirk by the sea. A clutch of Duncan's friends and relatives made the two-and-a-half-hour ferry journey and were put up in houses throughout the island, sleeping in spare rooms or on couches and camp beds.

There were a few awkward moments on the day when Cara threw the mother of all tantrums about the flowers and the bridesmaids' dresses, but her slightly manic mood was put down to nothing more than wedding nerves and jitters. Her long white dress was simple and elegant, white satin with a sweetheart neckline and a tight bodice that showed off her tiny waist. She had insisted on a long veil and artificial roses in her hair. Cara looked beautiful, although slightly feverish. Her eyes glittered and her cheeks were hectic red.

With no fatherly arm to lean on, she boldly marched down the aisle on her own, which made some of the older members of the congregation sniff with disdain. Cara brazened it out, pretending she didn't care, but she was bitterly disappointed. She'd secretly hoped her dad would somehow know she was getting married and turn up to share in the biggest day of her life. Right up until the last minute she looked in vain for him to burst into the church, proclaim he wouldn't have missed this for the world and proudly 'give her away'.

Resisting the urge to cry, she painted on her bravest smile, lifted her chin defiantly and beamed at her husband-to-be. Alongside him she would raise a huge, successful family. She would be better than the lot of them put together.

As he vowed to love her in sickness and in health, Duncan shed tears of joy and he kissed his triumphant bride. After the simple ceremony, a slightly stunned Duncan radiated happiness and shyly accepted congratulations from the boisterous band of newly acquired relatives. He felt he was the luckiest man alive.

5

Orkney, 2024

Freya swooped down to pick up Evie from the Foveran and take her to her cottage in Orphir, overlooking the sea. They hugged and cried in each other's arms. Freya was shocked to see Evie looking so frail and exhausted, but hid her concerns by giving her a massive dram of Scapa whisky and putting her straight to bed, saying they could talk in the morning and what she needed was rest and quiet.

Freya sat up that night, troubled and sleepless, worrying about poor broken Evie. Obviously, she was devastated by her father's death, but the defeat and despair in her eyes looked ingrained over a long, long time. She would need help to heal. For so many years, Freya had consoled herself that Evie had built a good life in London. Clearly, that was just wishful thinking.

Freya was also mourning Duncan. He'd always been good to her and treated her with kindness, respect and understanding. She felt so guilty about not telling him she was in touch with Evie. Maybe if she had, he wouldn't have gone downhill so rapidly and would have had something to live for. Freya loved Evie like a daughter, and it had almost killed her not to go down south and bring her back home.

She'd never found out why Evie had fled and cut all contact with Orkney apart from sending occasional letters and texts to Freya and no one else. She had tried gently over the past twenty years to persuade her to contact her dad, but she was well aware the link she had with Evie was so fragile it could easily break. She didn't want to risk losing touch altogether.

Now she reassured herself that Evie was home, and she could take care of her and maybe even try and get her to stay for good. Freya had overcome so much in her life and had always been wise beyond her years.

There weren't many who still remembered that long ago she'd grown up in Hrossey as a little boy called Magnus, while always knowing deep in her heart there had been some kind of mistake. There'd been a disconnect between the chubby lad she'd seen in the mirror and the person she'd truly believed she was supposed to be.

At the age of fifteen, Magnus had calmly told everyone that she was now Freya, the Norse goddess of love and war who cried tears of gold. Freya's parents and sister, Anne Marie, hadn't been exactly surprised by this announcement as they had eyes in their heads.

The aunties, uncles and cousins had just shrugged. Like everyone else on Hrossey they'd seen Magnus dress as a girl since well before he'd gone to primary school. Even sour-faced Mrs Linklater from the shop that sold everything had been nonplussed.

She'd sniffed and said, 'Magnus has always paddled his own canoe and that's the way of it. If his parents are all right with it then fair enough, although I must say we've never had such goings on in our family. But what can you expect from that lot?'

Old Mr Linklater took Freya's hand and said, 'You've a hard road ahead of you, my dear. You will need all your strength and courage. I'm sorry if I get it wrong sometimes and still call you Magnus. I'm a bit old and forgetful and I hope that you won't be too upset with me.'

Freya gave him a dazzling smile and a hug; from that moment Magnus was consigned to the past and she was Freya.

She was only five feet four with a round, generous face and big soft hazel eyes. A love of sweeties and all the fine Hrossey bread, cream and cheese made her pleasingly plump with cheeks like ripe peaches, and, it had to be said, a bit of a double chin and pot belly.

Freya grew her fair hair past her shoulders and painted her nails. Anne Marie helped her with clothes, both of them poring over catalogues and waiting for the packages to arrive so they could have their very own fashion shows in their bedroom.

Some people still called her Magnus, but never with malice, and she would gently correct them or just smile and say, 'I'm Freya now.' Every time she said it, she felt stronger.

There was inevitably a bit of bullying at secondary school in Kirkwall, but Freya was stoic in the face of it all, and had good friends from Hrossey, who looked out for her. It also helped that she was a genuinely kind person who just wanted to live her life in peace.

Most of the cruel comments at school came from thirteen-year-old Cara, who thought the little boy who wore his mum's clothes was a complete show-off. She maintained it was all attention-seeking and a phase that 'Magnus' would grow out of.

Cara had to tone herself down when even Duncan haltingly pleaded with her to leave Freya alone. As she didn't want him to think she was anything less than his perfect princess, she stopped goading Freya and, instead, decided to pointedly ignore her, while still holding her in utter contempt.

Freya was never academic so when she left school, she decided to stay on the Orkney mainland and work as a waitress in the Kirkwall Hotel. As old Mr Linklater said, it was indeed a hard road.

She lost count of the leers and jeers from young boys, and the funny looks from tourists off the big cruise ships, who descended upon Kirkwall like frantic locusts. They were so intent on ticking boxes and seeing everything, that they actually took nothing in, returning to their cabins with a fridge magnet and a vague recollection of ancient monuments and stories of World War Two.

Freya developed a waspish sense of humour to deal with their stares and whispers, and wore that like a suit of armour, but she knew most people who mattered quietly supported her. Duncan once threw a couple of idiots from Manchester out of the hotel bar for being disrespectful and calling her names.

'You clearly have no idea of how to treat a young lady who was trying her best to serve you some good food and drinks. You can come back when you have apologised and learnt some manners.' They were so scared of big Duncan that they never came back to the bar, or indeed to Orkney, ever again.

Freya was happiest on the beach looking out to the sea. In Orkney you were never far away from the water, and she loved the sounds of the waves and the birds overhead. She went there on her own as a teenager wearing her sister's plain black swimming costume and cried with joy when she ran into the sea, feeling free, happy and at peace.

Freya saved up her wages and her tips and headed south to begin her surgery when she was in her early thirties. She would never forget the physical and mental pain she had to suffer, but never once had any regrets. She stayed in London for a few years, working in various hotels, but she missed her family and her friends, the peace and quiet and the fresh Orkney air.

All of this called her back. She rented a cottage south of Kirkwall, close to the small ferry terminal of Houton with views of the crossing to the islands of Flotta and Hoy, and started to make delicate jewellery, inspired by the movements and colours of the sea and the land.

Freya could never quite decide what to wear so she ended up putting everything on at once, wearing bright bold colours and festooning herself in silk scarves and almost her entire jewellery collection. 'I am my own walking advert for my creations,' she would say. 'I need to let everyone see my wares and how fabulous they are.'

Freya considered herself a very happy woman. She had built herself a rich life on Orkney and was looked upon as a 'wise woman' with a large circle of friends who counted her as part of their family. She was always available to give help and advice, even if sometimes it wasn't really needed, because she just wanted to fix and mend everyone and everything.

She drained the remainder of her whisky and went to bed, determined to make Evie stay in Orkney and help take her sadness and pain away.

6

Orkney, 2004

Freya realised that young Evie was on the verge of hysterics.

'All right, my love, let's sit down in front of the fire and take a breath,' said Freya calmly. 'Then you can tell me all about it. Has Liv been up to her tricks again? Or have you had a fight with Brodie?'

At the sound of his name, Evie went white and started to gasp for breath.

Freya rummaged in Evie's handbag, handed her the inhaler and told her to use it and try not to panic.

'I am sure you and Brodie will be able to sort things out. He obviously adores you. He gave you that bonnie bracelet.'

Evie was shaking her head frantically.

'You don't understand, I just need to go. Somewhere far away from here.'

'Evie, believe me, things will be better in a few days. Why don't you stay the night with me and then we can talk about it in the morning? Everything always looks more hopeful when the sun comes up.'

'I can't. I can't tell you what has happened.'

Freya looked at the girl she loved like a daughter. Evie was the most level-headed and down-to-earth teenager and never made a fuss or caused a drama. This was obviously serious, but although she tried to get Evie to confide in her, she completely refused to say what had happened.

Eventually Freya said, 'All right. I will help you. Have you got a plan?'

'No, I don't, but just help me to go as soon as possible and I will try to find work and support myself. Please, Freya, I'm begging you, don't keep trying to talk me out of this.'

Freya nodded. She told herself that whatever Evie was going through, perhaps it would be no bad thing for her to get away on her own for a while.

She gave Evie a lift to Stromness to pick up the early ferry to the mainland and then Evie was headed south.

At the terminal, Freya gave her a hug and handed her an envelope containing two hundred and fifty pounds and the phone number and address of a hotel just outside London looking for live-in staff.

'The manager, Bernie, owes me a favour and he says there's a job going if you can get yourself down there. The money isn't great and it's a bit of a dump but it's a start until you get on your feet, and you won't have to worry about somewhere to live.'

She sighed and took Evie's face in her hands.

'I know I can't talk you out of this. God knows I've tried, but I will tell your family you are safe. If you can't or won't talk to them, please keep in touch with me so we know you are OK.'

Evie stood at the rails of the ferry watching Stromness disappear, hungrily taking in the views of the cliffs at St John's Head and the famous Old Man of Hoy, a sentinel pointing to the sky, a symbol of her home and all that she was leaving behind.

With her meagre savings and Freya's money, things were going to be tight. Evie had screwed up her courage, phoned the hotel from the ferry terminal and secured an interview, but it was clear that if she could get down there, the job was hers.

She booked herself a seat on the cheap fourteen-hour overnight bus from Inverness to London. From there she just had to get herself to the hotel in Crawley. It was a long and weary journey in darkness and pouring rain.

She dozed on and off, awakened by snores, grumbles and the occasional horn blast as impatient drivers tried to overtake the bus.

She couldn't get the nightmarish images of what had happened that night out of her head. How would she ever be able to live with the terror and guilt?

7

Orkney, 2024

Evie woke up in Freya's bright, comfortable spare room the next morning with the sun streaming through the windows and felt a brief moment of peace before the grief of her father's death made her whole body ache with loss.

She got up, put on a cute patchwork dressing gown that was hanging on the door, and found Freya in her sunroom. It looked over the water and was furnished with a comfy orange sofa and two squishy chairs with plump cushions and colourful throws.

One of Evie's portraits of Freya from over twenty-one years ago hung on the wall. Freya smiled at her as she handed her a cup of coffee.

'Do you remember doing that one?'

It was bittersweet for Evie to recall the teenager who had created that portrait with such love, and who'd spent long summer nights drawing and painting and making plans with Kate and Edwyn.

Everything had been so simple back then and they'd had it all worked out. Kate was going to be a hugely successful teacher, Edwyn a famous surgeon in Edinburgh and Evie was off to art school in Glasgow to become an acclaimed painter and sculptor. They were all going to make a such a big difference in the world.

She smiled at Freya. 'You don't look any different to when that portrait was done.'

It was true. Freya had grown plumper and greyer, but her smile was still the same and lit up her round face, which was surprisingly free of lines or any sign of ageing.

'Well, there's no wrinkles on a balloon as my old dad used to say about my mum,' said Freya. 'My moon face has come into its own as the years go by. But, don't forget, I'm older than your mother. I'm nearly eighty. Christ, even when I say it out loud, I can't quite believe it.'

'You look at least twenty years younger than that; I've always felt you were nearer my age than my parents.'

Freya was pleased and added, 'Anyway, because my eyesight isn't what it was, I can't really see any signs of ageing when I take my glasses off and look in the mirror to put on my make-up. Right, Evie, get yourself dressed. We have things to do.'

Freya was taking Evie to Kirkwall to sort out all the paperwork that always had to be tackled after a death. Evie was so relieved to have her help, especially with organising Duncan's funeral in a week's time.

Freya put a notice in the *Orcadian* newspaper and called everyone she could think of who had been close to Duncan to let them know the details. Although Evie's dad had become something of a hermit in the last years of his life, Big Duncan remained a highly respected and much-loved man, and she knew there would be a lot of people wanting to pay their respects.

Freya dropped Evie off at the solicitors in Kirkwall's main street at 11 a.m. for the reading of the will. Evie's stomach was churning with nerves and Freya picked up on her edginess.

'I know you are worried about Liv being there. Are you sure you don't want me to come with you? You know what your sister is like.'

'It's OK, Freya. I need to do this for myself.'

Evie walked through the door to where a bone-thin woman, clearly a stranger to soap and water, was ranting at a harassed-looking receptionist. Evie recognised the scrawny, filthy woman as her sister, Liv. Now aged forty-six, she looked decades older. Her skin had the deep furrows of a heavy smoker and the bags under her eyes were purplish black. Her hair was stringy and matted, and she looked like a starving hawk.

She was yelling furiously at the receptionist. 'I don't see why I should be kept waiting. There's no one else who is going to get anything in my dad's will. I know my rights. It's all coming to me.'

With a weary sigh the receptionist replied, 'Miss Muir. I've told you we are expecting your sister. In fact, this must be her now.'

Liv spun round, her face distorted with rage and shock.

With a voice dripping venom, she said, 'I can't believe you have the nerve to show your face after what you did to me. Don't think you will get a penny from the old man. You aren't entitled to a fucking thing. He hated you. We all hated you. You were told never to come back.'

The old feelings of guilt threatened to overcome Evie as she remembered the last time she had seen Liv. Her sister would never forgive her, and even the death of their father wouldn't change anything.

'Please, Liv, I can't deal with all of that now. I was told to come here for the reading of the will. I'm not after anything. I know I don't deserve it. I just want to know what Dad would have wanted us to do for the funeral.'

Glaring, Liv leant in closer. 'And then you'll go,' she hissed. 'You'll leave this island, for good. Otherwise, you know what will happen. I've kept your dirty little secret all these years. But maybe now is the time to tell everyone the truth.'

Evie felt a chill run through her at the thought of Freya, Edwyn and Kate knowing what she'd done. She nodded, miserably.

The receptionist coughed discreetly and said, 'Mr Sutherland is ready to see you now if you would just step this way.'

Evie recognised the young solicitor in the cluttered, over-heated office who looked at them both with sympathy and curiosity. He had been in the class below her at school.

He cleared his throat. 'Mr Duncan Muir made this will last year before he got really ill. There are details of his funeral requests, but I'm sorry to inform you that there's not much money. Your father seems to have taken out a lot of lump sums from his savings, especially over the last few years, and he wanted any money left over to go to you, Liv.'

Evie knew that would be the case. It was only right and fair after all that had happened. 'Well, thank you for your help,' she said formally. 'If that's all we had better get going as there's lots to do.'

'Wait, I'm not quite finished. Your father has left the family home and contents to you, Evie. There's no mortgage so it is yours outright. Mr Muir was very clear about it. It's a valuable asset, although I think it will need a bit of work.'

Liv was fuming. She stood up, her whole body vibrating with anger.

'You have got to be kidding me. She swans back here and gets the house after everything she's done. Well, don't think you have heard the last of this.' She jabbed a finger into Evie's chest. 'I want what's mine and I want you on the next plane south.'

Liv stormed out, slamming the door behind her so hard the windows shook and dust billowed up from the old legal files piled up on every available space.

The solicitor coughed and said, 'I'm afraid feelings do run high when it comes to a will reading, Miss Muir, especially when money and property are to be divided up between family members who might not get along. Let me read it out to you to clarify. Your father stated, "I want my youngest daughter Evie to always have a part of Orkney to come home to. My dearest wish is that she will return and live here in her childhood home where she belongs."

He handed Evie a slim envelope.

'Your father also left you this letter he gave to me for safe-keeping at the same time he made his latest will. Again, he was most insistent I made sure to hand it to you personally after his death.'

Evie's hands were trembling as she opened the letter.

My dearest Teenie,

If you are reading this then I am no longer here, but I couldn't leave you for ever without letting you know how much I have missed you all these years.

I think of you every single day and not being able to hear your voice and see your face is a constant pain in the deepest part of my soul.

I know you felt you had no choice but to leave us, but it has broken my heart that you cut me out of your life so completely. I have gone over that terrible night so many times wishing I could have taken back what I said.

I wish we could have had the chance to make things right between us. All I have ever wanted is for you to be happy. It was my job to keep you safe from harm and I failed.

I look back on my mistakes and I know that when you were a child, I should have helped you overcome your fear of the water, and I should have taught you to swim. Maybe that would have made all the difference.

So, I want you to forget the past and get into the water and swim like a selkie. I can only hope you have found someone who loves you as much as I do and that you have built a good life, and now that I am gone maybe you feel you can come home.

I love you. I will always love you, my Teenie.

Your dad xxx

Evie thought she didn't have any more tears to shed but they rolled down her face and dripped into her lap.

The solicitor didn't know where to put himself, confronted by so much sorrow. He wordlessly pushed a box of man-sized tissues towards Evie, and she gratefully grabbed a handful.

She somehow managed to thank him and ended up outside where Freya was waiting in the car. Not trusting herself to speak, she handed over the letter for her to read. Freya quickly scanned Duncan's words and put the letter down on her lap with a sigh.

'I told you he never stopped loving you, Evie, and here's the proof.'

'I should have come back years ago, but I was too scared. Time just went by so fast, and I will regret that for the rest of my life.' Evie murmured.

8

Orkney, 1963

With the bride and groom being so very young that technically they couldn't have had a drink at their own marriage celebration, everyone assumed Cara was pregnant and they'd had a shotgun wedding, but, as their first anniversary loomed and no baby appeared, it became clear it was a genuine love match. The lack of a baby wasn't for the want of trying.

In the first year of their marriage, Duncan would rush home for 'afternoon delight' after working on the farm since daybreak. They couldn't get enough of each other, and Cara channelled her energies into playing the role of being the most desirable as well as the most helpful of wives.

At first, Cara's restless energy was poured into making the 'perfect' home. She gutted the three small upstairs bedrooms, painted the walls white and polished the old wooden furniture until it gleamed.

She used her wedding money from her mother to have the dingy kitchen ripped out and refitted, although she kept the old cooking range and her late mother-in-law's beautiful, hand-crafted Orkney chair, created with such care from driftwood gathered on the beaches and straw from the fields.

No one knew exactly how old this chair was, but it had been passed down through the generations and, one day, she would in turn give it to her eldest child. When Cara had done all that was possible inside the house she turned her gaze outside, working tirelessly weeding the garden, and planting vegetables. She cooked *Desperate Dan*-sized meals for her huge-and-always-hungry husband who gave thanks every day for having Cara in his life.

She was building the ideal nest to be filled with a brood of their noisy, happy chicks. Then she could finally relax having achieved her dream of perfect motherhood.

In those early days, Duncan could not have been happier. He missed his gentle mother, but Cara had more than filled the empty place in his heart. He did sometimes wish she would take time to relax and enjoy their life together, but she was always in a rush. They lived in such a beautiful place, close to the water and near to Kirkwall, but still with a sense of sweet remoteness where the sunsets made your heart sing.

After a long day's work, he loved going down to the beach to swim and the cool water soothing his aching muscles. In the first year of their marriage, Cara would often join him, and she would shriek with laughter as he threw her up in the air as though she weighed less than nothing, but her visits became less and less as she became caught up in never-ending tasks.

Duncan longed to sit outside his house looking over Scapa Flow, quietly taking in the view and counting his blessings, but his restless wife would have a long list of jobs for him that needed doing right this minute, from putting up shelves to fixing outside lights and painting walls.

None of it was urgent, but he was never allowed to take a breath and rest and be thankful; however, he lived to please his Cara and loved to see her nod of satisfaction as she ticked off another completed job on her list.

Her busy brain was always thinking up new ways to earn money and she threw herself into all kinds of fads. She kept bees for honey and to make candles from the wax and planned to make scented soap to sell to the tourist shops, but somehow the bees all died, and the soap turned out like cloying, sweet cooking fat.

Each failure made her furious and even more driven to succeed, but she was extremely good at knitting, especially little yellow-and-white matinee jackets from the softest wool. These were put away in a special baby chest lined with tissue paper, eagerly awaiting the arrival of a newborn.

At first, she would tell herself after each monthly disappointment that it was just as well she wasn't pregnant as she had so much to do. When well-meaning neighbours and family asked her when they were thinking of starting a family, she would lie and say they were busy sorting out the house and the farm. There was time enough for babies in the future.

Inside, she was in despair. The blood of each period felt like a mark of failure. But just before their third wedding anniversary, Cara discovered she was pregnant at last.

After her second period was late, she did a test and hugged herself in glee and triumph when it was positive. She had finally done it. She was going to be a mother at last.

That will show them all, she thought with satisfaction.

She knitted a tiny pair of yellow bootees and served them up for Duncan's breakfast instead of his usual giant fry-up. He looked down at his plate, thoroughly confused, before it dawned on him what this meant. He let out a bellow of joy and got up to hug Cara, then stopped himself, fearful he might crush her and the precious baby.

'I can't believe we are having a baby!' he said. 'This is wonderful news.'

Then a cloud came over his face. 'Are you sure you are all right, though? Shouldn't you sit down? Let me make you a cup of tea and bring you a blanket. Do you want chocolate?'

Cara laughed. 'Duncan, behave. I'm not ill, I'm pregnant. You don't need to treat me like cut glass. I feel absolutely fine, and I'm so happy. We will be a family now and this is just the start. I want a whole football team.'

He grinned at her. 'You are going to be such an amazing mother. I can't wait to see you all fat and waddling about.'

'You are daft, Duncan Muir.'

'We'll need to get my old crib scrubbed and sanded down for the bairn. How my ma would have loved to have seen her first grandchild in it.'

Cara sat on his knee and hugged him tightly. Her eyes burned fiercely. 'Our baby will have the very best of everything. We can give it all that we never had.'

Duncan smiled at her. 'But, most of all, our baby will be loved and cherished. That's the most important thing.'

They had a long talk into the night about girls' and boys' names, and redecorating the nursery, and how their lives would change for the better.

As he was drifting off to sleep, Duncan turned to her. 'I promise both of you will want for nothing. I will work all the hours God sends. You aren't to worry about a thing. Just rest and eat properly and, please, Cara, don't overdo things. You push yourself too hard.'

She promised Duncan she'd take it easy, and maybe even believed it herself. But Cara couldn't keep still for any length of time and buzzed about the house cleaning and sorting her already immaculate cupboards, although she always made sure to be sitting down on her Orkney chair knitting yet another matinee jacket for the baby when Duncan came home.

'That's my girl,' he would say fondly. 'Taking it nice and easy. You look so beautiful. Being pregnant suits you. You are all soft and there's a glowing light on your face.'

Duncan had never loved her more, and he told himself that everything would be all right now.

Just a few days later, Cara woke up early with a terrible cramp in her stomach. She threw back the duvet and started to scream when she saw blood on the sheets.

Duncan was making her tea and toast downstairs when he heard her cries of despair and rushed up the stairs.

Cara was walking frantically backwards and forwards, her eyes glassy, wringing her hands. Her nightdress was streaked with blood. He wanted to howl in anguish, but he knew he had to be strong and mustn't panic Cara.

He tried to keep his voice calm and steady. 'Let me help you get dressed and I will take you to the hospital. They can take care of you. It will be all right. We will get through this together, but you need to let me help you.'

Cara lay down on the bloodied bed and curled up into a ball. Duncan knelt by her side and tried to take her hand, but she pushed him away and shut her eyes. She said flatly, 'Leave me alone. I don't want you near me. I don't want anyone near me. I've lost my baby. Everything is ruined.'

Duncan didn't know what to say or do. He felt utterly help-less and useless. All the plans they had made, all the hopes and dreams they had shared were nothing but dust. His Cara was like a broken doll. He had to say something to try to reach her.

'It'll be OK, Cara. I promise.'

She looked at him blankly and said coldly, 'You idiot. How can anything ever be all right ever again?'

He eventually managed to get her to the hospital where she was checked out and reassured by a kind doctor that this was very common indeed, but they could always try again. This made Cara livid with anger. She wanted to hang on to her rage because being angry was easier than sinking into a black hole of grief.

She didn't say a word to Duncan on the journey back home and went straight to bed, pulling the covers over her head. Duncan didn't know what to say to this chilly, remote stranger. This was the first time she had looked at him with indifference and dislike. He felt as though she was slipping away from him.

Duncan didn't know what to do with himself, so he went out for a long, lonely walk with the dogs. When he got back in the early evening, the door to their bedroom was closed and the spare-room bed was made up. He sat down on the bed, his head in his hands. He was heartbroken about the loss of their baby and in despair that he couldn't get through to his beloved Cara.

9

Orkney, 2024

The last time Evie had stood on this doorstep was twenty years ago and now, here she was, a grown woman of thirty-eight, feeling like a vulnerable child again. The spectacular view over Scapa Flow hadn't changed, but everything else about the solid farmhouse was almost unrecognisable. The overgrown garden was a tangle of thorns and weeds. The house looked unloved and forlorn.

Evie opened the faded, paint-blistered door and was appalled at the state of the place.

Her fastidious mother would have had an attack of the vapours. The living room and kitchen smelt of unwashed clothes, soup turned sour and general neglect. It was dark and dank and looked as though no one had lived there for months, even though Duncan had only been taken away to the hospital a week ago.

He'd obviously been sleeping on the old, busted sofa as there was a heap of grubby blankets on the floor and very little else. There wasn't even a TV, although judging by the dust marks on the old side table, one had been there until very recently. Her dad's radiogram and vinyl collection were gone. None of Evie's paintings were on the walls and her mother's prized display cabinet with its collection of crystal had also disappeared.

'I have a feeling I know who has been here and picked over the bones of everything when your dad was taken to hospital,' said Freya grimly, walking in behind her. 'Liv must have had help to load it up into a van. I reckon all the good stuff will have been sold already.'

Evie tried to keep the tremble from her voice. 'I really don't care about that, Freya. I'm just so sad that my dad was living like this.'

'I'm so sorry. I did try to clean up when he would actually let me in the house. Most of the time we sat in the garden. I'd take out the bins and do the dishes, but I thought sitting talking to him was of more benefit than giving the place a right going over.'

'Don't you dare apologise. You've done more for him than his own daughters.'

The two of them walked up the creaking stairs and looked around the sad, half-empty upstairs rooms. Evie swallowed hard as she pushed open the door into what had once been her tiny childhood bedroom. There were black damp patches on the ceiling and the wallpaper was peeling off in places. A few of her old books lay scattered on the floor. The carpet was covered in stains and cigarette burns.

What was she thinking coming back here to this house and imagining she could abide by her father's wishes? Let alone overcome her fear of water and learn to swim. The thought of going into the sea made her feel sick to her stomach. Her chest tightened and she knew she had to get out of this house full of ghosts and bad memories.

Freya bustled in. 'The bedsteads are fine, but you'll need new mattresses. There's not much worth keeping downstairs but that kitchen range is a beauty. The place just needs a bit of paint,' she added briskly, before catching sight of Evie. 'You look pale, love – let's catch a breath of fresh air.'

Outside sitting down on a battered bench in the garden, Freya asked her worriedly, 'Has this all been too much for you?'

'No, I'm fine,' Evie lied. 'But I do need to get the house sorted for when I sell up.'

Freya's shoulders stiffened. 'Sell up?'

Evie felt her stomach clench. She wished she could tell Freya that even if she wanted to, there was no way she could stay in Orkney, not with Liv threatening to tell everyone her secret. There was also the issue of money. She didn't have much to fall back on, and she couldn't stay away from work for all that much longer, even if her father had just died.

'I've got my life in London to be getting back to,' she said lamely.

'Ah, yes,' Freya said. 'Your life in London.' She narrowed her eyes. 'I'd like to hear more about that and why you would want to go back.'

I'm keeping secrets from everyone, thought Evie miserably. Secrets from Freya, secrets from Jeremy. But there was no other way.

'Maybe I could think about renting it out as a holiday home, for a bit,' Evie said to Freya, hoping it would keep the peace.

Freya sighed. 'Your dad wanted you to have a place in Orkney. A proper home here.'

Evie remembered just how stubborn Freya could be when she got an idea in her head.

'I know, Freya, but, whatever happens, I do need to get it fixed up. I don't suppose you know anyone who could help?'

'Well, as it happens, I know the very man,' said Freya. 'He's lived up here for ten years now. His name is Andrzej. He's an electrician by trade but he runs his own business, and he can turn his hand to anything. He built my sunroom and it's my favourite place in the whole of my house.'

'He sounds ideal,' said Evie.

Freya beamed. 'Aye, he's a lovely man. He first came to Scotland from Poland when he was a student years ago, staying in Dundee for the berry picking in Blairgowrie. He fell in love with a local girl, but it didn't work out. So, he decided to do a bit of travelling and headed north. He told me that as soon as he got to Orkney he felt right at home, and this was where he settled.'

'Have you a bit of a crush on him, Freya?' said Evie with a smile.

Freya spluttered with laughter. 'Och, he's way too young for me. He's only about forty-five, and he's carrying a torch for a lovely lass, which is a story I will tell you about another day.'

Evie got up and walked round to the outside of the old cowshed where she used to squirrel herself away years ago when playing hide-and-seek with her dad. There was what looked like a bundle of old firewood scattered across the grass. She moved closer, and saw it was the wreckage of her grandmother's beautiful Orkney chair that Cara used to polish with a frenzy until it gleamed.

Evie completely broke down. She had been trying to hold herself together, but seeing this wrecked chair was too much. It had been crafted with such love and care so many years ago, just to end up thrown aside as though it meant nothing.

'Oh, Freya. I loved this chair. Look at the state of it. It's been left outside, and it's ruined. There's cigarette burns on the arms. It's all broken into pieces.'

She ran into Freya's comfortable arms and sobbed her heart out.

'You have a good cry, my poor pet. You've had the stuffing knocked out of you. But you are home now, and you will heal,' said Freya. 'And there's enough of that chair left to be put back together and it will be as good as new. No, it will be even better.' *And we will put you back together too*, she vowed to herself.

'It's all such a mess. I don't know what to do.'

'Now. Listen to your Aunty Freya. You are coming home with me for a bowl of homemade soup and a nap. I will phone Andrzej and he'll come and see what needs to be done here. Until then you are staying with me. You need taking care of, my girl.'

Evie felt she didn't deserve such kindness, but Freya's words soothed some of her pain and it had been a long time since she'd been wrapped in unconditional love.

Back at Freya's, as Evie slept, Freya went into battle mode. First up she called Andrzej.

'It's an emergency. I need your help.'

'Good afternoon to you, Freya, and how are you?' Andrzej chuckled down the phone at Freya's usual manner of coming straight to the point with no social niceties when she wanted something done right away.

'Sorry, Andrzej. I'm just anxious to get things done for Evie. I told you about how she's come back to us.'

'I know, and I heard about her father. News travels fast here, as you well know. I'm so sorry, Freya. I know Duncan was your friend.'

'Aye, that he was. I think life just became too much for the poor man. Anyway, Duncan has left Evie the house in his will, but you want to see the state of it. It needs a steam clean, and it smells of damp. I'm sure there's dry rot and, of course, there's bound to be woodworm. It needs a new bathroom and kitchen, and the garden is a right mess.'

'Maybe there are still Italian POWs lurking in the under-growth,' Andrzej said with a deep chuckle. 'I've just been reading up on those prisoners who were held here in Orkney during World War Two.'

Andrzej was the kindest man in the world and obsessed with Orkney history. Freya knew he would be dying to tell her all he had discovered about the famous Italian chapel built on Orkney by POWs, and usually she was happy to smile and nod as though hearing it all for the first time.

Unlike some who made their home in Orkney, Andrzej didn't want to shake things up or interfere. He preferred to learn from the locals and fit in with the rhythm of their lives. That's why everyone loved and trusted him. But today, she needed to keep him on track to help Evie.

'There very might well be,' said Freya. 'So do you think you'll be able to take a look as soon as possible?'

'I'll see what I can do. Don't worry, your Evie will be my priority.'

Freya was on a roll. She had another very important task to get to. She had picked up every single splinter of the chair she could find at the back of the cowshed, and it was now in the boot of her car. Luckily, there were still craftsmen who specialised in making these fine chairs by hand. If she told them it was for Big Duncan's girl, they would surely be able to repair it. She knew the man for the job.

IO

Orkney, 1978

Cara was well able to get pregnant, but simply couldn't hold on to a baby full-term. She went through six agonising early miscarriages, each one breaking her heart. She'd been so sure she would have a brood of beautiful, bright children, the envy of everyone back home on Hrossey. That each loss made her feel like a failure.

She borrowed medical books from the library and scoured them trying to find an answer. Duncan was put on faddy diets and prevented from drinking any kind of booze. He was banned from wearing underwear and told to keep his tackle cool and well aired.

Sex, something he had revelled in with Cara, who was soft-mouthed and loving when they were in bed together, was now a clinical chore, precisely timed around ovulation, and afterwards Cara lay with her legs in the air, timing how long she thought it would take for his swimmers to reach their destination.

They went through a barrage of tests, going south to Aberdeen to see specialists, but doctors found nothing amiss with either of them. They were told to just keep trying and not to get too worried and that nature would take its course.

Cara would return home on the ferry after these appointments flinty-eyed and silent. Duncan would try to reassure her that they were both still young and strong, but she just sat like a statue with her eyes on the horizon. He was at a loss to know what to say and felt clumsy and useless.

Occasionally, she would head down to the beach, pointedly not inviting Duncan. There, she would slowly wade into the water and float on her back, letting the cold numb her body and her mind. It was the only time she felt free from the cycle of loss, hope and grief.

It didn't help that almost every year one of her Hrossey cousins added to their growing brood, and her mother kept sending her photos of various near-identical red-headed chubby cherubs.

Duncan constantly assured her she was more than enough for him and once, after another month of trying ended in tears of disappointment, he suggested they could foster or adopt.

'Cara, think of the life we could give to a bairn. We could take an older one and teach them about the farm. It would be brilliant, don't you think? You would be a fantastic foster mum and they'd have such a grand time.'

Cara was having none of it; she was desperate to take on the role of a mother, but it had to be on her terms: a baby born from her own body. Only then would she have the 'perfect family'.

'Adopt or foster? Are you kidding?' she snapped at Duncan. 'You would seriously want to bring up someone else's baby. You'd never know what you were getting. I can't believe you don't want your own flesh and blood. It's beyond my understanding.'

Duncan could only bite his lip when Cara went into one of her tirades. He let her rant then nodded his head and said simply, 'All right, Cara. We will keep trying and we don't need to talk about adopting or fostering ever again if it upsets you so much.'

And so life went on, with Cara becoming more and more shut down and despairing and Duncan feeling sad, stressed and guilty that he couldn't give his beloved wife what she wanted most. Then, just after their sixteenth wedding anniversary, Cara told Duncan she was once again pregnant.

The excitement of the very first time she'd broken the news, when they'd both been so very young and full of hope, was long gone. Instead of joy, there was anxiety, apprehension and the very real possibility of another devastating loss. The tiny box room, which Duncan had painted bright white and yellow with such love, had been demoted into a sort of all-purpose storage cupboard. The crib his mother-in-law had sent from Hrossey and taken him hours to lovingly sand, smooth and varnish, was wrapped in a sheet in the corner along with the box full of Cara's handknitted baby clothes.

Although they didn't discuss it, they both knew not to clear out or redecorate the little nursery until the baby was actually born; they were no longer filled with the joy of making plans for the future, discussing baby names and wondering whether the little mite would be cursed with Duncan's large nose and big hands.

They were both thirty-two now and had suffered crippling and devastating disappointment far too many times. So, Duncan simply nodded, wrapped tiny Cara in a big hug and kissed her forehead.

'Let's just take each day as it comes, love. I keep telling you that we have each other and that's enough for me. You need to rest and be calm and take care of yourself and let me take care of you too.'

'I don't want anyone else to know apart from the doctor,' said Cara. 'I can't stand the way everyone looks at me with pity in their eyes and I don't want my mum to make a fuss.'

Duncan smiled to himself. If there was a choice between who was more likely to cause a hoo-ha, his wife would win the gold medal over his mother-in-law, but it would be a close-run thing.

He wasn't a religious man, but he prayed that this time they would be blessed with a baby. He longed to be a dad, but he was also thinking what another miscarriage would do to Cara. He feared she would be broken beyond repair. He just wanted to fix her, in the same way he could mend faulty plumbing and ancient electrics.

This pregnancy was different though. Cara was violently ill almost from the first, something that hadn't ever happened before. 'I don't know why they call it morning sickness; I'm chucking up all the time, morning, noon and night, and I don't have the energy to do anything,' Cara wailed.

Duncan was there to hold her hair away from her face as she retched until nothing was left in her stomach but bitter bile. He applied cool cloths to her forehead and the back of her neck and tried to get her to keep down even a little bit of broth or dry toast.

The headaches and nausea were so unbearable that on one dark sleepless night, Cara told herself it would be a mercy if she died and the baby with her. The wind howled outside like a banshee, thunder roared, and lightning flashed, making the dogs howl.

Cara instantly regretted such dark thoughts and was terrified that she would once again miscarry. She became haunted by feelings of guilt and despair, and grew pale and thin, apart from her enormous pregnant belly, and it was a struggle for her to get out of bed most days.

She couldn't tell anyone how she felt. Poor Duncan was snappily dismissed as hopeless, and she didn't want 'pitying looks' from her mother or her cousins. She forced herself to go to the clinic for scans and check-ups but refused visits from well-meaning friends and neighbours, and shut her ears to any advice.

She felt exhausted, nauseous and terrified, but she didn't lose the baby. As her time came near, she allowed herself to think that maybe this time everything would be all right, and she'd finally have the chance to be a mother.

She had to hold on to that.

II

Orkney, 2024

The next morning, Evie woke up after being out like a light for ten solid hours. She found Freya in the kitchen making breakfast.

'I haven't slept like that for years. After everything that's been going on I thought I'd be awake all night tossing and fretting.'

'It's the air,' Freya replied, bringing hot rolls, bright yellow butter, homemade jam and freshly brewed coffee to the kitchen table. 'The Orkney air is magic.'

'I think you're right. Despite everything, it's good to be here.'

'And I am so glad to have you back and I want to help get you settled in.'

Evie gulped her coffee. 'But, Freya, I'm not staying. That was never the plan. I told you I'd be selling the place or letting it out. I still have a life in London.'

Evie knew she was kidding herself. She'd had a clutch of missed calls from Jeremy this morning, that she hadn't returned. She couldn't bear to listen to his voicemails. She had no idea how long she could keep on trying to pretend he didn't exist.

Freya decided it was wiser right now not to try to push Evie into staying, so instead she said breezily, 'Look, I've got things to do this morning but stay here and wait for Andrzej – he's swinging past before he goes over to the house to see what needs to be done. He will be here any minute. Give him a coffee, strong, a dash of milk and four sugars.'

Ten minutes after Freya had left, a massive man appeared at the door. He looked like the kind of fella a nervous billionaire would hire as a security guard. Evie took in the bald bullet head, thick neck and massive shoulders. He had a jaw that looked as if it could chop through wood like it was butter.

A massive paw was thrust into her hand.

'I am Andrzej, and you must be Evie? It is such a joy to meet a friend of Freya's. I am here to help you and I will give you all of my skills. But first we have coffee? Yes?'

Evie had just made a pot of strong coffee. She poured a cup for him, added milk then said, doubtfully, 'Are you sure you take four sugars?'

'Yes, Evie, I am cutting back,' he said gravely. 'I used to take six spoonfuls, but Freya said that was being an effing eejit and I would die of a heart attack. At least I think those were her exact words.' He looked at her kindly. 'I am very sorry about your father. He was a good man. I am afraid he drank too much beer and whisky, but he was very kind to me when I first came here and told me many stories about these beautiful islands.'

Evie smiled. 'I remember his tales. Did he tell you about when the Vikings came and all of the power struggles and murders? It was like *Game Of Thrones* without the dragons.'

'That he did. I think your dad always thought of himself as a Norseman. We spent many hours going over the Viking sagas and the story of St Magnus. Poor man to be murdered by his cousin. I will never forget my first sight of his magnificent cathedral in Kirkwall. The stone so bright and rosy red and inside so enormous that I felt very small.'

Evie thought it would have to take a huge and impressive cathedral like St Magnus to make Andrzej feel anything less than gigantic.

'He loved all of those stories. I'm glad he shared them with you.'

Andrzej placed a hand on his enormous chest. 'I have made it my life's work to visit all of Orkney's islands and to write everything down for my children.'

'Oh,' said Evie, 'That's so lovely. How many children do you have, Andrzej?'

'I have no children yet, Evie. None. But I live in hope.'

He looked so sad for a moment that Evie thought he was about to say more, but he merely drained his coffee mug, slapped his thighs and said, 'I must go and look at that house of yours and see what we need to do to make it happy again so you can come back and live here. Freya says this is where you belong, and I have learnt that she is never wrong.'

Evie smiled at this kind-hearted, well-meaning man, but she wasn't sure that she really did belong here any more. She wasn't sure she fitted in anywhere.

Freya pulled up outside a ramshackle bungalow on the outskirts of Stromness. She got out of her car and wasn't surprised to find the door was locked. 'Typical,' she muttered. 'She obviously has something to hide.'

Freya rang the doorbell, which didn't work, so she ended up hammering a fist on the door.

The door was answered by a bleary-eyed skinny bloke who Freya thought could do with a damned good scrub and might have been any age from twenty to fifty. When he opened his mouth, it was to reveal teeth like a row of condemned buildings.

'What do you want?' he demanded, trying to be tough and threatening.

'Not the monkey, that's for sure,' retorted Freya. 'Where's the organ grinder?'

He looked blank.

'Oh, for the love of Christ,' said Freya impatiently. 'Just let me by.'

It was the smell that caught the back of Freya's throat as she went into the living room: a mixture of sweat and cheap cigarettes. Through the gloom she saw Liv sitting on the sofa rolling a joint.

'Well, if it isn't the town freak,' drawled Liv.

Freya had dealt with insults all of her life far worse than even Liv could dream up. This was nothing more than a flea bite.

'I won't be staying long, but I wanted to let you know about your father's funeral. I have written down all the details. You've already got the black outfit obviously, but clean yourself up and try to stay off the bevvy and the drugs and show a bit of respect for the man.'

Liv bristled.

'Who do you think you are, coming in here and telling me how to behave at my own da's funeral? I doubt you will be telling your precious Evie the same?'

'Leave your sister out of it. She's been through enough.'

Liv gave a cruel laugh.

'You think she's been through it? You think you know it all, Freya, but you don't have a clue.'

'About what?' said Freya.

Liv narrowed her eyes. 'You all think she's perfect, don't you?'

'If you've something to say about Evie, spit it out.'

Liv scowled. 'Oh, fuck right off. Get out of my house!'

Freya didn't back down. 'Look, Liv, whether you like or not you're part of this community. We've all tried to help you, and we still want to. Don't cut yourself off, especially now.'

'I don't need anyone's help,' said Liv, her voice stony. 'Especially not yours. I can take care of myself, and I distinctly remember telling you to fuck off.'

Freya couldn't get out of the place quickly enough. She took in a deep breath of good clean air and drove off, with the windows down, to get rid of the noxious atmosphere.

Fortunately, her next mission was more positive.

She followed the road up to Dounby and found the sign for *Isbister and son. Orkney chairmakers.*

It was a small family business with the garage converted into a workshop and the beautiful chairs displayed in what would have been the front room.

Old Mr and Mrs Isbister lived next door in a house bought for them by their son, Ross, who was in his early forties. He lived upstairs above his workshop.

Freya rang the bell and went in. What a contrast to Liv's hovel covered in muck and bruck. The room smelled of fresh wood, clean straw and the tang of the sea.

A serious-looking young man who looked as though he had been born in southern Spain was putting the final touches to a beautifully made traditional Orkney chair with its distinctive hood to keep out the draughts. He had the blackest hair and eyes, and was completely unaware of how devastatingly attractive he was with his compact, sturdy body and bottom like a newly ripened nectarine.

'Ross, it's yourself,' said Freya. 'I'm so glad to find you in. Stop what you're doing right away. I have an important repair job for you.'

'Freya, I can hardly keep up with the orders I've got. So many tourists want an Orkney chair of their very own.'

'This one is extra special, and, if I'm honest, I'm not even sure if your incredible skills will be able to put it back together.'

Freya knew exactly what she was doing.

'Well, we'll just see about that,' said Ross, slightly affronted, 'Where is it?'

Freya had to stop herself from smiling at how well her ruse had worked. Ross was a man of few words, but such a master craftsman that she had high hopes he could repair Evie's chair.

'It's in a million pieces in the back of my car. Come and have a keek and see what you think.'

Ross looked at the wreckage and gave a low whistle.

'For the love of God, Freya, it's like the shittiest jigsaw puzzle I've ever seen. Should I not just make her a new one? It would be a hell of a lot easier.'

'I know you'll have to replace a lot of it as it's all so far gone, but it has to be the chair she remembers. A brand, new one just won't do.'

Ross looked unconvinced.

'Did I mention it was for Evie?' Freya added. 'You remember her, don't you?'

'I remember Evie fine well. Big Duncan's daughter. She left under a bit of a cloud if I recall. A bad business. I'm glad she's back. She's a nice lass.'

This was high praise indeed from Ross Isbister who viewed most women with deep distrust and had skilfully avoided being dragged down the aisle on numerous occasions despite the best efforts of most of the single women in Orkney.

'Well,' said Freya. 'Can you help? And can you do it fast?'

Ross rubbed his chin, looked heavenwards and eventually said, 'If I work at night and weekends, it might be possible, but it will still take me at least a month.'

'You've got a fortnight.'

Freya gave him a beaming smile and watched him muttering to himself as he gathered up all the bits and pieces of the chair. He'd need several days to clean the golden oat straw to remake the back of the chair. Then there was the driftwood to prepare to replace all the old bits, which would in turn have to be cleaned and polished, as well as the finishing stitching, and all of it done by hand.

It was a daunting job, but Freya knew Ross was up to the challenge.

She gave him a hug.

'Send the bill to me and I will see you at Big Duncan's funeral. Not a word to Evie, mind. This is a surprise.'

12

London, 2004

The Imperial Hotel was a faded, frowsy wedding cake that had seen better days, but Evie was welcomed effusively by Bernie, the general manager, who'd clearly been besotted with Freya when she had worked there.

'I can't believe it's been over ten years since I've seen her. Any friend of Freya's is a friend of mine. She's one in a million and I owe her big time.'

Evie just nodded at the man with the bad combover and shiny suit bursting at the seams. He had a face like a half-melted candle and an air of defeat, but he had a kind face.

'Can you possibly start right away?' he pleaded. 'We are so short-staffed. It's all hands on deck.'

Evie just nodded again.

'You don't say much do you. Let me show you to your room. You'll have to share, and it's a bit small. I see you are travelling light. Just that one bag? OK. Leave your stuff up there and then come back and I will let you know your hours and what I need you to do.'

Evie was given the title of chambermaid, but she really was just a glorified skivvy. Most of the other workers were teenagers and twentysomethings from Eastern Europe, over to improve their English and earn a bit of money before starting university back home.

Evie was sharing a room with Natalia, a flinty young Estonian student, outraged to discover that the Imperial was not a boutique hotel in the heart of London, but a crummy, sticky-carpeted relic used mainly by down-at-heel travelling salesmen and married men having affairs who rented rooms by the hour. Bernie called them the creepies from Crawley and never failed to snigger at his own joke.

Natalia loved listening to Evie speaking in her sing-song Orkney accent and decided to use 'peedie' for everything that was little, including her current boyfriend's penis. The poor fella never did cotton on that peedie wasn't an affectionate nickname for his manhood.

Despite how hard they tried, none of the staff could get Evie to open up about why she had left her home and her family to work in the ghastly Imperial.

They eventually gave up asking, but they all liked Evie who worked hard and was always willing to swap shifts and take on extra hours if they wanted to leave early. Of course, there was a reason for this. The only way she could get any sleep was to exhaust herself and then pass out the moment her head hit the pillow. Sometimes she couldn't believe how quickly her life had changed. She had gone from planning a future at art school and a future with Brodie to this sad shabby life.

She thought of Edwyn and Kate and felt ashamed and guilty for not being in contact with them.

Freya had called the hotel on her first day looking for her. A very deflated Bernie had told her Freya was on the line but hadn't given him the time of day.

'It's obviously very important she didn't even say hello to me properly,' he grumbled.

Evie reluctantly took the receiver and listened as Freya told her to come home.

Evie told her she needed more time away but promised to keep in contact. 'Tell my friends and family I'm all right but I need to be by myself right now. Please don't tell them where I am.'

Freya very reluctantly gave her word as long as Evie kept her promise to keep in touch. She sent Freya a postcard asking her to tell her family she was fine and wanted to be left alone.

Screwing up all her courage, Evie had called home late one night a few weeks after leaving, hoping to speak to her dad, but it was Liv who picked up the phone and ranted at her.

Evie could only listen in silence. She knew she deserved her sister's wrath.

On the phone Evie apologised to her over and over again and asked if there was anything she could do. Liv gave her bank details and demanded money every month not to tell anyone 'the dirty little secret'.

Evie said she would send as much as she possibly could.

She knew now she could never return home.

13

Orkney, 1978

Cara and Duncan's daughter, Olivia, came into the world two weeks early, red-faced and extremely angry with everyone and everything. She was in such a hurry to escape from the womb that Cara was badly torn up and needed dozens of stitches. For weeks she felt as though she was peeing through broken glass and her body ached all over. She had no energy and felt completely numb.

This wasn't how she had imagined being a new mother. Where was this feeling of unconditional love and the bliss of finally having a baby in her arms that she had always imagined? In the movie of her life, Cara had planned for a fat, happy, smiling newborn she could cover in kisses, not this grizzly, colicky gremlin who squirmed away from her and would not be comforted or cuddled.

Liv also refused to breastfeed, despite Cara's best efforts, which left her nipples on fire and her confidence wrecked.

Her baby would just about tolerate being held in her father's arms, greedily guzzling the milk from a bottle of formula while Cara watched them in tears, feeling guilty and hopeless, her leaky breasts swollen and painful. She told herself her baby hated her because of that one terrible moment when she'd wanted the pain and suffering to just go away.

It's all my fault she's such a difficult baby and she hates me, Cara thought. *I don't deserve to be a mother.*

Cara put on a brave face to all the kind visitors who brought her presents and made a fuss of the baby who they declared to be beautiful, even though she glowered like an extremely angry marmoset.

'They are going to have trouble with that one,' said the neighbours. 'Cara is a bag of nerves and Duncan is trying his best, bless him, but he is such a big, helpless galloot.'

They vowed to help as much as possible, but never to be seen to interfere. That was not their way. So, in the first few days and weeks, Duncan found that home-cooked pies and meals were left on the doorstep as well as baskets full of bread and cheese. Kind-hearted women popped in to babysit the fractious Liv, and somehow managed to find time to clean the kitchen and hang out washing while Cara dozed fitfully upstairs.

She would come down bleary-eyed and rant at Duncan for letting them do the housework.

'What will they think of me if I can't keep my own home nice and tidy and wash our clothes?' she fretted. 'Anyway, they don't do it all properly. Everything is in the wrong place. It's just more work for me. Tell them to leave us alone.'

Duncan didn't know what to do. He couldn't offend his generous neighbours, but he also didn't want to upset Cara. He also couldn't believe something so small as his baby daughter could cause such chaos and upheaval. He knew a baby would completely change his life. His pals in the pub joked often enough about the lack of sleep, zero sex and the sheer mayhem that comes with a newborn, but it was all done with a laugh and a joke. They loved their children dearly and were delighted that Big Duncan was finally a dad and hoped it would make Cara easier to live with.

Duncan couldn't tell them that he felt as though he was tiptoeing through a field of landmines and that Cara could go off at any time. There were tears and tantrums over the smallest of things, like burnt toast or a cup of tea going cold; Duncan didn't know how to make it better.

He also desperately wanted to love his bad-tempered baby daughter but couldn't help resenting her for causing Cara such distress, and then he'd feel horribly guilty.

Meanwhile, Cara was continually torturing herself. Her thoughts were going round and round in a vicious circle: *My baby knows I said I wanted to die and that she would die with me. That was such a wicked thing for me to think, even for just a moment, but I didn't mean it. I really didn't mean it.*

The tears would flow as Cara told herself, *I was never supposed to be a mother. That's what God was trying to tell me. I can't even feed her myself. She won't sleep at night, and I don't know what to do. This is all I have ever wanted. Why is it so bloody difficult. Why is this happening to me?'*

She couldn't bear to share these thoughts with Duncan. What would he think of her? The two of them warily circled each other in near silence apart from when Liv woke up and needed to be fed or changed.

Things came to a head when Sheila, Cara's mother, came from Hrossey to help. There was a terrible argument with Cara about Liv being left outside in her pram. Cara had her swaddled in hand-knitted woollens, and the baby was damp with sweat and shrieking in discomfort.

'She needs to kick her legs in the fresh air, Cara,' said her mother impatiently. 'She's far too hot. You need to leave her to sleep and try to get some rest yourself.'

Cara went ballistic, accused her mother of wanting the baby to catch pneumonia and ranting that she was an interfering old nuisance who had to stop telling her what to do. At that moment, Marie, the local health visitor, arrived. She had a long talk over a cup of tea with Sheila – Cara had run into her bedroom and banged the door shut.

'My Cara has always been highly strung,' explained Sheila. 'She needs everything to be perfect and she thought having a baby would be a Doris Day movie where you sit up in bed with perfect hair and make-up and the baby never cries or shits or vomits down your neck.'

'A lot of new mums find the reality doesn't meet their expectations,' said Marie diplomatically.

Sheila harrumphed. 'In my day you just got on with it and I brought Cara up myself. It's ridiculous, she's all worried about the house being a mess, when you can see it's a peedie palace. She's not sleeping and barely eating. I do what I can, but Liv isn't an easy baby. I'm too old to be a live-in nanny and the house is too small for both of us women to be in the kitchen at the same time.'

Marie was wise and very good at her job. She could see that Cara needed more than a well-meaning-but-rather-judgemental mother and an out-of-depth husband. In fact, Sheila declared she wasn't welcome and was getting the next ferry home. Later that day, Duncan drove his mother-in-law to the ferry as she bristled with anger against her daughter.

'She has you wrapped around her finger, Duncan,' said Sheila. 'I know you won't hear a word against her, but she's impossible and ungrateful. She always has been. I think it might be more than just baby blues. Have a word with that nice nurse, Marie.'

Duncan did tell Marie he was worried, and he was relieved when she popped round more often to keep an eye on his wife. As usual when she came to see her, Cara had a long list of questions and demands, but she never took the trouble to actually listen properly or take Marie's kindly advice on board.

Marie also put Cara in touch with a first-time-mother-and-baby group, hoping it would help her make friends and give her a chance to talk to other mums and share the highs and lows. Cara hated it. She had thought the other mums would feel just as unable to cope as she did, but, although they were all knackered, they were besotted with their babies and looked the picture of contentment even with leaky boobs and bits of toast in their hair. The other babies gurgled or breastfed happily, but Liv shrieked the whole time and wouldn't be comforted.

The mums asked Cara if maybe Liv needed to be changed or cuddled or just wanted a dummy tit. Cara couldn't tell them that this was just what Liv was like all the time. She was humiliated, upset and felt more isolated than ever. She never went back.

When Liv reached her first birthday, Cara was just about able to cope day to day, but she still couldn't bond properly with her child. She loved her daughter fiercely, but most of the time she didn't like her very much. That made Cara feel so incredibly guilty that, as the years passed, she would overcompensate, showering Liv with praise and presents. Not surprisingly she grew into a monstrous toddler and the terrible twos turned into the even more terrible threes and, by eight years old, she was a demanding little empress.

But Liv's life was about to turn upside down. If her parents felt she had been difficult before, they had no idea of the hurricane that was coming their way.

14

Evie lasted at the Imperial Hotel for nine years. Staff came and went, and Bernie gave her more responsibility, so she was effectively running the place.

Despite still sending Liv half of her earnings every month, eventually she had almost saved up enough to rent a flat and look for a job that didn't mean picking up bedding covered in unspeakable stains and cleaning up piss and shit from the bathroom floors.

Freya wrote to her regularly at the hotel. Just chatty letters with news of her mum and dad, babies being born and gossip about Kate and Edwyn, who were going steady and planning their wedding.

Evie was grateful that she never asked for an explanation as to why she wouldn't come home but, reading between the lines, she knew Freya lived in hope that one day she would confide all to her and return.

Evie would cry herself to sleep, going over the events that had led to her running away.

She rarely replied to these letters from home but cherished this one fragile link with her past and her heart leapt whenever she saw Freya's familiar handwriting on one of the very few envelopes addressed to her.

Freya's Cottage Orphir
2013

Dearest Evie

You have been on my mind a lot these past few days.

Your cousin Aileen's daughter Isla has had another boy. He's as fat and pink as a piglet with a gigantic head. God knows how she managed to get him out. She's so tiny and she gives birth to all these monstrous boys.

Kate and Edwyn still don't know I'm in touch with you, but the other day Kate said she wished she had your address as she wanted to invite you to their wedding. As I told you they are both back home. Edwyn wanted to work as a doctor here and Kate has a job as a teacher at the high school. Remember the three of you used to sit at my kitchen table and tell me of your plans for the future?

How long ago that seems. I have respected your wishes and I won't tell them where you are. I can't lie to you, Evie; they are very upset and would love to get in touch. I don't suppose you have changed your mind and I can let them know you are at the Imperial?

Do give Bernie my love. He's a grumpy old bugger but he does have a good heart. I don't know if he told you how I helped him when one of the guests accused him of breaking into her room and stealing her money. Bernie is a buffoon but he's not a thief. I told her we had CCTV in all the corridors (as if the Imperial would have such a thing) and could prove she was a bald-faced liar. She crumbled and he was pathetically grateful to me.

Your mum is the same, I'm afraid, and your dad is trying his best as he always does. Liv has gone completely off the rails and is the talk of Orkney. She is the instigator of so much trouble but somehow always manages to weasel her way out of it. I'm convinced she was behind that break-in at the Scapa distillery.

A gang of them swiped about a dozen bottles of whisky and then all got caught pissed out of their tiny minds on the beach in front. They are not exactly criminal masterminds. Liv got clean away as usual, but I know in my bones she was there. It was her gang of the usual suspects and she's unquestionably the ringleader. They all follow her like daft sheep.

Is there a proper message for your dad? Do you need anything? We miss you. Come home to us. Love Freya

Evie put the letter down and sighed. Liv was out of control, and it was all her fault for what she had done to her sister. Surely, if she returned to Orkney, it would only make things worse.

She was glad Kate and Edwyn had ended up with one another, it stung to realise they were moving on without her even if she was the one who left. Maybe she needed to do the same and try to build a better life here.

What she needed was a new start. She was restless and bored working in the hotel and was ready to move on. She had stayed on at school an extra year to do her sixth-year studies and her dissertation on the artist Hornel had been highly praised. She had passed all of her Highers in English, French, art and history with grades good enough for a place at art school, so, surely, she could get a decent enough job.

Over the next few months, she amassed a bottom drawer full of rejection letters, but finally secured an interview with an insurance company in the City looking for an office assistant.

With her quiet, well-mannered and obviously efficient manner, Evie made a good impression at the interview.

The large office was beige and sterile but compared with the Imperial, it was a palace. Evie hoped it would be her chance to leave the shabby seediness of third-rate hotel life firmly in the past.

She got a letter a week later telling her she had the job, earning three times as much as the Imperial.

Evie found a one-bedroom flat fifteen minutes' walk from the office that would have made her dad howl with rage at the exorbitant rent. She bought a cheap bed, a second-hand sofa and a TV.

Bernie told her to nick anything she wanted from the hotel, so she helped herself to crockery and cutlery. Knowing all too well what the towels and bedding had been subjected to over the years, she passed on those and bought new ones instead.

Her little flat was clean and tidy but it lacked any sort of warmth or personality. There were no family photographs or mementos of holidays or special occasions.

Evie had cut herself off from her past, but she had also buried the very essence of who she was.

The laughing girl who would run barefoot on the grass with her dogs, dressed in the brightest colours and singing at the top of her lungs, had turned into a drab, mousy dullard.

Evie had succeeded all too well with her plan to blend into the background. Her hair was scraped back in an unflattering tight ponytail, and she didn't bother wearing make-up.

She hid behind the most unflattering of clothes. She wore frumpy blouses that were too big for her, and trousers and skirts with elasticated waistbands in various shades of beige that would have made Freya shudder. Not to mention the most appalling shoes resembling a couple of undercooked apple turnovers.

But it had worked for all those years at the Imperial. No one really noticed Evie. She almost single-handedly ran the hotel, but guests could never quite remember her name or what she looked like.

Her first day on the new job found her almost sick with nerves and terrified she was going to have a full-blown asthma attack.

Everyone was far too busy to help her find her feet, and she was even starting to miss the hotel. At least there she knew where the toilets were, and which workers were arseholes and to be avoided at all costs.

Her harassed boss, Lucinda, a stick-thin woman dressed in a tight black shift dress with a slick of purple lipstick that had ended up mostly on her teeth, showed Evie to a desk and told her to wait for instructions.

After half an hour of sitting doing nothing she was beginning to think this all was a big mistake when a twentysomething girl around her own age sat down beside her and said,

'You must be the newbie. I'm Sophia, I work over there in market research. Basically, my job is asking people questions all day, and I am desperate to ask you this one: what the hell have you got on your feet, girl?' she said, laughing.

Evie blushed and said defensively, 'These shoes are very comfortable, actually.'

'Well, so are my pink bunny-rabbit slippers but I don't wear them outside of the privacy of my own home. What's your name and where's that accent from? You sound like you're singing.'

Evie found herself smiling at Sophia's words.

'My name is Evie and I'm from near Kirkwall in Orkney. It's in the very north of Scotland.'

74

'I happen to know where Orkney is, Miss Evie. I'm not a complete ignoramus. What brings you to the big bad city?'

'Well, that's a very, very long story. I've been down here for nearly ten years, working in a hotel but I wanted, well, I needed a change. I was getting so homesick, and the work was boring after a while and . . .'

Evie abruptly stopped speaking. She realised she had told this total stranger more about herself in just a few minutes than anyone else she had met since leaving home. Somehow Sophia was comfortingly easy to talk to.

Sophia smiled at her. She was a bright and beautiful woman with dark brown skin that looked as though it had been polished by angels. Her hair was cropped short, which made her eyes look enormous and her make-up was so perfect Evie thought it must have been done professionally.

'I'm from Bethnal Green – that's in the East End.'

Evie answered her with a smile. 'I know where Bethnal Green is, Miss Sophia. I'm not a complete ignoramus.'

Sophia laughed, a real, proper, infectious guffaw from her belly.

'I think you and me are going to get along just fine. But I need to take you shopping for shoes as a matter of urgency.'

In the days that followed, Sophia placed Evie firmly under her generous wing and helped her find her feet. And those feet found themselves in a pair of comfortable-but-elegant sandals and some trendy trainers.

'We also need to get your wardrobe sorted out, Evie,' said Sophia. 'You dress like a librarian. Are you sure you are only twenty-seven? My mum wears more fashionable clothes than you. Mind you, my mum is actually pretty cool.'

Sophia wouldn't take no for answer and marched Evie to Oxford Street to buy some cheap-and-cheerful dresses and practical skirts and blouses for work, but Evie simply refused to consider having an expensive haircut and colour, or facials and manicures.

Evie told her she didn't want to waste her money on such luxuries and dug her heels in, even though Sophia considered this sort of self-care as absolutely essential.

The two women, so very different, became firm friends, although Sophia always sensed there was a sheet of glass between them she could never break through.

Evie gave away very little about growing up in Orkney and would never talk about what made her leave. When she was a bit drunk after cracking open a bottle of wine with Sophia, she would sometimes talk about how she missed the quiet and taking the dogs for walks, but she never mentioned family and friends; Sophia instinctively knew better than to push her.

When she went to visit Evie and saw her spartan little flat, Sophia ached to cheer things up with some bright paint, fluffy cushions and scented candles but sensed that would be crossing a line.

She was only a year older than Evie but felt very protective of her friend and looked upon her as a little sister. As for Evie, she couldn't believe this vibrant woman had virtually adopted her and wanted to be her pal.

Sophia had her own flat close to her family in Bethnal Green, an untidy riot of clothes, scarves and jewellery, and smelling divinely of tuberose candles, but she also popped in and out of her mum and dad's house all the time.

The first time Sophia asked Evie to come over to her parents' for dinner and meet the family was a revelation.

She was welcomed with warmth and told to grab herself a seat and dig into the mountains of food on the table. A massive hearty spicy stew, bowls of buttery potatoes and vegetables, and hunks of what looked like homemade bread.

It turned out Sophia had bought her dad a bread-making machine for his birthday, and he was obsessed with it. His first few attempts had turned out to be dense cake-like oblongs, which were dutifully eaten by the family slathered with honey and jam, but he'd now perfected olive bread and his walnut loaf was his proudest achievement, apart from the two photographs of his sons on the mantelpiece in their university graduation robes.

In Sophia's parents' house, there was laughter and lively conversation over dinner. When Sophia knocked over her red wine, she just got up, grabbed a cloth and mopped it up. It was no big deal. Evie thought how her mother would have caused a scene and there would have been fuss and an uncomfortable silence that lasted for days.

For the first time since she'd left Orkney, Evie realised she hadn't spent the whole day eaten up with anxiety. Being with Sophia and her family was so relaxing, she felt maybe there could be some hope and happiness in this new life.

15

Orkney, 2024

The following morning, Evie was standing outside the huge Pickaquoy Leisure Centre just five minutes from the centre of Kirkwall, trying to pluck up the courage to go inside for a swim.

She'd remembered the excitement when the impressively modern 'Picky' opened and had been one of the first to go to the cinema to see the new James Bond movie *The World Is Not Enough* with Kate and Edwyn. She smiled ruefully at the memory of Edwyn rolling his eyes as she and Kate sighed over Pierce Brosnan as 007.

Evie watched as a group of laughing women headed to their Zumba class and a bunch of teenagers checked out the cinema opening times. She was almost knocked over by a noisy gaggle of toddlers leading their harassed parents to a birthday party.

She made up her mind to go inside. She'd been thinking about her dad's final wish for her to learn to swim and this seemed like a way to try it out without anyone knowing. If she couldn't actually stay in Orkney, perhaps she could do this one thing for him. 'Right, it's now or never. I need to do this,' she said out loud.

There was a good choice of sporty swimwear in the shop. She chose the cheapest, plainest one and headed to the big pool. Her already-wobbly resolve melted away at the first whiff of chlorine. Combined with the piercing shrieks of over-excited children and the hot humid air, her stomach lurched, and she remembered being full of terror when her dad had taken her to the old swimming baths.

Even here, the water felt like a malevolent threat. Evie had seen first-hand its devastating power to destroy lives.

She froze, images flashing through her mind. Liv screaming at her to help. The sound of the waves relentlessly booming and crashing. Appalled that she might actually throw up into the pool, she didn't even dip her toe in the water but ran back to the changing rooms, shivering and shaking. She couldn't do it. She got changed as quickly as she could and raced out of the leisure centre.

She hurried off and noticed another text had come through. But it wasn't Jeremy this time, it was Sophia, her only real friend in London. *Hey Evie – I hope you arrived safely. Can you just let me know you're all right? Sophia xx*

Evie couldn't bear the thought of Sophia fretting but she simply didn't know how or what to reply. She switched off her phone and went back to Freya's.

She had received another missed call from Jeremy last night and knew she couldn't keep ignoring him for ever, but she couldn't cope with his selfish demands and being dragged back to a life that had become unbearable.

When Freya got back home, she found Evie staring out of the window in a dwam. She looked sad and lost.

Freya sat down beside her and said gently, 'How do you feel about helping me make some of my jewellery? I always feel better when I have made something pretty.'

'Actually, I would really like that,' said Evie.

Freya set them up at her kitchen table, where she was making some ornate and very beautiful silver earrings. She had put Evie to work polishing pretty pebbles.

'And, if you feel like picking up a paintbrush and illustrating the stones with puffins or selkies, be my guest,' said Freya. 'The tourists go mad for them. They like the big rocks as doorstops as well as the peedie ones as souvenirs you can put on the kitchen windowsill. You could paint mermaids or whales and dolphins, if you like. Or some of your favourite scenes from right here.'

Evie was sorely tempted. She hadn't lifted a brush since leaving home but coming back to such glorious scenery with the Orkney light on the sea and the shore, had her longing to start again. She just didn't know whether she still could.

'I used to love mermaids when I was little,' said Freya. 'The idea that a woman could change her form. I remember dressing up as a mermaid when I was about six years old.'

'You would have been a gorgeous mermaid. I remember you told me you would dress up in your mum's clothes when you were a peedie thing,' said Evie.

'Oh my God, I did, and weren't they the ugliest things you ever did see? My poor mum had no sense of style. It was all brown and beige and elasticated waists and frumpiness.'

Freya took a glance at what Evie was wearing. 'No offence, Evie,' she said hurriedly. 'Each to their own.'

'None taken. I know my style is pretty pathetic.'

Freya smiled. 'I will take you shopping, and you can borrow anything of mine you like. I do love bright colours so much. Do you think sometimes I take it too far?'

Evie looked at her affectionately.

Freya was wearing a turquoise top and trousers, which were straining a bit over her soft belly, and a vivid, multicoloured silk floor-length house coat, which she declared was perfect for wafting. Her slippers were made of soft yellow wool, and she was festooned in silver jewellery of her own creation. She was a bedazzling plump peacock and carried it all off with great aplomb.

'You always look glorious,' said Evie.

'Thank you, my angel. That was the right answer and gets you a big dram later on.' Freya looked serious for a moment. 'You know, I was so lucky that my family accepted me. My mum was my cheerleader and Anne Marie was always on my side. Even my dad came round, although I know it was hard for him.'

She smiled at the memories. 'I remember him taking me to the hotel for a drink when I was eighteen and home in Hrossey for the weekend. He sat at the bar daring anyone to say a word about the fact I was dressed like an explosion in a lace factory. Of course, no one did. Not with him glowering at them. A couple of tourists off the cruise ship gave me odd looks but everyone else just accepted me. At school I wore frocks and was happier playing with the girls. And then I was me, Freya, and no one was really all that surprised. Of course, there were bumps in the road. Bloody big ones. But I didn't have the terrible problems that other people like me have to face.'

'Oh, Freya, I wish I was more like you,' said Evie. 'You're so brave.'

She looked totally downcast and started to cry.

'What's brought this on, love?' said Freya, setting down the jewellery she was working on.

Evie couldn't stop the tears from rolling down her face.

'I went to the Picky centre. I had decided that I had to do what my dad wanted and learn to swim. It was a disaster,

Freya, a complete disaster. I couldn't even dip a toe in the water. I'm a total coward.'

Freya took off her glasses and shuffled round to Evie's side. 'Listen to me. I know all about what happened on Hrossey with Liv when you were a nothing more than a baby. It's no wonder you're so scared of the water.'

Evie shivered. Freya was so kind, but she didn't know the full story.

'And your dad didn't mean for you to face your fear alone,' Freya continued. 'I think it's time I introduced you to my selkies.'

'Your selkies? Surely not even you have a group of pet seals?' said Evie.

'Very funny. That's what we call ourselves. Remember years ago, I wrote to you that I'd decided to start a swimming club?'

'Yes, you said everyone else had caught up with you now, but they were calling it wild swimming instead of just swimming.'

'Well, exactly,' said Freya. 'It's a really fun bunch of all ages. It started with just me and Kate, and then grew and grew. There's Agnes, who is a brilliant hairdresser. She works miracles with my unruly mop, and a lovely lass from Singapore who came here with Jack Randall after they got married over there. Delima is a shy peedie thing but she's fair coming out of her shell. She's a wonderful seamstress. You must remember Jack from school? Was he not in the same year as you?'

Evie did recall a big, handsome blonde lad who looked ridiculously like everyone's idea of a Viking with his sky-blue eyes and a body like Hugh Jackman in *Wolverine*. Freya smiled. She was very fond of them both.

'Anyway, Jack is an honorary selkie and a very handsome one at that. There's also Patsy, a fantastic joiner and carpenter who works with Andrzej, and then Maureen comes sometimes but she has a young son and takes care of her parents so she can't always make it, and she's not been looking too chipper lately.'

Evie saw a cloud pass over Freya's face and realised she must be worried about her friend Maureen.

'Freya, you make it sound wonderful, but I just don't know.'

There was no stopping Freya when she got an idea in her head.

'Tomorrow will be perfect. It's just me and Kate and Delima, and Maureen, I hope, if she's feeling a bit better.'

Evie opened her mouth to protest but Freya held up her hands.

'I know you don't feel up to actually going in for a swim, and I understand, but just come and get to know the gang. Like I've told you, they are a good bunch. You can just watch us having fun then have a coffee and a cake afterwards. That's the best bit anyway.'

Evie felt cornered and uncomfortable. She was worried about seeing Kate. She hadn't spoken properly to her friend and felt awkward.

'I'm not sure, Freya. I made such a fool of myself at the pool in the Picky. I know my dad wanted me to swim and I will. I am really trying to get over being such a feartie, but I just don't think I'm ready yet.'

'Well, as I've said you don't need to come in. You don't even have to go in for a paddle like a bairn. Just come along and see for yourself. I promise you there's nothing to fear.'

Evie sighed. Freya could be relentless sometimes and she obviously wasn't going to take no for an answer. 'OK,' she agreed. 'I'll come.'

*

The next day she found herself filling a flask of hot chocolate and packing a bag with homemade cakes and buns, and loading up the car with towels and hats and gloves.

'It will do you good to get some fresh air about you,' said Freya. 'You still look far too peelie-wallie, you need to get some roses in those cheeks of yours.'

It was a bright, warm day with a bit of a chilly wind, and the scent of rain to come. It was the kind of mild murr that wouldn't give anyone a proper soaking but would leave Freya and Kate with unmanageable mops of frizzy hair, which Freya couldn't give a toss about, but Kate found infuriating.

Freya and Evie made their way to the beach through the green grass and wildflowers where Kate, Maureen and Delima were already waiting. Evie had been hoping that Kate would greet her with the same warmth as Edwyn, but, as they approached, Kate's face was stony and she kept her gaze averted. Evie's stomach churned, but she understood. This was the first time she'd seen her childhood best friend in twenty years, and there had been no contact between them. She thought of all the important moments in Kate's life she had missed out on and felt a wave of sadness.

Maureen had on a wetsuit and Kate was in a practical sporty black swimsuit, while petite Delima was actually wearing nothing more than an itsy-bitsy-teenie-weenie bikini, which made Evie smile despite her nerves at seeing Kate again and being so near the water.

They all waved at Freya who 'yoohoo-ed' back.

'Hello, girls. A nice bracing one for us this morning,' said Freya

Kate rolled her eyes. 'It's always a nice bracing one, and you say that every single bloody time.'

Delima dimpled at Evie. 'Have you come to join us? It's great fun. Me and Freya go in without wetsuits.'

Freya looked at her with affection. 'Well, I have a fair bit of padding, but I just don't understand how a peedie thing like you doesn't feel the cold. You are as tough as nails.'

Delima giggled. 'It makes me feel all tingly and alive. I love it.'

'We all love it,' said Freya, busy stripping off to her bold purple costume with a little skirt she said made her feel like a ballerina.

'You are looking a bit better, Maureen. How are you feeling today? I wasn't sure you would come,' said Freya.

'I told you not to fuss, Freya. I'm fine. Just a peedie bit tired but I wouldn't miss this; it sets me up for the whole weekend.'

Kate still hadn't acknowledged Evie. She was busy scraping her hair up in a scrunchie. Evie felt her heart sink.

'Hello, Kate,' said Evie hesitantly. 'It's been a long time.'

Kate looked Evie in the eye. 'That wasn't my choice though, was it?' Kate sighed. 'Look, I'm sorry about your dad. He was very kind to me when we were young. When we were friends.'

'I hope we still can be friends,' said Evie hesitantly.

Kate chose to not answer. Instead she said, 'Right, are we all going in or what?'

'I will just mind the coats and be here with the towels and hot chocolate when you come out,' said Evie. 'Anyway, I don't have a cozzie with me.'

'Well, no one is going to run off with our coats,' said Freya, 'And you could always come in bare scuddie.'

They all laughed, apart from Kate who was striding purposefully towards the water.

Freya ran after her, bouncing like a glorious purple beach ball.

'Make sure you add a drop of Scapa to that hot chocolate. It's in my bag,' she yelled at Evie.

'I prefer Baileys,' said Maureen.

'Yuck,' said Delima. 'Has to be rum. Everyone knows that.'

Evie stood on the shore watching the four very different women enter into the water.

The sun had come out, that glorious golden Orkney light that turned the sky shades of azure and duck-egg blue and made the sea sparkle and shine.

Freya shrieked as she waded in. That first cold rush never failed to take her by surprise even after all these years. She was a surprisingly elegant swimmer doing the perfect breaststroke with a broad grin on her face.

Kate looked grimly determined and ran into the sea with a loud shout, diving straight under and coming up for air with a loud gasp.

Little Delima barely made a sound or a ripple. She just gave a bat-like squeak as the cold water hit her tummy then did a sort of cute doggie paddle.

Maureen took her time wading in and then lay on her back, her wetsuit letting her effortlessly float as she looked up at the big sky.

Evie watched them having a great time, splashing, swimming and laughing. She so wanted to join in and be part of their gang, but the water still terrified and haunted her. She didn't know if she could ever break through the barrier of her fear, and felt she was letting her dad down all over again.

16

Orkney, 1986

As she approached forty, Cara was convinced she was going through the menopause.

Her periods stopped, her waist thickened, and it was five months before she realised she was having another baby. There was no morning sickness and she sailed through this pregnancy, carrying her baby high and positively blooming with health.

A calmness came over her and Duncan glimpsed the lass he had fallen in love with so many years ago and who had proposed to him at Yesnaby Castle.

Even eight-year-old Liv seemed to respond to this new serene version of her mother, being less prickly and even succumbing to cuddles without making her body rigid with disdain. The three of them managed a few days at the beach, with Cara calm enough to leave her list of tasks and join in.

Although it was a chilly day with a brisk wind, she and Duncan paddled in the water, with Liv between them. The sea whirled around their ankles, and they laughed as the waves splashed against their legs. Liv begged for Duncan to take her in a little deeper, and he picked her up and waded in, Cara watching from the shore. It was a rare moment of peace, and each of them hoped that things would now be different.

Liv was, however, utterly disgusted when she found out there was a new brother or sister on the way. Living on a farm, she knew the facts of life and was horrified that her parents would still be getting up to such antics at their advanced age, and she had no intention of being usurped by a newborn.

Cara planned to have her baby at home.

'I want it all to be just right, Duncan. I can have her in my own bed, and you can bring me cups of tea and take care of us both.' She had decided to forget all the blood and the mess and the pain of Liv's birth, her stitches aching and itchy, breasts burning, a sense of hopelessness looming over every one of those early days.

This time, Cara told herself it was all going to be different, and she'd prove to everyone that she was the perfect mother. The unborn child in her belly ebbed and flowed like a mermaid and Cara loved the enthusiastic somersaults that woke her and Duncan up in the morning.

They had become so much closer, and he loved to put his hand on her swollen belly and feel the baby move around.

'We didn't do this with Liv,' said Cara. 'I was always feeling so sick and worried and out of sorts.'

'And I didn't know how to help you and felt like a big useless idiot,' he replied.

'I really think this baby is going to make such a difference to us, Duncan. Liv won't be on her own so much and she can help me. I really am worried that she hasn't made any friends at school, and she doesn't get on with any of her cousins. She told me she hates going to visit them and threw a tantrum the last time they came here. It was awful. She wouldn't play with them.'

Duncan sighed. 'I know. They are handful, your Hrossey mob, but they are good bairns, and we know our Liv isn't the easiest to get along with.'

Both of them went quiet remembering when Liv was banned from nursery school for biting the other children and how she had screaming fits when she didn't get what she wanted.

Cara's exasperated mother said she needed a good skelp on the arse to make her behave herself. Duncan could never imagine raising a hand to his daughter but had no idea how to deal with his difficult child.

One morning a few weeks before her due date, Cara woke up and knew right away something was badly wrong.

'Duncan! Wake up. The baby isn't moving.'

Duncan was bolt upright in a heartbeat and beside himself with worry.

'Oh, dear God, are you sure?'

'I can't feel anything at all. What will I do. I can't lose this baby. I can't.' Cara began to wail in distress.

Duncan could move fast for a big man, and he threw on his clothes, scooped up his distraught wife and shoved a sleepy Liv into the car still wearing her pyjamas. He drove to the hospital as though the devil was chasing after him.

'We can't lose another baby. Not at this late stage. It will kill Cara. She won't recover from this, and I can't bear to lose her.'

They got there just in time. The umbilical cord had wrapped itself around the baby's neck, but she was quickly and expertly delivered by emergency C-section.

She was a pale, perfect rosebud and barely whimpered as she was checked over. Duncan took one look at his daughter and felt a rush of protective love. The tiny baby turned her little face to her dad like a sunflower, opened her eyes, gazed directly at Duncan and effortlessly grabbed hold of his heart.

She's perfect, he thought. *The most beautiful bairn that has ever been born.*

He spoke to her for the first time. 'Hello, my beautiful peedie Teenie. Welcome to the world. I'm your daddy and I will love and protect you for the rest of your life.'

Evie was a beautiful child, with enormous blue eyes with flecks of gold that would soon turn a vivid shade of green, bright blonde curls and skin like a peach. She slept all night and loved being cuddled or carried around like a precious present by her doting dad.

With Cara making a slow recovery from her Caesarean, it was Duncan who did the feeding, nappy changing, burping and bonding.

Liv looked on, glowering at the usurper and refusing to have anything to do with her.

She declared Evie to be smelly, ugly and noisy and didn't even want to be in the same room as her little sister. She stomped upstairs to her bedroom, slammed the door and nursed her wrath.

Duncan loved Cara and tried his very best to love Liv, but with Teenie his love was overwhelming.

Which was why he would never forget the first time he almost lost her. One-year-old Evie had been gurgling happily outside with the dogs, Eric and Ernie, beside her pram, when she suddenly started gasping for breath. The dogs began barking to alert Duncan. By the time he had rushed to her side, Evie's lips were turning blue and her little body was struggling for air.

Duncan grabbed her and made for the car. He abandoned it outside the hospital and roared into Reception bellowing for help, a bull with his stricken calf.

Clear, cool heads took over. Evie was given an injection and her dad was only half-jokingly offered a sedative. She'd had a serious asthma attack and would need to be given medication, monitored carefully and come back for more tests.

Duncan's quick actions getting her to the medics on time had saved her life, but he was shaken to the core at the thought of anything happening to his Teenie.

It was his duty to keep her safe from harm and he would do anything to make sure she was protected. He vowed to carry an inhaler in his top pocket at all times.

Evie bounced back from her ordeal but her whole life had changed. She was deemed by her father as too fragile to be with other bairns, or to go to the beach to swim or even paddle in the sea. He would play their gentle game of hide-and-seek, but she was never to be overexcited or overtired.

Even the Hrossey cousins behaved themselves during family visits and treated Evie like a tiny Christmas tree bauble, liable to shatter with any sort of boisterousness.

She was an adorable child and when her proud dad first pushed her in her pram around Kirkwall, people would stop to admire her, with the older women pressing a silver coin into her tiny fist for luck.

Over the next couple of years, Duncan eyed her like a hawk as she started to babble and waddle like every other toddler, and there were no more bad attacks on his watch.

Cara eyed this with growing bitterness.

'You are suffocating her. She will rebel against you, and you are completely neglecting Liv. She is starting to really resent all the attention you give to Evie, and you are blind to it.'

'I know, Cara, but I just can't seem to talk to Liv. It's like there's a wall between us. I do try, but she looks so bored when I ask her about school or her friends.'

He looked out of the window and saw Evie waiting patiently in the garden.

'I promised Teenie I would play with her when I got back in from work. I won't be long.'

Cara sighed impatiently. 'She has you wrapped round her pinkie finger, Duncan Muir. You will live to regret it.'

17

London, 2014

As the months passed in London, Evie found to her surprise that she was really good at her job. She quietly sorted out her boss Lucinda's diary, instigated a proper daily meeting schedule and sorted spreadsheets for maximum efficiency. Old yellowing heaps of documents were sorted and filed, and, in a few short weeks, the department hummed with a sense of organised purpose.

Just like at the Imperial, Evie was so quiet and unobtrusive at work, people barely noticed she was there.

It was only on the rare occasion she took time off and the smooth running of the office stuttered and faltered that they all realised what a treasure they had on their hands. But Evie wanted to remain in the background, never drawing attention to herself, always keeping her head down.

When she was with Sophia Evie was more like her true self.

She hadn't made such a good friend since Kate and Edwyn, but even with Sophia she never talked about them or anyone from her past. Sophia continued to hope one day Evie would grow to trust her enough to confide in her because it was clear there was a sad story to be told.

They saw each other every day at work, gossiping during their lunch breaks, usually about Sophia's latest dating disaster, and the drudgery of office life, and now and again they'd meet for shopping trips on a Saturday afternoon.

Sophia had often invited Evie to come out at the weekends to a club or a pub with a group of her friends, but Evie always made up a lame excuse, and eventually Sophia took the hint and stopped asking.

She was very fond of Evie who was always there to listen to her woes about finding a decent man, or her frustrations in a job she found dull and stifling.

Evie gave thoughtful, sensible advice, and was fiercely loyal. She had mopped up lots of Sophia's frustrated tears when yet another fella turned out to be a big let-down and she'd walked away again. Evie would tell her they were eejits, and she would find 'the one' when she least expected it.

There was no need for Sophia to have to listen to any of Evie's man troubles, because she didn't have any. She hadn't even been on a date since leaving Orkney. Brodie was the only man she had ever slept with, and she had no desire to meet anyone else. The very thought filled her with dread.

Sophia quickly gave up trying to set her up with one of her friends and had to laugh at how appalled Evie was at her suggestion to try internet dating.

Evie was now twenty-eight years old and had been away from her home for ten long years. She had tried to bury her memories of Orkney, and now that past life felt almost dream-like, and, at times, especially in the wee small hours of the morning, horribly nightmarish.

For her birthday, Sophia had given Evie some gorgeous and classy underwear that she would put at the back of her drawer and keep 'for best', which drove Sophia to distraction.

Just like Freya, she thought that nothing should be saved for best and should be enjoyed every single day.

Freya had sent her a homemade birthday card and drawn a very odd-looking puffin on the front. She had decided that even these endearingly cheeky little birds with their red-and-yellow beaks weren't colourful enough and had given this one the full rainbow treatment.

Evie had giggled out loud when she'd seen it, but then experienced a wave of homesickness that had made her well up. She often thought of Freya, Kate, Edwyn and all the cousins on Hrossey, but especially her dad. She didn't dwell on the complicated relationship with her mother and any thoughts of Liv took her down a road that was far too dark.

As always Freya had sent her love but also the hope that Evie would one day come back.

On the morning of her birthday, she came into work as usual and went to make herself a cup of coffee. She was already feeling emotionally wobbly. Standing in the airless and grimy little cubbyhole where staff were territorial about 'their mugs' and put labels on the milk and sugar, she was reminded of the big cups of sweet tea she used to make for her dad. He demanded seven generous spoonfuls of proper loose tea in the huge brown teapot and said it had to be 'strong enough for him to dance on'. She felt teary and missed him so much.

'Cheer up, love, it might never happen,' came a voice she didn't recognise. She looked up to see a man around her own age, attractive in a weedy sort of way. His wiry brownish hair was starting to thin and sat in a lump on the top of his head like a sleeping guinea pig, but he had a handsome face. He smiled at her.

'Jeremy. Accounts. New here,' he continued, and she felt a clammy hand shaking her own.

He was lanky and Evie noticed his trousers and jackets weren't quite long enough to cover his bony wrists and ankles. She found that rather endearing and completely at odds with the confident man in front of her.

'I'm Evie. Nice to meet you.'

'Are you OK? You look so sad, as though you've had some bad news. Is there anything I can do to help?' he asked.

'I'm fine, really,' Evie said, touched that he had noticed she was struggling.

'Maybe I can cheer you up with a spot of lunch, and you can help me settle in as I'm new here,' Jeremy said.

Evie felt like she couldn't refuse, especially as Jeremy was being so very kind.

Sophia had been at a wedding and had taken the Monday off to recover, planning to spend the day in bed, hopefully not all on her own. Weddings, she declared, were 'rich pickings' and she never gave up hope she might meet someone interesting who wouldn't bore her to tears after a couple of months.

She was taking Evie for a proper belated birthday meal in Soho on Friday night, so today Evie had nothing to look forward to, but a sad cheese sandwich curled up at the edges because she had made it the night before.

So, she agreed to go to the café next door with Jeremy. He talked so much about himself that there was no time for Evie to fill him in on office gossip and politics.

Evie told him she would pay the bill, it was only a couple of toasties and two milky coffees, to welcome him to the workplace.

This made Jeremy immediately demand to take her out for a proper lunch at the weekend to pay her back for being so sweet.

He looked at her with such hope in his eyes that it would have been like kicking a puppy dog to refuse his request.

Anyway, everyone knew lunch wasn't really a date, not like dinner and a movie.

Not like it had been with Brodie.

'I bet HE thinks it's a date,' grumbled Sophia. 'I don't understand why you'd go out with him and not the guys I try to set you up with. I mean, you could do so much better than Jeremy.'

'No, I couldn't, and he seems nice,' said Evie. 'And he doesn't know anyone at work. I'm just being friendly.'

Sophia rolled her eyes.

'I suppose he's not awful-looking, but there's just something "off" about him. I can't put my finger on it, but I am never wrong about these things. He's one of those blokes who could suck all the fun out of a room just by being in it.'

Evie thought that was a bit unfair and it made her more inclined to look upon Jeremy favourably. If she was being honest with herself, she was secretly grateful that anyone was taking an interest in her at all.

Jeremy was the first person to ask her out in years and their lunch was a surprising success. He didn't ask Evie why she'd decided to leave Orkney and had ended up in London. He didn't really ask her anything about herself at all. She was so relieved she listened intently to his moans about his previous job and how, after just a week, he was thinking about leaving this one because he felt under-appreciated.

'I'm only on a temporary contract and I'm already fed up. There's a job coming up that I think I will apply for. My uncle knows the boss of this accountancy firm and promised to put in a good word for me. It's more money and really good chance of promotion, but, don't worry, Evie, this won't affect us. We will still see each other. I really must get to know you a lot better.'

He looked at her with such affection that she simply couldn't tell him he was taking a lot for granted and, besides, she wasn't really interested in having a relationship with anyone, but instead she heard herself say 'That would be lovely, Jeremy. I really hope you get the job, and it would be good to get to know you better too.'

Jeremy picked up the bill, tutted to himself and counted out the exact amount.

Evie said anxiously, 'Shouldn't we leave a tip? The service was really good. I've worked as a waitress in a hotel. It's a really hard job and the money isn't great.'

Jeremy was about to disagree but wanting to make a good impression on Evie, he left a couple of pounds for the over-worked and underpaid middle-aged woman working three jobs to pay for her daughter to go to college.

It was still early when they both went their separate ways at Leicester Square, Evie to get the bus home and Jeremy to get the Tube, but Evie thought to herself that it hadn't been as bad as she'd been expecting; in fact it had been a pleasant afternoon.

She gave Sophia a call as promised when she got back to her flat.

'Well, how did it go?' Sophia asked. 'Was there an undig-nified scuffle and did he try to pounce on you when you said goodbye?'

'No. Nothing like that,' said Evie. 'He didn't make any sort of move at all. He just said he'd see me at work on Monday.'

'Hmmmm. Interesting tactics. Was he as dull as he is in the office? I can't imagine there was any kind of spark?' said Sophia dubiously.

'No. Not really. But it was OK. No fireworks, but he's safe and somehow, I found him comforting.'

'Well, a hot-water bottle is comforting,' said Sophia. 'But you don't get much conversation out if it. Mind you, you don't get much interesting chat out of our Jeremy either. Will you see him again outside of work, do you think?'

'If he asks me. I probably will. He's applying for a new job, which is a good thing. I don't think office romances are a good idea. When they don't work out, it's really awkward for everyone.'

'Evie, you are talking about breaking up with a guy you aren't even really going out with yet.'

As it turned out, Jeremy's uncle must have called in some favours, because his decidedly average nephew was indeed offered that highly paid job in the accountancy firm.

There was the usual leaving 'do' in the office to see Jeremy off, warm Chardonnay in plastic cups and tooth-achingly sweet iced buns, while everyone made small talk around his desk.

Evie usually avoided these events and scuttled off home, but Jeremy had made a point of asking her to stay behind, saying it would mean so much to him, so she felt she couldn't let him down.

He was getting a bit red-faced and sweaty after a couple of glasses of wine and wanted to continue drinking. Evie and Sophia and a few of the lads joined him at the pub round the corner, but they all headed home after less than an hour. Sophia had a hot date and the lads found Jeremy a crashing bore, so Evie was left alone with him.

She was keen to get home; it was a school night and she had tights to rinse through and *Corrie* to watch.

'Have another drink with me, Evie,' said Jeremy. 'We are celebrating my escape after all.'

He waved his glass around expansively. 'I am off to bigger and better things.'

'Sorry,' said Evie. 'But I really must go.' She smiled at him. 'I really hope the new job goes well for you. Make sure you keep in touch and let me know how you are doing.'

Jeremy looked peeved but he forced himself to give Evie a slack-jawed grin. To her horror, he made a sort of lurch towards her and fastened his mouth on hers like a limpet on a rock.

He tasted of cheap booze and cheese-and-onion crisps. His tongue wriggled around in her mouth like a fat eel.

Evie was so startled, she didn't push him away, but when he finally came up for air, she told him firmly that she had to leave, right now.

He was baffled and affronted. 'I thought you liked me, Evie. You know I want us to be more than friends and now I have landed a proper job with the kind of salary a man like me deserves, I can look after you properly.'

Evie should have pointed out that she had been taking care of herself ever since leaving Orkney ten years ago and didn't need to be looked after. But never one to cause a fuss and always a people pleaser, she just grabbed her bag and fled.

Sophia laughed until Evie thought she would stop breathing when she told her about the 'lunge of the giant mouth eel'.

'You have had such a lucky escape there,' she gasped out. 'I don't even know why you considered going out with him in the first place. I kept on telling you that you don't need to settle for the first person who pays you any real attention.'

Sophia knew what she was talking about when it came to matters of the heart. No man had yet given her that wonderful feeling of stomach-flipping, tingling joy and excitement that came with falling in love.

She had dated some really decent blokes, but she was always the one to walk away because what she really wanted was the kind of love her parents shared.

Her dad lit up every time her mum came home from a shift at the hospital. He'd make her a cuppa, give her a foot rub and they would talk about their day. There was love, laughter, respect and she knew they still had a sizzling sex life, which she didn't really want to think about. So far no one had made her feel alive and goosebumpily like that, but she hadn't given up hope. Right now, Sophia was more worried about Evie drifting into a relationship with Jeremy. She thought he was bad news, and her instinct was usually right on the money.

Evie knew Sophia was only trying to help, but deep down felt even a man like Jeremy was more than she deserved.

What happened to make her leave Orkney all those years ago was never far away. It was the first thing she thought about when she woke up in the morning and the last thing she dwelt on at night.

She had forgotten what it was like to have peace of mind.

Evie tried not to think about her dad as it made her heart physically sore, but she knew no matter how much she missed him and her friends, she could never go back home.

The memories of Brodie and Liv made that impossible.

She still lived in her small flat, got the usual bus to work and only bought herself something new if Sophia practically forced her to go shopping or gave her a gift.

Ever since she'd left home, Evie had been sending more than half her wages into Liv's bank account. She knew it was guilt money, but hoped Liv was using it to make a better life for herself. Freya rarely mentioned Liv in her letters, which Evie thought must mean things were quieter and more settled.

Freya continued to write to her, but she rarely responded, and her friend's letters became fewer and shorter. She had received one a few weeks ago that had her missing home even more than usual.

Dearest Evie

I hope you are well.

Edwyn has had a promotion at the hospital. He's so highly regarded there, and the patients love him. He's kind and takes his time to talk to them and listen to their worries. Kate told me they are hoping to start a family soon. They still talk about you. I have told them as far as I know you are well and, to be honest, there's not much more I can say. You never tell me anything about your work and your friends. I am fine and Orkney is still here where you left it. Waiting for you.

Love Freya

18

Orkney, 2024

The sky was slate grey, and it was drizzling miserably as the mourners poured into the plain white kirk for Duncan's funeral.

As expected, every seat was taken, and there were even people huddled at the back who would be straining to hear the minister.

Evie sat with Freya on one side and Edwyn on the other next to Kate. They quietly shielded and supported her, and she was so grateful for their calm, comforting presence. She kept her head down and her gaze lowered as much as possible. She would have made herself invisible if she'd had the power.

Her aunts and uncles and a gaggle of cousins from Hrossey had turned up. They hugged Evie and said how sorry they were, and how much they had tried over the years to take care of Duncan, but he'd always rebuffed their invitations to come and stay, even when they'd turned up at his door hoping to drive him across on the ferry.

Evie wasn't able to say much to them and had barely exchanged a word with Kate. All she could do was thank them and it was Freya who promised they would both visit soon.

Evie could feel the weight of people behind her and the crushing sense that she was being weighed, measured and found wanting.

She knew she was being unfair because everyone had been so kind and sympathetic, but she felt awkward and ill at ease and, above all, utterly bereft at her dad's death.

She told herself she just had to get through the next couple of hours. She was dreading seeing Liv again and risked a quick glance back but there was no sign of her, though she did see Duncan's old friends, now grey and a bit unsteady on their feet, all there to pay their respects.

Andrzej had arrived with Maureen and her elderly parents and young teenage son, Rory. Andrzej made sure they were all comfortably settled and looked at Maureen with such love in his eyes it made Evie, already emotional, want to cry.

She also recognised the Nordic god with a daring blonde manbun as Jack Randall, sitting with his wife, Delima. Next to them, the Isbisters and their son, Ross, who made the beautiful Orkney chairs.

Just at the last minute when Evie thought Liv had decided not to come after all, her sister appeared. Liv's hair was scraped back, her clothes clean and ironed, and she walked steadily to the front and sat across the aisle from Evie.

Her face was a white mask with black kohl-rimmed eyes and carefully applied red lipstick. She held her head high in defiance, with her eyes fixed dead ahead, and didn't glance round once. Evie was relieved – she much preferred being pointedly ignored to an angry scene.

The minister cleared his throat, and the service began.

Evie could feel tears welling up again as the minister talked about how young her dad had been when he'd had to take over the farm after his father had died. There were smiles and nods as he told the story of Duncan living in a house of women; even his two beloved border collies were girls, but he insisted on naming them Eric and Ernie and on that he would not be budged.

Evie had decided she couldn't do a eulogy at the funeral. She didn't think it was her place and she wouldn't have been able to talk about her dad without breaking down. To everyone's surprise the minister announced that Duncan's daughter Liv wanted to speak.

Evie looked up in horror.

Was this going to be the moment Liv would tell everyone the truth about why she'd left Orkney? Would she really be capable of making the announcement at her father's funeral? Evie wondered desperately if she should make a run for the door, just as Liv walked slowly past the coffin and took a few steps up to the lectern.

Liv had to hang on to the lectern to stop herself shaking, partly because she was in dire need of a hit, but also because she was genuinely grief-stricken about her dad.

No one was more surprised than Liv how much the death of her father had hurt. She had been up most of the night sobbing like a child, but somehow managing not to take drink or drugs to numb the pain. It was her sort of twisted tribute to her dad, but she was paying the price now.

Liv had pretended not to care about her father and, for most of her life, shown him nothing but contempt, but deep down she had always yearned for his approval and been devastated that Evie was always his favourite.

She coughed and began to speak without any notes.

'I didn't prepare anything for the day,' she began, 'because I didn't expect to be speaking, but I wanted all of you to know that my dad was a fine, big man. He was good and kind to everyone. I know he liked a drink, but who doesn't?'

There were murmurs of agreement from the congregation.

'I wish I had seen him more often and I wish I had been a better daughter.' She glared at Evie. 'Both of us let him down and he deserved better.'

She looked over at his coffin.

'I'm sorry, Da. I really am. I hope you can rest in peace, and I wish I had been able to tell you how much I loved you.'

There was a stunned silence. Liv was in tears as she made her way back to her seat, scrubbing at her eyes with an old tissue, which came away streaked with black. For a brief moment, Evie had a glimpse of how different life might have been if she'd had a sister who was also a friend.

'The poor lass,' murmured Freya, as Liv sat down and buried her head in her hands.

Following the service, they went to the Ayre Hotel for the funeral wake and purvey. After getting married, Duncan and Cara had put by a small sum every month with the Co-op to pay for both their funerals. There was to be an open bar and lots of generous sandwiches, sausage rolls and thick homemade broth to soak up the booze.

Evie saw Liv grab a whisky from the bar. She downed it and wiped her mouth with the back of her hand. Evie took a deep breath and nervously started to approach her sister, intending to thank her for what she had said at the funeral.

'Look at these bastards pouring tenners down their throats,' Liv muttered to herself. 'They don't give a shit about my dad. It's fucking disgusting.'

Evie noticed her glassy eyes and belligerent expression and quickly turned away. Other people came up to Liv to offer their condolences, but Liv brushed them aside. She was downright insulting to Ben, one of her dad's oldest friends.

'He never liked you, you know,' she informed him bluntly as he tried to tell her a story about her dad when he was a schoolboy. 'He thought you were a boring old pain in the arse.'

Andrzej had been keeping an eye on Liv and gently led the old man away, saying, 'That's her grief talking, Ben. Don't mind what she said. Duncan thought you were a fabulous fellow and he looked forward to your visits tremendously.'

'Well, I didn't see enough of him at the end,' said Ben regretfully. 'I should have tried harder. But after Evie left and then what happened to Cara, he just didn't want to see anyone.'

Old Ben took out a well-worn, blue-and-white-spotted hankie, blew his nose and sighed deeply.

They were interrupted by the sound of breaking glass and angry voices. Liv had knocked her empty whisky glasses off the bar, and Evie had gone over to help pick up the smashed pieces and try to get Liv away in case she cut herself on the sharp shards.

Liv was drunk and furious. 'You aren't wanted here!' she shouted at Evie. 'You only came back to steal the house. You must have forged the will. Da said he left it to me. He left everything to me.' Her voice rose to a screech. 'I told you never to come back here. You are going to regret it!'

The room fell silent. Andrzej moved swiftly to take charge, telling everyone soothingly, 'We all know how emotional everyone gets at funerals. Poor Liv is distraught with grief. I am going to get her a taxi home so she can lie down and have a rest. I am sure you all understand.'

Maureen was looking pale and shocked. He turned to her and said softly, 'I will be right back for you.'

Evie felt she couldn't take much more of this. She followed as Andrzej held Liv firmly by the arm, leading her to Reception and asking them to call a taxi.

Evie was terrified Liv was about to blurt out her secret in a drunken rage and stood by the door straining to hear what she was saying to Andrzej, over the sound of chatter in the room.

Liv ranted at him non-stop. 'Get your paws off me. How dare you give me the bum's rush from my own father's funeral? Who the fuck do you think you are? You're just a bloody incomer.'

'I'm making sure you get home before you say something you really will regret, or you end up injuring yourself or someone else,' said Andrzej patiently.

'You really are one ugly big bastard. I see you mooning all over that Maureen. It's sickening. Do you honestly think she's going to look twice at an ugly gigantic fucker like you? You haven't got a hope in hell. Everyone thinks you are ridiculous.'

Andrzej's jaw tightened, but he didn't respond. The receptionist told him the taxi was there and he opened the door for Liv to escort her outside. Just as she left, Liv looked over and her vicious gaze focused on Evie. Her face twisted into a malevolent grin that made Evie's blood run cold.

A few minutes later, Andrzej came back inside, his face grim. *Has she told him?* Evie thought in a panic. She went over to him and gave him a grateful hug.

'Thanks so much for taking Liv away. Did she say anything?'

Andrzej gave her a weary smile. 'She didn't say much, Evie. Just the usual drunken, foul-mouthed insults. Nothing I haven't heard before.'

'She didn't mention anything about me?'

Andrzej looked at Evie in a slightly puzzled way. 'Not a thing. Now you must excuse me. I promised to take Maureen and her family home, and I cannot keep them waiting.'

Evie's secret was safe but for how long?

19

Orkney, 1989

It was a beautiful afternoon and Duncan was looking out to Scapa Flow with Eric and Ernie at his heels.

Eleven-year-old Liv was indoors stuck in her room in a huff and refusing to come out and enjoy the sunshine. He was playing hide-and-seek with his Teenie. These days being with her was the only time he felt truly content.

As long as she's happy, I'm happy, he thought to himself, and he could almost believe it was true.

Seeing rain approaching fast he decided to 'discover' Teenie and take her into the house.

'Teenie, where are you?' he called out, with mock indignation.

There were bell-like giggles from the tiny three-year-old.

He knew exactly where she was, where she always was, but had to pretend not to have a clue. He practised his best baffled expression to show her she'd once again outwitted him by hiding behind the cowshed, her favourite place.

But then he couldn't hear her giggles any more. As he drew nearer, he heard the little girl yelping in pain and distress.

He caught Liv squatting on her sister's chest and viciously slapping her. Evie's feet drummed feebly on the grass.

'Olivia, what the hell are you doing to your baby sister?'
Duncan was furious as he rushed towards both girls.

'Nothing,' Liv said sullenly.

'I saw you hurting her. She's still only a baby and you know
how fragile she is. What's wrong with you?'

He scooped up Evie and left Liv standing there, her fists
clenched and eyes bright with unshed tears.

He was so angry he couldn't trust himself to speak to her,
genuinely afraid he might lash out, and he would never be able
to forgive himself for raising a hand to his eldest daughter.

Duncan carried Evie into the kitchen where Cara was packing
for a trip north to Hrossey to see her mother and extended
clan of aunts, uncles and cousins who still hadn't quite forgiven
her for permanently moving south to the Orkney mainland.

Cara had become painfully thin with a cloud of frazzled,
dirty fair hair shot through with grey and a worried frown that
had caused deep furrows from her nose to her chin. Her dark
brown eyes constantly burned with nervous energy.

'Cara. We need to do something about Liv. I caught her
hurting Teenie. I can't talk to her, and I had to walk away
because I just wanted to skelp her.'

'I'm sorry, Duncan, but you will need to sort it out,' said Cara.
'I have enough to do preparing for the trip to Hrossey. The girls
were probably just playing, and it got a bit out of hand. You
always take Evie's side. I keep telling you it isn't fair on Liv.'

Duncan looked utterly defeated. He was in desperate need
of reassurance, but he would have no comfort or understanding
from his wife.

Little Evie was hot and sticky and hiccupping in distress, but
she seemed to have calmed down now she was safe in her dad's
arms. Duncan gave her a quick kiss and told her everything
would be fine. He patted his top pocket and reminded her she

mustn't worry as he always had her inhaler if she needed it, but thankfully she didn't seem to be in danger of one of her asthma attacks, which terrified the life out of him.

Cara sighed, briskly tore Evie from her father's arms and snapped at him.

'I keep telling you to stop treating Evie like a baby and how many times have I said that Liv is just going through a phase. Her nose is still out of joint because she's not the only spoiled princess any more. It's perfectly natural. But, of course, you never listen to me.'

Duncan thought, *I do nothing but listen to you. I have no choice. But you never ever hear me when I try to talk to you.*

Out loud he said, 'I hope you're right, Cara. I really do. I'm scared she will really hurt Teenie. We can't watch Liv every minute of the day, and I just don't know what's going on in her head.'

Cara was already on edge because of the visit back home and had been up at first light cleaning a house that was already immaculately tidy, and checking and rechecking the contents of their suitcases. They were getting the first ferry in the morning, but everything had to be ready the night before. As always, Cara and her family would be sitting in the car at the head of the queue ridiculously early for the journey. She'd be fretting and worrying about all sorts of disasters that would never happen.

She was working herself into a state and was in no mood for Duncan and her daughters causing her more anxiety.

'For Christ's sake, Duncan, finish loading up the car. We can't be late for the ferry tomorrow. We need to be all ready to leave first thing. And, then go and get Liv. It's sandwiches for supper. I don't want a mess in the kitchen. Well, what are you standing there looking at me for?'

Duncan knew it was better to simply shut up and obey his wife.

He couldn't understand her frenetic cleaning of a house that was already spotless, especially as they weren't going to be there for the next week. He also knew they had to do something about Liv, but he was browbeaten by his tiny wife.

Her wrath was something he had never been able to deal with, so he threw the cases into the boot of the car and then went to search for his eldest daughter as ordered. Not for the first time he wondered how Liv, such a longed-for child, created with so much love and welcomed with joy, had turned out to be a complete and utter nightmare.

She was a total mystery to him. But then he had to admit, so was Cara, even after all these years. For someone who fretted about the smallest of things, she couldn't seem to accept that Evie was vulnerable, and she refused to see that Liv's behaviour was verging on downright vicious.

In the movie of Cara's life transmitting inside her head, they were all playing the role of the perfect family and she wouldn't entertain anything that would damage that illusion even a tiny bit.

Duncan had dreamt of them growing old together and becoming closer with every passing year.

Instead, their home was a battlefield where he walked on eggshells for fear of upsetting Cara or sending her into one of her rages, or even worse an ice-cold remote silence.

If it wasn't for Teenie he would feel like a total failure, but her health was a constant worry, and now he felt as though he couldn't leave her alone with her older sister.

Only last week they had been called into the school after receiving a letter from Liv's teacher.

'They want to see us both,' said Cara. 'Apparently some of the younger bairns have complained about Liv. It's all nonsense, of course.'

'What do you mean? What has she been doing to them?' Duncan roared. 'Christ almighty, that girl will be the death of me.'

'Losing your temper isn't going to help,' snapped Cara. 'You know this is all your fault. You should have put your foot down with Liv. I'm so embarrassed. How am I going to face everyone at the school gate?'

'Cara, this isn't about you. It's about our daughter being a bully and we need to sort her out.'

There was a tearful scene at the school. Liv's teacher was a sweet-faced young woman who was extremely uncomfortable at having to tell Duncan and Cara their daughter had threatened a small five-year-old boy and stopped him from going into the toilet. The poor boy had wet himself in the corridor and was so upset and distressed he'd broken the pupil code of not being a clype and told his teacher what had happened.

Liv swore to her parents that it was all a misunderstanding and, of course, she hadn't stopped anyone from going into the toilet. The horrible boy was just embarrassed at peeing himself and had made it all up.

She was so convincing that Cara believed her, but her teacher wasn't fooled, and neither was Duncan. He knew how sly Liv could be, and he knew in his heart not only had she bullied that bairn but actually enjoyed seeing him suffer.

With Evie settled at the kitchen table, drawing pictures of the dogs with her crayons, he found Liv sitting outside gazing sullenly across the fields but looking very small and lost.

Despite his anger, he felt sorry for his eldest daughter. She always made him feel sad and guilty. At times like these he missed his gentle mother. She would have had wise words of advice and would have known how to talk to Liv. Even when she was a toddler, any attempts by Duncan to play games with Liv or spend time with her were always rebuffed. She hated being hugged. Her body would go stiff, and she never showed him any real affection unless he was buying her something.

And here they were. His daughter was the school bully and had really hurt his Teenie this evening. This wasn't the usual rough and tumble of family life.

Duncan felt way out of his depth, but he needed to try to get through to Liv. Shouting the odds never helped, so he tried another approach.

He sat beside her and said as gently as he could, 'Liv. You know that Evie isn't as strong as you and sometimes struggles to breathe. We've explained all that to you and it means we all have to take care of her, and you have to help us. We can't have her getting upset.'

Liv glowered.

'No one ever asked me if I wanted a baby sister. I don't want her. She plays with my stuff and she's always in the way. Everyone spoils her. It's not fair.'

'Liv. Me and your mum love you very much but you can't behave like this towards your peedie sister.'

She looked at her dad with scorn. 'All you care about is your precious princess. I will never forgive you for making me put up with her. She's a pest and I hate her, and I hate you.'

Duncan was shocked by her words, but he also felt guilty because truth be told, Teenie was his priority.

He thought about his in-laws and their children on Hrossey, constantly squabbling and arguing, but somehow always ending up laughing together. They drove each other to distraction, but there was such a lot of love in their warm, messy, disorganised homes.

He was completely flummoxed and just didn't know how to deal with Liv, and Cara was never any help. She refused to get drawn into what she called 'petty squabbles' and declared they were simply a couple of scratchy cats in a basket who would have to learn to get along.

Duncan just hoped this holiday wasn't going to be a complete disaster.

20

Hrossey, 1989

It was one of those glorious warm days where the Hrossey white sandy beaches and azure water looked like an advert for the Seychelles. The sea was flat and calm and the wind gentle and balmy.

Duncan took a deep breath of the fresh, sweet air. There really was nowhere else he would rather be than right here; he loved Hrossey almost as much as his in-laws did.

He'd left Cara at home with her mother after she'd declared she had a headache and didn't want to sit in the sun all day having to put up with all her cousins and their noisy children.

She'd made a big show about deciding not to come. In a high, long-suffering voice she'd whined, 'You can all still go. Obviously, you will have a better time without me. I will be fine here.'

Duncan was just about to do his usual and try to persuade Cara to come when his mother-in-law interrupted.

'Christ, the smell of burning martyr. Behave yourself, Cara,' said her mother tartly. 'If you aren't going, you can stay here with me. Take yourself off with your girls, Duncan,' she added. 'They will have a lovely time with their cousins. It's the perfect day for it. Get some sun on your faces.'

She looked at her daughter.

'Cara can help me make a big steak pie for tea. There's a sack of spuds to be cleaned and peeled. You'll all come back starving after being in the fresh air all day and you'll need food that sticks to your ribs.'

Sheila was in her element cooking for Big Duncan who always scoffed up seconds and would have eaten thirds if there was enough left.

Cara was fuming with her mother. Sheila had scuppered her plans of being cajoled into going to the beach, and now she'd have to spend the afternoon peeling potatoes.

Duncan and the girls happily went without her, laden with towels and flasks of tea and hot chocolate, and a picnic of sandwiches and homemade cakes.

After they'd gone, Sheila turned to her daughter. 'Cara, why do you work so hard to push happiness away. You could be having a lovely day with your family. I just don't understand you.'

At the beach, the families set up striped windbreaks and made a base camp with blankets and towels.

'Have you ever seen a selkie?' said Evie, and Liv pricked up her ears and listened for once.

'Och, yes,' said Duncan, thinking fast.

The girls widened their eyes in amazement.

'Really?' said Liv, and he nodded. 'What was she like?'

'It was only a glimpse,' Duncan said. 'But she was half woman and half seal, and the fastest swimmer you ever saw. You'll have to be quick if you want to see one.'

The bairns stripped off to their swimsuits and raced each other to the water, shrieking when the cold waves hit them, but soon becoming immune and playing elaborate games involving dolphins and mermaids.

Evie sat with her dad creating an elaborate garden in the sand with shells, stones and bits of seaweed, keeping watch out for selkies. She was desperate to go into the water, but her dad was worried the cold might bring on another asthma attack so here she sat.

Although she was disappointed, Evie played happily enough by herself but kept looking towards the sea where her cousins were now playing keepie up with a football. Even Liv had joined in.

Cousin Inga, who was expecting her first baby in a few months, waddled up to Duncan and asked, 'Will I take Evie for a peedie paddle? She can dip her toes in the water. Then we can build a fire and the bairns can have some hot chocolate to warm up. My Drew has got a hip flask tucked away. We can jazz up your tea with a dram, Duncan. That will keep the chill off.'

'Sounds perfect. Thanks, Inga. What do you think, Evie?'

The little girl was already taking off her socks and sandals. Inga took her hand, and they toddled off to where the waves lapped at the beach.

Evie was enchanted. She loved the sea and the stories her dad would tell of the brave Orkney fishermen who met all kinds of magical creatures on their voyages to other lands.

To Inga's surprise, Liv waved at them.

'Come on in a bit more, Evie, and play with us. It's not too deep. You can be on my team.'

Evie was stunned. First of all, her sister was addressing her by her name and she was being nice after being so horrible to her yesterday.

The little girl beamed.

'Can I go in a peedie bit deeper?'

'I promised your daddy we would just have a paddle, my lamb,' said Inga doubtfully.

Liv called out to her.

'Och, Inga, my dad won't mind. The water is only up to my knees. She'll be fine. Come in and take my hand, Evie.'

All of the other bairns splashed and laughed and were having great fun pretending to be orcas and diving into the water.

Liv took Evie out a bit deeper and, out of nowhere, a bigger wave than usual knocked everyone off their feet.

The others shrieked with laughter and bobbed up like corks, but little Evie went right under and didn't come back up again. Liv grabbed for her arm and held on to her tightly.

Inga was convinced Liv was actually pinning her sister down deliberately instead of trying to help her. Horrified, she panicked and started screaming.

'Let her go. Help. Somebody help! She's trying to drown Evie.'

Less than fifteen seconds must have passed by, but the world seemed be in slow motion. Another wave hit them all and Evie was still under the water; Liv wasn't strong enough to pull her back from the current and up to the surface and could only hold on grimly.

Duncan sprinted from the shore, waded in and managed to grab Evie by her arms and carry her out of the water.

A frightened-looking Liv was shouting, 'I was saving her. She went under and I was helping her.'

Duncan looked at Evie's pale, floppy body and feared the worst, but the little girl retched, spat out a salty waterfall, and started sobbing in fear and terror. She clung to her dad and wouldn't stop shaking.

'It's all right, Teenie, Daddy has got you. You're safe.'

He was furious and frightened and lashed out at Inga.

'What the hell happened? I told you just to take her paddling. Why did you let her go out so deep? She could have drowned.'

Drew was beside his wife, covering her with a soft woollen blanket. She was shivering with cold and crying in distress.

'Don't you dare shout at her. She saved your Evie. Liv was holding her under the water. You need to sort her out, Duncan, before something really terrible happens. There's something wrong with Liv. She's not right.'

He turned to his white-faced wife. 'Come on, love. I'm taking you home. You've had a hell of a fright and it's not good for you or the baby.'

He glared at Duncan and Liv and repeated, 'I'm telling you she's not right.'

The other children were all out of the water and being dried and dressed. Usually, they would be like a flock of restless little birds, chirruping and complaining about having to leave the beach early, but they were all completely silent.

Liv looked utterly stricken, her eyes wide and pleading.

'Dad. It wasn't my fault. A wave crashed into us, and we all fell over. I just grabbed her to keep her from getting dragged away. I was trying to help.'

Duncan couldn't bear to look at her. A few days ago, he had caught her viciously hitting his Teenie and today, as far as everyone was concerned, Liv had tried to drown her little sister. It was too much for him to take in.

Duncan was terrified Evie would have another asthma attack. He had her spare inhaler in his shirt pocket as always. He never forgot.

He said to Liv through gritted teeth, 'You have some explaining to do. But we need to get back right now. Teenie is freezing.'

Liv threw on her clothes over her wet swimming costume and trudged after her dad.

The others quietly packed up and headed home.

What should have been a golden day was completely ruined. Even the weather had changed with dark clouds scudding in, threatening a rainstorm.

When Duncan walked through the door, Cara went into full hysterical mode, yelling at him, upsetting Evie who had fallen asleep in her father's arms and making Liv dry heave in distress.

Sheila told her to shut up and stop making things worse, but Cara had never paid much attention to her mother, and she wasn't about to start now.

She continued shouting at Duncan, 'I told you not to go to the beach without me,' rewriting history as usual. 'If I had been there this would never have happened. We could have lost both of them. This is all your fault, you stupid, useless idiot.'

Duncan was too worried about Teenie to even register his wife's ranting, which just infuriated Cara even more.

Sheila was appalled to hear what had happened, but knew someone had to keep calm, so she ran a bath for Evie and Liv, who were shivering and covered in salty water, and put the kettle on for hot-water bottles and tea.

'Right, let's get these girls warmed up and into bed,' said Sheila. 'I will call over the road on Dr MacNeil. He's supposed to be retired but he'll want to give Evie the once-over just to put our minds at ease.'

Liv ran to her mother, clutching at her as she kept repeating, 'I tried to help Evie. They all think I wanted to hurt her, but I didn't. I swear I didn't.'

'We know that, my lamb,' said Cara. 'You wouldn't do anything to harm your baby sister. No one thinks that. Now off you go with Granny. It's all going to be all right.'

Alone in the kitchen, Duncan looked long and hard at Cara.

He tried to keep his voice down as he didn't want the girls to hear him.

'You weren't there,' he hissed. 'You didn't see what happened. Inga is convinced she saw Liv deliberately hold Teenie under the water.'

'Oh, for Christ's sake, Inga is an idiot, and you are taking her word over your own flesh and blood. You always think the worst of Liv, especially where Evie is concerned. I just refuse to believe Liv would ever do such a thing.'

'You didn't see the look in her eyes yesterday when I saw her hitting Evie. It was terrifying. Drew said today that she isn't right, and I agree with him. I think we need to get Liv help.'

Cara's voice rose to a shriek.

'Drew is even more of a simpleton than his thick wife. How can you possibly think that Liv wanted to kill her sister? That is actually what you are thinking, isn't it? You believe she's a monster and you want to send her away. Well, over my dead body. You don't love her the way I do. That makes you the monster, not Liv.'

'For Christ's sake, Cara, the girls will hear you. I can't talk to you when you are like this. I'm going out while you calm down.'

'That's right. Walk away as usual. You are so predictable and so pathetic.'

Liv was standing at the top of the stairs listening to her parents arguing and had heard every word. Her granny was singing softly to Evie as she put her into her own double bed. She would be sleeping with her tonight. Liv would be in the spare room on her own, feeling hard done by and misunderstood.

She really hadn't meant to harm her sister and had genuinely panicked when the little girl went under. She had grabbed her arm and tried to pull her to the surface but was battered down by the waves.

My mother believes me, thought Liv. *But she doesn't count. I shouldn't have hit Evie yesterday, but she was going on and on about wanting to go and see the neighbours' kittens. I had better things to do, and she wouldn't shut up about it. I lost my temper, and I lashed out. Anyway, who cares? I've had it with the whole lot of them. It would serve them right if I ran away and never came back, although I don't suppose they would even notice.*

Meanwhile Duncan found himself in the Thule Hotel bar telling his woes to Freya. She was sitting in the corner making plans to go to London for her final life-changing operation and trying to work out her finances.

Freya took one look at Duncan's face and beckoned for him to come over. 'You are a man in dire need of a drink. Sit there and I'll get it. Pint?'

'Aye. Thanks, Freya.'

They sat quietly for a few minutes before Duncan poured out the whole sad story. Freya always was a good listener.

He told her, 'I honestly can't say for sure that Liv deliberately tried to hurt Teenie, but then I can't rule it out either. I don't think for a minute she wanted to drown her, but I need to face up to the fact that I don't think it's safe to leave them alone together. Jesus, Freya, what am I going to do?'

'What does Cara think?'

'That I'm overreacting. She's completely blind to Liv's faults. You know she's been bullying the young bairns at school.' He sighed deeply. 'I'm frightened for her, Freya. She's my daughter and of course I want to love her; I don't want her to be like this. Do you think it's something I've done? Have I been too soft?'

It was unusual for Duncan to open up like this to anyone, but Freya was so easy to talk to and she never judged or gossiped.

Duncan knew anything he said to her would be just between the two of them.

'Maybe, but Cara lets her get away with murder.' Duncan winced, What about Sheila? Your mother-in-law is a wise old bird.'

'She is that. And she has the measure of Liv. She's one of the few people who can control her.'

'Well, use that, Duncan. Talk to her and ask her for help. Maybe Liv could come up here for the next school holidays on her own so her granny can keep an eye on her but also give her loads of attention. I'd help but you know Cara disapproves of me, and she's encouraged Liv to do the same.'

Duncan sighed. 'I'm more sorry about that than you will ever know. You are a good person, Freya, and a fine woman if you don't mind me saying.'

Freya could feel the tears well up as she grabbed his big hand. 'That means the world to me. I will always be here for you and your family. You know where I am if you want to talk some more. Anyway,' she said with a laugh, 'we will be giving the auld biddies plenty to talk about, both of us sitting here holding hands in a dark corner of the bar.'

Duncan laughed. 'You've done me the power of good. I needed to get things off my chest. I won't forget your kindness, Freya. And I hope you find happiness and someone who deserves you.'

'From your mouth to God's ears.' She chuckled. 'And Duncan, don't let Evie be scared of the water. Take her for swimming lessons when you get back home.'

Liv heard her father coming back in trying not to make a noise. He tiptoed into his mother-in-law's bedroom to check on Evie. Satisfied she was sleeping soundly with her granny, he left to go downstairs without looking in on Liv. She heard him sigh as he prepared to spend the night on the lumpy old couch in the kitchen.

Liv lay in bed glowering at the ceiling. *Look what I get for trying to be friends with that brat today. I saved her but they actually think I tried to hurt her. They believe I'm a monster. Well, that's exactly what I will be, and they will be sorry.*

From that day Liv declared war on the world, but especially on her father and little sister.

21

London, 2015

Evie continued with her unchallenging and unchanging routine. She was becoming dissatisfied with her job, which, although paid well, had become mind-numbingly boring, but she was too scared to make any sort of change. The years just drifted by, each one the same as the one before.

When Sophia left for an exciting new position in an advertising agency in Soho, she lost her only friend at work.

They saw each other now and again for coffee, but it wasn't the same.

Evie was always the last to leave the office, and when she switched off the lights and locked up, the weekend loomed ahead empty and lonely.

It was pouring with rain, but Evie never bothered with a brolly. She just put up the hood of her old beige anorak and trudged towards the bus stop.

A bright red sports car screeched to the kerb in front of her, drenching her feet and ankles with a wave of dirty puddle water.

She heard a voice bellow, 'Evie! Fancy bumping into you. Hop in and I'll give you a lift anywhere you like.'

It was Jeremy. To her surprise she was actually pleased to see him. The thought of being in a warm car instead of standing-room-only on the bus would be a blessing. She crouched down and clambered into the passenger seat, feeling as though her arse was scraping along the ground, but what a relief to be out of the rain.

'Oh dear. You are soaked,' said Jeremy, looking concerned. 'Luckily, I have leather seats so you being all damp won't spoil them. What do you think of her? Isn't she a beauty? Brand new and can do zero to sixty in five seconds.'

Evie had no idea what he was on about.

'It's a lovely car, Jeremy, and thank you for stopping, but what brings you back round here?'

'I had some business in the area and thought I'd swing past the old workplace. I sort of hoped I might see you, and here you are.' He grinned toothily.

'Well, it's very kind of you to offer me a lift, especially as we haven't spoken for ages.'

Evie tried to remember the last time she had heard from him.

'I know, Evie, it's been a long time, but I have never forgotten you. You are the one that got away.'

He guffawed and leant over to pat Evie on the leg.

To be honest, she hadn't given him a second thought, but now she felt flattered by his words and wondered if she had been too hasty. Maybe he deserved a second chance? Although he probably had a girlfriend who he drove about in his fancy car.

She heard herself saying, 'That's very sweet of you, and if you could drop me off at my flat that would be lovely.'

She gave him her address and he roared off far too quickly, talking about the new car all the way to the flat.

He insisted on coming up to 'spend a penny' and left Evie to clamber out of the sports car in a most inelegant fashion without offering her any help.

Jeremy followed her up the stairs and told her she must immediately take off her wet things before she caught her death of cold.

Evie disappeared into her bedroom, not realising he was right behind her. He suddenly lunged at her and started kissing her neck and groping her breasts. Somehow Evie found herself flat on her back in her single bed with her knickers and tights at her ankles being pounded by a red-faced Jeremy.

She was so shocked she couldn't tell him to stop and get off and lay there feeling as though she was looking down at this happening to someone else. *Why the hell am I letting him do this to me?* she thought. *What is wrong with me that I am allowing myself to be treated like this?*

But she didn't utter a sound.

After a mercifully short time he grunted, rolled off her and told her that he'd been looking forward to that for ages. He pecked her on the cheek and got up to go for a pee, shouting at her from the bathroom.

'Shake a leg, we are going out to celebrate being back together.'

She could hear him in her tiny shower bellowing a lewd rugby song off-key about four and twenty virgins going up to Inverness.

Evie lay there wondering why she didn't yell at him to stop, or push him off?

He had just used her for his own gratification. He wasn't kind or tender or loving. This was nothing like what she'd had with Brodie when they'd made love.

So why on earth was she just wiping herself, changing her clothes and meekly planning to go out with him tonight.

She could almost hear Sophia's incredulous voice roaring at her to stand up for herself and tell him to fuck right off, but her old ingrained feelings of guilt and shame had resulted in a crushing insecurity and made her genuinely believe Jeremy was all she deserved.

Evie sleepwalked with him to a cheap-and-cheerful Indian restaurant round the corner from her flat where she regularly picked up a weekend takeaway.

Jeremy immediately began boasting about his important job, while fretting about his car, which was parked round the corner.

'This is a dodgy area, Evie,' he said accusingly, as though she was responsible for the crime rate. 'Next time you can come to my place,' he continued smugly. 'That will be much more fitting.'

Evie barely said a word and didn't have the stomach for her biryani. Jeremy seemed not to notice her silence or lack of appetite.

He just prattled on about himself, and then scraped her uneaten dinner onto his plate saying, 'waste not, want not.' He paid the bill, without leaving a tip, and complained that the curry was too spicy and the chapatis were too small.

Jeremy left her outside the restaurant. It was still raining. He gave her a quick peck on the mouth, no tongues thankfully, said he would be in touch and ran off to his beloved car.

She trudged back to her flat in a daze, curled up in bed and cried herself to sleep. She was so ashamed and angry with herself.

She woke late on Saturday, threw on an old tracksuit, went to the laundrette and watched old repeats of *Upstairs Downstairs* in the afternoon while eating a bowl of cornflakes.

Her mobile rang just after midnight waking her up. It was Jeremy calling from a noisy pub. He slurred into the phone that he wanted to see her and that he couldn't stop thinking about her. She cut him off, but he called straight back.

'Not sure what happened there, Evie,' he yelled. 'Don't worry. I will come round tomorrow, and we can talk.'

At noon on Sunday, an extremely worse-for-wear Jeremy appeared at her door.

She was going to simply ignore him, but he kept ringing the bell and then shouting up at her window. Evie was only on nodding acquaintance with her neighbours, and she knew fine well they wouldn't take too kindly to a man roaring her name at the top of his lungs, so she decided to let him in.

Jeremy looked whey-faced and woebegone. 'Have you got any paracetamol, Evie? I'm dying. Never again. I think it was that crap curry I had with you on Friday night. I've not felt right since. Would you believe I feel so bad I can't even face making love to you?'

Evie disappeared into the bathroom and didn't know whether to laugh or cry.

Making love! What a sick joke. He had leapt on her like a sweaty, rutting wildebeest. She might as well have been one of those creepy plastic sex-shop dolls.

By the time she got back with a couple of aspirin he was on her sofa snoring loudly enough to wake the dead. She threw a blanket over him and went into the bedroom to read a book.

A few hours later she heard him throwing up in her toilet.

This was too much. Evie was furious and knew she had to call him out on his disgusting behaviour and show him the door. But Jeremy put her firmly on the back foot when he emerged from the toilet shamefaced and clearly upset.

'Oh, Evie, I'm really sorry. What must you think of me? I really wanted to make a good impression on you, and I've fucked up. Sorry, I didn't mean to swear. I really am so terribly sorry. I have fancied you for ages and I never forgot you. I've been plucking up the courage for years to ask you out.'

Evie couldn't believe this change in Jeremy. He was like a completely different person, contrite and begging her forgiveness.

He went on tearfully, 'Then I just jumped on you. I couldn't help myself. You are so gorgeous. I know that's no excuse,' he said hastily. 'And you didn't say anything, so I thought maybe it wasn't as good for you as it was for me. Then I just talked and talked at the restaurant and didn't give you a chance to say anything. I thought if I just kept rabbiting on, everything would be OK. I wouldn't blame you if you just want to tell me to piss off and never bother you again.'

He ran out of breath and just looked at her, clearly expecting the worst.

Despite herself, Evie felt sorry for him. *At least he's acknowledged it and apologised*, she thought reluctantly. *I suppose that counts for something.*

Eventually she sighed and said, 'Just go home. You look done in.'

'If you let me, I will make it up to you,' Jeremy begged. 'Just give me another chance. I know I don't deserve it, but you won't regret it. I promise.'

As she shut the door on him, Evie was already blaming herself for the whole fiasco.

She must have given him the wrong signals, and she didn't tell him to stop, so it really was all her fault. She went over the events of the past few days and started to make excuses for Jeremy, the same way her mother used to do for Liv.

Thinking about her sister, all the old feelings of guilt came back and hit her hard. How could she possibly judge someone else? She knew she would give Jeremy another chance.

22

Orkney, 2024

Maureen was sitting alone as the wake thinned out, leaving behind just the usual die-hard bar flies.

'I'm sorry I was so long,' said Andrzej. 'I wanted to make sure Liv got into the taxi.'

Maureen smiled at him. He felt his heart flip over at the sight of it.

'Quite right. That Liv was all ready to cause a scene,' said Maureen. 'We've been fine, but Rory ended up going back with my mum and dad. He'll get them settled back home. So, it's just me for a lift, if that's still OK?'

Andrzej was delighted. He didn't get all that much time on his own with Maureen and he treasured every precious minute. 'Of course. Let's get you back.'

To Andrzej, Maureen was the most beautiful woman in the world. He had been in love with her ever since he'd come to Orkney ten years ago.

He'd been quite simply hit by a thunderbolt when he'd gone to register at the GP surgery in Kirkwall and had seen Maureen behind the reception desk. His stomach had felt as though he was on a rollercoaster, every hair on his body had stood on end and he'd known for certain he had found his soul mate. He hadn't even known her name when he'd first laid eyes on her, but to himself he'd called her 'the girl with the worried eyes' and had vowed to make it his life's work to take that anxious look away and make her smile and laugh.

What he hadn't known was how much Maureen had been struggling after the recent death of her husband, David, who had been diagnosed with a particularly aggressive form of MS at just thirty-two.

It had been desperately hard for Maureen who'd loved him with her whole heart. Maureen's most beloved possessions were photos and videos of David with his son before he'd become too ill to even sit up in his wheelchair and hold his little boy.

The last months of his life had been especially tough as Maureen had promised to keep David at home for as long as possible. She'd also had to deal with a toddler who could sense that something was very wrong with his dad.

Maureen's parents had come to live with them and, at first, were a huge help, especially after David's death, but they were both getting on in years and struggled with the energy needed to run a household and look after a young boy. Maureen felt terribly guilty and wanted the two of them to have some peace to simply grow old together. She knew as time went on, they'd be able to help out less and less.

The family needed money and Maureen had to provide for her parents and her son.

Their pensions didn't cover the mortgage and Maureen was determined to keep the house David had loved so much, which is was why she'd found a job at the health centre.

The day Andrzej had come into the surgery, she'd been crying in the toilets, feeling alone and overwhelmed. Looking at herself in the mirror, she could see little trace of the woman

David has called his 'rose'; all she saw was a faded flower well past its best. He had loved her long, thick, dark hair, but since his death she always tied it up in a tight bun that made her look rather severe. She had high cheekbones and a wide generous mouth, but there were dark circles and deep lines of grief around her eyes, and she looked utterly exhausted.

She glanced up at the enormous, rather frightening-looking man in front of her who was sweating profusely and babbling nonsense. Maureen had no idea of the effect she was having on him; she just thought maybe Andrzej's English wasn't too good. Patiently, she took him through all the forms and as his heart started to slow down to its normal rhythm, he was at last able to string a few sentences together.

Andrzej wasn't at all proud of inventing an imaginary ailment to get a doctor's appointment a few days later, but it was the only thing he could think of to get to see Maureen again, even for a few minutes.

As luck would have it, he overheard her talking to the patient in front of him about needing work done in her garden, which had been neglected for years. He heard himself say in a slightly high-pitched squeak, 'I'm a gardener. I could do it for you. I know all about gardens and I am very cheap but I'm also very reliable. Shall I come round and take a look maybe?'

A rather startled Maureen said that would be wonderful. He took her address and told her he was feeling much better and didn't need to see the doctor, and he would come round to her house tomorrow.

He headed straight to the library to borrow and devour every book on gardening he could get his hands on.

Maureen wasn't kidding when she said her garden was over-grown, but Andrzej set to work digging up weeds, unthrottling rose bushes and even building a brand-new garden shed to replace the one that had fallen down. He worked as though his life depended on it, and when Maureen came home from the GP surgery, she would bring him a cup of tea and they would talk.

At first, it was just small chit-chat about the weather and the garden, but as they got to know each other Andrzej would tell her about his mother and his family back in Poland and how much he missed them.

Maureen talked about David and how brave he had been throughout his illness. Even in the last months of his life he'd never complained. At times she forgot he was dead and still expected him to be at home.

Just that day Rory had done well in an exam, and she found herself saying she must tell David, before realising he was gone for ever.

Andrzej could see that she had loved David very deeply and told himself she would never be able to even look at another man, certainly not a big lummox like him.

He vowed to take care of her and help in any way he could, but not to frighten her off by declaring that he adored the very bones of her and wanted to spend the rest of his life just breathing the same air.

It was surprising how many odd jobs needed doing and slowly Andrzej found himself becoming a big part of the lives of Maureen and her family. He refused to accept any payment for his work, telling Maureen a white lie that she was helping with his English (which was fluent) and her dad was an invaluable source and teacher of Orkney history, and he would have had to pay a fortune for his knowledge and all the books he borrowed from him. Maureen's mother, Peggy, doted on him, and her dad, George, loved the way he soaked up all his stories about Orkney's past.

His love for Maureen played a big part in Andrzej's obsession with his new home and by finding out more about the rich history of the place he had grown to love, he felt even closer to her.

When her dad told him all about Skara Brae, he took Maureen there to see for himself the place where people lived, laughed and loved long before the pyramids were built in Egypt.

She'd been taken as a schoolgirl to see the perfectly preserved Neolithic village, revealed after a massive storm hit Orkney in 1850 and ripped away the top of a sand dune to reveal dwellings with stone rooms, box beds and cupboards.

Seeing Andrzej enthuse about the site and the people who lived there made her look at it with fresh eyes and marvel at their ingenuity.

When they both went to the Ring of Brodgar, a giant circle of ancient standing stones, something about the magical and timeless atmosphere made him come close to declaring his love.

He took photos of her there looking so beautiful bathed in perfect sunlight. She took his breath away, but he backed down at the last minute, fearful to jeopardise what they already had, and so ten years flew by with Andrzej falling more and more in love with Maureen every day and yet never feeling able to tell her.

And here they were on their way back from Duncan's funeral.

As she sat in the passenger seat, Maureen once again blessed the day Andrzej had come into her life and become her friend. She was relying on him more and more. He was her rock, but she had absolutely no idea he adored her so deeply.

She shivered a little, tired from a draining day.

'Are you cold?' Andrzej said. 'I can put the heater up?'

'I'm OK,' said Maureen. 'Maybe I could just put your sweater on?' She had noticed a giant jumper of Andrzej's on the backseat.

'Oh, no,' said Andrzej, frowning. 'It's very old. Better that I just put the heating up.'

He didn't want Maureen putting on one of his smelly old jumpers. It probably reeked of oil and putty and, if he was honest, would also smell of his sweat. That would never do.

Maureen felt a bit rebuffed. She'd been hoping for a sign that Andrzej was interested in her. He was always so correct, sometimes to the point of being distant, that the thought never once occurred to her she meant anything to him in a romantic way.

Her own feelings for Andrzej had crept up on her and one day she realised she'd gone from liking him to loving him, but because she didn't want to damage their friendship, she kept quiet.

As the temperature in the car crept up, Maureen felt a deep weariness. She allowed her eyes to shut and was instantly asleep. Andrzej glanced across at her. He had noticed over the past few months she had been looking even more tired than usual and he was concerned. He slowed the car down and kept the speed steady to allow her to rest. Eventually, he pulled up in front of her house.

Maureen woke up and groaned.

Seeing Andrzej looking so concerned she tried to make light of how exhausted she felt.

'I'm so sorry I completely nodded off. And that's me without a drink too. I'm not much company, am I?'

'Stay there, Maureen, and let me help you out,' he said gently but firmly.

'It's fine. Don't worry I can manage.'

But as she tried to get out of the car, Maureen stumbled and would have fallen if Andrzej hadn't been there to catch her.

He picked her up and carried her in his arms as though she weighed little more than a tiny bird and gently told her to shoosh as she feebly protested that he should put her down.

Going through her front door that was always left open, he placed her carefully on the sofa in the big bright room he had helped transform into Maureen's happy place.

He'd fitted a huge window looking out to the sea and a new polished oak floor and made wooden shelves for her dad's collection of books. 'I'm making you some tea,' he shouted from the kitchen. 'And I'm putting sugar and honey in it.' But by the time he came back, she had fallen fast asleep once more. Carefully, he placed a soft woollen blanket over her and watched her sleep for a moment, before tiptoeing out.

As usual when he had a concern, Andrzej went to Freya for advice, and the next day he turned up on her doorstep.

'It's yourself, and you've brought the sunshine. Come away in. What can I do for you this fine day? Evie has gone into town for me. We need a few bits and then she's going to see Kate and the bairns.'

'Well,' said Andrzej. 'I can make a start on her cottage right away if she approves the plans. The team and I can get it back looking even better than she remembers. It will not take long, and she won't ever want to move back south.'

He paused for a moment. 'Freya, I need to talk to you seriously.'

Freya met his gaze. 'OK. Let me make some coffee. I think I might need more than one pot by the looks of your face. I will make it extra strong and so thick with sugar the teaspoon will stand up in it.'

Andrzej sat on the sofa in the bright and airy sunroom he'd built for Freya and took a sip of the sweet, strong coffee.

He sighed. 'It's Maureen. I think she's overdoing things. She has no energy and she's lost weight. I might just be over-reacting, and I just don't want to say the wrong thing. Do you think you could go and see her just to put my mind at rest?'

Privately, Freya had been wanting to knock both their heads together for years. It was obvious to everyone that he adored Maureen and that she loved him right back, but neither of them would make the first move.

'I will pop over later this afternoon. I'm glad she's only working part time now, and money isn't so tight. I'll tell her I want her recipe for millionaire's shortbread although between you and me, her baking is desperate.'

As much as he loved Maureen, he had to agree with Freya.

He had lost more than one filling to her scones and when he took some of her fruitcake home, even the wee sparrows wouldn't touch it, probably realising they wouldn't be able to take flight from the bird table if they had so much as a beakful.

'Don't worry, Andrzej. I am sure she's fine and there's nothing to worry about,' said Freya, reaching over to pat his arm reas-suringly. 'She might just need a bit of a break.'

23

Orkney, 1990

The ear-piercing shrieks made everyone turn round to look at a red-faced, embarrassed Duncan and his squirming four-year-old daughter in the Kirkwall swimming baths.

It was nine months after the disastrous trip to Hrossey, and Duncan thought it was time to try to get Evie to learn to swim, but she refused to get into the pool and no amount of cajoling, bribing or Duncan uncharacteristically losing his temper with her would make her budge.

Evie was adamant she wasn't going in the water and that was that.

Other swimmers tried to coax her in, telling her it was great fun, and one young girl offered to share her 'shivery bite' afterwards if she'd just pop her toe in the shallow end. But even the offer of half a pie and a macaroon bar didn't work, and Evie just shook her head.

'Please can we go home now, Dadda. I'm scared. I don't like it.'

She was so distressed she was finding it difficult to catch her breath.

Duncan knew the signs and took her hand, rushing into the changing room to get her inhaler.

'I'm sorry, Teenie. Don't upset yourself. Take a big deep breath of your inhaler and maybe we can try again another time.'

'I wouldn't bet on it, Dadda,' she said solemnly.

On their way out, a kindly woman Duncan had gone to school with told him there were special mother-and-baby classes on a Saturday morning where she could learn to swim with peedie toddlers, but Evie was having none of it.

'I don't want to learn to swim,' she wailed. 'Please don't take me back there. It's horrible and noisy and it smells like the house after Mum has cleaned it.'

Evie perked up later when her dad bought them hot, fat chips drenched in salt and vinegar, and two pickled onions.

They sat on a bench on the pier, far enough away from the water's edge so Evie didn't feel afraid, watching the ferry going across to Shapinsay, and Duncan realised he was dreading going back home.

Since returning from Hrossey, the atmosphere in the cottage had been Antarctic. In one corner, Cara and Liv united in their disgruntlement, and in the other, an increasingly unhappy Duncan and his Teenie.

The bitter irony was this time Liv really hadn't done anything wrong, but she had been blamed anyway. As far as she was concerned, her attempts to make her dad happy by paying attention to her despised sister had backfired badly. She believed her dad hated her so why bother making any effort at all.

Duncan had tried to talk to Liv but had met the usual brick wall. She merely told him she knew he didn't believe her, but that she didn't care. It didn't matter to her what he or anyone else thought.

How could Duncan know that ever since Evie was born, Liv had cried herself to sleep because she just wanted her dad to look at her with the same love and affection he showed his youngest daughter. But after what had happened on Hrossey, Liv had hardened her heart, and made up her mind never to let anyone, least of all her dad, make her feel like that ever again.

She also vowed to get her revenge on them all one day.

In the days and weeks that followed, there was no thawing of the frosty atmosphere at home and Duncan found himself suffering from terrible chest and stomach pains, and even Cara came down from her self-imposed moral high ground and nagged him to go to the doctor.

Duncan was sternly told by his GP that he was under too much stress, his blood pressure was sky-high, and he was in real danger of a heart attack. He'd also developed a stomach ulcer.

Cara got such a fright that she started speaking to him again. It was bittersweet for Duncan. He was saddened by how pathetically grateful he was to his wife for the truce. Their lives went back to some sort of routine, but there was always a simmering sense of unease.

Then one Saturday morning, Cara caught Liv threatening to cut off Evie's hair with the blunt scissors she kept in the drawer under the special Orkney chair, along with her wool and knitting needles.

Duncan was helping out at a neighbouring farm and Cara had decided to do an unnecessary wash of the bedding and towels. The house was in uproar, and she was outside putting out the washing when it started to rain. The white sheets billowed like sails in the breeze and were hard to grab, but Cara managed to get them in before the worst of the downpour.

She could hear shouting from upstairs. She ran up and burst into Evie's room to find her youngest daughter in a corner wide-eyed and terrified.

Liv tried to laugh it off and say they were playing a game, but even Cara couldn't swallow that one.

'You are frightening your sister. I heard you saying you would cut her hair off. I heard you. Give me those scissors right now.'

'I was only joking,' said Liv, full of indignation. 'She's such a baby and these scissors wouldn't cut through butter. I don't know why you are getting so worked up over nothing.'

Something inside Cara snapped. She'd always defended Liv, partly as Duncan doted so much on his Teenie, but also because she had never been able to shake off the feelings of guilt about that one moment she wanted to die when she was pregnant with Liv in her womb.

She also punished herself for being unable to bond with Liv when she was born and, if she was honest, she was also rather afraid of her eldest daughter.

She snatched the scissors away, grabbed Liv by the shoulder and started shaking her violently and screeching.

'Why do you keep doing this to me? What would people think if they found out the way you behaved. I'd be the talk of the whole of Orkney. You make me look like a bad mother. Say sorry to your sister and don't let me catch you doing anything like this again.'

Cara was in despair. This was not how she imagined her life would turn out. Liv's behaviour blew apart her carefully crafted illusion of the perfect family. She felt more and more suffocated by her husband's clinging adoration and frustrated by his ill health, and now Liv was actually laughing at her.

'You really are a piece of work, Mother. You want everyone to think we are this fantastic happy family. What a joke.'

This was too much and tipped Cara over the edge. She slapped Liv hard across her face.

The loud crack echoed around the room.

Cara put both her hands over her mouth.

'Oh, God, Liv. I'm so sorry, I should never have done that. Don't tell anyone, please.'

For once Liv was stunned into silence. She couldn't believe her mother had hit her. She was supposed to be her fiercest defender and now she had turned against her too.

Neither of them noticed Evie who had squeezed her little body into the corner of the room, trying to make herself as small as possible. She let out a whimper of distress and started to struggle for breath.

'Evie. It's OK. Where's your inhaler?'

Her mother took a step towards her, and Evie flinched.

The little girl was shaking as she took the inhaler out of her pocket and Cara helped her suck in a deep lungful. Evie began to feel a bit calmer as the medicine took effect.

Liv went into the bathroom to splash water on her face. There was a bright crimson mark where her mother had slapped her, and it still stung.

She looked in the mirror and willed herself not to cry. She needed to toughen up. She vowed she would never let anyone in this family hurt her ever again. Even at twelve years old she thought she could use this situation to her advantage if she played her cards right.

Downstairs in the kitchen as her mother nervously poured her eldest daughter a glass of creamy milk and gave her a plate of the best chocolate biscuits, she pleaded with her again.

'Don't tell your dad. He would be so furious with me, and you know the doctor told us he wasn't to get upset or he might have a heart attack. We wouldn't want that to happen now, would we?'

She is unbelievable, thought Liv. *Using my dad like that. And as if I care what happens to him anyway.*

Out loud she said, 'So, Mother, let me get this straight? You don't want me to tell Dad that you slapped me so hard I think a tooth might fall out, and you terrified his precious princess so much she nearly had another one of her life-threatening asthma attacks. Is that about the way of it?'

Cara looked jittery and uncertain. 'Well, Evie has already agreed not to say anything, haven't you, pet? You don't want your daddy to get upset and end up in the hospital.'

Evie nodded. Cara had absolutely terrified her by threatening that if she said anything, it might make her dad so cross he would drop down dead.

So, Cara knew she had nothing to worry about as far as Evie was concerned, but Liv was a totally different matter. She eventually deigned to answer her mother's pathetic pleas.

'OK. I will keep quiet but what do I get in return?'

'What do you mean?' said Cara.

'You need to make it worth my while otherwise I will tell everyone, including the police, that you assaulted me, and you'd never be able to show your face in all of Orkney ever again.'

Liv went to the dresser and tipped out all the coins in her mother's purse and the twenty pounds emergency money she kept under the fruit bowl.

'This will do for a start,' she said, smiling like a sleekit polecat and putting the money in her pocket. That was how Cara found herself resorting to bribery to ensure Liv's silence.

She slipped her extra pocket money every week and bought the expensive shiny black boots Liv had been craving for months. She also allowed her to stay out later at night and weekends.

Cara could never tell Duncan about the extra money as he would have gone ballistic.

She knew it was the coward's way out and didn't want to dwell too much on the fact she was being manipulated by a twelve-year-old.

Her eldest daughter would always believe she could get away with any sort of behaviour, and that her mother would bail her out or pay anything to keep up the illusion they had a happy home life.

It was their shameful little secret.

24

London, 2015

Looking at the four bare walls of her tiny flat, Evie realised it was more of a jail cell than a safe space and that she'd been hiding here, shutting herself away from the world. Maybe Jeremy was what she needed to get back out there and start living.

Sophia was the only person she could confide in. She called her up to give her the news about Jeremy appearing at the office to pick her up in brand new shiny sports car.

'Jeremy!' shrieked Sophia. 'The giant mouth eel? Why has he reared his ugly head?

'Please tell me you didn't have sex with him.'

Evie was silent.

'Oh, God. You did? What was it like? Was it terrible? Tell me everything!'

'I don't want to talk about it,' said Evie firmly. She could never tell Sophia the horrible tawdry details. Her friend would be appalled and want to call the police.

'Fair enough. You and your secrets.'

'Anyway,' said Evie. 'He turned up at my door yesterday morning totally hungover then threw up in my toilet and left.'

'Oh, dear God, it's not exactly *Pride and Prejudice* then.'

'Well, it was really odd. When he left yesterday he kept apologising and I felt really sorry for him. He looked so crushed, just like a little boy. I think underneath it all, he's a decent person really.'

'You are far too soft-hearted, Evie. I've told you he's not good enough for you. Listen, I have to go, but we need a right proper catch-up. I've loads to tell you and you've obviously a hell of a lot to tell me.'

'I'm so sorry, Sophia, I haven't even asked how you are doing or asked after the family.'

'I'm good. And everyone is fine. I will tell you all my news – how you fixed for Saturday? Fancy lunch? My treat. I will ping you the details.'

Evie never did make that lunch date with Sophia.

Jeremy appeared at her door on Saturday morning with the most enormous bouquet of expensive, fragrant flowers.

'I just wanted you to know how sorry I am and humbly ask if we can start again. I have a whole weekend planned for us. I want to spoil you. We can take a drive in the sports car to a lovely pub in the country for lunch and I've got tickets for *Les Mis* tonight. Really good seats too. Cost a fortune but you are worth it, Evie.'

'Oh, Jeremy, I'm so sorry I promised Sophia I would have lunch with her today.'

'Of course, I understand. You can't let her down. Don't worry, I will just cancel everything and spend the weekend by myself.'

He looked so downcast and disappointed that Evie said quickly, 'No. You have gone to so much trouble. She won't mind. We can catch up another time. I will let her know.'

She messaged Sophia to say she couldn't make their lunch but didn't receive a reply so was obviously in her bad books.

Instead, she spent all of Saturday and Sunday with Jeremy. He was a completely different man to the drunken, overbearing and intimidating figure from just a week ago. In fact, he was a total gentleman, dropping her off at her flat after the theatre, giving her a chaste peck on the forehead, opening the car door and saying he would see her tomorrow, and that he wanted to show her his place.

After a delicious Sunday brunch in Chelsea, they drove to his flat, a chrome-and-glass bachelor pad with an impressive view over the River Thames.

It felt like a corporate hotel room neglected by housekeeping, rather than a place where someone actually lived. It was dusty and unkempt, with sticky rings on the coffee tables and dust on every surface. There were no books or magazines, and Jeremy had nothing in the fridge but a few half-empty old cartons of leftover takeaways and a dried-up lemon.

'I don't have much in, as you can see,' he said apologetically. 'What this place could do with is a woman's touch.'

He looked at Evie hopefully and said, 'Do you fancy going for a nice meal? There's a lovely Italian place round the corner, and I booked it for dinner tonight. I want to make things up to you. I'm sorry I was such an idiot.'

'You don't have to keep apologising. It's OK.'

He looked grateful but just couldn't stop himself trying far too hard to impress.

'Would you like a glass of wine before we go out? I bought a nice bottle. I don't usually drink wine. I'm more of a gin or a lager man myself, but I hope it's OK? The man in the shop said it was a good one.' Jeremy proudly showed her a pretty decent bottle of Chardonnay that Evie actually rather liked, and made a fuss of pouring her a glass.

*

The meal was good, and Jeremy made a show of leaving a big tip, and when they were leaving, he asked Evie to stay the night. 'We don't need to do anything. You can stay in the spare room. I bought you a new toothbrush and you can wear one of my T-shirts as a nightie.' He had thought of everything. And he was being really kind and considerate. Despite what had happened the week before, Evie found herself charmed.

Around three o'clock, he crept into her bed and tentatively spooned her. Evie was half awake but she let him cuddle up to her, although she was very aware of his hard-on pushing against her thigh.

One thing led to another. It wasn't unpleasant. He was far gentler and took his time, but the earth stayed decidedly unmoved.

Six months later, just as Sophia had feared all those years ago, Evie found she had drifted into being one half of a 'proper couple' almost without realising it.

25

Orkney, 1994

Duncan and Cara were going out for the evening to an anniversary party. The house had been in an uproar all day with Cara fussing about arrangements and choosing something to wear. She rarely went over the door these days but everyone she knew would be at the party and she didn't want to be left out and have them all talking about her.

It was going to be the kind of special event where all of the women would be making an enormous effort, some even ordering dresses from the mainland and taking great care with their hair and make-up.

Cara told herself she had to look absolutely perfect and worked herself up into a frenzy because her new dress wasn't the exact colour she'd seen in the catalogue, and she had 'nothing to wear'.

Duncan was being driven to new heights of exasperation. Normally, he bit his lip and didn't say anything, but this time it was too much.

'For the love of God, Cara, this is why I never want to go anywhere. All this fuss and bother and you yelling at me and the girls. It's just not worth getting yourself into such a state. Let's just forget it and stay at home.'

'Are you kidding me?' shrieked Cara. 'I've had my hair done and bought this new dress.'

'I thought you said the colour was horrible and anyway we are only going to see the Balfours. They won't care what we look like, they just want us there to celebrate their silver wedding.'

'Huh,' said Cara. 'They want us there to show off and boast about their son at university in Glasgow. I give it ten seconds before they mention it.'

They caught each other's eyes and smiled. It was a rare moment of understanding in the battlefield of their marriage, but a truce was declared.

Duncan felt some of the tension leave his stomach, but these glimmers of peace were few and far between. He held on to it and told himself everything would be OK. When the girls were older Cara would relax and not be so stressed. It would all be worth it in the end.

He felt bad for yelling at her. All he had to do was hold his temper and keep her as quiet and calm as possible. Then it would be all right.

Cara had grown gaunt and grey, and looked far older than her forty-eight years. She fretted from dawn to dusk and never stopped cleaning, polishing and dusting her immaculate house. She no longer cooked big homemade meals every day as she said it made the kitchen too messy. Her best friend was the microwave, or she would call up for a takeaway. She'd use paper plates and plastic cutlery so there was no washing up or mess.

An hour before the taxi was coming to take them to the hotel, Cara was ready and drumming her fingers on the table. The dress was a sort of dingy apricot and drained all the colour from her face. Truth be told it would have looked bad even on a supermodel, but Duncan assured her she looked gorgeous.

The phone rang with the sharp tone that made Cara jump. 'If that's my mother, tell her I'm out,' said Cara.

That was her usual response to the phone going. It usually was her mum, Sheila, as not many people phoned the house these days. Cara hadn't been to see her family in Hrossey for a long while, and the old woman would always ask when she was coming north.

Cara simply couldn't be bothered with all the annoyance, planning and disruption of a trip, not even by plane, which took less than twenty minutes and was almost as easy as getting a taxi into Stromness.

This time it wasn't her mother, it was the babysitter, Jeanette. Duncan sighed heavily and put the phone down. 'I'm sorry, Cara. Jeanette can't make it. She's been asked to work late at the restaurant as they are short-staffed, and she doesn't want to let them down and . . .'

Cara cut him off.

'I don't give a toss about the stupid restaurant and whether they aren't organised enough to have the right number of staff.' Her voice rose 'Where does that leave me? All dressed up with nowhere to go, that's where.'

She was fuming. 'I told you we should have asked Liv ages ago to babysit, and now it's too late because she's out having a sleepover tonight. She's got a biology test next week and all the girls are swotting up for it.'

'Cara, we never asked Liv to babysit, and you know why. I still don't trust her to take proper care of Teenie.' And he thought to himself, if Liv was studying for an exam, he was a monkey's uncle.

'You and your precious Teenie. I've told you a thousand times that you smother her, Duncan.'

Duncan bit his lip and tried not to rise to the bait. 'Look. Maybe Liv's pals can come to study here and stay over instead.'

Cara rolled her eyes. 'And where would we put them all in this tiny, pokey house? And anyway, it's a complete tip; I wouldn't keep pigs in here, never mind teenage girls. What would they all think of me?'

'Cara, the house is a peedie palace and three bedrooms are more than enough for us. I've said we could move but you don't want to and . . .'

He abruptly stopped talking because he could hear his voice wobble and he felt so stupid to be a grown man on the verge of tears. He cleared his throat and shook his head.

I need to get a grip, he thought.

Breathing heavily, Duncan said he would go up and ask Liv if she would look after Teenie and then they'd be able to go out and hopefully have a good evening.

He was deeply ashamed of himself for actually feeling nervous at asking his sixteen-year-old daughter to babysit her own little sister.

He knocked on the door with the KEEP OUT sign. Underneath, Liv had scrawled THIS MEANS YOU EVIE MUIR. It had been done years ago when Evie was just a toddler and couldn't read anyway.

Liv eventually put her head round the door. She would have been pretty, but she wore too much thick make-up, and her face was arranged in a permanent disaffected scowl.

'What do you want?' she snapped.

'Liv, we've been let down by the babysitter at the last minute. Could you possibly change your plans and look after Teenie? Your mother is downstairs all done up like a dish of fish and she'll be really upset if she can't go and show off her new frock.'

Liv retorted, 'The dress is vile, and the colour makes her looks drab. I told her that.'

Yes, I'm sure you did, thought Duncan.

Liv's eyes narrowed. 'How much exactly are we talking about as a payment?'

'Well, we were going to give Jeanette four pounds an hour.'

Liv gave a harsh guffaw. 'Treble that and I'll consider it.'

He felt like telling her to go and get stuffed, but she had him over a barrel.

'OK, it's a deal. But behave yourself. Don't use this as an excuse to have your pals round for a party and raid our drinks cabinet. A few of the girls can come and study if you want and maybe stay over.'

'It's too late for them to change their plans,' she replied scornfully. 'And anyway, this house is way too small. Where would we all sleep?'

Not for the first time, Duncan thought she sounded just like her mother.

'Look, the taxi will be here soon. Take good care of your sister. She's in the sitting room watching TV and she won't be any trouble. She's had her tea and I ordered pizza for Jeanette to arrive at eight o'clock. You can have that obviously. Just make sure Teenie doesn't stay up too late. I know it's Saturday tomorrow, but she needs her sleep.'

'I'm not an idiot, Dad. The pest will be fine with me. As long as she doesn't want me to read her a bedtime story. I draw the line at that. Anyway, what kind of pizza did you order?'

'Pepperoni and extra cheese.'

'Large?'

'Aye.'

'I suppose that will have to do.'

It was like negotiating with a hostage taker. Duncan felt he needed a loudhailer and back-up, but at least Cara would be pleased.

She wasn't. She started flapping about like a damp duck.

'With all this upset, Duncan, I'm just not sure I'm in the mood to go now.'

'Cara, if I have to hoist you over my shoulder and carry you there, you are going to this night out whether you want to or not. I've squeezed myself into my old suit and this tie is choking the life out of me, but we are bloody well going to enjoy ourselves.'

'Fine.'

Why was it that whenever his wife said 'fine' in that tone it meant anything but fine? The exact opposite of fine in fact. This was going to be a fun evening.

As well as a surly Cara on his hands, Duncan also had severe doubts about leaving Liv in charge of Teenie.

His eldest daughter was tall for her age and thin as a rake. She wore skinny black jeans slung low on her tiny hips, tight black T-shirts and a scuffed leather jacket. She'd dyed her hair almost blue black and cut it herself in the spikey style of Chrissie Hynde from The Pretenders. Her dad said the long fringe made her look like 'a coo keeking over a dyke'. Liv's eyes were like two jaggy spiders caked in layers of black mascara and dark eyeliner that she never quite removed properly, but just piled more of on top every day.

He didn't know everything his daughter got up to, but he had some idea. There were rumours about her falling in with a rough crowd – he heard murmurs on the rare occasions he got to the pub, and he knew several people pointed the finger at Liv for a number of petty thefts.

When he tried to talk to Cara, she forbade him to confront Liv about her behaviour. She was still slipping her daughter secret 'hush money' but refused to admit that Liv was a problem and constantly made excuses for her.

Liv would regularly spin her a line that she was 'doing home-work' and would be staying at her friends' houses overnight.

Cara knew it was whopping great lie, but it made her feel better to cling on to the illusion that her daughter wasn't out all-night drinking and more than likely having sex, and was, in fact, diligently studying for her exams.

Duncan tried to tell himself that maybe by showing Liv he trusted her to take care of his Teenie, she'd step up and be responsible. They wouldn't be late, and Teenie would be in her bed early anyway.

They finally got into the taxi after a lot of fuss with Cara forgetting her handbag and then having to go back again for a shawl in case it got cold in the function room of the hotel.

On the journey she started fretting about the present they were bringing. Duncan had suggested a silver frame for the Balfours to show off a favourite photo, but Cara was now thinking that was a bit mean and they should have got them some silver goblets as well.

She nursed that worry all the way there.

Finally, they arrived and were engulfed in a warm crowd of happy people offering drinks and food and swapping stories. Duncan found himself with a pint in one hand and a fat buttery vol-au-vont in the other, surrounded by old friends and catching up with everyone.

Even Cara looked as though she was enjoying herself, gossiping with women she hadn't seen in ages. 'How is your bonnie Evie?' one of them asked. 'She's such a bright peedie thing. We see her a lot out with her dad.'

They all avoided talking about Liv. She already had a reputation as a troublemaker. Fathers didn't want their daughters to be in her company and mothers warned their sons about getting mixed up with the devil-eyed girl who was more than likely to find herself in the family way before too long.

As the night wore on, Duncan even persuaded Cara to slow dance with him to 'Yesterday', one of her favourite old Beatles songs. As he held her close, he remembered how they used to love just being together.

He still adored his wife, but he had sensed over the years she was slipping away from him. Tonight, felt more like old times. Maybe there was hope for them after all.

Duncan and Cara got into a taxi just after midnight. She'd had a few drinks and was happily chatting about how stuck-up the Balfours were, but that it had been nice to get out for once, and they really should do it more often.

Duncan was about to suggest they go out for a meal next weekend but as the car rounded the top of the road, they heard the thudding 'boom boom' bass of loud music.

'What the hell . . .?' Duncan muttered as they pulled up outside the front door. Every light was blazing, and the house was full of rowdy boozed-up teenagers; some of them had spilled into the garden. Duncan leapt out of the car and pushed past two teenage boys who were throwing up on the grass. The living room was a fug of cigarette smoke. Scuffles had broken out between young men drinking on empty heads and he could hear breaking glass and furniture being smashed.

Duncan was way beyond anger.

He rushed upstairs to Evie's room, to find a drunken couple on his daughter's bed, obviously looking for a place to have a fumble, and Teenie nowhere to be seen.

'Get out,' he roared at them, fear racing through him. *Where the hell was she?*

'Teenie, where are you, my lamb?'

'Da,' came a weak voice.

He looked around frantically and found Evie curled up under the bed, struggling to breathe and sobbing for her dad.

'Teenie, it's OK, I'm here. Take it easy. Where's your inhaler?'

'I left it downstairs in the living room, but I was too scared to go and get it and I can't find the spare one,' she said in a small, scared voice.

'Don't worry, I've always got one in my top pocket, remember.'

He gave it to Evie who inhaled gratefully.

'Are you OK now?'

She nodded.

'Right, I'm going downstairs to get rid of all these fuckers.'

Teenie managed a watery smile at hearing her dad saying a very naughty word, but she was badly shaken and still trembling.

Duncan bellowed at all of the half-drunk, drugged-up teen-agers to bugger off, and that he hoped their parents would give them a good hiding.

He couldn't believe the state of the house. It looked like they had been robbed by a gang of baboons. There were cigarette burns on the coffee table and someone had spilled cheap red wine over his favourite armchair. Liv was nowhere to be found.

He went back upstairs where Evie's inhaler had worked its magic and he stayed with her until she fell asleep. Sitting in the dark he grew more and more angry and upset.

This was the final straw. Something would have to be done about Liv.

He plodded wearily downstairs, his stomach sour from five pints of lager and rage at seeing his Teenie so frightened and his home completely trashed.

Cara was in the kitchen tidying away the empty cans and bottles.

'Now before you start, Duncan, Liv has explained that this wasn't her fault. A group of yobbos up here on holiday from Glasgow gatecrashed and Liv couldn't stop them. They threatened her, Duncan. She was really frightened. I've told her to go and lie down in her room and get some sleep. She looked so tired.'

'Are you actually blind, Cara?' raged Duncan. 'If Liv was so scared, she could have phoned us. I would have come right home and sorted all of this out. She's not tired, she's been at our booze and she's blootered.'

He looked around at the wrecked kitchen.

'Look at the state of the place. She obviously has no respect for us. I want her out of here. She can get a live-in job at one of the hotels or go to hell for all I care. I'm done with her.'

'You can't turn your back on your own child, Duncan. You can't. What would people say? How could I show my face ever again.'

'Cara. Teenie was terrified. She was struggling to breathe and didn't have her inhaler. She could have had another attack. She might have died.'

'Don't be ridiculous. You and your precious Teenie. This is what it's all about as per usual. Well, there's no way you are kicking Liv out. If she goes, I go. Although, you'd probably like that, wouldn't you? It could just be you and your Teenie.'

Cara burst into tears, and, once again, Duncan was left feeling guilty, hopeless, resentful and horribly frustrated.

For Christ's sake, he thought in despair. *I just want a bit of peace.*

26

Orkney, 2024

Freya was as good as her word and went up to see Maureen later that day in her house by the sea in Finstown, halfway between Kirkwall and Stromness, looking out to the Bay of Firth.

The afternoon sun flooded in through the window and made the wooden floors and furniture glow. It also shone on Maureen who was dozing on the sofa under one of her own colourful homemade blankets.

Freya smiled. Maureen's baking skills might leave a lot to be desired, but she could create the most beautiful woollen throws and blankets. Her smile faded when she looked closely at the dark circles under Maureen's eyes and saw her hollow cheeks. At the funeral, she'd been wearing a lot of make-up, which hid the waxy look of her skin. Andrzej was right. She looked really ill.

Maureen groaned and gave a gasp of surprise when she saw Freya.

'Oh, you gave me a turn. I must have dozed off for a moment. Can I get you a cup of tea?'

From Maureen's bleary expression, Freya guessed she must have been asleep for much longer than a few minutes.

'Let me do it,' said Freya. She went into Maureen's kitchen. The sink was full of dirty dishes and there were piles of damp clothes waiting to be hung up. Freya frowned. Maureen was usually so house-proud; it wasn't like her to leave things undone.

She set down two steaming mugs of hot, sweet, strong tea.

'You look a bit tired, love,' Freya began gently. 'How are you feeling?'

'Oh, right as rain,' said Maureen. 'A peedie bit weary after yesterday, but absolutely fine. I'll be needing to get on with the chores in a minute.'

'You're looking awfully thin,' said Freya.

'Do you think so? Well, I needed to lose a few pounds,' said Maureen with a fixed smile.

Freya hesitated, unsure what to do next. She glanced back at Maureen and saw that her smile was wavering. There was a flicker of apprehension in her eyes. What was really going on?

'I'm not the only one who's worried,' Freya said. 'Andrzej is too. He came to see me.' Maureen looked stricken.

'He's worried about me?'

Freya nodded. 'He is that.'

'I don't want to cause him any worry,' Maureen said, a tremble in her voice.

Freya got up and sat next to Maureen on the sofa, taking her hand.

'What's going on? You can tell me, and you know I won't let on to a living soul.'

Maureen hesitated, and a tear rolled down her face.

'I'm scared, Freya. And I do need to tell somebody. I found a lump, you know, on my, on my breast.'

Freya squeezed her hand.

'Plenty of women find these things, and there's often no need to be worried.'

'It's got bigger, though.'

'How long ago did you notice this?'

'Before Christmas.'

Freya was shocked. That was months ago, and Maureen worked at the health centre. She knew fine well how important it was to get checked right away.

'Please don't be angry with me,' whispered Maureen. 'I just hoped it might go away. I didn't want to face the possibility that it might be . . .' Her voice trailed off, before she added weakly, 'Not after everything my parents and especially my Rory have been through.'

'Oh, Maureen,' said Freya. 'You poor lass. I can't believe you've been carrying this worry all by yourself for so long. Look, we need to get you checked out as soon as possible. I'm sure it's nothing, but let's find out. Far better to know, don't you think?'

Maureen nodded but looked so miserable and scared that Freya's heart ached, and she made up her mind there and then that Maureen needed to be told about Andrzej, even if it meant breaking her promise to him.

'I am going to tell you something that I should have said long ago, but I try not to poke my nose into other people's business,' said Freya.

'That fine man Andrzej has been in love with you for ten long years, ever since he moved here. He adores you, Maureen, and he lights up when you come into a room. Surely you must know that?'

Maureen looked stunned and shook her head.

'No, you're wrong. He just sees me as a friend. I think he probably feels sorry for me. He can't possibly be in love with me. That's just plain daft.'

'He's never said anything because he's worried you are still in love with David, and he's scared that he might ruin your friendship.'

Maureen stared at her, and the first spot of colour came back into her cheeks. 'Are you really serious, Freya? Of course I will always love David, but he told me before he died that I should try to find happiness with someone else. He really was a special man.'

'And so is Andrzej. Tell me the truth, Maureen. Has he got any chance at all with you?'

Maureen gave a sort of choked gasp and delighted laugh. God, it felt good. She hadn't laughed properly for months.

No wonder Andrzej was so concerned about her; she'd been a right misery. Usually, he made her giggle and shriek with laughter. She thought about how he had enriched all of her family's lives. He was the kindest and most thoughtful man. She didn't know what she'd do without him.

She looked at Freya with tears of happiness in her eyes and said, 'I've loved him for years, Freya. I didn't want to mess up what we have. I honestly didn't believe he felt the same about me. I thought he mostly came round to see my dad and listen to his stories about Orkney history.'

'Well, for the love of God, Maureen, you need to tell the poor man. He will be made up. I reckon he will explode with joy.'

Maureen's face fell. 'How can I possibly tell him, Freya? Until I know whether I'm really sick or not.'

She couldn't say the word cancer out loud, but it thickened the air between them. Clouds covered the sunshine outside and cast a dark shadow in the beautiful room.

'You mustn't tell him anything we've talked about today, Freya. Promise me.'

With a heavy heart Freya gave her word, but only if Maureen made an appointment first thing in the morning and let her know the outcome. Maureen promised she would, but she looked so frightened that Freya said she would come with her.

If Maureen is really ill, thought Freya. *She would need Andrzej's strong arms around her, and he would be devastated if she shut him out.*

Evie was walking up the path to Kate's house, apprehensive about the sort of welcome she was going to get.

This would their first time alone together. At the funeral Kate had murmured her condolences, but there had been no time to talk, and it had been horribly awkward when they had seen each other on the beach with the other selkies.

Evie had brought toys for the kids along with wine and chocolate for Kate, hoping to start off on the right foot.

Kate answered the door carrying a basket of laundry. At least it solved the problem of whether they would hug or not as Kate had her hands full.

'Evie! This is a surprise.'

'If it's a bad time, I can come back?'

Evie thought she saw Kate ever so slightly arch an eyebrow.

'Well, you're here now. Come on in but ignore the mess. You can't have two kids and keep a tidy house like your mother did.'

'We couldn't eat a biscuit, but she'd have the Dustbuster under our feet sweeping away at the crumbs,' said Evie and she saw Kate half smile at the memory. 'Your place is lovely, Kate. It's a real home.'

The house was indeed bright and warm and smelled of home cooking and damp dogs.

A fat tabby cat was curled up on a rug in front of the blazing wood fire and two little girls were chatting happily and playing an elaborate game together with a huge wooden Noah's ark full of dinosaurs, Barbie dolls and plastic monkeys, but they went quiet when they saw Evie.

'Girls. Come and say hello. This is an old friend of mine and your daddy's. Her name's Evie. We were at school together a long, long time ago. Evie, this is my Louise and Claire.'

The girls giggled but were too shy to say anything.

The eldest Louise was dark-haired with a fringe that was endearingly wonky, and her two front teeth were missing. She was slightly chubby with bright red cheeks and big brown eyes. Claire was two years younger with fair, unruly curly hair and all skinny, coltish arms and legs.

Evie said hello but then stood awkwardly in the middle of the living room.

There was so much to say to Kate, but she didn't know where to start.

'I brought the girls a few peedie bits.'

Evie handed over the presents and the wine and chocolates for Kate.

Kate thanked her but in the way you'd thank a stranger for holding the door open for you.

Evie perched on the edge of the squashy sofa and there was an uncomfortable silence. She realised she still had her coat on but wasn't sure how long she'd be staying.

The sun peeked out, so Kate told the girls to go and play outside in the garden. Finally, she turned to Evie and said, 'Evie, I'll be honest with you, I'm struggling here. I don't want to upset you after the funeral yesterday, but don't you think you have some explaining to do?'

Evie realised coming here when Kate was on her own with the girls was a big mistake. She should have waited until the evening when Edwyn was back from work, and he would have been able to smooth things over.

Just when she thought about getting up and making her

excuses, two boisterous Jack Russells bounded into the living room, jumping up on Evie and demanding attention.

'Eric! Ernie! Get down right now. How many times have you been told?'

They obeyed immediately but not without giving Kate the side-eye, and padded off to sit in front of the fire, making sure to give the cat a wide berth.

Evie was so touched that Kate had named her dogs after her own pets all those years ago.

'Are they girls or boys?'

'Well, what do you think? Obviously, they are girls. We wanted to keep the tradition going for your dad. He did laugh when I told him. I was glad about that. He didn't have much to laugh about, the poor auld bugger.'

She looked at Evie straight in the eye for the first time since she'd arrived.

'He was a good man. We tried to help him, but he wouldn't let us. Maybe I should have tried harder, but I had the kids and Edwyn was working all hours at the hospital. Don't think we didn't make an effort.'

'He wasn't your responsibility, Kate. I was the one who left and stayed away. I will never ever forgive myself for that, and for not being there at the end. I can't bear to think of him all alone.' Her voice broke and she tried desperately not to cry. She went on, 'I'm so sorry, Kate. You've no idea how often I wanted to pick up the phone and talk to you. I was so homesick, and I missed you so much.'

The ice melted just a little bit.

'Your dad wasn't all by himself. Edwyn was there. And he didn't wake up. It was a peaceful end. You can take some comfort from that.'

Evie took a deep breath and her words tumbled out.

'I was so nervous about coming here today. I wouldn't have blamed you for slamming the door in my face and never speaking to me again. I wanted to talk to you at the funeral, but it wasn't the right time. There were too many people and Liv had caused a scene . . .'

Kate put her hand up.

'Wheest for a minute. Take your coat off for God's sake. I'm going to make some coffee and we are going to talk things out. You will be staying for your tea. You need some meat on your bones. I'll feed the girls in a minute, and I've got a good pot of stew on the go for me and Edwyn and there's more than enough for the three of us. He should be back around seven o'clock. But you know what he's like. So conscientious. They take a loan of him at that hospital.'

'He was always like that,' Evie said, as Kate set down the coffee and homemade cakes.

'Right,' said Kate. 'I need to say this, and you need to hear it. You know, Evie, you didn't just leave your family. You left me and Edwyn behind, too. We had no idea what was going on. We understood you wanted to get away for a while, but we thought you'd be back after a few days. It was awful what happened to Brodie, and no wonder you were devastated, but then you left, and we were beside ourselves with worry about you.'

She sighed and went on, 'You really hurt us, Evie. I don't understand why you couldn't have just written to us. We searched for you on social media, but you weren't on anything, not even Facebook. Eventually we just had to give up.'

Evie thought of all the times she had reached for the phone to call or text her friends or started a letter but could never find the right words. All her attempts ended up as sad, crumpled balls of paper in the bin. And, Freya had never stopped asking if she could give Kate and Edwyn her address. She was sorely tempted, but then always panicked and experienced waves of shame and guilt at the thought of having to explain to them why she had to run away.

She'd told herself it was far better not to have any contact at all, and they would soon forget all about her, but she had clearly underestimated the upset she'd caused.

Twenty years later, here she was being asked all the questions she'd always dreaded. She couldn't stop apologising to Kate, but she couldn't bring herself to tell her the real reason she'd left.

'I'm so sorry, Kate, more than you will ever know, and I will tell you what happened, I promise. I'm trying to pluck up the courage. I need to tell you and Edwyn and Freya together. I won't be able to tell the story more than once and I hope when you hear what I have to say you won't hate me too much.'

'Christ, Evie, you are frightening me,' said Kate only half-jokingly.

'I'm sorry. I don't mean to, but can we just talk about something else. I want to know about you and Edwyn. I'm so glad you got together, and your girls are just lovely.'

They could hear the sound of the children's laughter as Louise and Claire chased each other outside in the sunshine.

'They are good girls, and they get on so well. We are lucky. I think Edwyn would have liked to try again for a boy, but I've shut up shop. I think having two girls is just perfect.'

Evie thought of her mum and dad and how they might have felt the same when Evie was born. *We made them so unhappy*, she thought. Kate got up and began preparing tea for the girls.

Evie knew she had to tell everyone the truth and confess to what she had done, even although they would never be able to forgive her.

Her phone beeped. She looked down. A message from an unknown number.

GIVE ME THE FUCKING HOUSE OR YOU WILL BE
SORRY
LIV

She suddenly felt horribly clammy, and her stomach was churning. *Oh, God*, she thought. *I'm going to be sick.*

She managed to whisper, 'Kate. Where's the bathroom?'

Kate pointed to the hall. 'First on the left. Jeez, you look terrible. Are you OK?'

Evie ran to the bathroom and was just in time to violently vomit into the toilet and not all over the floor. She retched until there was nothing left but bile, then knelt on the floor blinded by tears and feeling very sorry for herself.

Kate was outside the door.

'Are you all right, Evie, love?

She croaked. 'I'm so sorry. I will clean myself up and then I'll go.'

'Rubbish! You are going nowhere. I'm going to get the girls and give them their tea. Go upstairs and have a shower. There's clean towels and I will leave you a sweatshirt and joggers to change into. I want Edwyn to have a right good look at you and check you over when he comes in. In fact, I'm going to call him now and tell him not to be late.' Evie opened the door.

'Oh, Kate, I don't deserve you being so kind to me.'

Kate sighed. 'Despite everything I'm still your friend and I'm really worried about you.' She left to call the girls inside and Evie wobbled upstairs on shaky legs.

It was such a comfortable house, all soft edges and bright colours. It was messy and a bit careworn. Joan Crawford the cat and Eric and Ernie the dogs had attacked the carpets and furniture, but it just added to a sense of home. Evie came back downstairs with newly washed hair and wearing Kate's bright pink sweatshirt and joggers, which were about four sizes too big, but soft and comfy and smelling of freshly cut grass and clean soap.

The girls were at the kitchen table having their tea of fish fingers, beans and poached eggs. Evie remembered Kate's mother used to make it for the three of them when they'd done their homework at her house.

Louise looked at her and said gravely, 'My mammy said you have a sore tummy. You can have my hot-water bottle if you like and my blankie. My granny knitted one for me and one for Claire. It's on my bed.'

Evie couldn't speak. She was choked up at how kind this little girl was being to a total stranger. Her little sister was busy feeding Eric and Ernie bits of fish finger under the table thinking that no one could see.

'Mammy, did you tell Daddy about the goldfish?' said Louise through a mouthful of beans.

'I didn't, my lamb. I thought you would want to tell him about it when he gets home tonight, but maybe Evie would like to hear the story.'

Louise looked at Evie. 'Do you want to know what happened to our goldfish?'

'Well, of course I do,' said Evie.

'It's a peedie bit sad because the goldfish we had in our class died. It was a shame, but we had been learning about the Vikings and we all thought it would be a good idea to give Ant and Dec, that was their names, a funeral like the Vikings had.'

'Right,' said Evie, who wasn't quite sure where this was going.

'So Ishbel's daddy made a peedie boat and her mammy made a red-and-white sail, and we wrapped up Ant and Dec in toilet paper and put them in the boat.'

'OK,' said Evie, biting her lip and trying to keep a serious expression on her face.

Louise continued gravely, 'Then we went outside to the beach and the teacher set fire to the boat and away they went to Havana.'

Kate and Evie were desperately trying to stifle giggles.

'I think they went to Valhalla, Louise,' said Kate gently. 'That's Viking heaven.'

Claire piped up. 'Will we do that for Eric and Ernie, Mammy?'

'No, sweetheart. I think we will just stick to Viking funerals for goldfish and not for dogs.'

Evie and Kate grinned at each other, and it almost felt like old times. She thought how lucky Louise and Claire were to have each other and to get along so well.

I never played with Liv the way those two played together today. Not once, she thought.

As she sat in Kate's house, wearing her clothes and chatting to her daughters, Evie knew she was on borrowed time and Liv would soon let everyone know about their secret, then no one would ever want to speak to her again.

27

Orkney, 2004

Evie had just turned eighteen. Liv had left home years ago, sofa surfing until she'd managed to rent a place. She'd occasionally come back home to ask her mother for money, or for a decent meal, but inevitably end up arguing with her dad and leaving under a black cloud.

The house had become quieter and less stressful without her, but sadly not any happier. Evie had learned to tiptoe around her parents' misery, trying to placate her mother and take the sting out of her waspish criticisms of her dad and attempting to lift his moods of weary sadness. She had become an expert in distracting them both from arguing with each other, but it was exhausting. To keep her mother happy she cleaned the house, weeded the garden and kept her room as tidy as the cell of a nun.

What made her dad happiest was her success at school. Evie worked hard and her report cards were full of As and Bs and she had turned out to be a genuinely talented artist, painting endless portraits of Eric and Ernie and beautiful sea birds. She was working hard on her sixth-year studies and building up a portfolio to get into art school.

Because of the tense atmosphere at home, she found herself spending more time with Kate and Edwyn after school and at weekends.

The three of them were inseparable and looking forward to spending the summer together. Evie wanted to try to paint landscapes over in Hoy where the scenery was spectacular, and she planned to visit her relations on Hrossey. They were always asking her to come and stay.

What she didn't know was that all those plans would be scuppered, because she was about to fall in love for the very first time.

She was weeding round the back of the house one morning, when her dad came out of the door and shouted for her.

'Come on, Evie, love, we are going into toon. I need your help.'

'Sure, Dad, but I'm a bit of a state. Can I have five minutes to clean up and change?'

Duncan knew that his daughter's five minutes meant at least half an hour. 'I'd really rather go now, Evie, if you don't mind.'

She had heard the raised voices and knew her parents had been arguing again. She took one look at her dad's tense, defeated face, threw down her hoe, wiped her hands on her dirty jeans, gave him a smile and declared, 'I'm ready if you are.'

She knew what the source of the trouble was. One of her dad's old school pals, Hugh, was coming back to Orkney for the summer with his nineteen-year-old son, Brodie. Evie had met the family years before when they'd hired a nearby cottage for a couple of weeks when Brodie was nine and Evie was eight.

She couldn't remember much about them. Hugh had been with his ex-wife back then, a bottle blonde with a sour face, and they'd broken up shortly afterwards. This was the first time Hugh and Brodie had been back to Orkney since.

Instead of their visit being greeted with pleasure, it had sent Cara into a complete meltdown. Evie had overheard another blazing row with Cara shrieking because her dad had invited Hugh and Brodie over for dinner that night.

'He never thought I was good enough for you,' shouted Cara. 'I'm not having him come in here thinking I can't keep a clean house.' Her mother had whined that she hadn't enough notice, despite Duncan telling her they were coming two weeks ago.

The house was turned upside down with a frenetic and completely unnecessary deep clean. She refused Evie's offers of help and put on her 'martyr's face' that made Duncan grind his teeth, and Evie disappear outside to work in the garden.

Cara had been up since five o'clock that morning frantically cooking and fretting and winding herself up into a state of high anxiety. In the end, and unusually for him, Duncan had put his foot down and cancelled the dinner, saying he'd take Hugh and Brodie for a pint and a pie in the local pub instead.

The cottage they'd hired was within walking distance of Kirkwall and just a ten-minute drive along the road from Duncan. He wanted Evie with him to buy some supplies and check that everything was ready for their stay, but he also needed her to cheer him up.

In the car, Evie tried her best.

'You will be looking forward to seeing Hugh again, Dad,' she said enthusiastically. 'You go back such a long way and you've not seen each other for ages.'

He nodded. 'Hugh is a good man, right enough.'

'Don't worry about tonight,' she added. 'Mum will calm down. It will be OK. You can catch up with Hugh down the pub and me and Brodie can come too.'

Duncan smiled at her. 'What would I do without you?' he said.

Evie felt torn in two as usual. She was glad she could help her father, but it came with a dead weight of responsibility.

He glanced at her fondly. 'It's fine, Evie. It's my fault. I shouldn't put that pressure on your mother. All I wanted was just a nice normal evening with a few drinks and a bit of supper. I wasn't after anything fancy, but there's no telling her. It's like she thinks she is always giving a performance and being judged.'

Evie wished her mother wasn't so highly strung, but also that her dad would stand up for himself instead of just being a rug for her to wipe her tiny feet on.

'Anyway, you're right, it will be grand to see Hugh and young Brodie. You might want to show him around a bit, Evie. He won't want to spend all his time with his dad and all of us old codgers.'

After stocking up at the supermarket, they went to the cottage. There was a key in the door, but of course nobody bothered to lock it. It was clean, basic and a great location for visiting all the sights.

Evie had already brought soft, clean towels and blankets from home just in case they were needed and started to unpack the shopping and stock up the fridge in the small kitchen.

She was just finishing up when they heard a car outside. She heard her dad roar a joyful greeting and looked out the window to see him and Hugh shaking hands. Even though her dad was delighted to see his old friend, they weren't the type for hugs, even manly ones, so a brisk handshake sufficed. She came out to meet them.

Hugh smiled at her. 'Surely this can't be young Evie? You are all grown up and so bonnie.' Brodie came up the path lugging their suitcases and grinned at Evie.

Now, just yesterday she and Kate had been talking about their ideal man. They'd decided tall but not too tall. Well built but not all muscles. A fire head of hair and perfect skin was a must. Brown eyes and good cheekbones would be a bonus. And, they had to have a kind and generous smile. Well, Brodie was all of that and so much more.

Evie felt her throat go dry and couldn't say a word. She had heard of girls melting at the flash of a man's smile and didn't believe a word of it, and yet here she was on the verge of collapse like a cheap umbrella.

Brodie had obviously said something utterly charming and devastatingly intelligent and was now waiting on her to reply. Evie was all over the place and couldn't hear a thing for the blood rushing in her ears and the thump of her heart.

Oh, bugger. He's going to think I'm a right eejit and I've come over here in my oldest clothes and wellies thick with cow muck and I didn't even brush my hair. I've even still got my woolly hat on. Why did my dad not tell me he had turned out to be so gorgeous? Wait until Kate sees him. But I saw him first. That has to count for something.

She gave herself a shake and tried to concentrate. Brodie smiled again. 'No pressure, Evie, but I know there's some great places here for live music, especially right now during the festival. Dad has already booked tickets for some highbrow stuff in the cathedral, but I fancy listening to some bands and having a beer. It would be good to meet your friends. And your sister Liv, of course. Although she never had much time for me as I remember.'

He laughed which made him even more ridiculously handsome.

Evie managed to get her act together enough to reply. She didn't really know anything about going to pubs to see bands as she was too busy painting and being a swot, doing her homework, and going for walks with Kate and Edwyn, but the last thing she wanted was for Brodie to think she wasn't the kind of sophisticated girl who knew her way around the local music scene.

'Yes, of course, absolutely. I can do that. No problem. I'm your woman.'

Duncan looked at them both fondly, but he put down a marker.

'Evie doesn't drink even though she's eighteen. She's too busy with her studies.'

Brodie looked at them both through narrowed eyes.

'Aye, right. And I'm sure you two never had a drink when you were younger than Evie. Don't you worry. I will look after her as though she were my baby sister.'

The last thing in the world Evie wanted to be was Brodie's sister. This wasn't going well at all, but when Brodie looked at her again and grinned, he made her feel like she was the only girl in the world and that gave her a bit of hope.

Duncan got up to go. 'Right then, we will leave you to get settled in. Do you both fancy a pint tonight then a bit of supper in the pub? I know I asked you over to the house for your tea, but Cara's not feeling too well. She's really sorry not to be seeing you but we can all catch up later in the week.'

'Course. No problem. Give her my love and tell her to take care of herself. I hope she didn't go to any trouble for us, Duncan. We wouldn't want any fuss.'

'No fuss at all,' he lied. 'Look, Evie and I will walk over around half six and we can all meander into toon and then you and me can stagger back later on.'

Evie asked her dad to drop her at Kate's, where Brodie was, of course, discussed in great depth. Then they both did a spreadsheet on all the pubs and venues where Evie could take him during his stay. Kate insisted she and Edwyn had to come along too to check up on him. Then there was a long and very involved discussion about what Evie should wear.

'Nothing too slutty. You don't want to look as though you are trying too hard,' said Kate with authority.

'I don't have anything slutty though. And neither do you. Do you think jeans and a T-shirt will do?'

'Wear that green one. You suit green but wash the mud off your face and do something with your hair. Don't wear a lot of lipstick in case he kisses you.'

'Do you think he might? Oh, I hope I don't make a right clown of myself, Kate. But mind I saw him first so hands off.' She wasn't kidding either.

As their dads reminisced in the pub that night, Evie and Brodie chatted together and found they liked the same movies and laughed at the same jokes. He wanted to know all about her life in Orkney and really listened to what she had to say.

Brodie had just the one bottle of lager and Evie would have loved a half pint of cider, but she knew her dad wouldn't approve. As they left the pub to walk home, Evie and Brodie let their dads go ahead of them and walked slowly side by side.

'I'm sorry your mum wasn't feeling well,' he said. 'I hope she gets better soon.'

There was something about walking beside him in the dark, and how genuinely kind and interested he was, that made Evie open up far more than she normally would to someone she hardly knew.

'She isn't really ill,' she said. 'She's just so highly strung and got herself in a right state about you coming over for a bit of supper. Everything is a drama. It's my dad I feel sorry for.'

'I know all about that,' said Brodie, his voice tinged with sadness.

Evie looked at him and felt real sympathy. 'My dad told me your parents had split up.'

'It was a while ago, right after that last trip to Orkney, but it was really tough, especially on my dad.'

'I'm so sorry.'

'Don't be,' said Brodie. 'They were miserable together. When we were up here, I can still remember my mum complaining about the weather and the remoteness, whinging that she wanted to go to the Costa del Sol and hit the bars and night-clubs. She left us soon after. I found out later that she'd been cheating on Dad. Some slick guy with a fancy apartment in Marbella.'

'Do you see much of her?'

'No,' Brodie said, his voice hard. 'She didn't want me cramping her style in Spain. But she still made Dad fight for custody. The lawyers cost a fortune. In the end, he sold the big house in Morningside, gave her half the money and bought the flat in Leith where we live now.'

'That must have been really hard.'

'Aye. It does hurt when your own mother doesn't want you around.'

Evie reached out and brushed his hand with hers. She suddenly remembered what he'd been like at nine. A bit over-weight and painfully shy. Her heart ached at the thought of his mother abandoning him.

'But me and Dad are just fine on our own, and I quickly realised they were better to have split up.'

Evie felt so comfortable with Brodie, she knew she could confide in him, and he would understand.

'I've never said this to anyone before,' said Evie slowly, 'but I feel the same about my parents. Sometimes I wish they'd call it a day. I honestly think they would be happier apart. Or at least my dad would, even though he still loves her. I think my mum just isn't good for him and I'm not sure she knows how to be happy.'

Brodie was nodding. 'And you do your best to keep the peace, right?'

'That's exactly it,' said Evie. 'I worry about what will happen to Dad when I leave home and go to art school, and how he'll cope without me.'

'That's what this trip is about for me and my dad,' said Brodie. 'I know he'll miss me when I go to university, and his dream is to take early retirement here in Orkney. I thought we could both explore some of the places where he might like to settle down.'

He added, 'I was supposed to be going to Thailand with my mates, but instead I booked the ferry and rented a cottage here until the end of August to surprise him.'

'That's so thoughtful,' said Evie. 'What a lovely thing to do.'

'Well, I am so very glad that I did,' he said, taking her hand and giving it a squeeze.

Over the next few weeks, Evie found herself spending most of her time with Brodie. She told him more about living in a house full of tension and stress. It felt as though she was betraying her parents but also, she felt a huge sense of relief to pour it all out. She hadn't mentioned Liv yet, she was building up to that.

She hadn't even told Kate and Edwyn what it was really like growing up with Liv, and how things were at home now, but she wanted Brodie to know everything.

28

Orkney, 2004

Evie was having a blissful time with Brodie. She would never forget their first soft-but-firm kiss that had melted her insides.

The next fine sunny day, he called Evie and suggested they go to the beach at Inganess.

'I would love to tell everyone I went swimming in the sea in Orkney and this one has got that brilliant old shipwreck you can easily reach. We could get a picnic and have a great time and, best of all, I will get to see you in a bikini.'

This was Evie's worst nightmare. She was still absolutely terrified of water. Despite Duncan's many patient attempts, she refused to go back to the swimming baths, and nothing would get her to even paddle in the sea. But she didn't want to tell Brodie. They were still at the stage of showing each other the best versions of themselves.

So, she said, 'I'm not a huge fan of the beach, all that sand going everywhere, and the water will be absolutely freezing.'

'I'll keep you warm,' he said. 'And we can just go in for a paddle.'

The very thought of going into the water even with Brodie holding her hand made Evie so anxious she had to think of a better excuse. 'Well, I don't actually have a bikini,' she said lamely.

'Can you not borrow something from Liv? I was just thinking it's strange I haven't run into her yet.'

'She doesn't come home much now she's in Stromness and she hasn't left much stuff in her room. I doubt she'd even have anything that fitted me, and I'd be killed if I borrowed anything from her.'

'Don't be daft, sisters are always wearing each other's clothes. Go and grab something, and can you pack a couple of towels and some snacks? We can get more food on the way. Come on, Evie, it will be fun. We need to make the most of the sunshine. Knowing Orkney, it might be snowing tonight.'

Evie put the phone down and, against all her instincts, entered her sister's room. Even though Liv no longer lived at home, everyone was too scared to disturb the belongings she'd left behind. The idea of Evie moving into the much bigger room wasn't even up for discussion.

An extraordinary number of black T-shirts were neatly stacked in Liv's chest of drawers, and under her tiny G-string knickers were suspicious-looking packets of what looked like something you'd feed to hamsters. And, right at the back, a tiny black bikini.

Evie made sure she put everything back precisely as she'd found it and went to her room to change. Looking in the mirror, she saw the bikini just about covered her important bits, although it was straining over her boobs, but she put on a big T-shirt and shorts as a cover-up.

Before she could have second thoughts, Brodie was at the door and they were on their way. The beach was busy with families taking advantage of the gorgeous weather and lots of little kids running into the water and squealing with glee.

Brodie and Evie set up base camp, with towels and a couple of cushions. It was so hot that Brodie immediately stripped off to his swimming trunks and talked Evie into taking off her baggy T-shirt. He had no idea she had such a sensational body.

Evie was thinking the same thing about him. Brodie was perfect in every way. He looked as though he had been sculpted by Michelangelo. The two of them had been enjoying long, blissful kissing sessions and lots of delightful exploring but, sensing what they had was special, they were taking things slowly.

Looking at Evie, Brodie found himself being aroused in the way only a nineteen-year-old boy can at the sight of a girl he fancies. There was only one solution. He needed to go into the water.

'I really have to cool off,' said Brodie. 'And you're coming with me?'

'Maybe later,' said Evie, attempting a smile. 'I'm just going to read my book for a while and enjoy the sunshine.' She wasn't sure how long she could keep up this act.

Her memories of almost drowning as a toddler were still vivid and she clearly remembered how the water closed over her head as she struggled to breathe. Then there were all the failed attempts at swimming lessons with her dad, with her terror intensifying every time.

She saw other young couples laughing together, running in and out of the waves, and wished she could be braver, but the thought of going swimming sucked the soul out of her body.

'Oh, come on,' Brodie said. 'I'll race you. There are little kids in there; it's not going to be that bad.' He couldn't understand why his normally sunny and affectionate Evie was so withdrawn. Her face was pinched and stressed.

'Just leave it,' she said in a harsher tone than she meant.

'Fine,' Brodie said. He ran into the water, hoping to show her it wasn't as cold as she thought, only to immediately jump back out again.

Christ almighty, that water is bollocking, he thought. *Those wee kids in there are hard as nails. It's taken care of my problem though. I must be shrunk to the size of a walnut.*

He waved at Evie and yelled, 'It's freezing, but we will get used to it. Come on in, Evie.'

She shook her head again. He ran back to her and gave her a hug. Evie pushed him away. 'Get off. You are all wet and cold.'

'What's got into you? I'm only messing,' he muttered, throwing himself down next to her.

Looking further along the beach, he saw a sloe-eyed, dark-haired slender woman in a pair of tiny denim shorts and a halterneck crop top. She wasn't conventionally beautiful, but he couldn't take his eyes off her. She walked with all the confidence of knowing she was attractive and desirable.

She came up to them smiling. 'Hello, there. Did I just hear you shouting for our Evie? You know she's my little sister? Have we met before? I'm Liv.'

Evie watched in dismay. This was seriously not good.

'Liv? I was wondering when I would see you again. I'm Brodie. We met years and years ago. I don't blame you if you don't remember.'

'Brodie! My, how you've grown. I'd heard you were back and hanging out with Evie, but I don't go home much.' She looked him up and down. 'I'm sorry to have missed you, though.'

Liv glanced at Evie, saw she was wearing her bikini, which was bad enough, but she was enraged that Evie looked better in it than she did. Liv narrowed her eyes. There would be a whole world of pain and trouble for Evie later. But for now, she was being as sweet as pie. Evie couldn't believe this Oscar-worthy performance.

'How was the water, Brodie? I saw you in there all by yourself.'

'I've been trying to persuade Evie to come in,' he said.

Liv looked stricken.

'Oh, no,' she said, her voice sickly saccharine. 'Poor Evie can't swim. Don't go asking her to get in.' Evie's face burned with humiliation.

'Can't swim?' said Brodie. 'You never told me that, Evie. I thought everyone here could swim, especially living on an island surrounded by the sea.'

'Not my poor baby sister,' said Liv with an exaggerated pout.

As usual Evie felt so intimidated by her sister, she just sat silent as a stone.

'You should have said something, Evie,' said Brodie. 'I'd have taught you to swim, I still could. We could start right now.'

Liv looked from one to the other and lit a cigarette. 'Good luck with that, Brodie. Anyway, I'd best be going. Got a hot date in town. I couldn't walk for days last time I saw him,' she added, with a wink. 'Evie, I hope you do get in the water. Especially in that lovely bikini.'

Brodie watched her slink off, leaving the scent of patchouli and cigarette smoke in the air.

'Your sister is really cool, Evie. Come on, let's go in for a swim. I told you I can teach you and there's nothing to be scared of. Trust me.'

'I'm sorry. No. I just can't. You go in again though.'

'But it's no fun on my own. I want you with me and I want to show you off. You look absolutely gorgeous, Evie.'

'I'm not a pair of trainers or a new watch,' said Evie, her voice rising. 'I don't want to be shown off. Actually, do you know what? I just want to leave. I knew this was a bad idea. I hate the beach.'

She could feel the tears welling up. She felt so humiliated.

'OK,' said Brodie. 'It's just a shame to spoil such a lovely day, but we can go home if that's what you want.'

She nodded.

'Sounds like your sister's heading off for a good time in town,' Brodie said, as they packed up. 'I guess she's pretty experienced with guys.'

This just keeps getting worse and worse, thought Evie. She already knew Brodie had had one or two girlfriends before her, and although he hadn't said, she was sure he'd slept with them.

Since she had started going out with Brodie, Evie and Kate had had endless conversations about what sex with him would be like, but they didn't have any personal experience to go on. They had fooled around a bit with boys but had never gone all the way.

They giggled and called themselves 'late developers' but the truth was they both wanted their first time to be special; to make love with a fine fella, preferably in a posh hotel with champagne after a bubble bath. But now, here was Brodie, openly admiring her sister's sexual experience.

'She's not the only one who's been with a lot of guys,' blurted Evie, the words out of her mouth before she could stop them. Brodie looked at her, taken aback.

'Well,' he said. 'You are full of surprises.'

Evie wanted to tell him that she had never been with another boy and she desperately wanted him to be her first, but he already thought she had ruined their day, so she kept quiet.

He gave her a hug and said, 'Look. I'm sorry about the beach, but it's going to be a lovely warm evening, so why don't I take you out tonight. Somewhere special.'

Evie gave him a wobbly smile. 'That would be great. I will get myself dressed up a bit.

He grinned. 'You can come in that bikini if you like. I guarantee you no one would mind.'

Later that evening, they went to a restaurant in Stromness harbour with seats outside full of people eating, drinking and enjoying the long summer evening. Evie and Brodie had ordered the seafood platter and a bottle of white wine and were feeling extremely sophisticated and grown-up.

Brodie was relieved she seemed back to her old self after her odd mood at the beach. They'd laughed and joked over dinner and talked about future plans together. As the meal ended, it seemed the perfect time to talk about the surprise he had planned. He took her hand.

'Evie, I've booked a room for us here upstairs. I've checked it out and it's really nice. I know we both want this to be special, and it will be, I promise.'

Evie felt herself freeze. She looked at him, his face so eager. 'I thought we said we'd take things slowly?'

'When I saw you in that bikini today and how gorgeous you looked, well, I know we said we would take our time, but I don't think I can.' He looked hopeful, eager and a bit shamefaced all at once.

Evie was panicking. He clearly expected sex tonight. And she'd given him the wrong impression that she was experienced. Why had she not just told him she was a virgin?

'I thought you'd be pleased?' he said, his face falling.

'We can't. My dad will wonder where I am,' she said.

'Our dads are out at that concert, and I told them we were going to see a band and would probably crash at some friends. Look, they know we're seeing each other. We don't have to sneak around.'

'I just feel like you've sprung this on me,' Evie said.

Brodie was hurt. 'I'm going back south soon, and I wanted you to know how special you are to me. I'm serious about you. I want us to be together properly.'

Evie shrank back in her seat and stayed silent.

'Please, say something,' said Brodie. 'I don't know what I've done wrong.' Although she could see Brodie getting more and more exasperated, Evie couldn't find the words to tell him the truth. She had backed herself into a corner.

'You know what, I feel like you don't trust me,' he burst out. 'Why didn't you just tell me today you couldn't swim instead of being in a foul mood? I just don't get it.'

'I don't know,' mumbled Evie, staring into her plate. He reached for her hand, and she pulled it away.

'And now you're freezing me out.' Brodie's voice was pleading. 'Please don't, Evie.'

She yelled at him.

'Stop it. You are being so needy. It's too much.'

Brodie had a horrible flashback to his mother saying exactly the same thing to him when he was a young boy before she'd left for good. He had felt abandoned and belittled and here it was happening to him again.

He said coldly, 'You know what, you're behaving like a silly little girl. You are so immature. You need to grow up.' It was one of the worst things he could have said.

'I don't need to listen to this. We're done,' Evie said tightly. She pushed back her chair and ran from the table.

'That's right,' shouted Brodie. 'Just leave. Without giving me a chance to explain.' Underneath his anger, his heart felt like it was breaking. How had he messed things up so badly?

He got up and went inside, heading to the bar to pay the bill.

I will need to cancel the room if it's not too late, he thought miserably.

He felt a tap on his shoulder and turned round to see Liv looking sympathetic. 'You look like a man in serious need of a drink,' she said.

He was relieved to see her. She'd been so kind and friendly on the beach. Maybe she could explain to him why Evie was acting so strangely.

An hour later Brodie's head was spinning. Liv had ordered several double Bacardis and then tequila shots, listening sympathetically to him pouring out his woes about Evie.

'Don't worry about her,' Liv said. 'She's always been a bit of a game player and known as a girl beginning with P and ending in teaser.'

'Has she?' said Brodie. He felt even more confused. That didn't sound like the Evie he had come to know.

Liv nodded. 'Take it from me. She's not what she seems. Now, I want to get to know you. Tell me about what you're going to study?'

She asked all about his plans to study architecture at university and what he wanted to do afterwards. She cooed with admiration at his ambition to help out in refugee camps and said she had always wanted to do something similar.

Brodie went to the bar for more drinks and could barely walk straight. He was having a good time with Liv, who'd told him that Evie was just stringing him along.

Evie can go to hell, he thought drunkenly but he still felt a stab of pain. He really thought she loved him as much as he loved her.

When he tried to order more drinks, the barman kindly suggested he have a pint of water and call it a night.

'I'll call you a taxi home,' he said.

He stumbled back to tell Liv.

She smiled at him.

'I've got a better idea. You told me you already had a room booked here? Why don't we put it to good use. You need a bit of fun.'

29

London, 2016

Another year passed by, and Evie had drifted into a dull and predictable routine with Jeremy. They rarely saw each other during the week. He claimed his work took up all of his time, but he would pick her up outside her office every Friday night so they could spend the weekend together at his flat.

She'd go out shopping during her lunch hour, frantically battling the crowds and staggering back to the office with her arms almost breaking from all the food and wine she'd bought to cook for them for the whole weekend.

As soon as they arrived, Evie would unpack the shopping and Jeremy headed straight for the booze saying he deserved a stiff 'drinky poo' and would pour himself an enormous gin and tonic.

She would disappear into the kitchen and prepare the school-dinner food Jeremy relished. At first, she'd made a real effort cooking up fish and seafood dishes she had loved as a child, and trying her hand at risotto, but Jeremy hadn't been at all impressed, and she'd found it wasn't worth the time and effort. He was far happier with sausage and mash followed by a heavy suet pudding. The most adventurous he ever got was a chicken tikka masala carry-out.

In those first months, when Jeremy had felt he still had to make an effort, he would take her for a Saturday pub lunch, or they'd go for a walk along the Thames. He would hold her hand and talk about his plans for the future and how he wanted to set up in business on his own. He boasted endlessly about 'friends' who were begging him to invest in their start-up companies and how he would soon make a fortune.

Back then, when he'd picked her up from work, he'd sometimes surprised her with chocolates or flowers, usually ones from the garage forecourt, but Evie had told herself it was the thought that counted.

Those days of wine and roses were long gone.

Now, on Saturday afternoons he watched rugby and cricket on the TV with cans of beer and food Evie had brought with her, usually a ready meal or pizza.

She'd tidy up and then it was the usual Saturday night ritual of a couple of hours in the pub around the corner with a white-wine spritzer for Evie and a couple of double gins and tonic for Jeremy, followed by a curry.

He liked staying up late on a Saturday to play his computer games that seemed mostly to involve shooting zombies or aliens. Evie thought he was far too old to be sitting in front of a screen until the wee small hours, but it meant that even though he woke her up stumbling into the bedroom he was too pissed and tired to want to have sex. So, there was that.

On Sunday morning, she'd clear up the debris from the night before, take out the rubbish, leave a snoring Jeremy a huge glass of water and a couple of paracetamols and head back to her flat.

If it was a lovely day, she would walk some of the way along the south bank of the Thames. One Sunday she realised that this walk was the only time she felt her shoulders drop and she could breathe and relax.

She had become utterly miserable at her work. There had been another a round of redundancies. Morale was low and Evie could do the admin work in her sleep. She was lucky that her salary was still relatively good, but her rent had increased, and she was still sending money back home to Liv. She also paid for all the food and drink that Jeremy guzzled and gulped down. There was little left at the end of the month, once she'd taken care of all of that. She often wondered how she had gone from feeling sorry for Jeremy and glad to have someone in her life to now feeling nervy and anxious in his company, and she fretted about money.

As the months wore on, Jeremy continually chipped away at her confidence, criticising her appearance and dress sense, even though he was the one who wanted her in unflattering clothes.

On the rare occasions she bought something new, he insisted on coming shopping with her and vetoed anything remotely figure-hugging or flattering. He would tell her that a dress she liked was too young for her and that she'd make herself look ridiculous, or that it was too tarty, and he'd be embarrassed to be seen with her.

She accepted this with a meekness that would have made Sophia enraged but, of course, Evie could never tell her friend. She felt too pathetic and ashamed.

Jeremy was always complaining about the cost of the mortgage on his flat, how expensive it was to run his car and to afford the right clothes for his high-powered job. He nagged her continually to give up her flat and move in with him permanently.

He told her, 'Evie, it's ridiculous for you to be paying rent and all the bills on your place when you are only there during the week. Think of all the money you could save if you moved in with me. It would be far better for both of us.'

He eventually wore her down and Evie gave up her little flat.

*

Jeremy actually rubbed his hands together with gloating glee when Evie handed back her keys. He informed her that as he was paying the mortgage, they would split the rest of the bills fifty-fifty.

He cleared out more space for her in the bedroom and bathroom, but Evie's possessions didn't take up much room. She missed her spartan little cell and the journey to work now took two bus journeys and meant she had to get up half an hour earlier, but it had stopped Jeremy harping on and given her a bit of peace and extra cash.

He persuaded her that as he understood finance far better than she did, they'd be better off with a joint bank account, and he could take care of everything. He was appalled to see how much she was sending home to Orkney, and, after their worst-ever argument, he browbeat her into cutting the money she sent to Liv in half.

Evie only agreed because she still had enough savings to top up the monthly hush money to her sister, but she spent sleepless nights dreading the day she would run out. Jeremy bought her a new mobile phone 'as a surprise', which he set up for her, so he knew her password and he got the detailed bill of her usage.

'Now I can see how much time and money you are wasting on Twitter and Instagram when you should be working,' he said with a fake laugh, but it was just another way of him controlling Evie's life.

Apart from Sophia, Evie didn't have any real friends, but Jeremy had none at all. He didn't mix with anyone from work. He told Evie that as their boss it wouldn't be fitting, and he never talked about pals from the third-rate public school his father had chosen, or people he had met at university.

So, all of his energy and attention was on Evie, and she was feeling increasing smothered. She was tempted to call Sophia and pour out her worries about being bored and devalued at work, and the way Jeremy made her feel so useless, but she knew her no-nonsense friend would simply tell her to leave him and to look for a new job.

They had managed to get back to a weekly catch-up on the phone. Evie didn't have much to say, but she enjoyed hearing Sophia's news about her family and her latest online dating disaster.

During one of their calls, Sophia invited Evie to a spa weekend. It was a freebie from a grateful client at the ad agency.

'Come on, Evie, it will be great fun. We can wear fluffy white robes and have champagne for breakfast while we get our nails done. We'll have blissful massages and facials, and it won't cost a thing.'

Evie was tempted but she knew it was impossible. 'It's kind of you to think of me, Sophia, but I don't know that I could get away for a whole weekend.'

Sophia was frustrated and hurt to have her gift rejected. She had planned to talk to her friend properly about her job and about her relationship and find out exactly what was going on. She retorted sharply, 'What you really mean is that Jeremy won't like it. Heaven forbid you should actually enjoy yourself for once. Come on, Evie. You need to stop being a doormat. Come with me and have a good time.'

Evie knew Sophia was right. Jeremy would be furious. It was bad enough when they argued over her giving up the flat and sending Liv money. She didn't have the strength to go through all that again.

Sophia told her that if she changed her mind to give her a call, but they both knew she wouldn't.

30

Orkney, 2024

Evie was in the kitchen with Freya, watching her bake her famous fruit scones. She had received yet another missed call from Jeremy and the texts were becoming increasingly threatening.

You really are trying my patience now. You know it was all your fault I lost my job and the flat. If you don't respond and call me back immediately, I am going to track you down and drag you back.

She tried to push him from her mind and focus on Freya. 'My baking never ever turned out like yours. I remember coming over here after school with Kate and Edwyn and you would be chatting away to us about our day while you just conjured up brilliant scones and cakes. You made it look easy. My efforts are worse than Maureen's.'

'God love her, but no one's baking is worse than Maureen's. It's a real skill how bad she is. Anyway, you mentioned our Kate. Are things any better?'

'We cleared the air, but she is still a bit frosty with me. I don't blame her though.'

'Well,' said Freya. 'She's a lovely girl but she does take everything to heart, and she really missed you. We all did.'

They both jumped at a knock on the door.

'Who could that be?' said Freya. 'Someone is playing silly buggers; no one knocks on my door here.'

Evie's blood ran cold. It had to be Jeremy. He had threatened to track her down and now he'd finally done it.

'I'll get it,' said Freya, pulling off her apron.

'No!' said Evie sharply, causing Freya to look at her in surprise. 'Let me.'

She couldn't bear the thought of Jeremy being horrible to Freya. She approached the door, her hands shaking, took a deep breath and pulled it open.

'SURPRISE!'

Evie was astounded to see Sophia on the doorstep.

She was her usual cool beautiful self with her cropped hair and immaculate make-up, and wearing a well-cut, fitted emerald coat that even Kate, Princess of Wales would have envied.

'What are you doing here?' Evie gasped out.

'I got the late flight, and they told me at the Foveran you were staying here. I had to come and see you. I've been so worried. You promised you would let me know what happened and I hadn't heard from you for over a week. And Jeremy's had the nerve to be in touch with me, asking where you are. I didn't tell him obviously, but I think he might have guessed. I wanted to be here if he showed his face.'

Evie reached out and gave her a hug.

'I'm so sorry, Sophia, I should have called and I'm so very glad to see you.' She ushered her inside. 'Freya, this is Sophia. She's my friend from London.'

Freya wiped her floury hands on her apron. She had so many questions to ask but first needed to make Sophia welcome.

'Come away in. You must be starving. I'll make some tea, or do you fancy something a peedie bit stronger? I think we could all do with a dram.'

'That sounds like a bloody good idea, Freya,' said Sophia. 'It's good to meet you. I'm afraid Evie hasn't said anything much about her friends or her life here.'

'Aye, never a truer word was spoken,' said Freya dryly as she disappeared into the kitchen.

Sophia looked at her friend with concern and sat down beside her, holding her hand.

'Evie, they told me at the hotel about your dad. I'm so sorry. The taxi driver that took me here knew him, and spent the whole journey telling me what a lovely man he was. How are you holding up, you poor love?'

Evie couldn't trust herself to speak but Freya had returned with a tray holding an unopened bottle of Highland Park and three glasses. 'You've come at just the right time. Evie needs all of her friends right now.'

'Has she told you much about her life in London?' asked Sophia.

'No, she has not,' said Freya.

'Well, you will have to come and see for yourself,' said Sophia. 'And we can show you the sights.'

Freya smiled tightly. 'That's kind of you, Sophia, but I have seen most of what London has to offer and I am very happy here. And, of course, there will always be a bed for you in Orkney and plenty of opportunity to visit Evie here.'

Sophia frowned a little. 'But I've come to take Evie back with me.' She turned to her friend. 'I thought you could move in with me for a bit. You've had such an awful time and I can look after you. I've been looking up flights and we could go the day after tomorrow, if it suits you?'

Freya put her glass down. 'Hang on a moment, I think it's obvious that staying here is doing Evie the power of good. She's got colour back in her cheeks.'

'Well, yes, for a holiday. But she's not lived here for twenty years.'

'It's her home,' Freya said firmly, and Evie could see the two women she loved most begin to size each other up.

'Please, both of you, stop,' Evie said. 'I know you've got my best interests at heart, but I just can't make such a big decision right now.'

Sophia and Freya both turned to her at the same time and with the same expression of bafflement.

'We were only trying to help,' they both said in unison, and then they looked at each other and laughed.

'Truce?' said Sophia.

Freya nodded. 'That calls for another dram.'

Sophia smiled. 'By the way, I love your dress and the jewellery you are wearing is spectacular.'

This was exactly the right thing to say to get on Freya's good side.

It had rained during the night and Sophia woke up in her hotel room to a bright new day where everything looked freshly washed and gleaming. The smell of grass and salty sea was intoxicating, and she breathed in deeply.

This was paradise. What on earth could have happened to make Evie stay away for so long? She was worried about her friend and called Freya, who said Evie was still asleep but that she should come over later. 'I don't want to leave her on her own, but you shouldn't waste this lovely morning.'

'I've actually decided to stay for a while,' said Sophia. 'I'm booked here for a week, and they've been so helpful and sorted me a car hire. I'll take a drive and do a bit of exploring but won't go far. Just ping me a message when Evie is up and about and wants to see me.'

After a hotel breakfast of fresh Orkney eggs and smoked salmon with hot buttered toast, Sophia headed off into Kirkwall for a walk around. She spent an hour mooching about the shops full of Orkney produce, handcrafts and souvenirs. The clothes, especially the handmade knits, were classically fashionable as well as being cosy and practical, and Sophia knew she would be doing some serious damage to her credit cards.

She was drawn towards the vast red sandstone St Magnus Cathedral in the heart of Kirkwall. Inside it was cool and calm. The enormous circular stained-glass window radiated colourful light and there was a sense of tranquil peace.

'This is so beautiful,' breathed Sophia. 'What an incredible work of art.' Coming out of the big wooden doors and down the steps, she checked her phone in case she had missed a call from Freya and bumped headlong into one of the most handsome men she had ever seen.

'Sorry. I wasn't looking where I was going. I was just visiting the cathedral. Isn't it big? And it's gorgeous inside. Seems even bigger. Like the Tardis,' she gabbled.

Oh, God, she thought. *I'm burbling on and acting like an idiot. He's going to think I'm a stupid soft-headed southerner.*

He grinned. 'It's impressive all right. Don't worry. No harm done.'

That smile made Sophia's stomach do a flip. This hadn't happened to her since second year at school when she'd fancied Joseph Kennedy. And, just like fourteen-year-old Joseph, this fella had the most spine-tingling, seductive Irish accent.

'I'm Finn. Nice to meet you.'

'I'm Sophia. It's my first time here. It's so beautiful and the weather is gorgeous. I had no idea it would be like this.

I had imagined it all chilly and dark and windswept, but it's spectacular and the shops are great, and the food is glorious, and everyone is so friendly.' *Why can't I stop rabbiting on. He doesn't need to hear all of this*, she thought.

'Surely you aren't here on your own?' asked Finn.

'I'm here to visit my friend, Evie.'

Finn's eyes lit up, making him even more ridiculously attractive. 'I met an Evie on the flight over. She was in a bit of a bad way when we landed. Had an asthma attack. I dropped her off at the hospital to see her da. But then I heard he'd died. I'm glad you are here for her; it's very sad.'

'Yes, that's my Evie. She's had a hard time of it. In fact, I'm going back to see her later.'

'Tell her I was asking after her, and, Sophia, I'm not sure how long you are staying here but if you want someone to show you round, it would be my honour. I'm here working for the RSPB and need to go back over to Hoy tomorrow. I'd love to show you the sea eagle chicks and we could even go for a stroll to the Old Man of Hoy if the weather holds. It's a lovely wander and I could bring us a picnic, or we could grab something to eat at the Be'neth Hill.'

Sophia only followed about half of what he was saying as she was too busy admiring his smile, but she said, 'That sounds lovely but I'm here to take care of Evie and I'm not sure I will have any free time.'

'Fair enough. But look, here's my number and if you fancy seeing more of Orkney give me a shout. It's very special here. I mean how can you not love a place that has a village called Twatt.'

Sophia burst out laughing. 'Seriously! Oh my God, that is brilliant. I really hope there is a sign where I can take a selfie.'

'Absolutely,' he said gravely. 'It is in fact the law enforced upon everyone who comes here. Now don't forget my offer to be your guide. I'm getting in first before everyone else asks you out.'

'Oh, so you are asking me out are you, Finn,' said Sophia archly.

For once Finn felt more than a bit discombobulated. He was completely bowled over by Sophia. She was stunningly beautiful, and he was intrigued by her. Of course, he was flirting unashamedly, which he did with every woman in possession of a pulse, but this was different.

He really wanted to get to know her, and he'd be crushed and disappointed if she didn't call. This was a new feeling for him, and he wasn't entirely sure he was all that comfortable with being the one who would be waiting by the phone.

'Promise, you will get in touch?' he blurted.

Sophia smiled and said she would think about it.

31

Orkney, 2004

Brodie woke up the next morning with the sun streaming through the window. He felt sick to his stomach, his mouth was as dry as the bottom of a budgie's cage, he ached all over and had a thumping headache.

Where the hell was he? He propped himself upright realising he was in the hotel room he'd booked and suffering from the hangover from hell. He could barely remember what had happened. He knew he'd drunk oceans of Bacardi and the guts of a tequila bottle doing endless shots with Liv, but after that it was all dark and murky.

The terrible fight with Evie came rushing back to him. He looked at his phone, but it was dead. Then it got worse.

Liv was lying in bed next to him. His stomach heaved. Surely not . . . Surely, they hadn't . . . Images came to him. Liv pushing him against the wall and kissing him. Taking off her bra . . . his hands on her breasts . . . He recoiled at the idea of it. She was still fast asleep.

He got out of bed, careful not to wake her, threw on his clothes and quietly left. As soon as he got back to the rented cottage, he charged his phone up. Eventually it beeped with a text from Evie, sent last night. *I'm really sorry. I shouldn't have left you like that. I don't want to fight. See you tomorrow. Usual place?*

He texted her right back, feeling hellish. If only he'd seen this last night before he went on his drunken binge. *I only just got this. My battery died. I should be the one apologising. I was being selfish. Sorry. Hope you can forgive me. I want to see you but I can't today. But soon. Xxxx*

Brodie couldn't face Evie right now. He felt as though she would be able to tell that he had spent the night with Liv. It was all such a mess.

It was a couple of days later before he saw Evie again at the beach down from Evie's house, and it was all horribly awkward.

They kept speaking over each other, repeatedly apologising and saying they were in the wrong and promising never to quarrel again. If Brodie looked more guilty and shamefaced than expected, Evie didn't notice. She was just so relieved they were together again.

She told him, 'I've been doing a lot of thinking and I need to be honest with you. I should have told you when you suggested us going to the beach that I'm absolutely terrified of the water. When I was a toddler, I almost drowned in the sea, and it has haunted me ever since. I don't know why I didn't speak up. I suppose it's because I am ashamed of being so pathetic.'

'Evie. You aren't pathetic. That must have been horrific. I just wish you had said something. I would have understood. I can't believe I was so angry when you wouldn't come in the water. I feel like a total arsehole. What happened? Can you talk about it or is it too difficult still?'

'Well, my dad and my mum's family blame Liv. They say she tried to hold me under the water, but I'm not convinced. I know she hates me, but surely even she wouldn't do that to me.'

Brodie was horrified. Liv was a piece of work and he'd been completely taken in by her.

'Evie, I am so sorry.'

'It's OK. It's my fault for being an idiot and not telling you.' She took a deep breath. 'I also need to let you know, and this really isn't easy to say, but I lied to you. I have never slept with anyone, but I got myself into a terrible fankle and I didn't want you to think I wasn't as experienced as Liv. You seemed to admire her so much. And, of course, I want you to be my first.'

Brodie thought, *More lies from Liv. She made out Evie slept around. God, how could I have been so bloody stupid to get tangled up with someone so manipulative?*

He said to Evie, 'Thank you for telling me but, look, why don't we stop putting pressure on each other and just enjoy ourselves. There's a gig tonight in Stromness. The band are really great, and I've got to know some of the lads from the pub there. They are a brilliant bunch. Ask Kate and Edwyn along and we can all have a good night.'

It turned out to be one of those fantastic evenings where the music was brilliant, the conversation crackled, and the laughter roared.

Evie had never looked lovelier or happier. Kate couldn't help being a peedie bit envious of her dazzling friend who was with one of the most handsome boys she'd ever seen, while here she was stuck with Edwyn.

But then something strange happened. Out of Evie's shadow, the normally shy Edwyn was turning out to be great company and a really good laugh. It could possibly have something to do with the pint of cider and blackcurrant she had downed very quickly, but Kate found herself looking at her old friend with new eyes.

I can't possibly fancy Edwyn, thought Kate. *He's my pal. It would be ridiculous and anyway he's always wanted to go out with*

Evie. He's never said anything, but it's obvious he has a massive crush on her.

She looked at Evie dancing with Brodie, slender and gorgeous with her shiny blonde hair, bright green eyes and big Julia Roberts smile; her friend was so effortlessly beautiful.

Kate grimaced at how she had spent a fraught couple of hours getting ready for tonight. She had stunk out the bathroom with hair-removing cream to get rid of her moustache and her upper lip was red and sore.

Studying for her exams and stress-eating junk food had made her pile on the pounds. She had tried on almost everything she owned trying to get something that still fitted. She'd gone for an oversized shirt and an old skirt that was stretched tight as a drum across her tummy. She felt fat, hot, uncomfortable, and very much in Evie's shadow.

Edwyn was smiling at her. 'Fancy a dance?' he said.

'You don't want to dance with me. Go and chat up some other girls over there. They are giving you the glad eye. I don't want to cramp your style.'

'Don't be daft, you are far bonnier than any of them and I don't have to worry about starting up a conversation or having to impress you. You are just Kate, my daft, funny, fabulous pal.'

'Yep, that's me all right. OK then, but don't do your usual goofy dancing; you are like a daddy long legs stuck on flypaper.'

He looked over at Brodie and Evie on the dance floor, engrossed in one another.

'I just hope he's good enough for her. She deserves the best.'

Kate's heart sank. He did fancy Evie after all. She was just second best.

Brodie was looking at Evie and thinking how lucky he was, and how close he had come to ruining everything.

While the band took a break, he joined the queue at the bar and was startled when he felt his bum being pinched hard. Thinking it was Evie he turned round, but the smile faded from his face when he saw Liv leering at him.

'Have you missed me? Wasn't very gentlemanly leaving me in a hotel room all alone,' she said, pouting.

He stuttered. 'Liv. I didn't expect you to be here. I didn't think this would be your scene or you were a fan of the band.'

'Of these clowns? Are you kidding me? They are utter crap, and the lead singer is a terrible shag, but I heard you would be here, and I thought it would be SO nice to see you again. Besides, you owe me an explanation and you owe my sister one too.'

Brodie pulled her outside. 'Liv. I'm sorry. I was so drunk, and it was all just a terrible mistake and Evie would never forgive me if she found out. I'm begging you. Please don't tell her.'

Liv's eyes narrowed.

'A terrible mistake. Is that what you think I am?' she said in disbelief.

'I've said I'm sorry. I really am, but what Evie and I have is the real thing. Our fight was just a misunderstanding. We are back together now. Please don't spoil things for us.'

He left her and went back inside. Liv couldn't believe what had just happened and was taken aback how upset she was by Brodie's rejection. She had targeted him simply to hurt Evie, but there was something about him that had got under her skin. It was more than just her bruised ego that was upsetting her. She felt genuinely crushed and deeply hurt. She angrily brushed tears from her eyes.

Once again, it would be her despised sister who would be cherished and spoilt and taken care of, while she was rejected and misunderstood. Liv vowed to have her revenge on both of them, and it would be a dish best served ice-cold.

32

Orkney, 2004

After a blissful summer, Evie and Brodie had said a sad
goodbye, vowing to keep in constant touch and counting
down the days until he would be back for the October half-
term holidays.

Evie missed him more than she even thought possible and
threw herself into her studies. She rarely saw Liv, which was
a relief, and she continued acting as a buffer at home to stop
her mother constantly nagging her father.

When Cara was about to embark on one of her rants about
Duncan being messy and untidy, Evie would quickly distract
her with some gossip about one of the neighbours while she
deftly put away the single mug on the sink that Cara deemed
was making the place look like a tip.

Evie was also taking driving lessons, and Duncan had bought
her a tiny little second-hand bright-yellow Beetle car that
she treated like a baby. She polished it until it shone, sent
away for massive fake eyelashes for the headlamps and put a
fresh flower in a little vase by the dashboard. She named her
Florence, which made Duncan shake his head, but secretly he
thought it was adorable.

He took Evie out for extra lessons, but the first time was a disaster with Duncan roaring at her to slow down. She burst into tears and walked home, and he vowed never to be in a car with her again. But, as she got more experienced and confident behind the wheel, they would go for long drives down to the bottom of South Ronaldsay or up to Birsay.

During these times her dad would talk to her about his childhood and the granny she'd never known, as well as life before Liv and Evie were born, and father and daughter became even closer. Evie was soon ready for her test, and desperate to pass so she could pick Brodie up off the ferry the very next day and surprise him by arriving in Florence.

Her dad was in the passenger seat, proudly accompanying her to the test centre.

'I remember when your mum took her test,' he said. 'It was so quiet that day the examiner asked her what she would do if she met another car at a junction. She replied that she'd wind the window down and ask where the other driver was going and if they had any gossip.'

Evie laughed. 'I can't imagine Mum saying something funny like that.'

'Your mum was quite the free spirit. I've told you how she proposed to me at Yesnaby.' He chuckled at the memory.

Evie couldn't believe that her stressed-out mother had ever been young and in love or had made cheeky remarks to driving instructors.

'I wish you could have seen her back then, Evie. She really was something. So full of life and she was happy. I know she was.'

He looked sad.

'Well, of course, she was happy. She met you. Tell me again about the wedding. I can't believe you hardly took any photos.'

Duncan laughed and told her that they were all too busy having a good time to take pictures of themselves having a good time. He looked at her, hesitated a bit and then asked, 'What about you, Teenie? You and Brodie. Is it serious?'

Evie had deliberately downplayed their romance but knew that both their dads would be chuffed to bits if she and Brodie ended up together, but only after they both graduated. They wanted the precious graduation photograph on their respective mantelpieces.

'We are good pals and I do think we could be more than that. Let's just see what happens when he comes back tomorrow.'

'I just want you to be happy, Teenie. I know you will be going away soon, and I can't keep you here for ever, but I hope you will always come back to me, and back to Orkney.'

'Of course I will, Dad. This is my home. You know how much I love it here.'

Duncan laughed. 'You kids are always going on about not having enough to do and being bored and wanting to go south to Aberdeen or to Dundee or Glasgow.'

'We don't really mean it though. We just do it to wind you all up,' said Evie with a grin.

'Right, here we are. Wish me luck.'

'I'll be waiting.'

He got out of the car as the examiner walked across. 'You'll ace it first time, love.'

As she pulled away in the yellow Beetle to take her test, Duncan knew that things were changing fast. Next year, Evie would be going to art school in Glasgow and Kate and Edwyn would be at university in Edinburgh. Then, he'd be left with Liv and Cara, and he really didn't know how he'd be able to cope. Liv barely registered his existence except to ask for money and Cara had become a cold and bitter stranger.

He felt like an unwelcome guest in his own house, just someone who brought in bruck and muck and wasn't even important enough to be actively disliked. He couldn't remember the last time he and Cara had had a proper conversation. How could it have come to this?

He had loved Cara so much and he thought she had loved him. All those years of disappointments, pain and grief when they had endured so many miscarriages had changed them both, and when Liv was born things had grown worse instead of better.

He was still baffled by his eldest daughter and although he could never understand Liv, he didn't worry about her. He believed she was made of steel, nothing and no one would ever pierce her hard shell. He knew she would break hearts but felt that hers was frozen.

His Teenie was a different matter altogether. She was so generous and kind, always willing to see the best in people, he fretted about her falling for the wrong man. *I don't want her to end up like me and her mother*, he thought. *She deserves so much more. I want her to be happy and loved. Maybe this boy Brodie would be the one. He seems like a good man with real prospects and Teenie obviously can't wait to see him again.*

An hour or so later, Evie and Duncan burst back into the house. Liv was there lounging on the sofa having 'borrowed' money from Cara who was furiously vacuuming, even though the carpet was as clean as the day it was newly laid on the floor.

'She passed, first time!' said Duncan proudly. Evie was beaming.

'Typical,' Liv seethed. 'The precious princess gets whatever she wants and what do I get? Nothing.'

Liv had never bothered learning to drive; she could snap her fingers and get dubious blokes on motorbikes or souped-up cars to give her a lift anywhere she wanted to go, but she was raging that her sister could now drive her own car.

Duncan wearily tried to be the peacemaker. 'Liv, you were offered driving lessons, but you took the money instead.'

'I'll give you a lift anytime you like,' said Evie.

'Are you kidding me?' Liv scoffed. 'I wouldn't be seen dead in that cartoon car. It's pathetic. The two of you look like Noddy and Big Ears.'

Evie stared at the ground, her excited, buoyant mood rapidly deflating.

Cara hadn't congratulated Evie. Instead, she chipped in, 'It's not fair, Duncan, you spoil Evie. Liv should get the same amount of money you spent on the car.'

And what in the name of God would she do with it? thought Duncan, but he said nothing.

He noticed Evie's forlorn expression and told her with exaggerated cheerfulness, 'Just imagine you can pick up young Brodie tomorrow and drive him all over the island.'

'Ah, yes, the perfect Brodie,' said Liv, her voice laced with venom. 'Do you ever think he might be too good to be true, Evie?'

Evie frowned. 'What's that supposed to mean?'

'Oh, I am sure you'll find out, soon enough,' said Liv.

She gave a smug smile and walked out the door.

That night Evie went over to see Freya, who'd offered to put Brodie up and was busy making up the bed in the spare room. 'I love your home, Freya, and so will Brodie. It's so restful and you do make the best cakes on the island. It's so good of you to let him stay.'

'Nonsense. He can come and go as he pleases, and I can make sure he eats properly.'

The two of them spent a happy evening putting on face masks and doing each other's nails, and had an absorbing conversation about when Evie should sleep with Brodie for the first time.

'I told you we decided to wait, but I feel ready now. I am just a bit worried I won't know what to do,' said Evie.

'When the time comes you will know. Like everything else practice makes perfect, but, Evie, you need to be careful. We talked about this.'

'I know I took your advice. Don't worry I'm on the pill. I won't get caught out.'

She kissed Freya on the cheek and said she would see her tomorrow with Brodie.

The next morning, she was up early and by seven o'clock had tried on every one of her outfits twice. She eventually settled on jeans and a green shirt that Brodie liked.

On her way out she shouted, 'Dad. That's me away to collect Brodie.'

'You are far too early, Teenie. The ferry isn't due in for hours yet. Getting there so soon won't make it arrive any faster.'

Evie couldn't wait and drove off in Florence, nodding and waving to people on the road who smiled at the cheerful daffodil-yellow car.

Watching the ferry slowly coming into Stromness harbour was torture. Evie was taut with frustration and hopping from one foot to the other like a toddler waiting in the queue to see Santa Claus.

For the love of God, she thought. *I actually think the thing is going backwards; it hasn't moved closer to me for the last fifteen minutes.*

Eventually, the ferry docked, and Brodie was the first passenger off, racing towards Evie, shouting her name and scooping her up in a massive hug.

'I've missed you so much and I've missed Orkney. It feels like coming home. Tell me everything. How's your mum and dad, and Kate and Edwyn and Eric and Ernie?'

'All good. Oh, it's so great to see you. I've missed you too.'

'Are you sure Freya doesn't mind me staying with her?' said Brodie.

'She's looking forward to it but be prepared to put on a least a couple of stone. She's a feeder.'

He laughed. 'How are we getting there? Did you book a taxi? Or will we just get the bus?'

'No need. Your carriage awaits. I passed my test yesterday and this is Florence, my pride and joy.'

'Well, hello, Florence, aren't you a beauty? We could paint the harbour wall with your eyelashes.'

Freya could not have made Brodie more welcome. He sank into her comfy couch as she clucked over him, urging him to eat more of the huge spread of homemade cakes, biscuits and scones she'd prepared.

Bette Davis sat beside him purring happily and allowed him to scratch her head and belly, which reassured Freya that Brodie was a decent lad as her cat was a canny judge of character.

Being away from Evie had made Brodie realise how much he truly loved her, and how stupid he had been to get caught up with Liv. He'd spent sleepless nights in Edinburgh agonising whether he should come clean and tell Evie about the night he'd spent with her sister.

The trouble was he wasn't sure what had actually happened but realised that sleeping in the same bed all night with her sister was more than grounds enough for Evie to dump him, and yet he knew he should do the right thing and tell her.

Freya discreetly left them both and shut the kitchen door while she noisily did the washing-up and turned up the radio. She knew they needed some time on their own.

Brodie was just about to confess when Evie whispered to him that she had missed him more than she'd ever thought possible and shyly told him for the first time that she loved him.

'I love you too, Evie. I am so lucky to have you and I don't deserve you.'

How could he tell her about Liv now, when she had so sweetly said she loved him and had looked at him with such open trust and naked adoration?

'Don't be daft,' she said with a laugh. 'You could have anyone you want. And you chose me. I am the lucky one.'

He got up and fumbled in his jacket pocket. 'I have something special for you. I hope you like it. My grandad bought it for my granny when they lived here in Orkney, and it means a lot to me, but I really want you to have it.'

He handed Evie a slim blue velvet box worn smooth at the edges with time. Inside was a delicate silver bracelet with a bright green stone in the middle of a Celtic love knot.

'Oh, Brodie,' she breathed. 'It's so lovely. Are you sure you want to give it me?'

He clasped it onto her wrist. 'Of course. I do. It was meant for you, and it matches your eyes, but you have to promise never to take it off.'

'I won't.' She kissed him deeply. 'Brodie . . .' she said. 'I've been thinking. I'm ready. For us to be together, you know, properly.' She blushed.

'Jeez-oh,' he said, laughing. 'If I'd known the bracelet would have had such magic powers, I would have given it to you the first night we met.'

She nudged him in the ribs and giggled.

He looked serious. 'Are you sure, Evie? I don't want to put any pressure on you. Not after last time.'

'Brodie, if we don't do it soon, I swear I am going to die, but I want it to be perfect.'

33

London, 2016

Evie wrote to Freya giving her change of address, but not that she had moved in with Jeremy. She'd never even mentioned him, as she knew Freya would never have approved of such a man.

Back home in Orkney, Freya looked up the London postcode and was pleased that Evie was living in such an upmarket area. She liked to think of Evie in a high-powered job, living in a gorgeous flat with lots of friends and having a wonderful time.

'No wonder she doesn't want to come back here. She would find us all very dull after living the high life in London.'

It made Freya feel less guilty that she hadn't told anyone she was in touch with Evie to imagine her carefree and happy.

She would have been distraught to see the reality of her life. Evie was more like a housekeeper who Jeremy had sex with. She made sure the place was clean and tidy, and that the fridge was always stocked up, but there were no books, photos or flowers to bring warmth and cheer, and Evie didn't have the heart or the money to try to turn the sterile flat into a home.

It took her so long to get back from the office, often all she had time to make was a microwaveable meal and this would result in Jeremy sulking all night. At first, she answered back, but his relentless petty jibes got to her. It was easier just to agree with him and tell him she would try to do better next time.

'Most guys wouldn't put up with this,' he whined, and she thought he was absolutely right.

Jeremy was coming home later and later every night, and clearly spent most of the evening drinking. He was belligerent and even more irritable than usual.

When Evie hesitantly asked him if anything was wrong, he flared up and told her to stop nagging. 'Can a man not have a few drinks after a long hard day? I need to unwind. You've no idea the kind of pressure I'm under. You might be in a dead-end job that doesn't matter but I do important work.'

That night Evie looked at him properly for the first time in ages and saw how seedy he'd become. His hair was thinning and greasy, he had red patches of 'gin blossom' on his cheeks and across his nose, and the bags under his eyes were like suitcases.

Evie remembered how Sophie had said he could suck the fun out of a room, and she was right, but it was too late. She was trapped.

She'd thought about leaving him many times, but by now she was so browbeaten, she couldn't go through with it. He'd done an expert job of breaking her spirit.

More and more evenings ended with her feeling as though a metal band was tightening around her chest.

Evie's phone pinged. It was a message from Freya. She'd persuaded Evie to give her mobile phone number, and Freya kept in regular touch, sending slightly blurry photos and cheery updates.

Evie had made her swear not to give anyone else her number, but she was glad to have this contact with home.

How's the high life in London? I see from the news you are all sweltering in the heat. It's glorious up here today. I've enclosed a photo of me on the ferry heading to Hrossey. The other blurry photo was me trying to take a snap of an orca, but he was too far away. You would have loved to see him and imagine the painting of him you would have done!! He was so beautiful and full of life, but a peedie bit scary.

Evie felt such a longing to be back in Orkney it was like a physical ache. She would have dearly loved to have seen an orca again, and it had always been one of her ambitions to try to capture its intelligence and fierce beauty in a painting.

She closed her eyes and could almost smell the briny air, but then she had a vivid flashback of that terrible night, her sister screaming at her, and her father looking at her in disappointment and anger.

'I don't deserve any happiness. A dead-end job and a useless lump of a man is all I'm good for.'

34

Orkney, 2024

As she was only in Orkney for a week, Sophia decided to call Finn that night after all. The following morning, she found herself getting the ferry from Houton across to Hoy to meet up with him.

She'd borrowed a small rucksack and Freya's oldest hiking boots with a change of clothes in case it rained. On the short ferry trip, she spotted a pod of grinning dolphins showing off for the passengers with joyful backflips and she had a stimulating-but-baffling conversation about birding with an elderly couple who lived on Hoy, and told her to pop in for a cup of tea if she was passing.

Finn waved enthusiastically as she got off their ferry and enfolded her in a massive hug. She thought, *I'm going to play it cool with this one. He thinks he can charm every woman he fancies straight into bed with that smile, but he's going to have to work a lot harder with me.*

He beamed at her. 'I'm so glad you could make it. Look at the day we have. It's going to be glorious. First, I want to show you the sea eagle nest, then we will head up to see the Old Man.'

By now Sophia had discovered that the 'old man' Finn was referring to was the famous sea stack and not one of his elderly relatives.

'Glad to see you have decent shoes on,' said Finn with approval. 'It's quite an easy walk but can get a bit muddy if it rains.'

Finn was full of enthusiasm as he talked about the introduction of sea eagles back to Orkney. He rattled on about how the first chicks had been born on Hoy in 2018 after they'd been wiped out back in the nineteenth century. He told her that seeing those chicks hatching was one of the best days of his life.

'I also have to take you to the Tomb of the Sea Eagles on South Ronaldsay. It's an ancient cairn where they found over six thousand sea-eagle bones. It's one of my favourite places.'

He glanced over at Sophia. 'Sorry, I've been banging on. I hope I've not been boring you.'

Sophia was actually enthralled, and she loved how he fizzed with energy and passion, but she just smiled enigmatically, giving nothing away.

'Here we are,' he said, pulling over at a layby. In the distance was a rocky hill face.

He eagerly lifted up his binoculars. 'Here, I've got you a spare pair.'

Sophia squinted into them and twiddled the knobs to try to focus. 'Can we really see them from here?' she said doubtfully.

'If you know where to look,' said Finn. 'See up near the top, next to the rock shaped like Shrek's head?'

Sophia found it. The nest was surprisingly big and very untidy. She saw one of the massive sea eagles land with a beak full of food for the hungry, demanding babies. A knot of excited birdwatchers and twitchers had also stopped and gathered around, keen to share stories and talk to Finn.

He became almost boyish in his keenness to tell them all about the sea eagles and Sophia found it impossibly adorable. They spent almost an hour looking at the massive pair of eagles flying off then circling back to feed their hungry, open-mouthed chicks.

Sophia's only experience of birds was when a pigeon in Trafalgar Square shat on her head while she was hurrying to get to the cinema. That was definitely not an evening to remember. This, however, was truly captivating and Sophia felt bad for dismissing birdwatchers as sad anoraks. They were so friendly and enthused about seeing these rare chicks and witnessing their massive parents soaring high above.

'Right, Sophia,' said Finn. 'Are you up for a hike now? It's not too far up the road and it looks like the weather is going to hold.'

They were driving north when Sophia noticed a little white headstone and grave on the hillside to her left.

'Who on earth is buried there, Finn? It's so far away from everything?'

'We can stop and have a look, but I have to warn you it's a very sad story.'

They made their way up to the little grave, which was surrounded by a small white wooden fence. There was nothing on the headstone but the simple words, "Here lies Betty Corrigan".

'This poor lass got pregnant around two hundred and fifty years ago,' Finn explained. 'But she wasn't married, and the father of her baby deserted her and ran off back to the sea. She decided she couldn't live with the shame and tried to take her own life by walking into the water. She was saved from drowning but, of course, now she was considered even more of a sinner.'

He sighed. 'Her life was in ruins and, a few days later, she hanged herself. No one wanted her to be buried in a kirkyard on consecrated ground and she wasn't even given a funeral. Instead, they dug a hole for her right here, out of sight and forgotten about.'

'That's so sad,' said Sophia. 'She must have suffered so much pain.'

'Oh, it gets worse. Much, much worse,' said Finn. 'Around 1933, a couple of fellas were digging for peat and their spades hit the side of a wooden coffin. They decided to open it up and there was Betty. Because she'd been buried in a peat bog, she was almost perfectly preserved. She had long brown curly hair past her shoulders and because of the peat her skin was just a little bit darker, otherwise it's said she looked as though she was sleeping. The story goes that the rope she'd hanged herself with was by her side but that it turned to dust as soon as it was exposed to the air.'

'Oh my God. Poor Betty. Was that the end of it?'

'Nope. They put her back in her coffin and back in her unmarked grave but less than ten years later, Hoy was a World War Two naval base. You saw some of the old buildings and the museum at Lyness where the ferry came in. Sadly, some of the troops didn't cover themselves in glory and unearthed her poor, wee body. She became a bit of a freak show until there was an outcry, and she was buried again, and her coffin covered with a concrete slab. After the war, an American minister put up the wooden cross and the fence around her and, in the seventies, there was finally a burial and a gravestone.'

Sophia shuddered at the story. Finn had known all along she wasn't as tough as she made out, and her compassion made him fall even more in love with her.

'Here's another strange thing though, Sophia, if you look closely at this gravestone, you can see it's made of fibreglass. Because, if it was a real stone one, it would sink into the peat.'

Sophia was quiet for a moment thinking about this poor, frightened woman and her unborn baby. So much pain and loss. She felt tears prick at her eyes. It had started to rain gently as they walked back to the car.

Finn looked troubled. 'Are you all right, Sophia? I wouldn't have told you the story if I thought it was going to upset you so much.'

She smiled. 'I'm OK. I just don't like to think of Betty so alone, but I won't ever forget her story.'

Finn glanced up at the sky. 'No one who visits her ever forgets. And don't worry. This rain won't last.'

'I'm not bothered about the rain. Freya says there's no bad weather in Orkney, just the wrong clothes, and she made sure I've come prepared.'

For the rest of the journey, Finn chatted away about his next trip up to North Ronaldsay, where grazing land was so scarce the sheep had taken to eating seaweed on the beach, and the birdlife was extraordinary.

'You should come with me, Sophia,' he said. 'It's just a wee hop on the plane, or we could get the ferry if you don't mind the chance of being bounced about a bit for three hours.'

He realised he was still chuntering on a bit, but he was desperate for Sophia to enjoy herself. He was worried that a girl used to the bright lights of London would think all of this was very dull.

Sophia was giving nothing away, but she was utterly enchanted by what she had seen of Orkney and so impressed by the stark beauty of Hoy.

Soon they had reached the start of the walk to the Old Man. It wasn't an arduous hike, and the path was easy to follow, but Sophia found herself panting a bit despite her weekly gym visits. Looking down from the top of the hill she saw the most beautiful sandy bay with impressive waves crashing on the shore, and a string of little cottages. She forgot for a second to be aloof and breathed in awe, 'Oh Finn. How beautiful.'

Finn smiled. 'That's Rackwick. Isn't it gorgeous? I'd love a cottage there. Can you imagine waking up to this every day. Come on, let's get to the Old Man before the rain starts up again.'

After about an hour's walk on an easy path, the Old Man sneaked up on them and Sophia found herself looking at the famous red sandstone stack with kittiwakes soaring above their heads and the waves crashing below.

It was all a bit overwhelming, and she felt light-headed and unsteady on her feet. Finn grabbed her before she stumbled.

'Don't fret. A lot of people get a touch of the vertigo when in the presence of the Old Man. I think it's something to do with the St John's Cliffs looming behind us. Let's have a sit down a wee bit away from the edge.'

Finn took a squashed biscuit from his backpack and poured her a coffee from his battered tartan flask.

'Are you warm enough? Do you want my jacket to wear on top of yours?'

'I'm fine, thanks,' said Sophia.

He really is kind and such a gentleman, she thought. *I could so easily find myself falling for him hard. I need to be careful.*

Sitting close to Sophia on the short, sweet grass, and without his usual blarney and swagger, Finn said humbly, 'I'm so glad you came over to see me today, Sophia. I love it here on Hoy, and it's really hard to get across how special it is. You just need to experience it for yourself.' He got to his feet and pulled her up. 'Right, we need to do a selfie and then we can get something proper to eat. I'm starving.'

*

On the drive back, they talked easily about Sophia's life in London and Finn's plans to publish a book on Orkney birds and wildlife.

'I know there have been lots of books on the subject, but I've had some really rare sightings and I've taken so many photos. I just want to share it with everyone, especially kids. Do you think I'm being daft?'

'Not at all. It's a lovely idea and will make people realise how fantastic this place is. I'm beginning to discover that for myself. Despite everything that's been happening with poor Evie, I feel like I belong here.' She shook her head. 'Now I'm the one being daft. I'm a city girl and I am telling myself this all feels like home.'

'Not at all. I'm a boy from a housing estate in Cork and I feel the same way. It reminds me sometimes of parts of Ireland, but Orkney has its own unique identity, and everyone is made welcome. Look at Andrzej, he came all the way from Poland, and this is now his home. He loves it here.'

'Evie says he's also in love with a woman called Maureen. Do you know her?'

'We all know each other. Andrzej and Maureen would make a fine couple.' He added, 'This is a good place to fall in love, don't you think?'

Sophia didn't answer and deftly changed the subject. 'All this fresh air is making me hungry too. You said you would take me for something to eat.'

'I did indeed, and I guarantee you the best homemade soup and sandwiches you'll ever have in your life.'

Down a winding road was a café with a garden for kids to play in and seating outside. The sun had reappeared, and it was pleasantly warm in this pretty, sheltered spot. Sophia was layered up like a Russian doll and took off her jacket, then her jumper and long-sleeve blouse, until she was just in her T-shirt.

The friendly waitress welcomed Finn back, took their drinks order and nodded approval at their choice of soup and a crab roll.

Sophia was curious about the name of the café. She asked the waitress, 'Why do you call this place called 'Beneth'ill'?'

'Well, it's at the bottom of the hill so it's underneath it, isn't it?' she replied. 'So, we thought that made sense.'

Sophia laughed. 'It absolutely does.'

Their food came and Sophia was in raptures over the fresh Orkney crab.

'This is incredible. Can I get another one, do you think?'

Finn was looking at her with a big grin on his face.

'Course you can. You know, we don't see women like you all that much here.'

She bristled. *Oh, here we go*, she thought. *I knew it was too good to be true.*

With a sigh, she said, 'Black women, you mean.'

He looked perplexed. 'Oh no, we see plenty of Black women. What I meant was I don't normally see gorgeous, captivating, bright, sharp, SINGLE women on Hoy. The good ones are always already taken.'

Relieved that he hadn't said something crass, but actually heartfelt and extremely flattering, Sophia said mischievously, 'How do you know I'm single?'

Finn looked panicked. 'I mean, well, I just presumed . . . here on your own . . . And you never mentioned . . . You are single, aren't you?'

'Well, what if I am?'

'Because I want to see a lot more of you, Sophia. You are a really special woman and I need to get to know you better.'

Sophia laughed. 'I am sure that line has worked for loads of your conquests, but I'm not here to have a holiday fling. I want to help Evie. In fact, I need to get back to get the ferry or I will be stuck here overnight.'

'Would that be such a bad thing?' said Finn, making his voice all soft and seductive.

'Nice try, but I really need to get back.'

'I know you do. Let me settle up and I will get you back to the ferry at Lyness, although I'm sorely tempted to pretend to run out of petrol on the way there though.'

He grinned and Sophia couldn't help herself – she had to laugh.

He really was irresistible, but of course she would never let him know that.

On the ferry back she looked out for the dolphins again, but they were off playing somewhere else. She did spot a lazy, sleek seal drying off on a rock looking as satisfied and stuffed full as a teenager who'd eaten an extra-large pizza and a jumbo tub of chocolate ice cream.

Finn had kissed her chastely on the cheek and told her he'd be over in a few days and would she allow him to take her out for dinner. She said she'd think about it, but she knew she'd say yes.

Walking off the ferry, still glowing from her day on Hoy, she saw a painfully thin young woman in tight black leathers hop off the back of a motorbike driven by a burly, grey-bearded middle-aged man.

The woman was purposefully striding towards her. She stopped and took off her helmet and Sophia almost gasped in shock. This was no young girl, but instead a hatchet-faced woman wearing altogether too much black eye make-up. Liv came right up to Sophia's face.

'You the one who is friends with my sister Evie, come up from down south?' She rasped belligerently.

'Who wants to know?' said Sophia, who'd overcome her share of bullies in her time.

'I'm her sister. That's who. You tell her that she has got twenty-four hours to get her arse off Orkney before I let everyone know why she left in the first place. I've kept my mouth shut, but she didn't keep her side of the bargain. I said I would stay quiet if she stayed away. But she's fucking back now so all bets are off.'

Sophia refused to be cowed. 'I don't know what you are talking about, but I don't take too kindly to you making threats about my friend, even if you are related.'

Liv looked at her up and down and despite herself, Sophia felt shaken. This was a dangerous and malevolent woman.

'Just make sure you let that bitch know.'

With that, Liv swaggered away and jumped on the back of the bike, giving her driver a thump to let him know she was ready to leave.

Sophia drove off in her hired car, deeply unsettled after the encounter with Liv.

She walked into Freya's house and didn't answer her question about how she had enjoyed her day on Hoy. Instead, she burst out, 'Evie, what the hell is going on? Your sister was waiting for me at the ferry. I didn't even know you had a sister. She made all kinds of threats and said you had twenty-four hours to get out of here or she would let everyone know why you left Orkney? What did she mean?'

Evie looked stricken. She'd been kidding herself that she had more time and even that she might somehow be able to talk Liv round.

She took a deep breath.

'It's time I told you the truth about why I left. Freya, can you tell Kate to come over? I want the three of you to hear what I have to say together.'

35

Orkney, 2004

Brodie spent most of his time at Evie's house, only going back to Freya's to sleep and have a hearty breakfast, which he worked off doing chores around the farm.

He was determined to make a good impression on Evie's parents and spent long hours helping Duncan with much-needed odd jobs. They repaired the roofs of the old barns, painted the outsides brilliant white and mended broken walls and fences.

Brodie was up for anything, even the dirtiest, muckiest jobs, and would be up at the crack of sparrows and only head back to Freya's when it grew dark. Duncan grew to like the quiet, hard-working young man and, although no one would ever be good enough for his Teenie, maybe he could just about tolerate someone like Brodie.

After one particularly gruelling day when horizontal rain lashed down on them both as they took care of the cattle, Brodie ended up falling on his arse in a pile of squelchy, stinking cow dung. Lying in the foul-reeking shit, the young man just laughed instead of angrily cursing. Duncan gave him a hand up and a grin and said, 'You'll do, son. You'll do.' This was high praise indeed.

Brodie had managed to effortlessly charm Cara, who had decided that he was prime son-in-law material. He bought her flowers and declared her far too young to be Evie's mother and that she looked more like her sister. He marvelled at her overly neat and clinical house and the cupboards full of tins lined up like soldiers with the labels all facing to the front. He helped Cara prepare meals, clear the table, wash the dishes and ensured not a crumb was spilled from his plate onto the pristine floor. No need for the trusty Dustbuster. Cara was enchanted to see him keep everything so neat and tidy.

He was handsome, eager to please and would have a steady job as an architect when he graduated from university. Brodie ticked a lot of boxes for Cara, and she knew he would give her valuable bragging rights over the likes of the Balfours.

As for Brodie, he could see his hard work was paying off and he was managing to become part of the family, but he still hadn't told Evie about Liv. It was the one enormous blight on his life. He tortured himself trying to remember what had actually happened during that sordid night and beating himself up for being such an idiot.

As he fell more deeply in love with Evie, he found it all the more impossible to tell her. There was just too much to lose, especially now they were officially a couple.

They'd finally slept together and although the first time had been a bit clumsy, and, if he was completely honest, over far too quickly, as they became more comfortable with one other their lovemaking was a wonderful way to express their feelings for one another. He was glad they'd waited, but he feared Liv was a ticking time bomb and she could obliterate his happiness with Evie whenever she felt like it.

Luckily, he'd barely even seen her since coming back, apart from one night when she was leaving and met him coming in the front door after his long day's grafting. She didn't even say hello, but merely blew smoke into his face, only stopping long enough to give him a look of utter contempt.

He'd heard rumours about her behaviour when he was in the pub, how she was supposed to be a small-time drug dealer and petty thief. No one would ever dream of saying any of this in front of Big Duncan, who was universally liked and admired, but also pitied for having to put up with his shrewish wife and hideous daughter.

What Brodie didn't know was that he was Liv's weak spot.

Liv might be hard-boiled with skin as tough as rhino hide, but not when it came to Brodie. He had somehow wormed his way into her black heart. She'd deliberately kept away from going home as she couldn't bear to see him with Evie playing happy families with her parents. The night she had passed him coming into the house as she was leaving had been agonising. She covered up her feelings by pretending to be disdainful of him, but he made her ache with longing.

It should have been her laughing with Brodie and making plans for the future, but as usual it was Evie the golden child who was showered with all the happiness and joy while she stood on the outside looking in.

Surely, it was only a matter of time before he dumped that pathetic, dreary little mouse and fell for a real woman like her? Initially, she was willing to bide her time, but that all changed. The turning point came when Liv was sitting in the kitchen talking to her mother.

'When's Brodie heading off back south then?' said Liv, affecting a slightly bored voice, pretending not to care.

'I'm not sure yet,' said Cara. 'But it's good to have him around the place.'

Liv responded tartly. 'Well don't get used to it. He will soon get bored of my dull little sister. Honestly, I don't know why he's bothered with her for so long. The novelty will wear off soon though. And then she'll be broken-hearted,' she said with satisfaction.

Cara shook her head. 'I'm not sure you're right about that. I overheard him the other night, saying goodbye on the doorstep. He loves her. He's talking about them having a proper future together. You never know, there might be wedding bells in the future. You may have to buy a hat.'

Liv was taken aback at how much her mother's news wounded her. So, Brodie did truly love Evie. Her sister had won the battle, but the war was by no means over, and Liv had a plan.

She pinged Brodie a text. *We need to clear the air. Please meet me at the beach down by our house tonight. I want to make things right. See you at 8 p.m.. Please come.*

She got a reply right away.

You are right. We do. Don't worry. I will be there.

Liv arrived early and built a wood fire on the sand, wrapping herself in thick blankets to keep out the chilly evening air and sipping a beer from a six-pack she'd brought.

She heard Brodie approaching and put on an act of being all sweetness and light.

'Long time no see. Thanks for coming. We really do need to talk.'

He looked wary and anxious, but as handsome and desirable as ever. Liv was furious to think of her weakling of a sister having this fine young man for ever. It was so unfair, but she forced herself to say, 'Don't look so worried. Sit down and have a beer.'

She handed him a bottle and gave him a false beaming smile.

'I hear you're getting pretty serious about Evie?'

He took a swig of his beer.

'You heard right. I love her very much,' he said seriously. 'She's the most important person in the world and I'll do anything to make sure she doesn't get hurt.' He knew he had to tread carefully with Liv, but he also had to be honest. 'You and I made a big mistake but if I'm going to become part of your family, and I really hope I will, we need to put whatever it was that happened behind us. Don't you agree?'

The waves relentlessly broke on the shore, and the wind picked up and began to howl.

'I'm not sure that's going to be possible, Brodie. But let's wait until Evie gets here.'

Brodie looked appalled. 'She's coming here. But why would you do that?'

Liv shrugged. 'I thought it would be nice for us all to hang out together.'

Brodie shook his head. 'I know you. You haven't asked Evie here for any other reason than to cause trouble.'

The fire that Liv had lit earlier didn't seem warm and comforting anymore. It cast an eerie glow on the beach. He looked up and saw Evie coming towards them; it was just a ten-minute stroll from the house. She had no idea what she was walking into. She was smiling and waving and looked so innocent and happy. He just wanted to spare her from whatever Liv had planned.

Evie arrived, gave him a kiss on the cheek and sat down on the sand. She turned to her sister. 'I got your message that you were here with Brodie, and you wanted to talk to me. What's it all about?'

Brodie thought Evie had never looked more beautiful. The silver bracelet he'd given her glinted on her wrist. She had promised him she would wear it always. He felt as though he was driving a car with no brakes heading straight for a brick wall and there was nothing he could do to stop the impact.

The wind had picked up, and so had the waves. Sparks burst from the fire and the surface of the water turned deep black with flecks of reflected orange. It was becoming much colder.

'I thought we could have a cosy chat,' said Liv.

'Well, you could have maybe picked a warmer spot, like the pub; that wind is freezing, and your fire is struggling.' Evie laughed.

She was actually really touched that Liv had asked to meet her. She was so happy with Brodie she wanted everyone to be just as full of joy. Even her sister. Maybe this would be a fresh start and they could be friends.

'Oh, I think this is the perfect place for me to let you in on a few things.' Liv smirked. The wind was now churning up the sea and blowing Liv's hair up and away from her face. She looked like a malevolent banshee.

'Evie, I want to go,' said Brodie abruptly. 'Right now.' He got to his feet. Evie looked confused.

'Sit down,' hissed Liv.

'What's going on?' said Evie, uncertainly.

'I have some news for you, little sister. You might want to have a drink first though. You won't like what I have to say.'

Brodie looked at her pleadingly.

'Liv, please don't do this. I'm begging you. I will tell her myself.'

Evie looked from one to the other, 'What's she talking about, Brodie? What's going on?'

'Well,' drawled Liv. 'I think I owe it to you to tell you that your so-called perfect boyfriend has been very naughty indeed. I know for a fact he has cheated on you.' She laughed gleefully.

With a sinking heart, Evie realised once again her older sister actually enjoyed inflicting pain upon her and watching her suffer. She would never change.

'You are a liar. Brodie would never do that to me,' she said vehemently. Liv gave a smug smile and said nothing.

Evie looked from one to the other.

'Brodie, say something. Is she just being cruel and trying to split us up or have you really been with someone else?'

He couldn't look at her.

Liv cackled.

'He hasn't got the balls to tell you. Because, you see, the person he slept with is very close to home.' She paused dramatically. 'In fact, it was me.'

Evie laughed in derision. 'God, Liv, you are so pathetic. Brodie, let's go. I've listened to enough of her bullshit.'

Liv's eyes narrowed until they were slits of black. She looked demonic in the firelight.

'Remember your big fight back in the summer? Brodie booked a room, didn't he, but he was left all alone and frustrated after you flounced off. Well, the two of us made sure the bed in that room didn't go to waste if you get my drift.'

Evie gasped. 'How did you know about the room? Brodie, how did she know about that?' Brodie couldn't look at her. He was so ashamed. That's when she knew for sure he was guilty. She said hoarsely, 'So it's true, you slept with my sister?'

He sprang up, taking her hands in his and knelt before her on the sand.

'Evie, I'm so sorry, I was going to tell you. Please don't hate me; it had nothing to do with how I feel about you. It was just a mistake. A huge mistake. I was so drunk; I was so upset . . .'

'You didn't seem that upset when we were in bed together,' said Liv.

Evie couldn't believe what she was hearing. Of all the people in the world, Brodie had betrayed her with the sister who loathed her. She pushed him away.

'You were my first. I thought I was special, but you slept with me after having sex with my sister. How could you do something like that? I would never have gone to bed with you if I'd known the truth.'

'The truth is that I love you, and only you,' said Brodie, his voice breaking. 'Evie, please. I didn't tell you because I knew I had behaved appallingly. I didn't want to lose you. I was trying to protect you . . .'

'Protect me?' Evie said incredulously. 'Protect me?'

Liv was rocking backwards and forwards hugging herself, watching the scene unfold. This was playing out even better than she'd hoped.

To her surprise, Evie felt unnaturally calm.

'I never want to see you again, Brodie. As far as I'm concerned, you two deserve each other.'

She got up to leave. Brodie caught her wrist.

'Evie, I am begging you. Liv just slept with me to hurt you. I don't even remember what happened. I know it's no excuse, but I was so drunk. I must have blacked out.' He added desperately, 'Let's leave together, just the two of us. Now, tonight. And we don't look back. We never have to see her again.'

Evie wavered as she looked down at him, the man she loved with all her heart.

'Well,' said Liv, slowly, relishing her big moment. 'That's where you are wrong. We will always be part of each other's lives. There's something else you don't know. I am expecting a baby and it's yours.'

Brodie looked utterly shattered. Evie couldn't believe what she was hearing.

'Have you got nothing to say, Evie? You are going to be an aunty. Aren't you pleased?'

A terrible wail burst from Evie. She wrenched Brodie's bracelet from her wrist and threw it with all her strength into the sea. Without thinking, Brodie waded into the water to try and to rescue it.

The water was ice-cold, but he crouched down and was scrabbled in the sand for the precious bracelet, when a huge wave knocked him over. He was completely drenched with freezing salt water.

As he tried to get up, he felt the strong current pulling him under and out of his depth. He couldn't swim because his heavy boots, jeans and jumper were sodden with sea water, the weight dragging him under.

On the beach, Liv was watching in alarm.

'Brodie, come back,' she yelled. 'Leave that stupid bracelet.'

She looked down at her sister. 'Evie, tell him. He'll listen to you.'

But Evie was in such a state of shock, she didn't even register her sister shouting at her.

'Brodie,' yelled Liv. 'Get back here right now!'

She watched his body go limp and his head loll from side to side with the movement of the waves. Liv grabbed her phone and called her dad, screaming that they were on the beach, Brodie was in the water and in trouble.

Duncan rushed for the door and shouted at Cara to call 999.

Liv saw Brodie disappear completely and waded in. She was a strong swimmer and managed to reach him as he came back to the surface again.

She tried desperately to hold on to him, but he was so heavy she knew he would soon slip from her grasp. Liv kept screaming at Evie to come and help but she couldn't or wouldn't respond.

In the water, Liv saw Brodie's eyes roll back in his head, and he slipped from her grasp and disappeared under the black, relentless waves.

Duncan was running down to the beach. He saw that Evie was safe on the shore, but Liv was in the water. Duncan waded in and swam quickly to her side.

She was white with fear and cold.

'Dad. I couldn't hold on to him. He's just gone under again.'

Duncan dived down and groped frantically for Brodie. It took him several attempts, but he managed to grab him under the arms and drag him to the shore.

Liv was kneeling and keening beside them, utterly distraught.

Duncan felt in vain for a pulse and then started mouth-to-mouth and CPR, but there was no sign of life. He kept pressing Brodie's chest firmly, tears streaming down his face, and then he sobbed in horror when he heard a loud crack as Brodie's ribs broke under the pressure.

'Oh, Brodie, son. I'm so sorry. I've hurt you. Come on now, you have to stay with us. Think of your dad. Come back to us, Brodie, come back.'

Two paramedics arrived and quickly and calmly took over. Liv, Duncan and Evie, all shivering uncontrollably with shock and cold, were wrapped in foil blankets.

Duncan told them tearfully, 'I think I hurt him badly. I didn't mean it. Tell him I'm sorry. Do you think you can save him?'

'You stand back now,' said the older paramedic gently. 'We will do all we can.'

They used a defibrillator in an attempt to get Brodie's heart beating, but the sight of his poor body being severely jolted was too much for Duncan to bear. He scooped up Liv and went to Evie, who still hadn't said a word, and wrapped his arms around both of his girls and prayed that Brodie would survive.

After what seemed like an eternity, it began to rain, the fire hissing and going out, but the medics never stopped their efforts to save Brodie. Eventually, they shook their heads. The older paramedic said, 'There's nothing more to be done.' He added wearily, 'We all tried our best. It looks like shock from going into the cold water. His heart just couldn't take it.'

He said gently to Duncan, 'You need to leave him with me now. I will take care of him, and my colleague will get you and your girls home. I'd like you all to get warmed up and checked out. I especially don't like the look of your youngest.'

Liv was incoherent with grief and racked with sobs, but from Evie there was nothing. It was as though she was made of stone.

36

Orkney, 2004

The house was in turmoil. Evie, Duncan and Liv had arrived back about half an hour ago, and Duncan had broken the news to Cara, who'd immediately unleashed a barrage of hysterical questions that he couldn't answer.

'I need to call Hugh,' Duncan muttered to her, his face ashen. 'He has to hear it from me, but I am scared it might finish him.'

Evie watched her dad shuffle into the hall to call his friend. He looked so old and weary. He picked up the phone and dialled Hugh's number. She stood at the door of the living room where she could hear him.

'Hugh?' Duncan said. 'I'm sorry to be calling so late. I've got . . . I've got some hellish news.'

Her father's voice broke as he told him that Brodie had died, had drowned, in a terrible accident. Hugh couldn't take it in. At first, he accused Duncan of making a sick joke. Then he shouted angrily then he crumbled.

'Not my boy,' he cried over and over. 'Please, Duncan, not my boy.'

Duncan wiped tears from his eyes. 'I'm so sorry, Hugh. We did everything we could. Liv went straight into the water after him, trying to pull him out, but he was too heavy for her. I was there as soon as she called for help and we both got him out together, and I tried to bring him back. The paramedics were there quickly, and they tried everything, but they just couldn't save him.'

Hearing her father say out loud that Brodie was dead, finally made Evie realise that this was real. He was gone. She had been completely numb since Liv had broken the news she was having Brodie's baby. The last thing she remembered properly was throwing his bracelet into the sea and him going in after it. Everything that came afterwards felt as though she was sleepwalking.

Now, she let guilt and shame wash over her because she'd done nothing. If she'd been braver, she could have helped Liv. Those vital few moments might have made all the difference. They both could have saved him. She had a terrible thought: what if deep down she wanted him to die because he'd betrayed her.

Then she was hit by a tidal wave of deep, dark loss. She couldn't believe she would never see him again. Earlier that day they had been laughing together and making plans for Christmas and New Year, but now she would never see him again.

Duncan was speaking softly and slowly to Hugh, and Evie turned away and stood at the living-room door and watched her mother comforting Liv. In a rare moment of tenderness, Cara had her arm round her eldest daughter, who looked young and vulnerable and was clinging to her mother.

'I watched him die in front of me.' Liv's voice broke. 'And I couldn't save him. I tried so hard.'

Cara kissed the top of her head and told her, 'You were incredible. You were a true heroine, and I am so proud of you. You have nothing to feel sorry about.'

Evie felt as though she had been punched in the stomach. She knew she would never be able to atone for her behaviour tonight. Duncan hung up the phone. When he turned around, his face was white.

'Evie, go and sit down in the living room with your sister.' His voice was suddenly firm with an undercurrent of cold rage. She immediately obeyed.

Cara and Liv picked up on his demeanour. They both sat upright and, for once, Cara didn't say a word.

'I have just broken the news of Brodie's death to his father,' said Duncan. 'As you can imagine he is completely shattered.' He stared at both his daughters. 'He had one question I couldn't answer. What the hell was that boy doing in the water in the first place?'

Evie felt sick to her stomach. She couldn't speak. She didn't know what to say.

'I won't ask you again. Tell me what the hell was he doing in the water?' Duncan said, raising his voice.

Suddenly, Liv leapt to her feet and pointed at Evie. 'It was her fault,' she yelled. 'She threw that stupid bracelet he gave her in the sea, knowing full well he'd have to go and get it! And then she stayed on the beach refusing to help me, and she—'

Something in Evie broke. Twenty years of being bullied by Liv, of enduring her taunts and torments, unleashed a fury in her. She whirled round to face Liv and screamed in her face.

'You took the only thing that was precious to me! And you ruined it like you do everything else!' She grabbed Liv's shoulders and dug her fingers in, her eyes wild. 'I hate you. I hate him. And I cannot bear that you are having his baby.'

Cara and Duncan gasped.

'What baby?' said Cara, her voice barely audible.

'What is going on?' said Duncan.

Evie felt almost hysterical. She blurted, 'Liv's pregnant. She's pregnant, and it's Brodie's.'

For once, Cara was so shocked she had nothing to say. Her mouth opened and closed like a guppy fish, but no sound came out.

'Brodie was going to be a father,' said Duncan. 'I should . . . I should tell Hugh . . . But I don't understand. He loved you, Evie.'

Liv burst out, 'I loved him. He's the only person I've ever loved. I don't know why, but there it is. And maybe, just maybe, he could have loved me too. But we never got the chance to find out did we, Evie?'

Evie squared up to her. 'I don't believe for one single second you loved him. You just wanted him because he was mine. You are incapable of loving anyone but yourself. And you will be the worst mother of all time.'

'Evie. Stop,' said her dad. 'Just stop it.'

Cara was sitting with a wondrous look on her face. 'I'm going to be a granny. Something good will come out of this. I can start afresh with my grandchild and do it right this time. Duncan, don't worry, it's all going to be fine.'

'For the love of God, Cara, the boy is dead, and he might still be here today if . . .' He stopped abruptly. He couldn't say it aloud.

Evie looked at him with intense pain in her eyes. Her dad had always had her back and been on her side, but now he was looking at her with anger and disappointment. She whispered, 'You think he would still be alive if I hadn't thrown away the bracelet he gave me, or if I had helped Liv to try to rescue him? Well, you're right. He would. And I will never ever forgive myself.'

Evie felt as though the walls of the house were closing in on her. She had to get out of here. She had to leave now. She thought desperately, *Freya will help me. She will know what to do. I need to get to Freya.*

Out loud she said, 'I can't stay here.' Evie rushed to the door, but Liv blocked her way.

'That's right, run away and play the victim,' she hissed. 'Isn't it about time you had another one of your attention-seeking asthma attacks?'

All the pent-up fury that Liv had slept with Brodie and was now having his baby burst from Evie and with a cry she shoved her sister hard into the wall.

Liv staggered and fell, her body twisting as she landed heavily on the floor. She cried out in pain, putting a hand on her stomach and writhing in agony. 'The baby. Something is wrong. Mum, Dad, I can feel I'm bleeding. I'm going to lose the baby.'

Evie watched in horror as her parents scrambled to help Liv. Duncan knelt beside her. 'Keep calm, love. We'll get you to hospital.'

He raised his head and looked at Evie with anger and contempt. 'Just get out. I don't want to have to see your face.'

Evie rushed into the hallway, grabbed her coat and her handbag and fled out into the night. That was the last time that Evie ever saw her father.

37

Orkney, 2024

Evie had almost come to the end of her story. She paused and looked around at her friends, their faces ashen. She forced herself to continue. This wasn't the full story, not yet.

She swallowed and said tearfully, 'That wasn't the end of it. I spoke to Liv, just once, after I left. She told me that she had lost the baby. It was so bad they had to perform a hysterectomy. She said my mother was utterly distraught and almost lost her mind, and my dad never wanted to see me again.'

There was a sharp intake of breath from Kate. The room was thick with emotion. 'That's why I left, and why I stayed away,' said Evie. 'I couldn't face any of you knowing what a terrible tragedy I'd caused, and now I don't blame you if you never want to speak to me again.'

There was a stunned silence. The three women, Freya, Sophia and Kate, couldn't look Evie in the eyes.

She kept talking. 'I'm the reason Liv is such a mess. She lost the baby. I ruined her life. I made my dad so unhappy he gave up and died, and then there's my mother, and poor Brodie. That lovely young man with his whole life ahead of him. The post-mortem showed he had an undiagnosed heart condition. The shock of getting in the water killed him. I've gone over it in my head so many times. If only I hadn't thrown that bracelet in the water, he'd still be alive.'

Freya was the first to speak. She looked utterly shattered. 'I wish you had told me all of this years ago. I begged you so many times to tell me.'

She now looked directly at Evie. 'Do you know how hard it was to keep it to myself that I knew where you were? I should have made you come home. I should have gone down to London and dragged you back here to make things right. I had a stupid notion that I couldn't betray your trust.'

She took a deep breath. 'I had finally made up my mind to tell your dad where you were that day I went to see him and found him on the floor, but he never regained consciousness. I will regret that to my dying day.'

She started to cry. Freya never cried. Evie felt sick to her stomach.

'Oh, Freya. I'm so sorry I put you through that.'

Freya blew her nose. 'I honestly thought I was helping you, but you were just a kid. I should have sorted it out. Maybe I liked being the only one you could talk to. But what a mess. Liv is a wreck. Duncan died never having seen you again and Cara. Well, Cara is lost to us all.'

Freya lapsed back into silence. Evie felt small and scared. She turned to Sophia, who was twisting her hands together. 'Sophia . . .' Evie began. 'Please, say something.'

Sophia swallowed hard and then said very slowly and quietly, 'It's a lot for us to take in, Evie. I mean, you kept all of this from me. You know everything about me. You stayed with my family, and, now, I just wonder if I know you at all.'

'You do. Of course you do,' Evie said despairingly.

'But why didn't you trust me?' said Sophia. 'I thought you had no family and friends because you never wanted to discuss the past. It feels like you have always lied to me.'

'I am trying to make sense of it and understand why you didn't stay and try to sort things out.'

Evie said in a tiny, exhausted voice, 'They all wanted me to go. Liv said she hated me, and my mother told me she couldn't stand the sight of me. Even my dad thought it best I leave.'

Sophia wasn't convinced. 'But, Evie, that was in the heat of the moment. They didn't mean it. Not really. Your dad certainly didn't want you to cut all ties with your family and your friends. You should have stayed.'

Freya added, 'And I shouldn't have helped you to leave. I blame myself for that. Every day.'

Evie looked at Kate. Her face was pale, and her lips were pressed tightly together. She was furious.

'I've had enough of this,' said Kate. 'This is ridiculous. Both of you are looking for excuses for Evie. I, for one, am scunnered. There's only one person responsible for all of this, so don't you two dare let her off the hook. She nearly fooled me when she came to see me. I actually felt sorry for her. But not any more.'

She looked at Evie with complete disdain. 'No wonder your sister is such a mess. I feel terrible now for being such a cow to her for years. I blamed her for the fact you left. I thought she'd done something terrible to you. All the time she was suffering from losing her baby. I can't begin to imagine what she went through. And your poor mum and dad as well. I honestly don't know how you can show your face here.'

Freya took charge. 'Kate, please stop. We are all overwrought. Don't stay things in the heat of the moment that you will live to regret.'

Kate wouldn't listen. She started furiously gathering up her things.

'Please don't go, Kate,' said Evie. 'I want to try and make things right.'

Kate glared at her.

'You could have done that by staying here and facing up to what you did. Not by running away. Anyway, Edwyn's picking me up after his shift. He'll be outside now.' She left, slamming the door behind her.

Freya, Sophia and Evie were alone. Evie couldn't bear the hurt and disappointment in Freya's eyes. For the first time she looked like a woman on the verge of her eightieth birthday.

Evie started to apologise again but Freya raised her hand. 'Let's not say any more tonight. We will sleep on it. Things are always better with the dawn of a new day.'

But for once she didn't really believe it.

As soon as she got out of Freya's front door, Kate took some deep gulps of fresh air.

She had never been so angry. She simply couldn't believe Evie had come back and unleashed all of this on them.

Edwyn pulled up in the car and she got in the passenger seat.

'Good night with the girls?' he said, driving off.

'Hardly,' Kate said. 'You're not going to believe what I have got to tell you.'

As they drove slowly home, Kate recounted everything Evie had said. 'Can you believe it?' she finished up, having made herself furious all over again. 'All this time, she was hiding the truth and now she's come back and expects us to welcome her with open arms and actually forgive her! Well, bollocks to that.'

Edwyn didn't say a word. He was deep in thought. Something didn't add up. Evie's story just didn't make any sense. Everyone in Orkney knew about what had happened to Brodie. Any tragic death here was a rarity.

They all realised that Evie had needed some time on her own after he died but could never understand why she never came back. Now the rest of the tragic story was revealed. Liv had lost her baby and the baby's father all on the same night. It was horrific.

'Are you not going to say something?' said Kate.

Edwyn shook his head. 'I'm trying to take it all in. There's something about this that doesn't feel right. This doesn't feel like our Evie.'

Kate went ballistic. 'So, you can't believe your precious, perfect Evie could be capable of doing something so disgusting? I don't know why I'm surprised.' Her voice was shrill. All of her fears were coming true. 'It was always Evie, wasn't it. You were devastated when she left. She was your ideal woman, you put her on a pedestal, and no one could match up to her. Not even me. Be honest. I've always been second best.'

Edwyn was shocked and baffled. 'Kate. What the hell are you talking about? Where is this all coming from? You were just as upset as I was when Evie left.'

Kate looked at him with a mixture of despair and exasperation. 'You know the truth is, part of me was glad she went, because then I had you all to myself. Evie was prettier and cleverer, and you only turned to me when she took up with Brodie. When you came back from university and got a job here in the hospital, we spent all our time together, and eventually you stopped talking incessantly about what had happened to her.'

She sniffed. 'I remember on our wedding day I overheard you telling your brother that we "rubbed along well together" and I told myself that would be enough. I could accept that, and we could build on it. One day you would love me properly. We had our girls and I thought that we were finally happy.'

Edwyn was flabbergasted: 'Kate, I don't know what you are going on about. I don't even remember saying anything like that.'

He wanted to reassure her and tell that he loved her. Kate and the girls were his whole life, and all he felt for Evie was friendship and pity. Nothing more than that, but he hated talking about his emotions and lost the chance to placate Kate who was off on another rant.

'Even after what she has just told us, you still think the sun shines out of her backside. Don't you get it? She caused her sister to lose her baby. Then she runs away to leave everyone to deal with the mess. Well, she's back now and you are welcome to her.'

The rest of the journey was ice-cold and silent with Kate refusing to talk to her husband and Edwyn exasperated by her accusations. At school, he'd admittedly had a crush on Evie, and he'd been desperately upset when she'd left, but way before then he'd fallen properly and deeply in love with his Kate and genuinely had no idea she still nursed such resentment and was so insecure.

Back at the house, Edwyn paid the babysitter and Kate got into their comfy bed, accompanied by the girls, who'd woken up when she'd slammed the front door hard. He lay in Louise's narrow single bed with his feet hanging out of the end feeling sick to his stomach about what he had heard tonight about Evie, and also from the row with Kate.

The two of them never argued unless it was about Joan Crawford the cat bringing in a mouse. Even though Edwyn was a doctor he couldn't bring himself to dispose of the poor dead creatures and Kate always had to do the honours, which made her shudder and shout at him.

There was also something nagging away at him about Evie's confession. It was just out of his grasp, but he felt it was hugely important.

38

Orkney, 2024

Evie got up the following morning, having tossed and turned for most of the night. Bleary with lack of sleep, she made a cup of tea in the kitchen. Sophia shuffled in, having spent the night on Freya's sofa wrapped in blankets.

'Tea?' said Evie and Sophia nodded. The two women sat around the kitchen table.

Sophia sighed. 'It's just going to take me some time to get my head round all of this.'

'I know. I don't blame you. Can we please talk about something else? You didn't tell me about your trip to Hoy and how you got on with Finn.'

At the mention of his name, Sophia blushed.

'Why don't you go and see him today?' said Evie. 'You should do something fun for yourself rather than everything being about me and my troubles. Anyway, I've made up my mind to go and see Liv later this morning.'

Sophia looked dubious. 'Are you sure? Then let me come with you.'

'That's good of you,' replied Evie. 'But I need to do this on my own. I thought if I go early enough, she might not be drunk or drugged up.'

'I understand but remember I'm here to help you anyway I can.'

'Even after what I told you?'

Sophia sighed. 'You are still my friend but are you sure you are up to seeing Liv? It's not going to be easy.'

'I need to. Even if it is just to tell her to do her worst. I've let the people who matter to me most know what happened. You and Freya have been amazing. But I'm so sad about Kate.'

'Give it time,' said Sophia. 'She might come round.'

An hour later, Evie drove up outside Liv's house in Stromness. She chapped on the door and waited. She noticed a batch of flyers caught in the letterbox, and a sign stuck up on the door. An eviction notice. She knocked again and heard movement from inside.

'It's open! Come in for fuck's sake!' came a harsh shout.

Evie pushed open the door and was appalled at the state of the house. There were empty beer cans, old pizza boxes and every surface was covered in cigarette butts. Liv had run out of ashtrays, so saucers and side plates had to stand in.

She was slumped in a dirty armchair in the middle of the chaos. She looked up and spat, 'Oh, for fuck's sake. Did I not tell you if you didn't go back to where you came from, I would make sure everyone on this island knew your dirty little secret?'

Liv had just woken up and her voice was raspy. She lit up her first fag of the day.

The stench of dirty clothes and neglect was stifling, and Evie took a hit of her inhaler so she could breathe. Liv barked a laugh.

'Still pretending to have a deadly illness, I see. We all know there's nothing wrong with you, baby sister. You used those fake asthma attacks all our childhood to get sympathy. You are so full of shit.'

Evie looked for somewhere to sit down. She cleared a pile of newspapers from a greasy, grubby chair. At least Liv was on her own with none of the usual motley crew of drunks, junkies and poor lost souls who huddled at her house and supplied her with booze and drugs.

Evie took a long hard look at her sister. In the morning light, she was even more raddled. The roots of her hair were greyish white, and her skin the colour of sour milk.

Evie remembered how cool and dazzling she'd been as a young woman and how she'd envied her swagger and confidence. She felt fear replaced by something else. Pity.

'Liv. I'm here to tell you that I have confessed everything to the people here I care about. I needed to tell them myself before you broadcast it all over the island.'

Liv narrowed her eyes as though she wasn't buying any of this.

'I also told my friend Sophia who is up from London,' said Evie. 'But you already met her. She and Freya were shocked but have said they understand. They are willing to give me a second chance. But that's not what matters most right now.'

She leaned in closer to Liv, meeting her eyes. 'I just wanted to come here and tell you that I'm so sorry about what happened. There's not a day goes by when I don't feel ashamed of myself and regret the pain I caused you.'

She added, 'I kept my promise to stay away for twenty years, but I know now that wasn't the right thing to do, even though it was what you wanted. I tried to feel better by sending you money, but that was a mistake too. I should have stayed here and made it up to you and tried to help you.'

Evie was in tears now. 'I know I don't deserve your forgiveness, Liv, but I'm asking for it anyway. I just want to salvage something from this whole mess.'

255

She couldn't say anything else as she was so choked up. Liv got up on her feet and began a slow clap.

'Well, what a performance. The Oscar goes to Evie Muir for being a hideous phoney and talking absolute shite. I bet you gave your friends a totally sanitised version of what happened that night.'

'Honestly, Liv, I told them everything.'

'Why should I believe you? When will you get it through your stupid thick skull that I will never ever forgive you. You ruined my life. Because of you I never got to be a mother and I live like a pig in shit. I know what people say about me and I have been so tempted over the years to tell them all the truth about you, but I wanted your cash. Believe me. That's all that stopped me.'

She got up and jabbed Evie in the chest. 'I wanted to tell them it was the blessed sainted golden child who destroyed everything. You killed my baby, and you killed Brodie. You made my mother go mad and you destroyed my father. He died the day you left, and you know it.'

Evie stood up. 'I deserve that. I know I do, but please let me try to make things right. I can get someone in to clean up the place and I can get you proper help to stop drinking and to get off the drugs. I saw the eviction notice on the door, Liv. I want to help you. Please let me help you.'

'You can help by fucking right off.'

Evie looked at her sister. Liv's eyes were glittering and defiant, but Evie saw that they were also filled with despair.

'I just want you to find some sort of happiness,' said Evie.

'Aye, right,' Liv retorted, her voice dripping with scorn. 'You want me to find some peace only because that will make you feel better. Just get out and don't come back. If I see you in the street, don't talk to me. All I want from you is money. Otherwise, you are dead to me.'

Evie left; there was nothing more to be said. She took a deep breath of fresh sea-salted air. She had tried her best.

When she got back, Freya was bustling around preparing lunch, and Evie filled both her and Sophia in on her visit. 'I tried, but she won't accept my apology. I don't blame her. I offered to help her to get clean and find somewhere to live, but she wasn't having it.'

Freya sighed. 'It sounds like your sister is just beyond help. Whether or not that changes in the future, we don't know. But at least you made the effort.'

Evie nodded. 'It was the least I could do, and I've been thinking. I'd like to go and see my mum.' Freya looked dubious.

'Evie, are you sure? She's not in a good way.'

'Is she still here on Orkney?' asked Sophia. 'What happened to her?'

Freya answered for Evie. 'It's a sad story, Sophia. Cara was always highly strung. Poor Duncan had a hell of a life with her, but he loved her, and he protected her for years. None of us knew just how bad things were and it must have been about eight years after Evie left, she was finally diagnosed with Alzheimer's.

'She went downhill very fast. She's in a private nursing home on the mainland near Wick. That's where most of Duncan's money went. I made the arrangements when he could no longer cope, and Cara became a danger to him and to herself. He was never the same after she went away.'

Freya turned to Evie. 'Are you absolutely sure you want to go? I hate to say it, but she might not even recognise you.'

Evie nodded, determined. 'If there's the chance to make things right with my mum, I have to take it.'

39

Orkney, 2024

Freya and Evie walked up the driveway to Cara's nursing home. It looked more like a splendid country house hotel, with beautiful, well-tended gardens. Evie was nervous. This would be the first time she had seen her mother since Cara had told her to get out of the house almost twenty years ago.

She felt almost as apprehensive as when she had told her friends the truth about what had happened that terrible night. 'Just give me a minute,' she said to Freya, who nodded.

'Take as long as you need. I wasn't sure whether to tell you this, but I feel I should prepare you. The last time I brought Duncan here, it was a disaster. I used to take him on the ferry to visit your mum, but she'd often refuse to see him, or worse she wouldn't recognise him and just sit staring out of the window. The poor man didn't know what to do.'

She went on, 'Physically Cara is healthy, and she will probably outlive us all, but she's in a bad way in herself and she can be very paranoid and delusional.'

Freya remembered sitting in the care home with Duncan on what was his final visit. Despite, the delightful exterior and lovely gardens and the enormous monthly cost, inside the home was that unmistakable foetid odour of pee, disinfectant, and boiled cabbage.

Cara was bone-thin, wearing a brown cardigan and a long tweed skirt that was far too big. Her face was deeply wrinkled and her hair wispy grey, but her brown eyes still burned fiercely in her cadaverous face. She had fixed her gaze on Duncan and, in a clear voice, asked him to stop spoiling Evie and to pay Liv some attention.

She added that he looked a shambles, needed his hair cut and he had better be keeping the place tidy so that when she got out of this prison, she wouldn't have to spend all of her time getting everything back to normal. Then a door seemed to slam shut and she turned her face to the wall and wouldn't say another word.

When Duncan got up to go, she grabbed his arm with a claw like talon and hissed, 'Don't come back here. You are not wanted. I know who you are, and I despise you. I always have.'

Freya had tried to tell him Cara wasn't in her right mind, but Duncan barely said a word on the whole journey back and went straight home to disappear into a bottle of whisky.

The last thing Freya wanted was for Evie to be subjected to something similar. But Evie drew back her shoulders with a look of determination on her face. 'I need to see her, Freya. I have to do this and thank you for coming with me.'

They walked together into the home and were welcomed by the crisply efficient matron.

'Your mother has her moments, Miss Muir,' she said to Evie. 'I know when your late father and Freya came to visit her last month, she was very angry and upset, but recently I have to say she's become as good as gold. Nothing seems to bother her, and she loves to listen to her radio. Her arthritis has stopped her from knitting, which is a real shame, but she's one of our easier clients.'

Freya was astounded and Evie unconvinced. The matron led them to Cara's room. They knocked and went in. Cara was sitting in a chair with her back to them looking out of the window. She turned around and greeted them both with a big smile.

Evie saw a tiny little woman with wispy grey hair and twisted, gnarled hands. She wouldn't have recognised her own mother if she'd seen her in the street. Her restlessness had been replaced with a quiet calmness.

Evie looked at her with sadness and compassion. Her once-vital mum was now so fragile it felt as though the slightest breeze would blow her over and waft her away like a dried-up autumn leaf.

She looked at Evie and said in a faint, tremulous voice, 'Hello. Are you here to take me back to Hrossey? My mum will be waiting for me, and you know my dad is coming to visit us at last.'

Evie didn't know what to say. She crouched down beside her mum and took her hand, all twisted with blue ropey veins.

'Do you want to go to Hrossey?' said Evie gently.

'Maybe not today. I'm a little tired, but soon. Will you take me?'

'Of course I will take you, if that's what you want.'

'I'd like to see my mum again,' said Cara. 'It feels like such a long time has gone by since I heard her voice and I need to get sorted out for the big school. I have to go to Kirkwall, you know.'

Looking at this frail, elderly woman trapped back in her childhood, Evie silently begged her forgiveness for that terrible night and decided not to reveal she was her daughter. It was clear that would just upset and confuse her. Far better to leave her in a happy state of hope looking forward to seeing the father she'd never known.

Just as they were about to go, Cara looked at Evie as though seeing her for the first time. She suddenly looked sharp and alert.

'Don't go. I know you. You are my Evie. I haven't seen you for so long. Your dad will be so pleased you are here.'

'Yes, Mum. It's me. It's Evie.'

'You were always such a happy baby. I loved you very much, you know, but I couldn't tell you in case SHE got upset. Is she here?' Cara looked around anxiously. 'I'm a bit scared of her, you know, but as long as she gets her money, she leaves us in peace.'

She patted Evie's hand and smiled at her. 'You were always a daddy's girl but don't ever forget your mum loved you too.' Freya snuffled into her hanky and Evie clutched her mother's hand.

'I love you, Mum, and I know you did your best.'

'I hope you have a better life than me, Evie. Tell me, are you happy?'

Evie stared into her mother's eyes, unable to answer. Her mother turned away from her.

'I wish I'd been braver,' murmured Cara softly. 'I pushed happiness away.'

'Oh, Mum,' began Evie, wanting to say something to console her, but Cara looked back at her in confusion.

'Who did you say you were again, dear?'

The fog had descended but, for that brief moment, Evie felt they had made their peace. Evie thanked the staff for taking care of her mother and vowed to visit again soon.

On the ferry back across the Pentland Firth, which thankfully wasn't as choppy as it could have been, Evie stayed outside on the deck to feel the wind blowing in her hair and reflected on her mother's words. *I wish I'd been braver. I pushed happiness away.*

Freya stood by her side.

'You are in a bit of a dwam. Are you all right?'

'I'm thinking about what my mum said.'

Freya nodded. 'Maybe it's a kindness her memory is fogging over, and she doesn't have to live with regrets all the time.'

'I hope you don't mind me asking, Freya, but we've never talked about it before. Did you ever have someone special in your life? Did you ever fall in love?'

'Well, I've had my moments,' said Freya, 'but to be honest nothing that lasted the course.' She frowned and gathered her thoughts. 'I think I just wanted someone to see ME. Not Freya, a trans woman. Just me. Freya. And to be accepted and loved for who I am. I was badly hurt in the past by men who just wanted to show off how "right on" they were by going out with someone trans. I was like some sort of badge of honour for them. It wasn't about me. It was about what I represented. That was a hard lesson to learn.'

Evie waited for her to go on. It wasn't often Freya talked about her past.

'When I was in London, I met a really good man. He was a fair bit older than me, and we lived together for a while. Not much sex though. To be honest, I didn't really fancy him like that, but he was a good friend and he taught me a lot. He got me reading decent books and taking an interest in the world. We had a good few years together, but then he got very sick with heart problems. I was looking after him and we were doing fine, but his only niece insisted on putting him in a home because she wanted to sell his house. I visited him there until he died.'

Freya sighed. 'But I wasn't wanted at the funeral. We loved each other in our own way but it wasn't a big passionate affair. Just two lonely people huddling together.'

'I'm sorry,' said Evie. 'You deserved better, Freya.'

Freya took her hand. 'Thank you, Evie. But I'm content with the life I have built. It brings me a lot of joy.'

Evie stayed silent. Her mother's words kept echoing in her mind and Evie realised they could equally apply to her. She should have been a braver person and she also pushed happiness away. Evie didn't think she deserved to be happy and living a rather sad life was her punishment.

'I was thinking,' said Freya, breaking the silence. 'When we get back, why don't you pop down to your house and check out what Andrzej and his team have been up to? I know it's only been a couple of weeks, but the man is such a grafter, I bet he's made great progress.'

'He's such a hard worker,' said Evie. 'I think he could turn his hand to anything.'

Freya sighed. 'I just wish he would have the gumption to bestir himself and propose to Maureen.'

'How's she doing?' said Evie. 'She was very kind to me at the funeral, but I thought she looked exhausted.'

'Well, there's a reason for that.' Freya looked grim, but she added quickly, 'Anyway, Andrzej has loved her for years. He worships the ground she walks on. He helps her with her elderly parents, and he's been like a second father to her boy, Rory. And she adores him right back.'

'Well, that's wonderful. They are obviously the perfect match. What's the problem?'

'Oh, I could bang their heads together, Evie. I promised not to say anything but I'm sick of keeping so many secrets. Well, I don't need to tell you that.'

Evie winced and Freya continued, 'The thing is that both of them are worried that by declaring their feelings they would ruin their friendship. So, I told Maureen that Andrzej loves her but thinks she just looks upon him as a pal.'

'Well, some might say you were interfering,' said Evie. 'But I think you did the right thing. What happened then? She told him how she feels, I hope?'

'No.' Freya's face twisted with sorrow. 'She won't tell him.'

'Why ever not?'

Freya's eyes glistened, 'She has breast cancer. She found out for sure this week. It's not good. We are just waiting to hear on the treatment plan and, of course, there's still hope. Oh, Evie, you should have seen her face when I told her Andrzej loved her. She lit up, but then the light just switched off again, because she thinks it's hopeless. She swore me to secrecy because she doesn't want to be a burden on him.'

'So, Andrzej has no idea that Maureen loves him?' said Evie. 'Oh, Freya, he needs to know. They deserve some happiness, especially now.'

'I can't tell him, Evie,' said Freya. 'I promised Maureen and she'd never forgive me.'

Evie gazed at the grey sea and the rolling waves that still made her fearful, but she resolved to do something brave.

'But I can tell him. Obviously not about her cancer. But surely, I can let the poor man know what her feelings are, then it's up to him to decide what to do next. I'm sorry, Freya, but I can't stand by and see them both miserable when they could find happiness with each other, even if it turns out they might not have all that long together. Don't worry, I will be discreet. Your name will not be mentioned, but I need to try to fix this.'

40

Orkney, 2024

At Evie's house, Andrzej was making the most of the good weather to finish fitting the new windows and to paint the outside gleaming white. Inside, the bathroom and kitchen were being installed and there was a sweet smell of fresh sawdust and a hum of hard work.

Andrzej beamed at Evie. 'We are making progress. I am very pleased that your house is being brought back to life. It is a beautiful strong building and now it is no longer sad.'

'It's wonderful, Andrzej,' said Evie. 'You've done so much already. I had forgotten how beautiful it is here. The view really is very special. I don't think I truly appreciated it when I was young. It was just there.'

She thought, *Maybe I could start again here. Even with everything that happened. Could I possibly get a second chance?*

'Well, now,' said Andrzej. 'I wanted to talk to you about something. Freya tells me you are an artist. She has one of your creations on her wall and it is very good. I am thinking you could set up your easel in the big room downstairs where there is now even more wondrous light and paint this glorious view. What do you think?'

'The light is lovely, but I haven't picked up a brush since I left here, apart from helping Freya with her pebbles. I honestly don't know if I can still do it.'

'Of course you can, it is just like riding the bicycle and what beautiful work you could create here with inspiration everywhere you look,' said Andrzej, gesturing with his arms wide.

Evie smiled. Andrzej was so positive and kind you couldn't help but feel better just by being in his company. And he was right. There was inspiration all around her especially now the house was coming back to life. Before it had been filled with shadows and pain, now there were real possibilities.

'I will think about it. I promise.' She hesitated, knowing she would need to choose her next words with care, but she had an idea.

'Actually, I did want to ask you a favour. Could you see if your girlfriend would make me one of her lovely throws for my sofa? She did one for Freya and it really is beautiful.'

'You are mistaken, Evie. I don't have a girlfriend.'

'Really,' said Evie, feigning innocence. 'But I thought you and Maureen . . .'

Andrzej shook his head. 'No, we are friends. Good friends.'

'But I saw you both at my dad's funeral; it was clear how much she adores you. And I saw the way you look at her too.'

She looked at him hopefully. She really wasn't very good at this. Freya would have known exactly what to say and Kate would have come straight to the point. Then again, Andrzej hadn't denied that he loved Maureen. So, she decided to keep going. 'You looked so happy together.'

Andrzej shrugged and gave a hollow laugh. 'I think you are mistaken, Evie. I am not exactly a catch, you know. Why would Maureen ever think of me like that?'

'Are you kidding me?' said Evie. 'I haven't known you very

long, but you are one of the most decent and kindest men I
have ever come across. Freya can't speak highly enough of you,
and that says it all as far as I'm concerned.'

He looked at Evie with such hope in his eyes it made her
heart ache.

'Andrzej,' said Evie gravely. 'It's obvious you love her, and
I know she feels the same. Some people never get the chance
to find their soulmate. You need to tell her how you feel.'

'Maybe in a few months I'll tell her,' he murmured. 'She has
too much on right now, and I want to support her, but just as
a friend. That's all she wants from me.'

Evie couldn't tell him about Maureen's diagnosis; that wasn't
fair. But time might not be on their side. She had to convince
him somehow.

'Andrzej, listen to me,' she said. 'None of us know what's
round the corner. I met someone when I was very young, and
I thought we would be together for ever. But we only had one
short summer.' She swallowed hard, remembering how much
she had loved Brodie and how little time they'd had together.

'We just don't know what fate has in store for us. Please
don't wait to tell her. Sometimes, there is only the one chance
at happiness. You have to take it.'

Andrzej looked at her very seriously.

'Evie. Are you sure? You see I love Maureen very, very much,
but I have always believed that she considered me to be nothing
more than a friend. So many times, I have almost plucked up
the courage to tell her, but I have been too nervous and afraid.
She loved her husband so much, and I always thought that no
one could take his place in her heart.'

'She will always love him, Andrzej, but he would have wanted
her to be happy. And you do make her happy. The two of you
are meant to be together. You are made for each other.'

'I have the confession,' said Andrzej. 'I have been carrying this around with me in my inside pocket for years thinking one day I will have the courage to propose to Maureen.'

He brought out a worn box that contained a golden ring with a small-but-beautifully cut diamond.

'It belonged to my great-grandmother, and my mother gave it to me to one day give to my bride. Do you think it will do?'

'It's absolutely perfect,' said Evie. 'Well, what are you waiting for. It's past six o'clock. You and your squad have done enough grafting for me for the day. Get cleaned up and then go and see your Maureen.'

When Andrzej and his workers had left, Evie walked through the fresh, bright cottage, climbing the stairs up to her old bedroom. It looked so small – little more than a cupboard – but it had been her sanctuary when she was growing up.

She hesitated before opening the door and going into Liv's room, still scared of her wrath after all these years. Inside was a bare, sunny space that surprisingly held no ghosts. It was just a room with a beautiful view and would make a lovely place for Sophia to stay when she came to visit.

Listen to me, making plans to have guests staying over when I haven't even decided to stay here, she thought. Andrzej had managed to erase all the bad memories and he really had given the house its happiness back. Her parents' old room had stunning views over to Scapa Flow, a beautiful sight to wake up to every morning.

Evie knew she would sleep well in this lovely room. She gazed out at the sea and thought again of her dad's wish that she would learn to swim. She imagined herself stepping into the water. For the first time, the terror wasn't overwhelming. She had a sudden image of herself going in deeper, the cool water surrounding her, and then the magical moment of beginning to swim like a real selkie.

Stepping downstairs and into the old living room, she realised Andrzej was right. The huge new windows meant the space was filled with light, making it the perfect studio if Evie wanted to start painting again. She'd already decided she wanted the kitchen to be as cheerful and colourful as possible – bright yellow walls with blue tiles and shelves covered in plants and books. Maybe she could also create some paintings to really make the house into her home.

She had loved painting so very much but had abandoned it like everything else that had given her joy as a form of self-punishment. Perhaps it was time to do something that made her forget her past troubles.

On one of their visits to the house, Evie and Freya had found the key to the old garage that was overgrown with weeds and bracken. Clearly no one had been in there for years. She decided to explore further.

Opening the half-rotten wooden door with difficulty and amidst a scurry of mice and spiders, she saw a hint of yellow in the gloom. Half hidden under an old tarpaulin was Florence, her beloved Beetle car. How on earth had it managed to escape Liv, who had stripped the rest of the house bare? She would surely have sold it if she'd known it was here. Florence was dirty and rusty, and it looked as though animals had been living in her wheels, but Evie just knew she could be brought back to her former glory.

Andrzej had gone straight to Maureen's. He softly called her name before coming into her living room. She was sitting on the sofa looking out at the view with a beautiful woollen blanket in her hands.

She smiled up at him. 'I'm so glad to see you. I've just finished this one and I wanted your opinion before I send it on to the shop.'

'It's beautiful, Maureen, and I know exactly who would love it as much as me. Just today Evie was asking if you would make one for her. She wants it for the sofa in her house.'

'Well, that's settled. She will have it as a housewarming present from me. I can do another one for the shop. How's the work coming along at Evie's?'

'It's good. It's very good and I think Evie would be happy there, if that is what she chooses. Freya wants her to stay, and you know what Freya wants she always gets.'

Maureen laughed. 'She does. You always manage to build a proper real home for people rather than just a house with four walls. Look at this lovely place you made for me and Rory. And my parents are so happy in the flat downstairs where we can keep an eye on them.'

A look of sadness and worry crossed over Maureen's face, and, in that instant, Andrzej knew he had to gather all of his courage and finally tell her what was in his heart.

'Maureen. I have something to say to you that I should have told you a long time ago.'

He took a deep breath. This was a speech he had rehearsed many times but never had the courage to deliver.

He launched into it. 'I have loved you from the moment I saw you and my love for you has become deeper with every passing year. I should have told you years ago, but I didn't feel I was worthy of you, and I didn't want to ruin what we had.'

For a moment, Maureen gave one of the smiles that made Andrzej's heart sing, but then she covered her face with her hands and started to sob. Andrzej looked appalled.

'My little love. My darling. What is wrong? Oh, I have upset you. I am a big, stupid oaf. I am so very sorry. I was afraid of this.'

'Oh, Andrzej. I should have told you that I have loved you for such a long time and now it's too late. I thought you just wanted to be friends with me and that it was really my dad you came to see to hear all of his old stories.'

'My lovely Maureen. You really truly feel the same? I am so happy and so relieved. Oh, we are both such fools and have wasted so much time.' He smiled at her. 'Of course, I am very fond of your father, but I do not want to marry him. It is you I wish to wed. Please say you will do me the honour. I will be a good husband and I know I can make you happy.'

He cradled her in his arms and realised that it was like holding a tiny bird.

Much as she wanted to stay in his embrace, Maureen gently pushed him away. 'Andrzej, I'm sorry but I can't marry you.'

'Well, we don't have to get married straightaway . . .' Andrzej began, but Maureen raised her hand to make him stop talking.

'Andrzej, you have to listen to me. It wouldn't be fair of me to agree to be your wife.' She looked stricken. 'I need to tell you something that I have been dreading.'

Andrzej drew her closer. 'I know you aren't well. You have looked so tired and anxious, and I have been waiting for you to tell me what's wrong so that I can help you.'

'Andrzej, you need to know . . .' She hesitated and then blurted out, 'I have cancer. I ignored it for months, and finally got checked last week. I don't know what the prognosis is, or the treatment. I might be living on borrowed time already.' She choked on her next words. 'So, you see, I can't possibly marry you.'

Andrzej kneeled at her feet and rummaged in his pocket where he found his great-grandmother's ring.

'Maureen. My love. I am now asking you properly down on one knee. Will you make me so very happy and do me the honour of being my wife?'

Instead of answering, she said gently, 'Didn't you hear what I said? I can't be your wife. I don't know what the future holds. I don't know what treatment I'll have to go through. I don't even know how long I have left.'

'None of us do, my Maureen. So don't you think we should make the most of every minute. I want to look after you and we must seize the day together.'

Maureen let out a sound that was half a sob, half a laugh. 'You truly are the most extraordinary man.'

Andrzej held her hand. 'We will face the future together, whatever it holds. But, Maureen, you haven't answered my question, do you love me enough to marry me?'

'I adore you. You know that now. But we don't need to get married. Can't we just go on like before? Except we would be living under the same roof.'

'Maureen. I am shocked,' said Andrzej with a laugh. 'Surely, you know you need to make an honest man of me, or my mother will never speak to me again.'

She smiled at him through her tears, and he knew everything was going to be all right.

They had love and they had hope.

41

Orkney, 2024

Since the night of Evie's confession and their dreadful quarrel, Edwyn and Kate had become polite, cold strangers in their own home. The silence had allowed bad feelings to fester, turning a crack into giant chasm growing ever wider between them.

Kate thought Edwyn's distance proved her fears and insecurities were right, and she really had always been second best, meanwhile Edwyn was deeply hurt that Kate wouldn't believe he only looked upon Evie as a friend.

He didn't know how to convince his wife that he truly loved her. He was fearful of risking another argument, so he just kept quiet and made everything so much worse.

The two of them put on an act in front of their girls at breakfast but the little ones knew something was wrong and became very quiet over their cornflakes and toast. Normally, mornings were busy and loud with the girls chatting away while getting ready for school, and Edwyn gulping down his first cup of coffee of the day before giving them all a quick kiss goodbye and rushing to work.

Now, Kate walked them to school in stony silence and Louise and Claire held hands and looked worried. Their safe, warm world had changed overnight, and they both thought they had done something terrible.

Louise believed it was all her fault because she had eaten the whole pack of Bounty bars her mum kept hidden at the back of the cupboard, and Claire was sure she was to blame because she hadn't tidied up her toys.

Edwyn was relieved to get out of the house and lose himself in his work at the hospital but knew things couldn't go on like this. His marriage seemed broken and he feared it might be beyond repair.

He'd done a lot of soul-searching and realised that he hadn't told Kate often enough how much she meant to him and that he would be lost without her. He just assumed she knew.

He wasn't at all romantic and they had never been a lovey-dovey couple. They both thought Valentine's Day was a big con and they weren't big on anniversary celebrations.

He remembered how the nurses had teased him mercilessly when he'd told them he'd bought Kate a pressure cooker for her birthday. He'd wailed that it was what she wanted, but they'd told him he needed to seriously up his game. He wished he'd listened to them.

He had taken Kate for granted and now the world had shifted beneath his feet. He needed to make amends and he had the beginnings of an idea. He called Kate, hoping she would pick up, but he ended up leaving a message on her phone. 'Can we try to talk things through tonight? I will get your mum to pick up the girls from school and they can have a sleepover so we can have a chance to speak properly.'

About an hour later he received a text from Kate. *OK. I am going to be out at Freya's all day. Back at eight.*

It was terse but at least she had got back to him and agreed to hear him out. He couldn't believe his rock-solid marriage to

Kate was crumbling because she thought he was in love with Evie. It was ridiculous.

It had always been Kate for him, but he was too emotionally constipated to tell her how he really felt, and it was his fault she believed she was the consolation prize all these years. He just hoped his plan would work. He had a lot to do before tonight.

When Kate walked into Freya's house, she was furious to find herself alone with Evie. 'I'm sorry but Freya has had to go and pick up Delima. She won't be long. Jack's out with the lads planning Andrzej's blackening.'

'I'll come back later when Freya is here and you are not,' said Kate coldly.

'Kate, please. We need to talk.'

'I honestly have nothing to say to you, Evie.'

'I know you are angry about what I told you, but both you and Edwyn mean so much to me.'

Kate, snorted. 'You mean, Edwyn really means so much to you.'

Evie frowned. 'What? I don't understand. The three of us were really good friends.'

'Really, Evie? Don't act so naïve. You know he's in love with you.'

'What on earth are you talking about?' said Evie. She was so shocked she let out a laugh. 'I'm sorry, but . . .'

'You think it's funny? That my family is falling apart?'

Evie's face dropped. 'What on earth do you mean?'

Kate sighed. 'He's clearly been in love with you since you were teenagers. I don't know, you might feel the same. Maybe you've been making all sorts of plans behind my back.'

Kate's eyes glimmered with tears. Evie realised that her friend wasn't thinking straight.

'I haven't seen him since I came to visit you. Kate, please sit down and listen to me. Are you seriously going to throw your marriage away and put those two wonderful little girls through hell? And for what? Some daft idea you've had since you were a teenager that Edwyn is in love with me. It's crazy. You must be breaking his heart.'

'You really haven't seen him,' said Kate, looking doubtful.

'I've been with Freya planning the wedding or at the cottage with Sophia. I'd love to show you how we are getting on there. I want us to get back to normal.'

'Normal! That's rich coming from you. The day you left normal went out of the window. We all had to cope with the chaos you left behind.' Kate went on, 'You know what, I knew that as long as you stayed away, I would have Edwyn to myself and, once the girls came along, I knew he wouldn't leave me, but I dreaded you coming back.' She gave a hollow laugh, 'The daft thing is that I also missed you – how screwed up is that?'

'Kate. Please, this is really important,' pleaded Evie. 'Edwyn doesn't love me. He never did. It was always you. He just didn't know how to tell you at first and I bet he's still the same. You know how buttoned-up he is when it comes to talking about his feelings.'

Evie searched her memory. 'Remember at his granny's funeral he never shed a tear, but you told me when everyone left the house after the wake, you found him in the cupboard under the stairs sobbing his heart out.'

Evie sensed Kate was softening a bit and continued hurriedly. 'Remember when you broke your arm, and he wouldn't leave your side. He was beside himself with worry, but he couldn't tell you, but he gave you his favourite Action Man. For Christ's sake, he had to take the day off school when his hamster died. He told everyone he had food poisoning, but we both knew better.'

Kate gave a grudging smile. 'Of course I remember the hamster. God, he's such an idiot.'

Evie swallowed hard.

'Kate. You have no idea how much I envy you. You have a husband who loves you, two fantastic kids and so many friends here. You have the kind of rich life that most people can only dream of. Please, please don't throw that away because of an idea you have in your head, that simply isn't true.'

A silence fell between the two women. Evie could sense that Kate was thinking seriously about what she had just been told.

Evie went on desperately, 'Look at me. I have made a total mess of everything. Sophia is my only true friend, and I never told her anything about my life here or why I left. I can tell it's made her look at me in a different light although she's being really kind and trying to understand.'

Finally, Kate looked at Evie properly. 'I'm glad we have talked and you know, that really was a terrible time. I'm so sorry that Brodie died. I have wanted to say that to you for years. I just didn't get the chance.'

Evie felt tears prick at her eyes.

'Thank you.'

'It must have been so hard for you. Losing him.'

Evie nodded. 'It was. It still is, sometimes.'

Kate sighed. 'And here I was all set to blow up my own life. You have given me a lot to think about.'

'Just talk to Edwyn,' said Evie. 'Please don't add the fact I buggered up your marriage and ruined more lives to my long list of sins.'

Kate sighed. 'I know I overreacted that night,' she said. 'But it was the way Edwyn defended you. I have always been worried that I wasn't good enough for him. He's so bright and always getting offers to go south, and I worry about me and the girls holding him back.'

'Kate. Freya told me that your Edwyn is one of the happiest people she knows. OK, he doesn't give the impression of a man riding a unicorn with rainbows shooting out of its arse, but that's not his style. You have made such a good life together. Why would he want to leave what he has here? I'm asking you again: why would you want to throw that away? It doesn't make any sense.'

Kate held up her hands. 'You've made your point, and you are right. I've been an idiot. Not an easy thing to admit, but I have.'

She went on, 'Look, put the kettle on. The two of us haven't talked properly since you got back. You've told us so little of your life in London. Did you ever meet anyone else?'

It was time for Evie to be honest, with herself as much as with Kate.

'I am sort of with someone. He's called Jeremy and we live together.'

'You never mentioned him!' said Kate. 'Come on then, tell me, what's he like? I bet he's a cracker.'

Evie stared at the floor. 'He makes my life a misery,' she said, slowly. 'He's a bully, and he constantly criticises me. For years, I thought that was all I deserved. I should have left him a long time ago.'

Kate was appalled. 'Evie, no one deserves to put up with a man like that. Why have you stayed?'

Evie paused. 'I don't know. I suppose I thought of him as my punishment.'

'Well, you absolutely cannot go back to him, Evie. Promise me you won't. You have a home here. We will talk a lot more about this over several bottles of wine.'

She got up and put on her coat.

'I think I've made a bit of a fool of myself. I need to go home and make things with Edwyn right, don't I?'

Evie nodded. 'Friends?'

'Not yet,' said Kate, 'but we will be.'

42

It was Evie and Jeremy's ninth anniversary and Evie decided to make a real effort. She planned to cook his favourite shepherd's pie followed by jam roly-poly and custard; basic nursery food that made him nostalgic for his school days even though he'd told her he hated every minute.

She'd bought some decent red wine and hired a noisy, gloomy *Batman* movie lasting over three hours, she knew he would love. Jeremy had given her a cheap gaudy bracelet, which brought tears to her eyes, not due to the unexpected gesture, but because it brought back memories of Brodie and the happiest and saddest times of her life.

While she was in the kitchen, he did his usual sneaky trick of checking her phone. As always there were messages from Sophia, whom he loathed. Despite his efforts to wean Evie away from her, she still hung around refusing to budge, to his intense irritation.

He kept scrolling, eyes darting to the kitchen in case Evie caught him out. *Christ, that ghastly fat old woman on a ferry again, and those hideous red-headed children really are gruesome*, he thought as he once again deleted Freya's new photos and all her unread texts.

He sloped off to the pub on his own around six o'clock after spending the afternoon watching golf and told Evie he would be back soon after a couple of 'sharpeners'.

By nine o'clock, he still wasn't back. The pie was burnt, the roly-poly was like rubber and the custard had skin as thick as Boris Johnson's. She knew he would come rolling in drunk as a skunk and couldn't face his belligerence.

At eleven o'clock, she heard his key rattling in the lock. He staggered in, banging into the walls and demanding to be fed. 'Don't start with your nagging. I got talking to some chaps in the pub. I'm starving. Where's my dinner?'

She looked at him with a mixture of apprehension and disgust. 'You're too late. Your dinner is ruined and it's in the bin. I'm going to bed. You can sleep in the spare room.'

He snarled back at her. 'Who the fuck do you think you are talking to? You're supposed to have my meal ready when I want it. Not that your cooking is ever any fucking good. You are hopeless at everything, do you know that?'

Evie would normally never answer him back. She had realised early on it wasn't worth it and would just result in a tirade of abuse and a toxic atmosphere that could last for days. But this night, she had had enough. She was sick of being bullied and badgered.

So, she stood her ground. 'Shut up. Just shut up and leave me alone. You are completely pissed and I am not prepared to put up with your shitty behaviour any more.'

He went purple with rage.

'You useless bitch. You've got a fucking cheek. How dare you talk to me like that? You should be down on your knees thanking me for putting up with you.' He lifted his hand, and, for one terrifying moment, Evie thought he was going to hit her.

She ran into the bathroom, locked the door and slumped down onto the cold floor wondering how her life had come to this. In the flick of a switch Jeremy turned from an enraged drunk to a maudlin mess.

She could hear him outside the bathroom door slurring pleas of forgiveness. 'Evie. Please come out. I shouldn't have said that to you. I'm sorry. You know I love you really.'

He went on whining apologies until she tentatively opened the door and found him sitting in the hallway with his head in his hands, rocking backwards and forwards and blubbering like a child. He crawled over to her and wrapped his arms around her legs like a toddler after a tantrum. He kept wailing that he was sorry and didn't know why he said such terrible things.

'Please don't leave me. I couldn't live without you, Evie.' Against all her instincts Evie still felt sorry for him. It happened all the time. He'd behave appallingly and then blame it on booze or stress at work. He'd tell her he was sorry, and it would never happen again. But it always did.

She realised with a sinking heart she had nowhere to go. She was sending a chunk of her wages and savings to Liv, she paid all the bills as well as their food and drink. She felt that was only fair as he was taking care of the mortgage.

Wearily she told him to stop crying and go to bed and they would talk in the morning. He staggered off to the spare room, while she lay awake most of the night trying to work out what to do next. For the first time, she had felt really frightened that Jeremy would physically hurt her.

She knew she couldn't go on like this. She had always been too embarrassed and ashamed to tell Sophia what life was like with Jeremy, but now realised she needed her help.

On Sunday morning she was up early and could hear Jeremy snoring in the next room. She couldn't bear the thought of him waking up and making the usual snivelling apologies and tearful promises he would inevitably break.

She headed out for an early breakfast at the local café and called Sophia. 'Hello, it's Evie, I haven't woken you up, have I?' she began apologetically.

'That's OK. For once I'm not nursing a Sunday-morning hangover. I was on a very boring date last night and home tucked up in bed by eleven, all on my own. What's up?'

'Can I come and see you. I need your help.' Evie could hear her voice wobble.

Sophia cut across her. 'Get in a cab and get over here right now. I'm putting on a pot of strong coffee.'

Sophia listened quietly as Evie told her about Jeremy. Even now she still made excuses that he was under pressure at work and that caused him to drink too much, but Sophia was having none of it.

'Just tell me the facts, Evie, and stop blaming yourself. I knew there was something not right about that guy. He's a coward and a creep and you are far too good for him. You do know that you need to leave him?'

Evie lowered her gaze and nodded.

Sophia went on firmly, 'Good. You need to draw the line. No more of this. Go back and get your things and come and stay with me for as long as you like. Do you want me to come with you?'

'No. I don't want another scene. Can I go back in the morning when he's at work and then I won't have to see him?'

'Evie. You don't need to ask my permission. You can make your own decisions. If that's what you want to do, then that's fine.'

'OK. I will call work and say I am sick. I never do that so hopefully they won't mind and then I will head over to his flat to pick up my stuff.'

'Another thing, Evie, you really must look for another job. I know the money is good, but you are miserable there and they walk all over you.'

The next day, letting herself into the cold, soulless flat, Evie headed into the bedroom, hastily grabbed her clothes and toiletries and shoved them in a bag. There wasn't all that much to show for the past five years. She heard a noise in the living room and froze. It was Jeremy, bleary-eyed and obviously fallen asleep drunk on the sofa.

'What the fuck are you doing here?' he yelled. 'You should be at work, and where the hell were you last night?'

He saw the bag full of her belongings and instantly knew she planned to leave him.

'Oh, no, you don't. You're going nowhere. You know you can't stay away from me, Evie.'

She tried to remain strong, to show she wasn't scared of him. 'I'm going, Jeremy. I'm not taking any more crap from you,' but her voice was trembling.

He looked her up and down and started to laugh. 'Do you honestly think any other man would put up with you? You are scrawny and ugly, and you are crap in bed. It's like shagging a corpse. You are pathetic.'

Emboldened by her talk with Sophia, Evie snapped back, 'I'm pathetic? You're the one smelling like a brewery in your stained Y-fronts at eleven o'clock on a Monday morning. Why aren't YOU at your work, or have they found you out and given you the boot?'

He flinched and Evie realised that she had hit on the truth. For weeks, he had been coming home early and moaning more than usual about the cost of everything. She had suspected something was up.

'Oh my God. You've been kicked out of the firm. Why didn't you say anything? Where have you been going when you were supposed to be at work?'

'What are you fucking talking about. Of course I haven't been fired. I've just had my hours cut back a bit. I didn't tell you because it would have given you something else to moan about. I've had to take a temporary pay cut so you can say goodbye to the sports car and this flat.'

Evie shook her head. 'I never wanted any of that, Jeremy. I just wanted someone to love me, but you are incapable of that.'

Evie turned to leave and Jeremy pounced on her, grabbing her handbag and scattering the contents all over the floor.

He shouted at her, spitting with fury, 'I say when you can leave. Pick all that shit up and put your things back.'

Evie calmly put her stuff back in her bag and headed for the door again.

'You know you can't leave me. I won't let you.' He raged.

Evie didn't say a word. She just walked away ignoring Jeremy's angry rants, knowing full well that in a few minutes he would start tearfully whining and begging her to stay. She went out the door and didn't look back.

It was only when she returned to Sophia's she realised her phone was missing. It must have fallen out of her bag when Jeremy grabbed it. It would still be at the flat, but she couldn't face going back.

Sophia asked, 'Have you still got your keys? Give them to me and I will go and get your phone right now.'

'No, it's fine. You don't need to do that. Let's leave it for couple of days for him to cool down. I will be fine. No one calls me apart from you anyway.'

Sophia was baffled.

'You can't be without your phone, Evie. How will you function?'

'I can manage just fine. Honest. It's no big deal.'

Evie told her that Jeremy had been in the flat instead of at work, and claimed it was because his hours had been cut, but Sophia didn't believe a word of it.

A couple of days later she got her assistant, Stuart, to call Jeremy's office pretending to be an old friend of his he'd invited to stay, but mislaid the address.

Stuart was coldly informed that Jeremy had been sacked several weeks ago for gross misconduct. Jeremy was also being kicked out of his rent-free company flat tomorrow, so he had better look for somewhere else to stay.

Sophia was fuming. He'd lied to Evie that he was taking care of the mortgage but had also made her pay all the bills and spend her hard-earned cash keeping him in booze and food.

'That slimy bastard,' she muttered. 'I hope he's in when I go round there to get Evie's phone. I have a lot to get off my chest.'

Sophia let herself into the flat with Evie's keys. There was no sign of Jeremy, but his stuff was still there waiting to be packed up by tomorrow when he would be frogmarched off the premises.

Sophia hunted around for Evie's phone and found it by his bed. The battery was dead.

On her way out, she picked up a pile of letters by the front door. Among the pizza flyers, leaflets from the council and the usual bills, was a letter for Evie with a postmark from Orkney. She left the rest and put this one in her handbag.

Back at her flat she told Evie, 'Well, that wanker has been telling you a pack of lies. He was sacked, and they are kicking him out of the flat. He never owned it, Evie. It belonged to the company and so did the car. He has been leeching off you for years making you pay all of the bills. What an utter asshole. I found this letter under a pile by the door but I'm not sure how long it's been there. I hope it's not important.'

Evie recognised Freya's handwriting right away. She tore it open.

Dearest Evie,

*You need to come home as soon as you receive this. I have been
calling and texting you for over a week, but you never replied.
I can't believe I'm having to write to you instead. I'm sorry
to say your dad is very ill. It's not looking good. I know you
didn't ever want to come back but that doesn't matter now.
You need to get here as soon as possible.*

Please, please come as quick as you can.

Love Freya

'Oh, Sophia. I need to go home right away.' Evie was trembling.
'I have to see my dad. Freya says he is really sick. I don't understand why I didn't get all of Freya's messages on my phone last
week. It doesn't make any sense.'

'I'm so sorry, Evie. Let me find out what I can do to get
you there as quickly as possible.'

The first available flight was early the next morning, from
London to Dundee and then onwards to Kirkwall. Sophia
offered to come with her, but Evie told her that she had done
enough and she needed to do this by herself.

'Well, let me drive you to the airport tomorrow at least,'
said Sophia.

Sophia was worried Evie would find it too difficult to cope
with her dad who was clearly seriously ill, especially after all
the upset with Jeremy.

Although Sophia had no idea what had happened twenty years
ago, she knew her friend was going home to face her demons.

'You must let me know what happens, Evie. Please take
care of yourself, you've been through such a tough time, and
I'm worried about you. Are you absolutely sure I can't come
with you?'

Evie smiled at her friend.

'I will have Freya. She has always had my back and I'm tougher than I look,' she said, hoping it was true. 'You've been brilliant, Sophia. You are such a good friend, and I don't deserve you. Thank you and wish me luck.'

I'm going to need it, she thought.

43

Orkney, 2024

Kate stepped through her front door into a scene of utter bedlam. There was a horrible smell like burned blubber, and broken glass and wilted flowers strewn across the sodden rug. Eric and Ernie were in the corner looking utterly disgusted and Joan Crawford the cat was on top of the bookcase with an expression beyond disdain.

Edwyn was in the middle of it all looking deranged. He had a cut on his forehead, a blackened eye and was wearing just a shirt and boxer shorts.

'Don't go mad. I can explain,' he said hurriedly. 'I was making you paella because it's your favourite and it was bubbling away. I just left the room for a minute to get changed, but then I spilled that aftershave you bought me all down my trousers, so I took them off and then I smelt burning so I rushed down the stairs, but I tripped over Ernie and banged my head on the chair.

'Everything scuttered off the table including the roses I had bought you. That's why it's all wet, and so I went to get the Hoover to clean up the glass in case the dogs stood on it but, by that time, the paella was burning so I had to throw a tea towel over the pan and it caught fire but I managed to put that out and that's when you walked in,' he finished lamely.

Kate had to press her lips together very firmly to stop herself bursting out laughing. She looked at her usually unflappable, calm, logical husband and shook her head.

'I'll never for the life of me be able to work out how you can keep cool in a life-and-death situation, but you're completely defeated by an ordinary stove, a bunch of rescue animals and a Hoover.'

In a small, defeated voice he said, 'I wanted to surprise you. I thought I'd make you a nice dinner and I bought your favourite wine. I opened it and poured two glasses, but it's all ended up on the rug.'

It was too much for Kate. She couldn't keep it in any longer. She put her hands to her mouth and started to make peculiar wailing noises. Edwyn was distraught. He rushed to her side.

'Don't cry, love. I was so terrified I was going to lose you, so I wanted to do something special, and I know it's all my fault for not telling you how much I love you and taking you for granted. Please don't be upset.'

'You utter buffoon. I'm not crying. I'm laughing. It's the funniest thing I've ever seen.' Kate was almost unable to breathe through her guffaws.

She waved him off. 'Go and get cleaned up and put on your comfies. I will sort things out down here. I've a pizza in the freezer and we can sit and eat it in front of the TV like barbarians.'

Briskly and efficiently, Kate got rid of all the broken glass, mopped up the wine, salvaged most of the flowers, threw out the remnants of the dodgy paella and the burnt pan, fed the dogs and the cat who were looking at her as if to say, 'We all know he is useless, but we still think you should keep him.'

Kate agreed. She had been so touched he had gone to all that effort to try to make things up to her. Edwyn came downstairs in his well-worn blue tracksuit. The cut on his head was just a scratch but he would have a cracking purplish bruised eye in the morning.

'That's some keeker you've got there. Let me have a look.'

He sat down and she looked more closely at the cut, fussing over it with some antiseptic cream. She noticed his hair was thinning on top and felt a rush of love for him that was most unlike her.

It struck her forcibly that all she wanted was to grow old with Edwyn. It had always been him and it always would be. She gave him a hug and a kiss and mussed up his hair.

'God knows why, but I do love you even though you are a complete eejit.'

He looked impossibly grateful. She went on, 'I've had a heart-to-heart with Evie and I realise I got it all wrong, but you have to take some of the blame for not talking to me.'

He took her hand and spoke from his heart.

'I know and I'm sorry. We aren't very good at the soppy stuff but that doesn't mean I don't love you very much. You should have told me you thought Evie was some kind of threat. She never was, Kate. You need to believe me.'

'I do,' she said, and they looked into each other's eyes for a moment, the silent, loving, trusting gaze saying more than their words ever could.

'Right, I'm putting that pizza in the oven,' said Kate. 'And let's make the most of the girls being away. There's just time for a quickie. What do you say?'

He didn't have to be asked twice and chased his laughing wife up the stairs to their bedroom. Later on, as they munched on pizza on their comfy old sofa in front of the TV, Kate turned towards Edwyn and asked, 'What was it you were saying about Evie's story? That you didn't think something was right with it?'

'This isn't the time for thinking about Evie,' murmured Edwyn. 'It was just a hunch. And there's other things I'd rather focus on right now.'

He leant over and gave her a kiss. They both tasted of tomatoes and garlic, and it was clear the old sofa was going to get a bit of a battering.

At work the next day, a much happier and mightily relieved Edwyn was joking with the nurses who were making fun of his keeker. His poor eye was like a rotten piece of fruit.

'You ought to see the other guy,' he told them. They laughed and sent him off on his rounds.

His first patient was a difficult one and needed all of Edwyn's kind bedside manner. A young woman who had suffered an ectopic pregnancy had been kept in overnight, as she'd suffered heavy bleeding. She and her partner were distraught, but Edwyn did his very best to reassure them.

The girl, who was only twenty-two and looking forward to her first baby, was convinced it was somehow all her fault. Edwyn sat down and told her gently, 'You didn't do anything wrong, Lizzie. Sometimes these things happen. It's desperately sad and I am so sorry you had to go through it. I'm just glad that Peter brought you in so quickly. He did the right thing, and you are going to be just fine.'

The poor young man looked shattered. 'I honestly thought I was going to lose her, Doctor. She was in such a lot of pain. Thank you for everything.'

'You are very welcome. We will just get the paperwork done and you can take her home. I know you might not want to think about it now, but you can try again when you are ready, and I'm here if you have any questions. Just take care of each other.'

After he'd written up the case notes, he began thinking again about Liv, who had also lost her baby and suffered such heavy bleeding she'd had to undergo a hysterectomy, leaving her unable to have children. It was a tragedy that had destroyed so many lives, and the aftershocks were still being felt.

What a terrible thing for Liv that she never got to be a mother, he thought. *Maybe it would have changed her whole life.*

He remembered back to all the times he'd seen her getting in and out of trouble, sometimes sober for a while, most times not. He could picture her so clearly, stumbling into the pharmacy when he'd worked there, demanding her medication.

He frowned. Something didn't add up. That unsettled feeling he'd had when he'd first heard Evie's sad confession was coming back. Edwyn stood stock still right in the middle of the busy ward, as his memories came back to him. Quickly, he turned around and marched back to the office. He had to find out the truth.

44

Orkney, 2024

The phone rang in Evie's house at six o'clock just as she was thinking about what to have for her tea. She loved to cook in her bright shiny new kitchen and try out different recipes. What a change from takeaways and reheated microwave meals in London. Already that felt like a long time ago in another life.

'Evie? It's Edwyn. I need to see you urgently. Will you be at home for the next hour?'

'Of course, but you sound upset. Is everything all right?'

'It will be, I hope so anyway. Do you mind if I come over soon?'

'Of course not. Do you need your tea?'

'No, that's OK, thanks, but we might both need a stiff drink afterwards.'

Edwyn got out of his car, which he'd parked outside Liv's rundown house. He was furious with Liv but knew he had to keep his temper in check if he was going to persuade her to come with him to see Evie.

The door was open, and he walked into a wall of stale smoke. He yelled into the gloom, 'Liv. I know you are in there. I need you to come with me to see Evie. We need to talk about what happened to you that night she left.'

He heard a toilet flush and Liv appeared in the hall. 'So, she really told you what she did to me. She actually told you everything?'

He nodded and gave what he hoped was a sympathetic smile. Then he lied through his teeth. 'Evie is willing to keep paying for your silence, but she wants to see you right now. I can assure you it will be worth your while.'

Liv looked at him through heavy-lidded eyes. 'It had better be. I don't want to spend any fucking time with her at all, especially in the house she stole from me.'

On the journey, they sat in silence. Liv lit up a cigarette, Edwyn pointedly opened the window, but she refused to take the hint. As they approached the house, Liv's jaw tightened.

The last time she had been here was to strip it bare of anything worth selling. Now the outside was transformed. It was clean and bright; the garden was neat and tidy, and it looked as through someone had poured love into every nook and cranny.

As they both went inside, Liv was filled with fury and jealousy to see the freshly painted walls, polished floors and glowing wooden furniture. This should have all been hers, but as usual she was overlooked in favour of her despised younger sister. Evie came into the hallway looking shocked to see Liv.

'What's going on, Edwyn?' The atmosphere was thick with guilt and mistrust.

'Let's go into the living room. We need to straighten out a few things and you both need to listen to me very carefully, especially you, Liv, because this is not going to be easy to hear.'

'What the fuck do you mean?' said Liv. 'What exactly is this all about? When am I getting my money?'

'Just sit down and be quiet. I had to get you here and the promise of cash always works. If you say another word, you won't see another single penny, I promise you that.'

Liv was so taken aback at the usually gentle Edwyn fiercely giving orders, she obeyed and slumped on Evie's couch.

Then he turned to Evie. 'I knew something was wrong when Kate let me know everything you told her, but your version of what happened just didn't add up.'

'What do you mean? I told her and Freya and Sophia everything. Honestly, I swear I did.'

Edwyn turned to Liv.

'I'm giving you a chance to come clean and tell the truth.'

Liv glared at him, her eyes glittering. 'The truth about how she wrecked my life. Stole my future away from me? Left me with a whole load of shit to deal with while she ran away?'

Edwyn raised his hand. 'Enough.'

Evie's heart was pounding. 'What's going on? Please. Tell me. I need to know.'

Edwyn turned to her.

'You most certainly do. Both of you need to hear me out.' He continued, 'After you went away and when I was at university, I worked in the local pharmacy during the holidays. I mostly stacked shelves and dished out repeat prescriptions and I remembered Liv coming in and demanding hers, and that's what has been nagging away at me.' He paused. 'Evie, her prescription was for contraception. Liv was on the pill.'

'I don't understand,' said Evie.

'No, it doesn't make any sense does it,' he replied grimly. 'Why would Liv be taking contraception if she'd had to have an emergency hysterectomy and couldn't possibly get pregnant?'

He looked at Liv. It was dawning on her that she was in deep trouble. Her eyes were desperately darting all over the place looking for an escape.

'I did a bit of digging because I had to find out the truth. I looked at Liv's records and discovered the night she came into the hospital, she'd been kept in overnight for observation after claiming she had hurt her head. In fact, it turned out she had suffered little more than bruising. There was no mention of a miscarriage or a pregnancy, let alone a hysterectomy, in her notes.'

Evie was dumbstruck.

'To make doubly sure, I also spoke to a retired nurse who was on duty that night and remembers you vividly, Liv. She said you screamed at everyone not to let your parents in and demanded they be sent away and told nothing about your condition.'

Liv opened her mouth to speak.

'I thought I told you to keep quiet,' said Edwyn. 'I'm not finished. Liv got a taxi to take her back home the next afternoon, and that allowed her to keep up the pretence she had been through a major operation. Duncan would have had no idea that anyone having a hysterectomy would have to spend several days in hospital and didn't question her story, and Cara wouldn't have been thinking straight, even back then.'

He glared at Liv. 'I think that's how you were able to keep this disgusting lie going.'

He relentlessly continued, 'They felt sorry for you, didn't they, Liv? And for all those years they were so grateful that you kept Evie's deep, dark secret. There was no one to put them right because they didn't tell anyone else what had happened. They thought they were protecting Evie.'

Liv was raging, but also scared stiff. How had Edwyn, who she dismissed as a pathetic clown, worked it all out? Of course, he was right. It was a giant lie that had spun out of control.

She'd meant to destroy Brodie and Evie's perfect relationship by telling her they had slept together, but then had taken it further by faking a pregnancy. But then Brodie had drowned, and she'd had no choice but to keep on lying.

The only way out had been to fake a miscarriage, and by doing so, she'd got rid of Evie, and, God, that had felt good, especially as she'd had all of her parents' attention and sympathy for once.

She had stayed in her room pretending to suffer, asking for tea and whisky and crying crocodile tears about her supposed lost baby, wailing that her sister had ruined her life.

She had kept up the act for weeks until she'd got bored and realised Evie was never coming back. It was mission accomplished and Liv had quickly gone back to her old ways, but this time Cara and Duncan had felt they had to indulge her because she had been through such a terrible ordeal.

Liv drank because she was depressed. Liv took drugs to dull the pain of never being able to be a mother. Liv stole because she was traumatised.

Edwyn glared at her. 'Let's be honest, your parents wouldn't have dreamt you would be lying to them. Who would do such a despicable thing? But the truth is, there never was a baby. You lied about that, and you lied about the hysterectomy, and you have been lying every single day of your life ever since.'

Evie had gone milk-bottle white. She whispered, 'Is this true, Liv? Did you really lie to me and to our mum and dad, and to poor Brodie? Why would you do that? Have you any idea of the pain you have caused?'

Evie couldn't take this all in. For the past twenty years she had been living with the crushing guilt that she had been responsible for the death of Brodie and that she had killed Liv's baby. She'd thought she was the one who had torn her family apart and made her parents suffer so badly.

'It was all a lie. It wasn't my fault. I could have stayed here even after Brodie drowned. I could have tried to rebuild my life somehow.' She looked at Liv in utter bewilderment. 'Tell me. Is it true?'

Liv refused to look at her sister. 'I don't need to stay here and listen to this utter bollocks. You've got no proof.'

Edwyn sighed in exasperation. 'Were you not listening to me, Liv? I've seen your medical records. There's no mention of a pregnancy, a miscarriage or a hysterectomy.'

Liv knew the game was up but refused to back down.

'You are full of shit, and I hope she has suffered every single day for the past twenty years.'

Evie found her voice. 'Oh, I suffered all right. I was in a dead-end job I hated. My boyfriend made my life hell and I always felt so guilty because I thought I had ruined your life, and now I discover you made it all up. And I can't believe you lied to Brodie.'

For the first time Liv looked genuinely upset and guilt-ridden.

'I never meant for him to die. I never wanted that. He was a lovely lad, and he didn't deserve for that to happen.' For once she was telling the truth. 'Why do you think I take so many drugs and drink myself into oblivion? It's because I can't cope with the guilt over his death, but it's not all my fault. I am not taking all the blame.'

She pointed a shaking finger at Evie. 'You are the one who caused this and I'm glad you've had a shit life, because you destroyed mine. From the day you came into the world I was ignored. It was always all about you. They all even thought I'd tried to drown you when we were kids, when I was trying to save you, but no one believed me.' She looked at both of them defiantly.

'So, yes, I lied. I did it for revenge and because I could. And I got away with it. The old man died a drunk before you could have a tearful bedside reunion and ask for his forgiveness, and our dear mother is nothing more than a vegetable. So, I've won. Fuck you.'

Edwyn was disgusted. 'No, you haven't won anything. You need help, Liv, but I fear it's too late.'

He turned to Evie. 'I really think we should go to the police. Your sister has been blackmailing you for years. That's a crime.'

Liv looked unnerved and scared at the mention of the police. 'We can go now,' said Edwyn. 'Get this sorted.'

Evie held up her hand. 'Just give me a moment. Please.'

She looked at her sister and instead of a monster she saw a sad, pathetic wraith. Someone who was so consumed with jealousy she had destroyed any chance of her own happiness.

'No, I won't do that,' said Evie wearily but firmly.

Liv looked at her uncertainly, and then stared at the floor. Edwyn looked appalled. 'You can't let her get away with this.'

Evie replied, 'She's been punished enough. Look at her. She's a wreck. Despite everything you've told me tonight, I still feel sorry for her.'

She looked at her sister sadly. 'And if I do end up staying here, we are bound to run into each other at some point. We can try to stay out of each other's way. Is that what you want, Liv?'

Liv didn't answer. She just nodded tersely. She looked broken and defeated. All of her bravado and bluster had oozed away as she turned her back on them and slunk out the door of her childhood home.

There was a moment's silence before Evie said urgently, 'Edwyn, it's cold outside. She's not got a coat on, and how's she going to get back to Stromness?' He rolled his eyes.

'Oh, for the love of God, Evie. You can't be serious.'

'I am. She's my sister when all is said and done, and I don't want to see her stranded or having to walk into Kirkwall or get the bus.'

He looked at her in resignation. 'I suppose you're right. OK, I will give her a lift back if she doesn't tell me to take a running jump to myself. Will you be all right on your own?'

'I think so. I'm sure I will. It's a lot to take in though, and I haven't even thanked you properly.'

'No need. That's what friends are for. Call me if you need anything but I will see you tomorrow.'

She gave him a hug. 'You are a good, kind man, Edwyn. I'm so glad you are still my friend. You're like the big brother I never had.'

'Och, away with you, Evie Muir. Right, I better try and catch that piece of work, although with a bit of luck she might have flown back home on her broomstick.'

After he had gone, Evie sat down and wrapped herself in a blanket. She lit a candle and stared at the flame, trying to process it all. So, Liv hadn't been pregnant with Brodie's child, and Evie hadn't been responsible for her miscarrying. She sighed. It was desperately sad. She had spent so many nights lying awake feeling guilty and thinking how things could have been different. If she had been able to swim and brave enough to go into the sea, maybe she could have saved Brodie.

But, if Liv hadn't lied in the first place, she wouldn't have been angry with him and thrown her precious bracelet into the sea, and Brodie wouldn't have gone in after it.

'Enough,' she murmured to herself. 'Enough now. I can't dwell on this any more.'

Picking over the past would do no good. It wouldn't bring Brodie back. It was time to look to the future, whatever that might hold.

The next evening Evie, Edwyn, Kate and Sophia gathered at Freya's house. Sophia and Freya had no idea what was coming. Evie had thought long and hard about what she was going to do and wanted to get this over as quickly as possible.

'Thanks for coming,' she said. 'Firstly, I want to make it clear that what I tell you stays within these four walls.' She looked around at her friends, each of whom nodded slowly.

'I'm telling you this not because I want to be vindicated or because I think I am blameless. What happened in the past is complicated. I want you to know the truth because I think you have all been affected too. I know you've wondered if there was more you could have done to help me and my mum, and especially my dad. I hope what I say puts your minds at rest.'

Evie took a deep breath and explained what Edwyn had found out. The fact there was no baby. No miscarriage. No hysterectomy. By the end of her story, Freya was lost for words, an event that no one could recall ever happening before.

Sophia was the first one to make a move. She gave Evie a hug and asked if she was sure Liv deserved to get away with her lies and blackmail.

'Honestly, I just want to put it behind me and concentrate on the future,' said Evie. 'Liv punishes herself every day with her self-destructive behaviour. I've no wish to add to that. And this secret goes no further. I don't want Edwyn getting into trouble about patient confidentiality.'

Freya looked at Evie with concern. She obviously had passed a sleepless night and looked completely exhausted. 'You are right about Liv. She has to live with what she has done. That's maybe punishment enough, but are you sure you are OK, Evie? This is such a lot to take in. It has really knocked us all sideways.'

'I don't think it's sunk in properly. To think she really was lying about everything.' Evie's voice broke. 'And I didn't kill her baby. Do you know I often thought about what Liv and Brodie's baby would have looked like and, in reality, there never was a child in the first place.'

Freya took Evie's hand. 'At least we know the truth now.' She got up on her feet. 'I don't know about you lot, but I need a stiff drink.' She poured them all a generous dram, which they downed in one.

Freya declared, 'Can we hear it for Orkney's very own Inspector Rebus?' They all cheered as Edwyn turned bright pink.

Evie smiled, but she could feel her chest growing tight, and her breathing was becoming more difficult. 'Could you get my inhaler, please, Kate?' she said wheezily. Kate ran to fetch it from Evie's bag. After using it, Evie calmly waited for the attack to die down. She'd had so many emotional batterings since arriving in Orkney it was no surprise her body had reacted with another attack.

'I'm OK.' She smiled at them. 'Just all the drama and upset.'

'You sure?' said Edwyn, who had been watching her with concern. She nodded.

'Any more attacks, call me straightaway. We should leave you now in Freya's capable hands and get some rest. That's doctor's orders.' He got up to leave and then stopped abruptly. 'I'm so sorry. There's something I needed to give you; I completely forgot. It's actually from Liv.'

'From LIV?' said Evie, looking confused and apprehensive.

'She gave it to me after I dropped her off last night. It was a pretty awkward journey. She barely said a word, but she was in tears when she got out the car. She told me to wait and then she gave me this for you and said you might want to keep it. She said it fell from your father's top pocket the last time she saw him.'

He placed an old inhaler in Evie's hands. Sophia said, 'Did your dad have asthma too, Evie?'

'No, he didn't.'

She looked closely at the inhaler and exclaimed. 'This is mine. Look. It's faded, but it has my name on it and the year is when I left home. My dad must have kept it all this time waiting for me to come back.' Everyone felt themselves choking up.

Only Evie was clear-eyed. 'Liv must have known how much this would mean to me. My dad really did love me. I have to hold on to that, don't I?'

Freya nodded. 'That you do. Love lasts, Evie. It endures and it's passed down. It's how we live on in the hearts of the people who remember us.'

45

Orkney, 2024

Evie awoke at Freya's the next morning feeling lighter than she had in years. It was as though a heavy, dark shroud had been lifted from her head and a leaden weight from her heart.

She still couldn't understand why Liv had told such vicious lies and was angry with herself for being so easily manipulated into leaving Orkney.

She felt renewed regret and sadness about Brodie and what might have been. It was so long ago now that she could barely remember what his voice sounded like, although she would never forget his face. She gave herself a shake. This was her chance to start afresh. She could begin to make proper plans for the future. For years now she had been just drifting, lost and aimless. That was all going to change.

She heard off-key singing in the kitchen and smelt fresh coffee. Freya was up and making breakfast. Evie threw on one of Freya's fabulous silk dressing gowns and called out, 'Good morning.'

Freya beamed at her and gave her a hug. 'How are you feeling? Did you sleep well?'

'Do you know what, I actually did. I don't think I realised the weight of guilt and unhappiness I've been carrying for all these years. I feel a bit like I'm floating.'

Freya was making French toast. Evie used to love it when she was a girl and she thought comfort food was a good idea this morning. She said, 'I can't believe Liv told those whopping lies. It beggars belief.'

Evie poured herself a cup of coffee. She said thoughtfully, 'I know. She's my sister, but she's always been a stranger. It would all have been so different if we had been closer. I'm finding it hard not to look back and wonder what might have been.'

'Well, we can all torture ourselves doing that, my love, but you have to look forward now. I know it's a bit soon, but have you made any plans?'

'I have been doing a lot of thinking—'

'Freya, Freya, are you in? I really need your help.' It was Maureen looking flustered and wild-eyed.

'Come away in. What on earth has happened to get you into such a state? Sit down and take a deep breath. Evie will bring you a cup of tea and you can tell us all about it.'

Maureen sat down but was so agitated she stood back up again. 'Oh, Freya, I have had a call from the hospital and I've a date for the start of my treatment.'

'Well, that's good news, isn't it?' said Freya encouragingly.

'NO. It isn't. You don't understand. It's in just three weeks. That's going to completely scupper our wedding plans. I hoped we would have been able to get married before the chemo started, but I didn't realise it would be so soon. We will have to put it off.'

On the verge of tears Maureen added, 'I don't know how hard it's all going to hit me. I don't want to be feeling sick and be throwing up on my big day, and what if all my hair falls out? I know I'm being ridiculous, but I wanted to look and feel my best for Andrzej. Am I being really pathetic?'

She looked so forlorn that Freya knew she had to reassure her.

'Absolutely not. It's perfectly natural to feel like that. Obviously, you can't postpone your treatment, but you can still get married afterwards. Can't she, Evie?'

Evie nodded and handed Maureen a mug of hot sweet tea. 'Course you can. What does Andrzej think?'

Maureen managed a watery smile. 'Well, he says he doesn't care if it has to be postponed, and he said I would be a beautiful bride even if I look like a boiled egg.'

Maureen started to cry, and Freya made her mind up.

'Here's an idea. Why don't we just bring everything forward and you get married in a couple of weeks and then you start your treatment?'

Maureen looked at them both with hope in her eyes. 'Do you really think that could be possible? But I haven't sorted anything. I haven't even chosen what I am going to wear yet.'

Freya wasn't completely sure that it was doable, but with great confidence she declared, 'Well, of course it is, and we can organise it all for you, can't we, Evie?'

Evie nodded again, although she thought even Freya might be out of her depth putting together a wedding in less than a fortnight.

Maureen dried her eyes. 'I couldn't possibly ask you to sort out my wedding, Freya.'

'You haven't asked me. I am insisting. Leave it to me. Everyone will help and I promise you and Andrzej will have a day to remember. It will be our present to you both. Right, finish up your tea and this is what I want you to do. Go home and make me a wish list of what you want, and we will do our best to make it all come true. Then I want you to rest up and pamper yourself. Your only job from now on is to prepare to be a glorious bride.'

'Oh, Freya. I don't know how to thank you. I was in a right tizzy. Are you sure?'

'Absolutely. I will get on it right away. Don't you worry about a thing.'

When Maureen left and was safely out of earshot, Evie looked at Freya and said doubtfully, 'Can we actually do this?'

'If we all work together, I think we can,' said Freya determinedly. 'I mean, we can't possibly let Maureen and Andrzej down, but I'm going to need your help, and we need to round up the selkies. Are you up for it?'

'I'd be honoured.' Evie had become very fond of Maureen and Andrzej and was delighted to have the chance to help them, and to feel part of the community again.

Freya was all full of bustling business. 'We really need to push the boat out. I want banners and balloons and doves. We must release doves. Oh, and maybe owls to carry their wedding rings.'

Evie had a feeling she would have to rein in Freya, so she said gently, 'But we need to make sure that's what Maureen would want. It's her big day after all.'

'Yes, of course', said Freya. 'I know I'm getting carried away, but I really want everything to be perfect. I know it sounds silly, but I feel that if we make this wedding a big success then it means they will have a long and happy future together. It's just that she's so ill and we don't know what going to happen . . .' Freya's voice broke, and she couldn't carry on.

'Right,' said Evie briskly. 'Rule number one when planning this wedding. No tears. Unless they are happy tears. Rule number two. No sadness. It's simply not allowed. We focus on making this a joyful day for Maureen and Andrzej.'

Freya smiled at Evie. 'You are quite right. Thank you, love. Let's get down to work.'

A few hours later they had made good progress. Every call for help had been enthusiastically received and everyone was delighted to muck in. Kate had volunteered to make the cake. Maureen wanted a simple plain sponge and white icing, but Kate vowed to go to town on the decoration. Patsy, who worked with Andrzej, was in charge of cars for the wedding party and Agnes was doing Maureen's hair and make-up.

Delima had some beautiful raw silk material she'd brought over from Singapore she knew Maureen admired and was using it to make the bride's outfit. Delima was also in charge of flowers and ordering white roses and white freesias with little blue thistles for the bouquet, as well as button holes and corsages, and special baskets of rose petals for Kate's daughters who were to be flower girls.

Delima had come up with some good ideas for floral arrangements for the venue, but that was the one thing that was providing Freya and Evie with a headache. Hiring a suitable place for a wedding happening in a fortnight was proving impossibly difficult.

Freya refused to get stressed about it. She looked at Evie over the kitchen table buried in lists and notes and half-empty cups of coffee.

'We just need to think outside the box. It will come to us. Let's have another coffee and a cake then come back to it. I've got feelers out all over the place, but we also need to discuss our weddings outfits. I will definitely need something new.'

Evie agreed. 'Me too. I desperately need to get myself some decent clothes, and I want to buy some really silly shoes, even if they turn out to be too painful to walk in.'

Freya clapped her hands. 'Praise the Lord. That really is good news. I didn't want to say anything to you about your dress sense but now I feel I can.' She took a deep breath. 'No offence, Evie, but your clothes are the absolute worst. They aspire to be frumpy. I didn't know there were so many varieties of sludgy beige in the world.'

'None taken, Sophia has been saying the same for years.'

'Well, it's about time you listened to both of us. Also, might I suggest a trip to the hairdressers in Kirkwall for a good cut and maybe a few highlights.'

Freya went on happily, 'I always feel a hundred times better when I get my hair done at Agnes's. I don't care if it sounds trivial – when your hair is right you feel much more confident, and you can take on anything. Agnes is a genius and she'll fit you in tomorrow if I give her a call.'

'Well, let me walk before I can run, but a new hairdo sounds perfect, and we all need to look spectacular for Maureen's wedding.'

46

Orkney, 2024

Freya had instructed Sophia to meet Evie in Kirkwall and not to come back until she had an outfit for the wedding and as many new clothes as possible. In the meantime, Freya was going to bundle all of Evie's offending 'griege' clothes into a bin bag for the charity shop.

She'd made a morning appointment with Agnes for Evie to have her hair done in the salon, and, at that moment, Evie was squinting into the mirror trying to see the back of her hair. Agnes had played a blinder. Evie now had shiny golden loose curls with bright highlights. It took years off her.

She was thrilled with the results and felt more like that young girl who had left home so long ago. She could sense her confidence coming back. 'Agnes, thank you. I love it. I can't remember the last time I was in a salon.'

'I could tell,' said Agnes, laughing. 'You have neglected your poor hair for far too long. This one is on the house as a welcome home, but I want to see you every eight weeks from now on for a cut and colour. You need to treat yourself. A peedie manicure wouldn't go amiss either.' Sophia came into the salon and Agnes gave her a nod of approval.

'Now, that's a woman who knows what hairstyle suits her perfectly. It's your pal, Sophia, isn't it? She's gorgeous.'

'Yep,' said Evie, seriously impressed once again with the way people here knew everything about everyone.

Sophia came up to them. 'Wow, Evie. You look fabulous. That style really suits you.'

Evie grinned. 'All thanks to Agnes here. She's one of Freya's selkies.'

'Great to meet you, Agnes. Freya says I must come on your next swim at the weekend. You know she has to be obeyed in all things.'

'That's an understatement. You'd be more than welcome.'

'I look forward to it. Right, Evie. We need to hit the shops. Finally, I'm getting her out of those unflattering elasticated waists. See you later, Agnes.'

The two of them walked up the high street with Evie glancing into shop windows to check out her new hair. She couldn't remember the last time she had looked at herself and didn't feel inadequate. She had become adept at avoiding seeing herself in mirrors. Jeremy told her so often she was plain and ugly that she believed him.

She saw a bright emerald-green cotton summer dress with a sweetheart neckline in the window of Hume Sweet Hume that sang out to her. She shook her head and was about to walk past when Sophia stopped her.

'You'd look great in that, Evie. Let's go in and you can try it on.'

'It's too young for me and it's such a bright green. People will think I'm a right show-off if I wear something like that.'

'Excuse me, but I've got something very similar at home and I don't think I'm too old to wear it,' said Sophia in mock indignation.

'You'd look good in a bin bag. I'm better in more subdued colours.'

'I swear to God, Evie, if you buy one more beige polyester blouse, I'm going to rip it off your back and set fire to it in front of you. Those days are gone.' Sophia smiled at her to take the sting out of what she'd said. 'Look at you. You are a lovely woman with fabulous hair and brilliant boobs. It's about time you realised that. Now get inside and try on that gorgeous dress.'

Evie giggled. 'I must admit I've always wanted to go in and ask for the outfit in the window and walk out of the shop wearing it.'

'So, let's do it,' said Sophia.

The emerald dress could have been made just for Evie. It fitted perfectly and the colour made her skin glow and brought out the green in her eyes. She thought, *I look so different. I look more like me. Jeremy would never have let me wear this. He would have said something cutting and made me feel stupid and worthless.*

Aloud she said, 'Jeremy would hate this dress.'

'Well, Jeremy won't be wearing it. You will, and as you well know Jeremy is an arsehole.'

Sophia was right. She would have to do something about Jeremy. She couldn't keep on ignoring him and hoping he'd go away.

Sophia had found Evie a gorgeous turquoise silk off-the-shoulder dress perfect for the wedding for her to try on, and she teamed it with a sassy little fascinator, and a cheeky pair of silver sandals.

'This is what I would call a good start,' said Sophia as they waited for their purchases to be beautifully wrapped. As she had always dreamt, Evie left the shop wearing the emerald sundress.

Sophia made a note to herself to give her friend's old clothes away to a jumble sale. She said to Evie, 'We are also going online tonight over a bottle of red and buying you more outfits and some decent underwear. I couldn't help but notice in the changing room you are wearing applecatcher knickers and that bra is older than Justin Bieber.'

After visiting just about every shop in Kirkwall and laden with shopping bags, they were sitting having a coffee across from the cathedral when Sophia said, 'Do you think we've got enough time to see the Italian Chapel before we head back? I've been reading up about it after Andrzej told me all about it. Is it too far away though?'

'Not at all. This will be a good time to visit as we will have missed most of the bus tours. I need to make one quick stop on the way for something really important for the house though.'

Evie drove them out of town and followed the sign for Isbister and Sons, makers of Orkney chairs.

'I will only be a minute, I want to treat myself to something really special.'

Evie had one big regret – the beautiful Orkney chair passed down through the generations that had been so smashed and destroyed she'd thought Freya had to throw it away.

She remembered her mum sitting on the chair knitting in front of the kitchen range on the long, dark winter evenings. It was one of the few times she'd seemed happy.

Ross came in from his workshop at the back of the house to greet them. He saw Evie and blushed as red as a fog lamp. 'What are you doing here?' He faltered. 'I'm afraid it's not finished yet but don't tell Freya or I'll be killed.'

'What's not finished?' said Evie, puzzled.

'Nothing. I don't know. I'm not sure. What have you heard?' Ross blustered.

Evie was completely confused by this sweaty, red-faced albeit gloriously handsome man who was stuttering and stammering.

She glanced sideways at Sophia, who looked equally bemused and shrugged.

'It's Ross, isn't it?' Evie said as though talking to a five-year-old. 'I remember you from school. I was just here to see if I could order an Orkney chair from your mum and dad, but it looks like you are the man I need to talk to.'

'Yes, I run the business now and anyway sorry for the confusion. I thought you were here to pick up a thing I was making for Freya that's not quite ready.'

'What thing?'

'Er. It's, well, it's a peedie chair she wants for the cat and it's not quite ready.' Evie was flummoxed. Freya might be eccentric but getting an Orkney chair made especially for Bette Davis the cat seemed over the top, even for her.

'Please don't tell her you were even here,' said a frazzled Ross. 'Or even mention the cat chair to her.'

'Okaaay. Don't worry, Ross, I won't tell her that the cat chair isn't finished yet. But here's my number and let me know when we could talk about you making a chair for a human being to sit in.' Ross completely clammed up, and only nodded.

'Bye then,' said Evie.

He nodded again.

The two girls walked to the car. Evie glanced back to see Ross staring after them. She whispered to Sophia.

'Do you think he's all right? He seemed very confused.'

Sophia smirked as she got in the car, and they set off on the road to the Italian Chapel on Lamb's Holm. 'Evie, he obviously fancies the pants off you.'

'No, he doesn't,' said Evie, giggling. 'My new haircut isn't that fabulous, and it will take more than a new green dress to make me attractive.'

'Come off it! You are looking so much better, Evie,' said Sophia. 'The Orkney air has given you roses in your cheeks and you've lost that frightened look as though you were waiting for someone to be horrible and yell at you.' She winced. 'Oh, God, Evie. I'm so sorry. Me and my big mouth, but you know what I mean. You let Jeremy walk all over you. You are much less tense now. Even your voice has changed; you sound more like Freya. It's as if you are singing again.'

Evie smiled at her friend. 'I don't want to waste today talking any more about Jeremy, I would much rather talk about you. Tell me about Finn. He is totally smitten.'

Sophia needed no encouragement to talk about him. 'Well, after I went to Hoy with him, we've been seeing a lot of each other as you know. To be honest, Evie, I have never felt this way about anyone, but I don't want to show him that I might be falling in love with him because then he will run a mile. I reckon he's one of these men who likes the thrill of the chase and then gets fed up and moves on to the next challenge, or in his case the next woman. I need to keep him on his toes because I don't want him getting complacent. It's a bit of a dance but if it means he wants to stay with me then that's the game I have to play.'

'Sounds exhausting,' said Evie.

Sophia laughed. 'Believe me, it's worth it. I've been staying with him in his cute little flat in Stromness and I thank the Lord the walls are so thick otherwise the neighbours would be mortified.'

Evie laughed. 'So, is this just a fling, or do you see it going somewhere?'

'I'm not really planning anything, Evie. I do need to go back to work on Monday, I've already stayed here much longer than I planned, but I will be back for the wedding obviously, and Finn only has a yearly contract for this project so who knows?

I'm just taking each day as it comes, but the longer I stay here the more I realise how magical it is.'

Evie smiled. 'Well, you wouldn't be saying that in the middle of winter when it's as black as arseholes in the afternoon and the waves are lashing over these barriers and there's nowhere to get your oat milk latte and quinoa salad.'

Sophia laughed. 'Fair point, but I will come back then and find out for myself.'

They'd arrived at the first of the famous Churchill barriers, massive square blocks of concrete that looked as though they'd been hurled by giant ogres to build a solid bridge between the islands.

'Why are there shipwrecks on either side?' asked Sophia.

'Oh, they were scuppered deliberately during the war so German U-boats couldn't sneak up to bomb the British Navy in Scapa Flow. That's why the barriers were built in the first place. As a bonus it meant all the islands in the south are now linked by road. We just take these causeways for granted now. Right, here we are coming up to Lamb's Holm. Can you spot the Chapel?'

'Oh, is that it?' Sophia sounded a bit crushed. 'I'm sorry but it doesn't look much from the outside.'

'Just wait,' said Evie.

Inside the two Nissan tin huts, homesick Italian POWs captured in North Africa and sent to Orkney to help build the barriers, had created a little miracle. Using bits of scrap metal, paint and concrete, these talented men turned two bleak huts into a glorious chapel filled with light and love. The painting above the altar of the Madonna and Child was copied from a tiny prayer card given to one of the POWs by his mother, and the ornate lights hanging down from the painted ceiling were crafted from old tin cans.

Sophia was in complete awe. 'It's a little jewel. I can't believe they made something so beautiful with so little to work with. I'd love to get married somewhere like this. It's so romantic and atmospheric and small enough to be really intimate.'

'Does Finn know you are planning the wedding?' Evie laughed.

Sophia grinned a bit ruefully. 'He'd run screaming for the hills. I'd never dare mention the words bride or marriage to him.'

On the way out, Evie's phone rang. It was an utterly distraught Freya.

'Oh, Evie, despite our best efforts I can't get a venue for the wedding. It's just too last minute. I don't know what we are going to do. We can't let Maureen and Andrzej down.'

Evie glanced around her. 'Freya, don't worry. I think I might just have had an idea.'

47

Orkney, 2024

Evie walked slowly around her house, looking at all the changes she had made. She'd bought a second-hand sofa and chair from a couple in Finstown and new mattresses and bedding in Kirkwall, as well as mugs and crockery when she was with Sophia in town the other day.

Once the furniture was in, she'd given the whole house a thorough dust and made up the bed in her parents' old room, where she would sleep that night for the first time. Delima had insisted on making cheerful curtains for the bedroom, and she still needed to put those up. Freya had brought her essential supplies: milk, bread and butter, tea and coffee, homemade cakes and, of course, bottles of Scapa and Highland Park.

Draped over the sofa was the gorgeous blanket from Maureen, which she'd brought round as promised. She'd said the colours were inspired by the view from Evie's window: the sea, the sand and green grass. Evie absolutely loved it, and it was all the more special because Maureen had made it herself.

She heard the sound of a vehicle pulling up outside and went to the front door where a sweating Ross Isbister was wrestling with an enormous parcel.

'Hello, Evie. I've a special delivery for you.'

He carried it into the kitchen and placed it in front of the newly polished old range. He looked at Evie shyly and said, 'I'm not sure where you want this to go, Evie, but I hope you like it. It's been an honour to put it all back together for you.'

Evie felt her heart racing. It couldn't possibly be what she thought it was. She quickly tore off the wrapping and there was her family's old Orkney chair, beautifully restored and right back where it belonged.

'Ross, is this really our old chair? But it was in a hundred pieces. I can't believe you managed to repair it. It's absolutely perfect.' She gave him a massive hug and started sobbing on his shoulder.

Ross didn't quite know what to do. Feeling baffled, he just patted her back as though she was a puppy with colic.

She broke away and laughed through her tears. 'When I came to see you, you told me you were making a cat chair for Freya. And I was daft enough to believe you.'

Ross raised his eyes to the ceiling.

'It was Freya who arranged for me to fix your chair, but she said I had to keep it secret. God, that was a terrible excuse right enough. It was the only thing I could think of. You must have thought it was a right eejit. I mean, I know she loves her cat and all that but . . .'

'Even for Freya that would be taking it too far,' Evie finished for him. They smiled at each other.

'Aren't you going to sit down on your throne and see if it fits your royal behind, Your Majesty? said Ross with a grin.

Evie sat down with a happy sigh. 'I will be spending a lot of time in this chair, Ross. I might even take up knitting. I honestly don't know how to thank you for bringing it back to its former glory. You've no idea what it means to me. Along with the house, the chair is the strongest link to my past, the good and the bad. I just don't know how to repay you.'

Despite himself, Orkney's shyest and most elusive bachelor found himself mumbling, 'Maybe we could go out for a drink or something, Evie?'

'I'd really like that. Here's my number, give me a call and let me know what suits you, but it's my treat.'

As soon as Ross had left, Evie rang Freya.

'I've just had the best surprise', she burbled. 'Ross has just brought the chair round. You went to all that trouble for me. It's absolutely beautiful – thank you so much.'

'You are welcome. I know how important it was to you. I hope Ross did a good job.'

'He really did. He is so skilled. I'm going to take him for a drink to thank him.'

'Well, don't expect him to turn up. He never goes out with girls, or boys for that matter.'

'But he was the one who asked me,' said Evie.

Freya was flummoxed. 'Are you telling me Ross Isbister actually asked you out? Well, I thought I'd heard it all, but this really is something else, and another thing that struck me, he rarely does home deliveries. I think he's fallen for you in a big way. It must be all this love in the air with the build-up to the wedding. He is a real catch and very good with his hands if you know what I mean.'

'Behave yourself, Freya. That's the last thing on my mind. I'm taking him for a quick drink to say thanks and that's it. There's no other motive.'

'Well, he is very easy on the eye,' said Freya. 'And a peedie bit of a romance might do you the world of good, but he's not the kind to give his heart away lightly and I don't think he would be interested in a mere fling. Just about every girl in Orkney has tried to get off with him, but they've never managed to catch him.'

She went on, 'Be careful with him, Evie. He's a good lad and I wouldn't want him to get hurt. If you aren't interested in anything serious, let him know.'

'I hear you. Don't worry. His heart is safe from me. Besides—'

Freya interrupted her. 'I know what you are going to say. You've got this Jeremy fella in London that you never talk about, and when I ask Sophia about him, she just looks scunnered and won't tell me anything either.'

Evie sighed. 'Can we talk about a proper romance? How are you getting on with booking the Italian Chapel?'

'No news yet,' said Freya. 'I'll keep trying. I'm not prepared to be defeated on this one.'

'If anyone can make it happen you can, Freya. Keep me posted. Talk later.'

After Evie hung up, she went back into the kitchen to gaze on the chair that was so much a part of her history. The gentle granny she'd never met had rocked her dad to sleep in this chair when he was a baby, and her own mother had been at her calmest and most content sitting there knitting. It felt like the final piece of the jigsaw was complete.

This was so much more than just a chair. It was a symbol of hope and healing and coming home. And now it was hers. She sat down and looked out over the view. So much had happened since she had come home.

She began to think of what a new life would look like here at home. She had her pension from work and some savings left over, and now she didn't have the drain of blackmail cash to Liv, and paying Jeremy's bills, she could get by, and she could get a job in one of the bars or hotels to bring in some extra cash. She knew she couldn't go back to her soul-crushing, dead-end job. The very thought made her shudder. She could never be happy working there.

Of course, the dream would be to sell her paintings when she picked up a brush again, but she didn't know if she was still any good or if people would actually be willing to pay money for her work.

Evie's confidence was slowly coming back but she could still hear the distant echo of Jeremy's nasal drone telling her how useless she was. His bullying had corroded her self-esteem for years. Then there was all that needless guilt over Liv and Brodie, but she was getting stronger every day. She was ready to do something she had been putting off since she had arrived here.

Freya mentioning Jeremy had made her think about the texts and messages she had sent about her dad being ill and how Evie had never received them. Jeremy must have deleted them. Her anger spurred her on to finally dial his number. He answered almost immediately, and the sound of his voice made her want to hang up, but she was determined not to allow him to upset her ever again.

He was furious. 'What took you so long to get back to me? Get yourself on the next flight. I won't ask you a second time.'

Evie took a deep breath.

'No, Jeremy,' she whispered.

Jeremy couldn't believe his ears. 'What did you say to me? Who the bloody hell do you think you are talking to? I've had enough of your stupid games. Get your sorry backside down here where you belong. I've found us a new flat. It's not the best area and you will have to pay half the costs, but we can do it together. You know you can't stay away from me.'

'No, Jeremy,' Evie said again, her voice trembling.

'You are utterly pathetic. You know you have no other choice,' said Jeremy, his voice like ice. 'Who else would put up with you or want you?' He then switched instantly to a wheedling tone that turned her stomach. 'You know that no one else cares for you like I do.'

Evie had believed that was true for years, and that Jeremy was all she deserved. But no more. She looked at the house her dad had left her as a way to show he loved her. A home that had been brought back to life with kindness and skill and filled with gifts from friends who really cared about her. She stood up holding onto her precious chair and suddenly her voice was strong.

'Jeremy, listen to me. I am never coming back. I am staying here where I belong. You are an arsehole and a bully. You will never see me again. Now do me a favour and go fuck yourself.'

She hung up on him ranting and raving, gave a broad satisfied grin and happily blocked him from her phone and from her life. She poured herself an enormous dram and sat back down on her chair like a queen.

48

Orkney, 2024

The phone rang, interrupting Freya from her quiet afternoon nap on the sofa. She swore she never actually fell asleep and everyone who popped in and found her gently snoring would tiptoe away without disturbing her slumber. She woke with a start and fumbled for her phone.

'Freya, it's Keira. I got your messages. I'm really sorry but as I feared the Italian Chapel is actually going to be closed on that Saturday you are after. Unavoidable, I'm afraid.'

Freya's heart sank.

'You're joking, Keira.'

'I'm sorry, Freya, but we just can't do it. We needed more notice. And, if we make an exception then we can't refuse anyone else who wants a quick wedding there.'

Freya thought desperately, *But the one thing we may not have, is time.* Aloud she said, 'But, Keira, she's our Maureen. You went to school with her. Are you really going to stop her having a wonderful wedding day because of daft red tape. Anyway, what's so important that it can't be moved to another day?'

'It seems there's actually a wedding going ahead that day I

forgot to mention,' said Keira. 'Between a couple called Andrzej and Maureen. Not sure if you know them?'

'Oh, Keira. You had me going then,' said Freya, not knowing whether to laugh or cry. 'That's amazing news – thank you so much. This will mean the world to them. Well, to all of us.'

'I'm just glad we could sort it. Look, I'll send some of the boys over to make sure the grass is cut and will put flowers around the door. Will white roses be all right do you think?'

'Keira. Pee-the-bed dandelions would be all right, but white roses will be so much better. Perfect, in fact. You are an angel. I will never forget this.'

'Just make sure that lovely lass has the best day. Take lots of photos and remember, I'll be sending all the demands from brides wanting to skip the queue and get married in the chapel directly to you, so you can turn them all down and experience the full force of their Bridezilla wrath.'

Freya hung up the phone and breathed a sigh of relief. It really was going to be all right.

Andrzej had one very important job to do before the wedding. He asked Maureen's young son, Rory, to come sea fishing with him, something the two of them always enjoyed. Rory was a quiet boy who'd inherited his mum's thick dark hair and fine cheekbones. He had a scattering of freckles across a snub nose and seemed older and wiser than his fourteen years. He'd had to grow up fast after his dad died and took his responsibilities as 'man of the house' very seriously.

He hero-worshipped Andrzej who'd taught him to play football, how to steer a boat and the best way to catch and gut a fish. Andrzej always listened with keen interest to Rory's worries about school and rejoiced with him when he came top of the class.

When Andrzej and Maureen had told Rory they were getting married, Andrzej had made it clear he wasn't trying to replace Rory's dad, although he had grown to think of the lad like his own son.

All Rory had said was, 'Me and Granny and Granda have always thought you would end up together. Just don't get too soppy and start kissing and cuddling all the time.'

'We promise,' said Andrzej gravely.

'Nothing will really change, son,' said Maureen. 'Andrzej wants us to move in with him, but we will still be close to your granny and granda.'

'But you don't need to move if you don't want to?' said Andrzej hastily. 'I can come and stay with you.'

Rory just grinned and said, 'The internet is better at your place anyway.' So that was settled.

They were out on the fishing boat munching on ham sandwiches and sharing a conspiratorial smile as they dumped Maureen's homemade shortbread over the side for 'the poor peedie fishies,' said Rory, sympathetically.

Andrzej turned to him. 'Rory, I have something I need to ask you and I hope you will accept, as it would mean so much to me. I'm very nervous about this wedding and I need someone to help me through it. I would be so happy if you would stand beside me as my best man. What do you say?'

Rory blushed with pleasure. 'I'd be very proud to be your best man, Andrzej,' he said gravely. 'And I promise I will do a good job.'

'I know you will, son.' They shook hands solemnly.

Rory hesitated. 'Can I ask YOU something man to man?'

'Absolutely. Man to man,' said Andrzej seriously.

'Is my mum OK? She hasn't been feeling well and she has been lying down a lot and sleeping really late. It's not like her and I'm worried.'

Andrzej and Maureen had talked about this and agreed Rory needed to be told the truth, especially if he asked either one of them directly. Andrzej knew he would have to be honest, the boy deserved that, but he also needed to give him hope.

'She is very sick, Rory, but she is going to get the best possible treatment and I am certain she will be absolutely fine.' He continued gently, 'I am so sorry, but she has cancer, but you know your mother – she is strong, and she has so much to live for.'

Rory fought back tears. 'I'm glad you didn't tell me a lie. I knew it was something serious.'

Andrzej looked at this brave boy who had already lost his dad and had now been given such heartbreaking news about his mum.

'So, do you really think she will be all right? You aren't just saying that?'

'Of course I do.' Andrzej had convinced himself his Maureen would be cured. He wouldn't accept any other outcome.

'And she will be so happy you have agreed to be my best man. We both hoped you would say yes, but now we have a lot to plan before the wedding. And, look, you have a bite and it looks like a big one. There will be fish for our tea tonight.'

49

Orkney, 2024

On the morning of the wedding, it started lashing down. Proper serious rain. Freya kept looking at the sky as if by sheer force of will, she could stop the deluge.

'The forecast said light showers then sunshine this afternoon. If this doesn't stop, we are all going to be soaked getting into the chapel and we won't be able to do the photos outside. I'm raging. I wanted this day to be perfect.'

'It doesn't matter, and we can't do anything about it,' said Evie. 'Let's head over to Maureen's and help her get ready. Agnes will be there already to do her hair and Sophia is in charge of make-up. Are we still changing into our outfits at her place?'

'Absolutely. I've already packed.' Freya wheeled in a massive suitcase bursting at the seams.

'Freya, what have you got in there? You need one outfit, a pair of shoes and a handbag. You look like you are going on an expedition to the South Pole.'

'Well, I can't quite decide what to wear so I'm bringing a few choices, just in case. It's a big day and I don't want to be underdressed.'

Evie smiled to herself. There was absolutely no chance of Freya ever not being dressed to up to the nines and beyond. She festooned herself in silks and satins just to take the bins out when there was no one to see her but a few startled hooded crows.

'I don't think there will be any danger of that,' Evie said fondly. 'And you will look gorgeous as always.'

'Shoosh,' said Freya, but she was chuffed at the compliment. 'I can't wait to see Maureen; she's picked such a pretty outfit. A wee bit plain for my liking, but she will look beautiful.'

When Delima had shown Maureen the pale blue raw silk fabric from Singapore, they'd both known it was perfect. She'd made Maureen a shift dress and matching coat from the beautiful material. It was elegant and classy, but the only problem was Delima kept having to make alterations as Maureen continued to lose weight. It was easy for everyone to forget how ill she was in the middle of all the wedding excitement, especially as she seemed so full of energy and had never looked happier.

When Freya and Evie arrived, Maureen was sitting at her kitchen table, wearing fluffy slippers and a dressing gown with *Bride to Be* emblazoned on the back Sophia had bought her as a present. Agnes was blow-drying her hair, while Sophia was carefully painting her nails a pale coral.

Maureen's mum, Peggy, was getting ready downstairs and her dad had been up since daybreak and was now pacing the kitchen, full of nervous excitement. Freya had brought snacks and was pouring everyone a buck's fizz, taking care not to make it too strong as this was going to be a long day; everyone toasted Maureen.

'I'm convinced it's going to clear up by three o'clock,' said Freya. 'And the sun will shine on us all.'

'Poor Freya', said Delima fondly. 'It's the only thing you can't control, but, don't worry, Jack says that it will definitely clear up later and he's far more reliable than any weather forecast. Now,' she added. 'Maureen, I have made something for you that I want you to try on before Agnes starts putting in the big rollers.'

She carefully opened a large box stuffed with tissue paper and brought out the most beautiful fascinator in the same raw silk as Maureen's outfit with a matching blue feather.

'Although I say it myself, I'm really pleased with how this turned out, but there's no pressure and, if you hate it, I won't be offended, well, maybe just a bit, but you all have to give your honest opinion.'

Delima placed the fascinator on Maureen's head, and everyone gasped. 'It's absolutely beautiful,' said Maureen.

Freya said, 'But is it enough of a statement? Should we add some different-coloured feathers or maybe a few bits of jewellery to jazz it up?'

'No,' said Maureen, smiling. 'It's just perfect as it is. Thank you, Delima. It's the finishing touch I didn't know I needed. You are so kind. All of you have been incredible. I would never have been able to get all of this done in such a short space of time without your help.'

'Ooh, it's just like Queen Camilla's hat when she got married,' said Agnes. 'Except better because it's a lovelier colour and, let's be honest, her hat looked a peedie bit like porcupine spikes and bullrushes.'

Evie changed the subject quickly before die-hard Di-fan Freya objected to the 'Queen' bit of Camilla's title even though she was officially crowned and on the front of all the tea towels.

'Right,' said Evie. 'Come on, Freya, we need to get ready. I can hear giggling outside; that's got to be the girls with Kate.'

Maureen clasped her hands together. 'Oh, I can't wait to see them in their dresses. I'm so lucky to have such beautiful flower girls.'

Louise and Claire had been so excited to be part of the wedding, and Delima had worked long hours at her sewing machine to make them both ankle-length fairy princess dresses in pale blue satin with white roses around the waistbands. Delima made the finishing touches of headbands of fresh roses and little baskets filled with rose petals and tied with fat blue silk bows.

'Aunty Evie, do you like my dress,' said Louise, doing a twirl.

'The two of you look beautiful,' said Evie. 'Like those two characters from *Frozen*.' This was exactly the right thing to say. The girls beamed.

'Look what Delima has made you,' said Kate. 'Princess crowns of flowers and you have these lovely baskets full of petals, and you know what you have to do.'

The girls had been practising for days, up and down the hallway of their house using dog treats instead of petals, much to the delight of Eric and Ernie, until Kate stopped them and got them to draw and cut out paper roses instead.

'Just before Maureen walks down the aisle you need to scatter the rose petals like me and Daddy showed you,' said Kate.

The girls nodded gravely. They knew they had the most important job of the whole day and were taking it all very seriously.

Patsy walked in to gasps of astonishment. She was wearing a tight-fitting bodycon purple dress with green strappy sandals and looked as though she was going to explode or fall over. Or both at once.

'Don't say an effing word. I'm wearing this bloody dress for Maureen. It's hugely uncomfortable and I feel like a right eejit.'

'Patsy.' Freya spluttered. 'Are you actually wearing high heels?'

'I borrowed them. They are killing me, but I wanted to fit in with everyone else and not spoil Maureen's wedding photos.'

'You could have turned up naked or wearing a bin bag,' said Maureen. 'As long as you are here, but I really appreciate you making the effort and you do look very striking.'

Patsy grimaced but looked pleased all the same. 'Well, I know you've got already something auld because you are marrying that silly bugger who will never see twenty-one again, and—'

Kate tutted 'Patsy!' She jerked her head towards her daughters. 'Little ears!'

Louise chirruped, 'Is Uncle Andrzej a silly bugger, Mammy?'

Claire added, 'What IS a bugger, Mammy?'

Kate rolled her eyes. 'Patsy, you need to stop cursing like that in front of the bairns. They pick up everything.'

'Shit, Kate, I'm really sorry. Oh, fuck, I said shit. Right, I'm just going to shut up now.'

'Good idea. You looked so ladylike until you opened that mouth of yours,' but Kate said it with affection.

'Anyway,' said Patsy. 'We have established you've got something auld in Andrzej, but I wanted to give you something new, something borrowed and something blue all combined.'

She shyly handed Maureen a beautiful handmade wooden box with the initials M&A and the date carved on top entwined with a Celtic knot. Inside was a beautiful blue garter wrapped in a silk handkerchief.

'The box is new,' said Patsy. 'I've been working on it all week. The garter is something blue and the hanky is something borrowed, in case Andrzej needs to blow his nose and dry his eyes; you know what a sap he is. It belonged to my dad.'

'Oh, Patsy, it's all so beautiful and thoughtful of you. Thank you.' Maureen was overwhelmed with all the kindness she had already received today, and the best was still to come. She just hoped she wouldn't get too exhausted as she didn't want to let everyone down and fall asleep at her own wedding.

'Right,' said Evie. 'Time is marching on, and we are getting picked up at half two in the posh minibus, so we need to be ready. I haven't even got my mascara on. Freya, you need to pick your outfit. If you can't choose one, then just wear everything.'

There was a flurry of activity as everyone put the finishing touches to their hair and make-up with lipsticks being borrowed and perfumes sprayed. Maureen disappeared into the bedroom to put on her wedding finery and for Agnes to help her with the fabulous fascinator.

'How are you feeling, Maureen?' asked Agnes.

'I'm a bit nervous to be honest. I'm not used to being the centre of attention and not really sure what to expect. Evie and Kate promised to rein Freya in, but you know what's she's like. She's so kind but . . .'

'She's a peedie bit over the top,' finished Agnes. 'I know. But I have seen all the plans and you have nothing to worry about. It's going to be lovely. You just make sure to enjoy every second. Now and again stop for a minute today and take it all in, because it will go past in a flash.'

'Life does go by too quick,' said Maureen. 'I know that more than most.' She saw Agnes's chin wobble and said hastily, 'Don't worry, I'm not going to get all maudlin on my wedding day and upset everyone, and I'm not going to cry and ruin this beautiful make-up. You are right and it IS going to be lovely, even in the pouring rain.'

At exactly twenty past two, Maureen stepped into the living room dressed in her bridal finery. Evie, Sophia and Delima welled up at the sight of her. Even Patsy had a tear in her eye. Kate was openly crying, and the little girls were clapping and cheering. Freya had the biggest smile on her face.

'Maureen,' she said. 'You have never looked more beautiful. Andrzej is going to be beside himself. How do you feel?'

'You all keep asking me that. I feel fantastic, all fizzy and full of life. I just want to hold on to this feeling for ever.'

Freya kissed her on the forehead. 'No one deserves happiness more than you, my love.'

Evie popped downstairs to tell Maureen's mum and dad she was ready and on her way. The usually stoic Peggy was blinded with tears at the sight of her radiant daughter. 'Oh, you are a bonnie bride, my darling. I'm so happy for you.'

There was the toot of a horn outside.

'That's our ride, everyone,' said Evie. 'Sophia, Kate and the girls, Delima, Faye and Agnes, get yourselves into the minibus. It's the posh one and it's all clean and shiny. Freya and I will take Maureen's mum in the car. Maureen, you are obviously going with your dad and your lift is at 2.45 p.m. precisely.'

It was like herding cats, but Evie managed to eventually usher them all downstairs. 'Right,' said Evie. 'We have booze. We have serious underwear to hold ourselves in. We have uncomfortable high heels. We also have flat shoes for the dancing later. I think we're all set.'

They all bundled into the minibus shrieking about the rain ruining their outfits and trying to put on their seat belts without crushing their dresses. There was a panic when Claire's basket overturned and the petals fell onto the seat just as Sophia was about to sit down, but everyone scooped them up before Claire could even think about starting to cry.

'Finally,' said Evie, waving them off. 'Freya, let's take Peggy and get her settled in the car. Don't worry about your mum,

Maureen. Jack says he will take her home if it all gets too much for her and we will be with her all the time.'

Maureen was left alone with her dad, George, who had been quiet all day. He could hardly speak he was so emotional. He took her hands. 'Maureen, you look like a film star. I couldn't be prouder of you, my fine, brave girl.'

'Don't make me cry, Dad, or my mascara will run down my face and I will look like a panda. I don't want to spoil Sophia's hard work.' He hugged her tightly.

They heard a car pull up and Jack appeared at the door. He was ridiculously handsome in his wedding attire. He'd left his long hair loose down to his shoulders; Hollywood's idea of the perfect kilted warrior. He was beaming with happiness and carrying a massive umbrella to shield Maureen from the pelting rain.

'Your carriage awaits, madam.'

Jack had hired his cousin's vintage white Mercedes and polished it until it gleamed. He'd also festooned it with giant white bows, which had gone rather limp in the damp.

'Oh, this is too much,' said Maureen. 'I'm really being spoilt now.'

'We will be there in about half an hour, Maureen; I'm to take it nice and slow. We don't want you turning up bang on time.'

'Jack, even if you drive backwards, it surely won't take us that long to get to the registry office. It's only down the road.'

Her dad smiled at her. 'This is the biggest surprise of all, Maureen. Don't worry. You are going to love it.'

The rain had eased off and Maureen was wondering why the streets were so quiet; usually everyone stood outside their shops and houses to wish a bride well as she went on her way. She saw they were taking the road down to South Ronaldsay and over the barriers. Where on earth were they going?

Coming onto Lamb's Holm, she saw a huge crowd in front of the Italian Chapel. As they swept up into the car park and Jack opened the door for Maureen, the sun came out, bathing her in a glorious golden light.

There were hundreds of people outside clapping and cheering their congratulations. They'd come from all over the island to give the couple their best wishes. No wonder the streets had been so quiet. Everyone was here. Maureen was completely overwhelmed.

As she walked up the path to the chapel, so many friends and little ones gave her flowers and cards and lucky horseshoes. Jack collected them all as Maureen kept saying thank you over and over again.

At the door, Louise and Claire were waiting to perform their duties as flower girls. Maureen heard the most beautiful sound. The St Magnus Cathedral Choir were outside and came round both sides of the chapel singing 'Give Me Joy In My Heart'. It was glorious.

Her dad whispered, 'Are you ready, Maureen?'

A slightly dazed Maureen replied, 'I am so ready, Dad. Let's do this.'

The doors opened and the two little girls wearing their most serious expressions went ahead, perfectly scattering rose petals at the bride's feet. The tiny chapel was full to the brim and, at the altar, stood Andrzej and his best man, Rory.

When Andrzej saw Maureen coming towards him, he couldn't help himself, and exclaimed. 'Oh, Maureen. You are so beautiful. Everyone look at my bonny bride.'

His mother, who had flown over from Poland, clapped her hands and blew kisses towards her son. Everyone else burst into applause as Maureen slowly and carefully made her way towards her husband-to-be, arm in arm with her proud dad. She handed her bouquet to Freya and turned to face Andrzej.

The ceremony was a simple one but full of love and joy. There were sniffles when they vowed to take care of each other in sickness and in health, and more applause as the minister pronounced them man and wife.

In a clear voice, Maureen told her new husband '*Kocham cie*'. It meant I LOVE YOU in Polish. The choir outside started singing 'Love Is In The Air' and when everyone came out of the church in bright warm sunshine, a giant rainbow appeared right over their heads. The bright colours in the sky were outshone by Freya in a red-and-orange swirling silk kaftan. The well-wishers outside threw confetti and cheered themselves hoarse.

Andrzej's mother was enchanted. 'There's so much love for you both,' she said to her son. 'And the rainbow is a sign from God that you will be truly happy together for ever. This marriage is indeed blessed.'

She turned to Maureen. 'I have always wanted a daughter, Maureen. I have all of these big boys and they are very good to their old mother, but now I am so happy to have you and a grandson too. I hope Rory can call me his granny and you can all come to see me in Poland for many years to come.'

Andrzej had tried explaining to her that Maureen was about to undergo treatment for cancer, but his mother refused to believe that someone who looked so pretty and happy could be seriously ill. She was sure all would be well for her dearest son and his bride.

Jack was trying to get everyone in front of the chapel with Maureen and Andrzej in the centre to take lots of photos, but no one was paying any attention until Patsy bellowed, 'Come on, everybody, stop tit arsing around. Let's get the bride and groom in the middle and just huddle together. The bad news is you all have to look at Jack. If you can see him then you won't be hidden, and we will see you in all of the photos.'

Jack shouted, 'Give us a big smile for the *Orcadian*. Maureen, you will be this week's cover girl.'

'Away with you,' said the bride, but her smile was as wide as the Pentland Firth.

50

Orkney, 2024

Outside the Italian Chapel, each click of the camera captured all the joy of the big day. Jack was nearly done, apart from one final shot of the bride and groom.

Andrzej and Maureen gave each other a kiss and the crowd went wild. Andrzej looked at the faces of his friends and neighbours as well as strangers who had come to congratulate him and his bride.

He was determined to thank them all and began by saying, 'On behalf of my wife and I . . .' This resulted in another massive cheer from everyone and more applause.

'I just want to tell you all that my heart is full. When I came here many years ago, you made me so welcome, and you have all been so very kind. I fell in love with Maureen almost as soon as I arrived, but, fool that I am, it has taken me until now to finally ask her to marry me. There cannot be a happier man in all the world. I am so lucky and so grateful that she said yes, and we both got to share this day with everyone, and also that the sun shone for us.'

Maureen smiled at him. 'My husband is very sentimental,' she said, giving him a kiss on the nose. 'So, who's going to be next? Let's see who will catch my bouquet.'

Maureen threw the flowers high into the air. Evie automatically stretched out her arms and the bouquet landed right in her upturned hands to applause and jokes about who would be the lucky man to win her heart. She blushed furiously and just so happened to catch the eye of Ross Isbister, looking almost criminally handsome in his kilt.

They both averted their gazes and while Evie thought she just wasn't ready for another relationship, seeing the love between Maureen and Andrzej meant she couldn't rule it out completely either. Sophia saw Finn looked rather disappointed that she hadn't managed to beat Evie and catch the bouquet for her herself. She smiled and congratulated herself that her tactics were working.

Hand in hand, Maureen and Andrzej made their way to their car through a blizzard of confetti. Jack held the door open and told them they were heading to the Foveran for the reception.

Sitting in the back of the car, where it was calm and quiet, Andrzej said, 'Well, my dearest wife. How are you?'

Maureen gazed at him. 'So, so happy, my lovely husband. What a beautiful ceremony and wasn't it amazing that so many people turned out to see us and wish us well? And the choir too.'

'I know,' said Andrzej. 'And in the Italian Chapel. I don't know how they managed to sort that for us. I had no idea until this morning when Rory told me.'

He looked lovingly at his new wife. 'I've never seen you look more beautiful. When I saw you coming down the aisle towards me you looked like an angel. You aren't too tired?'

'Honestly, I'm fine. All I need is a cuddle and a glass of cold bubbly.'

Jack stopped the car.

'Oh, God, I'm an idiot,' he said. 'Freya will kill me.'

From the boot of the car, he brought out a bottle of champagne and an ice bucket and two carefully wrapped crystal glasses. He poured them both a glass.

'Don't tell her I forgot, will you?' Jack pleaded. 'I was supposed to pour you both a glass before we set off and then I'm under strict instructions to drive slowly so it won't spill.'

'Your secret is safe with us,' said Maureen. She raised her glass to her husband. 'Cheers, Mr Kowalski.'

He beamed at his Maureen. 'Cheers, Mrs Kowalski.'

Meanwhile, Evie had quietly walked to the beach at the edge of the water beside the Churchill Barrier. As soon as the bouquet had landed in her arms, she'd known what she wanted to do, and it was something she had to do alone.

The beach was deserted. The sea was calm today with the sound of the waves lapping gently on the shore. Evie realised she wasn't afraid. She walked over the white sand and gently placed the bridal bouquet of flowers on the water. She watched it drift away.

'This is to say a proper goodbye, Brodie. I never got the chance to do that. I will never forget you and I am so sorry about what happened to you. In another life, it might have been you and me getting married in the Italian Chapel. Rest in peace, my one and only love.'

She joined the rest of the guests piling into the minibus, glad that the hustle and bustle of everyone getting on meant that her absence had gone unnoticed. Freya gave her a sympathetic look. 'Are you OK, Evie?'

Evie nodded. She would keep the moment on the beach to herself. 'Yes, I really am. For the first time in a long time. Now let's go and celebrate a beautiful love story.'

*

Maureen and Andrzej had already arrived at the Foveran to see all the staff outside clapping and cheering and an enormous homemade banner over the door emblazoned: 'Congratulations Maureen and Andrzej' with the red-blue-and-yellow cross of the Orkney flag beside the Polish red-and-white.

The dining room had also been festooned with flags and each table decorated with white roses and thistles. The manager told them both, 'We've reserved the big guest room for you if you want to freshen up or have a peedie rest or just five minutes to yourselves. We thought you'd want to greet everyone right here as they come in the door. Let me pour you a glass of champagne or would you like anything a bit stronger?'

'I'm sticking to the bubbles,' said Maureen. 'But I'd better go easy, or I'll be asleep before the first dance.'

The guests soon arrived with lots of hugs and kisses, gathering in the sunshine on the balcony and the lawn with their drinks, taking in the view and chatting happily. As they heard the skirl of the pipes start up, they took their seats, and the piper played the bride and groom up to their top table.

Young Rory made a beautiful speech about how glad he was that his mum and Andrzej had decided to get married at long last.

He finished by raising his glass and saying, 'To my mum and my new dad. I love you both.' This reduced Andrzej to happy tears and then to everyone's surprise Maureen stood up to say something.

'I know it's not traditional, but I just want to say how proud I am of my son for being Andrzej's best man and doing such a wonderful job. I am so lucky to have such a splendid boy, and obviously I want to say thank you to my husband.'

There were more cheers and applause, and when it died down Maureen told them all, 'Andrzej actually wanted me to do this speech because he said he wouldn't get through it without crying and, as you can see, he's already sobbing like a bairn.

'I also want to say thanks to our dearest friends for organising such a wonderful day. It's been perfect and more than I could ever have hoped for. I can never thank you enough, Freya, Kate, Patsy, Agnes and Delima. And Evie who has come back to us with her friend Sophia. And thank you all for coming here today. It means the world to us both.

'As you all know, our future, well, my future, is uncertain,' said Maureen. 'But none of us have any idea what's around the corner. That's why I wanted to tell you all to seize the day and make the most of every single minute. Never take your friends and family for granted. Never go to bed on an argument. Keep those you love close and don't ever be afraid to tell them just how much you love them. Our time here is short, but it's very, very sweet. Now, let's enjoy this gorgeous meal and I know you will all be up for a bit of dancing later.'

Eyes were dried and everyone started chatting as they were served fresh Orkney scallops to start, followed by delicious roast lamb then homemade ice cream for pudding, followed by large platters of Orkney oatcakes and cheeses.

For their first dance, Maureen had chosen 'The Wind Beneath My Wings'. 'I know it's cheesy,' she said. 'But I don't care. It's a song that means a lot to me and Andrzej actually is the wind beneath my wings. He always will be.'

The DJ knew his stuff and soon everyone was up on the floor. Freya was twirling and birling and having the time of life, as happy dancing by herself as with all of her friends. Kilts were swinging and the older women looked on in approval as it was very clear the men had all obeyed the rules and gone commando.

Sophia and Finn were glued together even during the fast songs, although she told him she was disappointed he was in a suit rather than a kilt.

'I would have enjoyed giving your bare peachy bum a right good squeeze,' she told him.

He laughed. 'You do that anyway. I'm surprised my bum isn't like a bruised peach.'

They kissed each other passionately and Patsy told them to behave themselves and get a room, but she did it with a smile. Love was in the air.

Evie bumped into Ross at the bar. He smiled at her. 'You look lovely, Evie. It's good to see you.'

'Thank you. We never did get that drink. It's a free bar tonight. What can I get you?'

'Oh, nothing, thanks. I'm driving. I brought my mum and dad in the car. In fact, I need to take them home now. They've had a great day. It really was good to see you.'

Evie watched him go, surprised at how disappointed she felt to see him leave.

Around nine o'clock, Maureen whispered to Andrzej, 'Husband, would it be very bad if we were to just slip away. I'm feeling a peedie bit tired.'

'Of course not. Let me just tell Jack.'

Under strict instructions from Freya, Jack had manfully abstained from booze all night so he could drive the bride and groom back to Andrzej's house. They held hands on the journey back, no words needed as she rested her head on his shoulder.

Andrzej gently scooped Maureen out of the car and carried her over the threshold. She was as light as thistledown and almost asleep. Inside, Freya and the girls had worked more magic. The bed was sprinkled with rose petals, and they'd hung up twinkly lights around the room.

'Let's get you into bed. You need your rest. It's been a wonderful day, but you must be exhausted. I will be here holding your hand until you fall asleep.'

'Oh, Andrzej, I really am puggled, but are you sure? It's our wedding night after all.'

'We've talked about this, my love. There will still be time for us to share a bed properly and anyway I have eaten so much wedding cake I am going to burst. I am just so happy to be your husband.'

'I don't deserve you. I don't deserve all this.' Maureen started to sob.

'Oh, my little wife, please don't cry.'

'They are happy tears,' said Maureen. 'You've made me so very happy.'

A few minutes later she was fast asleep. Andrzej lay beside her on top of the bed holding her hand, until he too closed his eyes and drifted off.

51

Orkney, 2024

A month after the wedding, on a Friday evening, Evie called Freya. She'd been sitting on her 'special' chair in the kitchen thinking about how much her life had changed since she'd returned home. She had sloughed off her old meek, apologetic self and emerged brighter, happier and looking to the future with optimism.

It was as though she had been living in a black-and-white world and now everything was in Technicolor. There was, however, a very special promise she still had to keep to her dad. Even when he was no longer here, he had taken care of her, giving her a home where she was able to heal. She owed it to him to overcome her fears and finally get into the water and swim.

When Freya answered, Evie told her, 'I'm ready. It's time.'

'At last! I'm so pleased and the girls will be too. We are meeting at our beach tomorrow as usual at 10am.'

'How's the weather looking?' said Evie.

'It's going to be positively tropical, of course,' said Freya, laughing. 'Well, we will probably get a peedie murr of rain but nothing to worry about. Does Sophia know you're coming? She could pick you up tomorrow morning.'

'You just want to make sure I'm going to turn up. I know you too well,' said Evie with a laugh. 'I'm just about to call her and let her know.'

After telling Freya she had made her decision, Evie felt a sense of relief, but at the same time she was still apprehensive. She told herself she felt strong enough to get into the water and, of course, she'd have her friends to support her, but it was such an enormous step.

What if she backed out at the last minute and couldn't go through with it? Everyone would be so disappointed in her. She needed to gather all her courage and think of Dad and make him proud.

Early on Saturday morning, Sophia sat in Evie's kitchen with her hands wrapped round a mug of freshly brewed coffee. She was up for the weekend and staying with Finn.

The commuting was proving to be a strain with bad weather and delayed flights, and he lived in constant fear she'd get fed up and dump him. Now he knew how those women whose hearts he had broken must have felt.

'You really have got this place looking gorgeous, Evie. I love all your original artwork and that seascape you're working on now is gorgeous. You need to start getting your paintings into the shops and galleries.'

'Freya and I have talked about it a lot but let's take one step at a time.'

One of Evie's first completed paintings when she picked up a brush again was a portrait of a vivacious young woman with a beautiful smile and dark brown eyes that somehow seemed to sparkle and shine.

It was Liv when she was a teenager and, although Evie didn't remember her sister smiling all that much, when she had it had been like the sun coming out. She wrapped it up carefully and left it at Liv's door in her new one-bedroom council flat quietly sorted out by Freya and paid directly from Liv's benefits.

She hadn't had a reply yet, but Liv also hadn't thrown her gift back in her face, so she had hope that one day she and her poor damaged sister might manage to be in the same room as each other.

Sophie smiled at her. 'You are miles away – are you having second thoughts about going into the sea today with me and the other selkies?'

'Not at all. It's something I have to do for myself and for my dad. I can't say I am looking forward to it though. Do you think I'm being daft?'

'Of course not,' said Sophia. 'It's a big deal and I think you're being really brave. I remember having to be persuaded to plunge myself into the freezing cold water for the first time up here. I was bribed with a hot rum toddy if you recall, but, I promise you, afterwards you'll feel incredible.'

'I will take your word for it.' Evie was starting to feel a knot of anxiety in her stomach.

'You will be fine. Now we need to get going. Have you got everything you need?'

'I've got my cozzie on already. I've a huge, big towel and Kate is bringing me an extra dry robe. I've a flask of coffee with a peedie nip in it. Well, it's quite a big nip actually, to be honest.'

'Then you are all set. Let's go. We don't want to be late, or Freya will think we aren't coming.'

On the short car ride to the beach, Sophia asked Evie something that had been on her mind.

'I notice you haven't mentioned a certain Ross Isbister?' said Sophia. 'Have you seen him at all?'

'Not really. We bump into each other now and again but, believe it or not, we still haven't had that drink.'

'Well, he's a fine-looking fella. Your "bairns" would be stunning. See, I'm learning the lingo.' She laughed.

'Behave yourself,' said Evie. 'He is a good man, but I'm not looking for any sort of romance right now.'

It was sunny but there was a bit of a chilly breeze at the beach. The sand was soft white sugar and the sea a swirling blue grey. Evie breathed in the sharp salty smell. She would never take the clean Orkney air for granted ever again.

The other selkies were on the beach already, in various stages of undress. 'It's invigorating today!' Freya declared.

'Translation: it's bloody freezing,' muttered Kate, but with a wink back at Freya.

Freya saw Evie and Sophia making their way down to the beach and waved enthusiastically. Kate whispered to Freya, 'Are you sure Evie wants to do this? She really is terrified of the water, and I don't want her to panic and bring on an asthma attack.'

'She wants to, and she needs to,' said Freya. 'It will give her such a confidence boost and she'll feel reborn.'

She smiled reassuringly as Evie and Sophia joined them.

'Here you are,' Freya said heartily. 'We've a good day for it.'

Evie's stomach was churning like a washing machine. 'So, tell me exactly what the plan is,' she said hesitantly. 'You do know I can't swim at all?'

'Of course we know,' said Freya. 'It's very simple. We will all just slowly wade in and then see how we go. We can support you if you get a peedie bit out of your depth. Then you can float, just for a moment. We will all be right there. You will be safe, my love, I promise.'

Evie gulped nervously. This was going to be harder than she'd thought.

The other selkies, Patsy and Agnes, were also there, but Delima was at home being pampered by Jack, decorating their nursery and planning baby names. There would soon be a new life for everyone to celebrate.

Andrzej had driven down with Maureen. Although she wasn't well enough to go into the water, she wanted to be there for Evie. Maureen's chemo was making her feel weak and nauseous, but she was determined to live each day to the full.

There was no bucket list of skydiving, going up in a hot-air balloon or having a holiday in the Caribbean. Maureen just wanted to do ordinary everyday things with Andrzej and Rory, making memories and counting their blessings, just happy to be together.

She said to Evie, 'I'm so proud of you for doing this. I just wish I could go into the water with you, but my husband and I will be here to cheer you on.' Calling Andrzej her husband still gave Maureen a happy thrill, and he beamed with delight every time she said it.

Evie looked at this brave woman who had a long, hard road ahead of her, and yet still had come today to give her love and support.

She thought: *what I'm about to do is absolutely nothing compared to what Maureen is enduring.* She vowed to channel some of Maureen's courage and strength to stop feeling so scared.

Looking up, Evie saw a slight, lonely figure at the top of the hill. It was Liv. Evie raised her hand and her sister waved back briefly before turning around and walking away. It was a start.

'Right, everyone, let's do this,' said Kate. 'Evie, are you ready?'

'I think so,' said Evie. 'Just don't let go of me.'

'Don't you worry, I'm right here by your side. You will do just fine. We can take it as slow as you like but it's better just to take the plunge.'

Evie had Freya on one arm, Kate on the other and Sophia ahead of her, smiling into her eyes. Patsy and Agnes had already run in, shrieking from the cold at first, and then swimming like graceful sea otters. They bobbed in the waves, shouting encouragement.

Evie gasped as she entered the water. It was freezing but strangely exhilarating. She felt her skin begin to tingle.

They all walked in further until the water was almost up to her shoulders. Soon her feet would no longer touch the ground. She felt a jolt of fear and uncertainty and turned to look back at the shore. Andrzej and Maureen suddenly seemed far away.

Freya encouraged her gently.

'We've got you. Just lie back and let yourself float. We'll hold you up.'

Evie nodded and leant back. To her surprise, she didn't sink. She found herself being lifted by her friends and by the water, looking up at the bright blue sky and feeling safe and loved.

'You're a proper selkie now,' Freya said.

Evie smiled, and felt a tear roll down her face, mingling with the salt water. She felt alive. She felt free and at peace. She floated in the water for a few minutes longer before her feet found the seabed again.

She was gasping and laughing with her hair wet and her whole body atingle. Her dad would have laughed with pride and joy.

'Will you all do me a big favour?' she said.

'Of course, my love, anything you want,' said Freya.

Sophia and Kate added, 'Anything. Just say the word.'

Evie paused, taking in the magic of this moment in the water.

'Now and then, will you call me Teenie?'

Acknowledgements

Thank you to everyone who worked on *The Island Swimmer*.

Thank you to Carly Cook. And Miranda Chadwick and Jamie Slattery from Mirador.

To my editors at Orion Sam Eades and Sophie Wilson.

A special thanks to my husband Steve and my daughter Rosie for their patience and understanding.

And to Paul, Helen, Elise and Leona Doull and all the people in Orkney who have made me and my family so welcome over the years.

For those wanting to discover more about Orkney I urge you to visit. Most of the places in the story are inspired by real life locations on the islands, apart from Hrossey which is from my imagination!

Credits

Lorraine Kelly and Orion Fiction would like to thank everyone at Orion who worked on the publication of *The Island Swimmer* in the UK.

Editorial
Sam Eades
Sanah Ahmed
Sophie Wilson

Copyeditor
Francesca Cowan Brown

Proofreader
Suzanne Clarke

Audio
Paul Stark
Jake Alderson

Contracts
Dan Herron
Ellie Bowker

Design
Charlotte Abrams-Simpson
Joanna Ridley

Editorial Management
Charlie Panayiotou
Jane Hughes
Bartley Shaw

Finance
Jasdip Nandra
Nick Gibson
Sue Baker

Marketing
Lindsay Terrell

Production
Ruth Sharvell

Publicity
Francesca Pearce

Sales
Jen Wilson
Esther Waters
Victoria Laws

Toluwalope Ayo-Ajala
Rachael Hum
Ellie Kyrke-Smith
Sinead White
Georgina Cutler

Operations
Jo Jacobs
Dan Stevens

The Island Swimmer – Q&A

1. What made you decide to set the story in the Orkney islands? Is it a place you have visited before?

I love ORKNEY and have been visiting the islands since the early eighties. My husband Steve and I travel up there at least once a year. It's my happy place and as soon as I land by plane or on the ferry I can feel the stress oozing out of my body. I always wanted to write about Orkney and to make this special place at the heart of my story. I've had a lot of ideas buzzing around in my head and I knew I had to write them down and just carve out the time.

2. How important is the theme of swimming in the story? Have you ever been cold-water swimming?

I LOVE cold water swimming. I've had a dip in Antartica and also in Orkney as well as in the cleanish bits of the Thames. It's exhilarating and obviously an important part of *The Island Swimmer* as my main character Evie has to come home to Orkney and face her fears as well as her past.

3. There is such a strong sense of community in this book. Did you have fun creating a cast of characters? Do you have any favourites?

Writing the book has been one of my greatest challenges but I LOVED it and it was so exciting and absorbing creating the characters and storylines.

I hope I've managed to convey the sense of community and the rich lives being led in this glorious part of the world.

My characters are complex and the relationships I've written about between mothers and daughters, sisters and friends can be tough. They all have their anxieties and difficulties but there's also love and trust and laughter.

I hope people will identify, sympathise and be moved by how my characters tackle their challenges and celebrate their times of happiness.

My favourite is Freya who is at the heart of the book. She's a wise woman with a fascinating back story. I would love her to be my mentor and best friend!

4. Which authors have inspired your writing?

I adore Maeve Binchy. She was such a brilliant storyteller and created worlds that were so real and utterly absorbing. I re-read her books all the time. I also greatly admire Marian Keyes who is also a genius at making you keep wanting to keep turning the pages to find out what happens next.

5. What does the future look like for Evie and the island swimmers? Will they return in future books?

I am currently working on the second book which continues the story of Evie, Freya and all of the other characters because I'm just not ready to say goodbye to them!